Contents

I. Sis Hetta's Child—The Ante-Bellum Years

II. "Mine eyes have seen the Glory"— The Civil War Years

III. "Forty years in the wilderness"— Reconstruction and Reaction

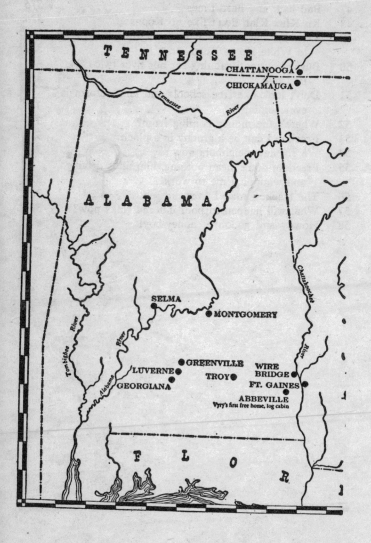

TENNESSEE

CHATTANOOGA

CHICKAMAUGA

Tennessee River

ALABAMA

Chattahoochee River

SELMA

MONTGOMERY

Tombigbee River

Alabama River

GREENVILLE

LUVERNE   TROY   WIRE
                                    BRIDGE

GEORGIANA   FT. GAINES

                ABBEVILLE
                Vyry's first free home, log cabin

FLOR

ATLANTA
Post Civil War capital

MILLEDGEVILLE
State capital 1807–1867

MACON
Confederate munitions works

ANDERSONVILLE
Civil War prison

DAWSON
The Dutton plantation
Randall Ware's blacksmithy & grist mill

LOUISVILLE
Old slave market

SAVANNAH
Missy Salina's home

GEORGIA

Flint River

Oconee River

Ocmulgee River

River

Ogeechee River

River

Savannah River

Atlantic

Ocean

F L O R I D A

I   *Sis Hetta's Child*

THE ANTE-BELLUM YEARS

Swing low, sweet chariot,
Coming for to carry me home . . .

1 Death is a mystery that only the squinch owl knows

"May Liza, how come you so restless and uneasy? You must be restless in your mind."

"I is. I is. That old screech owl is making me nervous."

"Wellum, 'tain't no use in your gitting so upsot bout that bird hollering. It ain't the sign of no woman nohow. It always means a man."

"It's the sign of death."

Grandpa Tom, the stable boy, and May Liza, Marster's upstairs house girl, were sitting on the steps of their cabins in the slave Quarters. It was not yet dusk-dark. An early twilight hung over the valley, and along the creek bank fog rose. The hot spring day was ending with the promise of a long and miserable night. A hushed quiet hung over the Quarters. There were no children playing ring games before the cabins. The hardened dirt-clay road, more like a narrow path before their doors, was full of people smoking corncob pipes and chewing tobacco in silence. Out on the horizon a full moon was rising. All eyes were on the cabin of Sis Hetta, where she lay on her deathbed sinking fast.

Inside Sis Hetta's cabin the night was sticky hot. A cloying, sweetish, almost sickening smell of Cape jessamine, honeysuckle, and magnolias clung heavily to the humid night air. Caline, a middle-aged brown-skin woman with a head of crinkly brown hair tied in a knot on her neck, imposing eyes, and the unruffled air of importance and dignity that one associated with house servants, stood beside the sickbed and fanned Sis Hetta with a large palmetto fan. Caline knew Hetta was dying. As soon as supper was over in the Big House, Caline came to see what she could do. Aunt Sally, cook in the Big House, couldn't get away with Caline but she sent word, "Tell em I'll be along terreckly." Fanning Sis Hetta in the hot night seemed all there was left to do for her, and so Caline kept fanning and thinking: Sis Hetta was a right young woman, younger than Caline, and she got with all those younguns fast as she could breed them. Caline had no children. She had never known why. Maybe it was something Old Marster made them do to her when she was a young girl and first started working in the Big House. Maybe it was the saltpeter. Anyway, Caline was glad. Slaves were better off, like herself, when they had no children to be sold away, to die, and to keep on having till they killed you, like Hetta was dying now.

Out on the Big Road, May Liza and Grandpa Tom could barely discern a man in the distance. As he drew nearer they could see he was riding a small child on his shoulders.

"Brother Zeke," breathed May Liza.

"Yeah," and Grandpa Tom took his pipe out of his mouth and spat.

"That's Sis Hetta's last child she had for Marster, Zeke's riding on his shoulder."

"How you know?"

"I hear tell they done sent clean over to Marster's other plantation cause Hetta wants to look at her youngun."

"Be her last look, I reckon."

"Yeah, I reckon so."

Now in the tricky light of the half-night they saw a figure wearing long trailing skirts of a woman. She was walking slowly at a short distance behind Brother Ezekiel.

"Mammy Sukey's coming too."

"You know she ain't leaving that gal out of her sight. That's Marster's youngun they give her to raise."

"Marster don't care nothing bout that youngun. Mammy Sukey's got her cause Jake won't leave her be in peace with him and Hetta. They say he pinch that gal when she wasn't nothing but a suckling baby."

"Wellum 'twarn't no use in that. Jake knowed Hetta been having Marster's younguns long as they can remember."

"Reckon how he knowed?"

Hetta was twenty-nine years old, although this was a fact she could not verify. After having given birth to fifteen children, all single births, she was waiting for death in childbed. Her thin bony fingers clutched nervously at the ragged quilt that covered her. Evidently her mind wandered back over happier and earlier days, for her quick beady eyes, glittering with fever, sometimes lighted up, and although she was nearly speechless, Caline fancied she heard the sick woman muttering words. Hetta was a woman who had never talked much.

Another black woman, small, and birdlike in her movements, moved in and out the cabin carrying china washbowls and pitchers of hot water; moving blood-soaked rags and clothing, watching the face of the sick woman to whom she had fed laudanum to ease the pain of these last three days. Granny Ticey was deeply dejected. She moved to keep her hands busy and occupy her mind. She had always been proud of her reputation of rarely losing her patients. Babies she lost, but mothers seldom. She had been uneasy all week about Hetta. It wasn't the first time this heavy breeding woman, whose babies came too fast, tearing her flesh in shreds, had had a hard and complicated time. She did not like either the looks or the actions of Hetta and she told Jake and Marster, or at least tried to communicate her fears to them. Of course it was true there wasn't anything too much she had to base her fear on. Hetta was sick every day this last time. Toward the end she rarely left her bed. She was bloated and swollen beyond recognition. But Jake said nothing, as usual, and Marster only laughed. Eight days ago when Granny Ticey saw the quarter moon dripping blood she knew it was an evil omen. When Jake came for her and said Hetta's time had come she did not want to go, because she knew nothing was right. But she went and she stayed, and now grim and wordless she watched the night lengthen its shadows outside Sis Hetta's door.

One thing Granny Ticey had done. When the baby was born dead, and Hetta started having terrible fits and hemorrhaging, she made Marster send for a doctor, but two days went by before the doctor came. Meanwhile Granny Ticey made tansy tea and bathed Hetta in hazel root, and used red shank. All these did no good. On the third day when the white doctor came, he barely stayed ten minutes, and he did not touch Hetta. Instead he spoke angrily to Granny Ticey.

"What you want me to do, now that it's plain she's dying? You didn't get all that afterbirth. How many times do I have to tell you to get it all? Don't know why you had John to get me way out here for this unless it was just to make him waste money over your carelessness."

Granny Ticey said nothing. Her lips were tight and her eyes were hard and angry in an otherwise set face. But she was thinking all she dared not say: How was he expecting me to get all the rotten pieces after a dead baby? That's exactly why I sent for him, so's he could get what I couldn't get. If he had come on when I sent for him, instead of waiting till now, Hetta might not be dead. No, I'll take that back. She was going to die anyway. She had to die one of these times. The last two times were nothing but the goodness of God. I guess it's just her time.

When the doctor went away he must have told Marster that Hetta was dying. Early in the afternoon when dinner in the Big House was over, Marster came down to Hetta's cabin. Granny Ticey was there alone with Hetta. Jake was in the fields. Marster was a tall blond man barely thirty-five years old. John Morris Dutton scarcely looked like the Marster. He still looked like a boy to Granny Ticey, but a big husky boy, whose sandy hair fell in his face and whose gray-blue eyes always twinkled in fun. He liked to hunt and fish, and he was always slapping a friend on the back in good fellowship and fun. He never seemed to take anything too seriously, and his every other word was a swearing, cursing song. He was a rich man with two plantations and sixty slaves on this one. He was a young man with hot blood in his veins. He could eat and drink as much as he liked, sleep it off quickly, rise early ready to ride far and enjoy living. Now he came down the path whistling, and only when his rangy form stooped to enter Hetta's cabin, and he saw the disapproving gravity in Granny Ticey's solemn eyes, did he hush, and ask, unnecessarily, "Where is she?"

Granny Ticey pointed behind the heavy quilt hanging from

top to bottom of the cabin and separating the cooking corner of the fireplace and iron pots from the place where Hetta slept. Marse John pushed the quilt aside and stood over Hetta. A fetid odor made him sick for a moment, but he saw her eyes looking at him, and he called her name . . .

"Hetta?"

"Yassah." He voice was so weak and soft he bent lower over her.

"Hetta, do you know me?"

"Yassah, Marster, I knows you." But her voice was only a whisper.

"How you feeling?"

"Poorly Marster, mighty poorly."

"I'm sorry. Is there anything you want? Something I can do for you?"

"Nossah, Marster, nothing nobody can do now. Hetta ain't long for this world."

"Oh, shut up! You're going to get well in a jiffy; be up and around in no time, as usual. You just feel bad cause you've had a bad time."

"Nossah, that ain't it. I'm dying, Marster, and I knows it. Just one thing I wants . . ."

"What's that?"

"I wants to see my youngun Vyry, fore I dies."

"I'll send for her. Now you lay still and get well. I'll be back to see you tomorrow." And he patted her hand and went outside. But when he went out he was not gay. He thought, "By God, she might be dying at that!"

And he began to think through the years when Hetta was a young girl and there was no thought of her dying, ever. His father gave him Hetta when he was still in his teens and she was barely more than a pickaninny. He remembered how she had looked growing up, long legged like a wild colt and just that temperamental. She looked like some African queen from the Congo. She had a long thin neck and she held her head high. She must have imagined herself, he thought, in an African jungle among palms and waterfalls with gold rings coiled around her neck. Her small young breasts tilted up, and even her slight hips and little buttocks were set high on her body. When she moved lightly and they switched lazily and delicately, they titillated him and his furious excitement grew while watching her walk. It was all his father's fault. Anyway it was his father who taught him it was better for a young man of quality to learn life by breaking in

a young nigger wench than it was for him to spoil a pure
white virgin girl. And he had wanted Hetta, so his father gave
her to him, and he had satisfied his lust with her. Because in
the beginning that was all he had felt, a youthful lust. He still
remembered her tears, and her frightened eyes, and how she
had pleaded to be left alone, but he had persisted until she
had given in to him. And things went along like that for a
good while, until he began to think about getting married.
At least his father thought about it first. His father kept
pestering him to find a lovely young lady and make her his
wife. It was time he assumed his responsibilities and settled
down. So he went traveling and hunting for a wife. Between
courting times he came back to Hetta. At home he took her
as a matter of course, but when he went away he thought
about her and he could see her and feel her and smell the
musklike odor of her body in his mind. Clean enough to
bathe twice a day and quiet enough never to annoy him with
chatter, she provided him with all the physical release he
needed. When she began having babies it was no problem. He
gave her Jake for a husband and that was that.

But finally he found a wife, a beautiful young lady of quality
from a fine old family in Savannah. And he married Salina.
He was sure that she was madly in love with him, and when
she kissed him demurely and let him hold her hand he felt
sure there was enough fire in this pretty brunette girl to excite
him forever. There was an elaborate wedding. He still remembered the drinking, and Salina's mother crying because her
daughter was leaving home for the first time and going into
the backwoods of Georgia. He could still see Salina's father
grasping John Morris Dutton's hand and getting all choked
up, and begging him in a voice hoarse with drink as much as
anything else, "Boy, take care of my little Salina." Salina
wasn't little. She was a big-boned girl, tall, and inclined to
get fat. And John Morris got all emotional himself. Inco-
herently he promised, no, vowed like a knight on a charger
to protect her with his life and to be good to her all the days
of his life. Then they rode away in a buggy amidst a shower
of rice, Salina laughing and crying, and John Morris Dutton
just a wee bit tight.

They had a long journey, and a new house waiting, and he
could understand why his wedding night was not a night of
love, why she begged off with fatigue. What he never understood was why Salina acted outraged and shocked when he
finally made love to her. She was pious and romantic and

she locked her door most nights against him. When she finally became pregnant and suffered morning sickness his hopes ended. He went back to Hetta.

Everything was the same for a long time after that. Salina made him understand that sex, to her mind, was only a necessary evil for the sake of procreation. When she had presented him with a son and a daugher, she further informed him that her duty as a wife had ended. She simply would not, no, she simply could not go through all that suffering again. She did not want any more children, and consequently there was no more need for sex. At first he was stunned. He got drunk and got up nerve enough to tell her a few pointed facts, but beyond a few curse words nothing prevailed over her tears. His next shock came when she found out about Hetta. She pitched a lovely tantrum then. She threw things at him, called him a beast, cried three days in a row, and even packed to go home to mother. But when he encouraged her to go, offered to pay all her expenses there and continue to provide for her after she got home, only leave his children with him, she relented. Although she never forgave him, she never left him. Miscegenation was no sin to Marse John. It was an accepted fact of his world. What he could not understand at first was where Salina had been given such romantic notions, and how her loving parents had kept the facts of life from her.

Now, Hetta was dying. He would miss her. Perhaps Salina will be pleased, he thought, except for the child. With a sudden jolt, he remembered Vyry.

Vyry was two years old. Mammy Sukey had been keeping her as she kept all Marster's bastards till they were big enough to work. She and Brother Ezekiel had nearly a two-mile walk bringing Vyry to see her dying mother, Hetta.

Brother Ezekiel was a powerfully built, stovepipe-black man. He was neither young nor old. He was the plantation preacher, at least among the slaves. He could read and write, but the white folks did not know this. Now as he came along with Vyry on his shoulders, and Mammy Sukey walking behind, he was humming a song—

> Soon one morning,
> Death come knockin at my door . . .

When they got to Sis Hetta's cabin door Aunt Sally met them. She was still in her voluminous apron, had her head rag on, and she went inside with them.

Jake was sitting inside with a little black girl on his knees. Her eyes looked big as saucers in her thin face, and she had her thumb and two fingers in her mouth sucking on all three hard as she could.

Granny Ticey, Aunt Sally, Brother Ezekiel with Vyry in his arms, and Mammy Sukey all stood around Hetta's bed. Jake had not moved from his corner, but he sat where he could look behind the quilt. Granny Ticey spoke first.

"Hetta! Hetta! Here's Brother Zeke with Vyry. He done brung your youngun to you."

But the sick woman seemed in a stupor and hard to arouse. Brother Ezekiel moved forward while Aunt Sally and Caline stood on both sides of the bed, and while Granny Ticey propped Hetta's head higher the other two women lifted her up just as Brother Ezekiel held the child down over her and spoke, afar, "Sis Hetta, here is Vyry."

Mammy Sukey stood aside, a wizened old crone with a red rag on her head and her arms akimbo. Now the urgency in Brother Ezekiel's voice seemed to rouse the dying woman. Her eyes flickered, and her lips moved. She put up her bony hands and fluttered them like a bird. A scarcely audible and muffled sound came from her lips. Then with great effort she spoke, raspy and indistinct, but clear enough for them to know she was saying, "Vyry?"

Brother Ezekiel held the child down close to her mother's face and said, soothingly, "It's your mama, Vyry, say hello to your maw." The child spoke, "Mama," and then she whimpered. Hetta fell back on her pillows and Ezekiel handed the child to Mammy Sukey, who quickly took her outside into the night air.

After a moment Brother Ezekiel spoke again to the dying and exhausted woman.

"Sis Hetta, I'm here, Brother Zeke, it's me. Can I do something for you?"

"Pray," she rasped, "pray."

He fell on his knees beside the bed and took her hand in his. The night was growing darker. Despite the full moon outside, spilling light through the great oak and magnolia trees, inside Granny Ticey had lighted a large tallow candle. It flared up suddenly, and eerie shadows searched the corners and crowded the room. Brother Ezekiel began to pray:

"Lord, God-a-mighty, you done told us in your Word to seek and we shall find; knock and the door be open; ask, and it shall be given when your love come twinklin down. And

Lord, tonight we is a-seekin. Way down here in this here rain-washed world, kneelin here by this bed of affliction pain, your humble servant is a-knockin, and askin for your lovin mercy, and your tender love. This here sister is tired a-sufferin, Lord, and she wants to come on home. We ask you to roll down that sweet chariot right here by her bed, just like you done for Lishy, so she can step in kinda easy like and ride on home to glory. Gather her in your bosom like you done Father Abraham and give her rest. She weak, Lord, and she weary, but her eyes is a-fixin for to light on them golden streets of glory and them pearly gates of God. She beggin for to set at your welcome table and feast on milk and honey. She wants to put on them angel wings and wear that crown and them pretty little golden slippers. She done been broke like a straw in the wind and she ain't got no strength, but she got the faith, Lord, and she got the promise of your Almighty Word. Lead her through this wilderness of sin and tribulation. Give her grace to stand by the river of Jordan and cross her over to hear Gabe blow that horn. Take her home, Lord God, take her home."

And the sobbing women listening to him pray breathed fervent amens. When Brother Ezekiel got up from his knees he put the hand of Sis Hetta on her cover. But she no longer seemed to hear what he was saying. Her eyes were fixed and staring above her, and her throat made raspy noises. Brother Ezekiel went outside and sat in the dampening night air. Caline got a dipper of well water and with a clean rag began to drop water in Hetta's mouth and moisten her throat. But the water trickled out of the side of her mouth and ran down her chin, and the noises in her throat grew more raspy.

Jake got up to lay his black baby on a pallet, and then with a terrible groan he walked outside where the friends of Hetta sat waiting for her to die.

A few yards from the cabin Granny Ticey had built a fire under a big, black iron wash pot. Pine knots and hickory wood sputtered and burned with sudden spurts of bright flame, emitting an aromatic smoke and discouraging mosquitoes and even the lightning bugs. At odd intervals Granny Ticey threw something in the pot and something on the fire. Each time a hissing noise of water boiling over the flames, and fresh knots catching fire flared up, it startled the watchers. When the flames flared they lighted the faces of the slaves sitting watch, and when the pot boiled over they jumped in fear and suspense.

Jake did not feel sociable. He wanted to go off alone in the woods or work in the fields and not be here when Hetta died. Whenever her eyes closed in death, his fate would be sealed. Marster would have no further use for him and he would be sold. Maybe not right away, but sooner or later, it would happen after awhile. What would they do with his helpless black child then?

Hetta had been a good wife to him. He remembered how she kicked and screamed first time he "knocked her up" and he remembered the bitter dry taste in his mouth when he realized she was Marster's woman. Marster had broke her in, and then "give her to me." She kept the cabin clean and she cooked good greens and corn pone. She never went to the fields and she always smelled clean. She made him bathe every day when he came from the fields and she never showed him her nakedness, but she never refused him either. Often when he found her crying after Marster's visits while he, Jake, was in the fields he would get mad, but she never would talk except to keep him from doing foolish things. When their children were sold away and some babies never cried she would cry and grieve over their helplessness. She was a sullen-looking woman with a pouting lip who rarely smiled and almost never talked and who kept her hair wrapped in endless clean little rags. Once, when she was young and shapely, she was proud and she walked like she owned the earth. He felt sometimes because she was Marster's woman that maybe she thought herself too good for him, but she never said so, and no, she never acted that way either. But maybe it was just an evil thought in his mind anyway.

Jake's path seldom crossed Marster's. He stayed out of his way as much as possible, but if by chance they ever came face to face, Marster laughed and slapped Jake's back and talked down to his slave, Jake, like he did to one of his good hound dogs. Jake hated Marster and despised himself and looked at Hetta and got mad and evil. But that was the end of it. He never dared say anything or do anything about it.

Now she was no longer young and slender and lovely. Her breasts were long and flabby; her belly always bloated, whether she was big in family way or not, and her legs and thighs were now covered with large broken blood vessels that made it painful when she stood long or walked far. Only her black face was still the same, serene, dignified, sullen, and quiet by turns. Even her neck was changed and looked shorter. Her hair was still the same, and her hands and feet were still small, and she still believed in everything being spotlessly clean.

"Well, now she is dying, and they'll send me away. I guess in a way I ought to be glad. Guess in a way I am glad to get away from here. Marster's always said he'll get a fair price for a good stud like me."

Midnight came and thirteen people waited for death. The black pot boiled, and the full moon rode the clouds high in the heavens and straight up over their heads. The child, Vyry, stirred in the arms of her nurse, the old black crone, Mammy Sukey. Aunt Sally, sitting near Tom and May Liza, had made a place for her son, Sam, the carriage boy, to sit beside her. It was not a night for people to sleep easy. Every now and then the squinch owl hollered and the crackling fire would flare and the black pot boil. Aunt Sally kept wondering what would happen to the little girl, Vyry, not only now, but when she got too big for Mammy Sukey to keep her. Would Marster bring her in his house as he had done all his other bastards? Even though they never lasted long in the Big House, what would Big Missy Salina say? Aunt Sally looked again at the child sleeping in Mammy Sukey's arms and thought how much she and the little Missy Lillian in the Big House looked alike. In her mind she thought, "They could pass for twins—same sandy hair, same gray-blue eyes, same milk-white skin. One of them was Hetta's child, and one of them was Big Missy Salina's. But they were both Marse John's and there was no mistake about that. What was even more interesting, they were nearly the same age. Granny Ticey had been granny for both and Hetta had wet-nursed Miss Lillian just like her own Vyry. Big Missy had been pleased as punch with her daughter's resemblance to her father until she learned about Hetta's child and a few weeks later had seen Vyry. Aunt Sally glanced up at the Big House, and, just as she had suspected, the light was still burning in Marse John's room. All the rest of the house was dark.

Sometime between midnight and dawn the night subtly began to change. Those who had been wakeful were now drugged with sleep, and those who had slept too long and hard were now wakeful. Even before the first thread of light shot like a ribbon across the tenuous line where earth touched the sky, there was a stirring of sleeping people and animals in preparation for the coming of the morning. It was four o'clock, getting-up time for the field hands, and the cocks began to crow loudly for day. In that changing hour Sis Hetta breathed her last and slipped quietly away.

It was Granny Ticey who closed Hetta's eyes. In annoyance and chagrin, and partly in genuine sadness, pity, and grief, tears rolled down her wrinkled black cheeks. With her lips tightly set, and her eyes brimming, she pulled the coarse sack sheet over Hetta's face.

Outside the cabin the watchers were half asleep, half nodding, half dozing. Now the rasping noises had ceased, and in the long, thick silence that followed they realized that Hetta was gone.

The black pot was still and the white ashes were cold. In the growing daylight the moon's wan light was lusterless on the far horizon. Soon it would be time to bathe the dead body and prepare it for an early burial, but suddenly Granny Ticey gave a bloodcurdling yell, startling all the watchers and making them all sit up wide awake. She ran out of the cabin into the dawning daylight. Gathering up all her ample skirts, coarse petticoats, and apron, she threw them over her head, showing her aged nakedness while covering her face, and thus she ran blindly and screaming down the road.

In less than a minute, the death wail went up out of every cabin in the Quarters, and Brother Ezekiel began the death chant:

> Soon one morning,
> Death come knocking at my door.
> Soon one morning,
> Death come knocking at my door.
> Soon one morning,
> Death come knocking at my door.
> Oh, my Lord,
> Oh, my Lord,
> What shall I do?

When Israel was in Egypt's land—
Let my people go.
Oppressed so hard they could not stand—
Let my people go.

2   *Along the Big Road in Egypt's land . . .*

"Vyry, wake up child, wake up so's we can make haste and git along."

Mammy Sukey shook the sleeping child and she stirred in her sleep.

"Wake up, wake up! Sun's up, and us got a far ways to travel. Git up, now, git up and make haste, I says."

Vyry was seven, and the old crone, Mammy Sukey, was all the mother she had ever known or could remember. Today was special. When Vyry remembered, she jumped up from her pallet, rubbing her eyes with her fists and nudging her legs and feet together.

"Today I'm going to the Big House to stay!" she thought to herself.

"What you gone say when you sees Big Missy?" and Mammy Sukey's words shook her out of her reverie. Vyry bowed herself and crossed her legs in an elaborate curtsey, and with a solemn face and soft voice said, "I'm gone say, 'Morning to yall, Missy.' "

"What you gone say to Marster?"

"Morning to yall, Marster."

"And the young Missy Lillyum?"

"Morning, Missy!"

"And young Marster John?"

"Morning, Marster!"

After the slow and serious rehearsal Mammy Sukey nodded approval.

"That's good. That's good. That's just like I showed you. Mind your manners good, and be real nice and polite. You a big gal now, but you ain't gone be no field hand and no yard nigger. You is gone wait on Quality and you got to act like Quality. Go to now—eat your vittles."

While she talked she fixed their breakfast, pulling out of a flour sack two tin plates. She went outside her cabin and from the smoldering fire, dying away into ashes, she brought a hoecake of bread and scraps of fried salt meat. Together they ate, after Mammy Sukey muttered a blessing over the food. The child mixed the bread and the sweet thick syrup with her fingers as she had long watched the toothless old woman do, and together they washed down the food with a gourd dipper of cold water, Mammy Sukey drinking first, and then Vyry.

When they started down the Big Road toward Marse John's Big House, nearly five miles away as the crow flies, dew was still on the grass, but the rising sun was already beaming down on Vyry's bonnet and on Mammy Sukey's head rag. At first the cool, damp grass and the moist earth felt squishy under Vyry's bare feet, but soon they were on a hot dusty clay road. Occasionally she felt pebbles and roots roughen her way so that she stubbed her toes, and sometimes she stumbled.

Ever since she could remember Mammy Sukey had been bringing her along this dirt road, taking her to the Big House many times. Sometimes they picked a pail of blackberries early in the morning before the sun was high. Sometimes they went fishing and caught catfish for their supper. Most times they ambled along just enjoying the summer and the Georgia countryside—butterflies and will-o'-the-wisps, and pretty pink flowers with deep cups of gold pollen that grew along the wayside, or scarlet-colored cardinals and blue jays chattering and screeching and flying over their heads.

But today was different. Today they were in a big hurry, and Mammy Sukey held her hand so tightly it felt hot and sweaty, and her fingers felt cramped. The old woman muttered to herself, and sometimes she seemed to forget the little girl who was trudging along beside her.

"Ain't make a speck of difference nohow. Politeness and cleanness and sweet ways ain't make no difference nohow. She gone stomp her and tromp her and beat her and mighty nigh kill her anyhow." And the child listening was puzzled and troubled, but she did not question Mammy Sukey.

She had been to the Big House many times and she knew what to expect. Marse John was always kind to her when he was around. He would tell the little Missy to share when he brought bananas and oranges and other goodies. "Give Vyry some, too," he would tell her and Miss Lillian would do as her father said. The two little girls often played together making mud pies, or running over the hillside playing hide-and-go-seek and playhouse under the big live oaks and shouting and laughing in fun. On a hot summer's day Vyry had sometimes seen inside the Big House and stood in awe at the dark coolness inside and the richness of the lavish furnishings. In Big Missy's bedroom there was a great oaken bed whose headboard nearly touched the high ceiling and the high mountain of feather mattresses always was covered with a snow-white counterpane. In young Missy Lillian's there was a tester bed with a canopy of sprigged pink and white cotton while the Marster and young Marster had rooms with massive dark furniture with silk furnishing in dark greens and reds and blues. Vyry would go from room to room, tiptoeing in awe and not daring to touch all the wonderful things she saw and the beauty of the rooms that seemed endless. Now, when she thought about it, she wondered why she did not feel happy about going to the Big House to stay.

She vaguely felt, however, that neither young Marster John nor his mother, Big Missy Salina, liked her very much. They were never kind and Mammy Sukey was always trying to keep her out of their way. Why this was true Vyry did not understand, and she did not ask. It was not her place to ask and Mammy Sukey taught her never to get out of her place.

There was that time when Big Missy had company from

Savannah and Vyry was at the Big House playing in the yard with Miss Lillian. She heard the lady ask Big Missy, "My, but those children look so much alike, are they twins?" Vyry jumped when she heard the question and dared not turn her burning face in Big Missy's direction. Big Missy's cold angry voice hastened to correct the mistake. "Of course not. Vyry's Lillian's nigger maid. John brought her here to be a playmate to Lillian because they're around the same age, and Lillian has nobody else to play with. I must say they're near the same size, but I never have seen where they look alike at all."

The woman must have realized what a terrible mistake she had made, for she fumbled with the ivory fan that hung around her neck, at the same time changing color and muttering incoherent phrases in half-apologetic and half-frightened tones. But Vyry had a staunch champion in Miss Lillian. In those early years the little Missy did not mind saying to anyone, "Yes, Vyry's my sister, and I love her dearly, and she loves me, too, now don't you, Vyry?" And Vyry would mumble, "Yes, Missy, I reckon I does." But that was child's talk and had nothing to do with their elders, Big Missy and Marse John.

Marse John was forty years of age and slowly settling into a man of serious purpose. At this time of morning he was just getting out of bed. His little daughter, Lillian, still in her long white batiste nightdress with insertions of pink ribbon and lace, ran in to kiss him good morning and confide happily, "Vyry's coming today!"

"Oh, is she? I guess that means making mud pies all day?"

"Oh, no, she's coming to stay. She's going to be my own individual maid all the time, isn't she, Mama?" And Lillian clapped her hands in happy anticipation. Marse John dropped one of the heavy riding boots he was about to put on and turned a questioning look on his wife, Salina, who was standing before a large and ornate mirror arranging her hair.

"What the devil is the child talking about?"

"What she said. The nigger Vyry starts working today as Lillian's maid. Run along now, Lillian, and let Caline get you dressed and comb your hair. Breakfast ought to be ready in a little while."

He put on his boot and then stood fully dressed except for his riding coat. As soon as the child was out of earshot he turned on his wife, "What in hell is going on around

here? Why the devil wasn't I told about what's happening in
my own house?" His voice was pitched low and well controlled to keep the slaves in the upstairs hall from hearing
him, but his face bespoke his deep hostility and anger.

"Because you were either not here when I made the decision, what with all your new political notions and hunting
all night in the swamps—if that is what you are really doing
all night—or else you were too drunk to notice. And anyway, the house is my affair. I run things here as I please.
Unless you change your ways overnight, which isn't likely,
I'll have to run the whole plantation. Everything's going to
rack and ruin, what with all your nigger-loving ways. You
were going to bring her in here anyhow when you got good
and ready, just like you've brought all your other bastards.
I just beat you to it, and you've got the nerve to be angry."

For a full moment they eyed each other without speaking,
and then in an oddly controlled voice he said, "I'm riding
over to the Smith Barrow and Crenshaw plantations. They've
got some horses and dogs for sale that I want to see."

"You going before breakfast?"

"I don't want any breakfast."

"Humph, well remind them about the dinner party, will
you?"

"I will not. That is really your affair, so you attend to it
yourself." And grabbing up his riding cap he rushed out of
the room slamming the door behind him.

Downstairs, out of the house, and on his way to the stables
his mind was busy with a half-dozen things, the confusion
of the morning, his abrupt leave of Salina, Vyry and Lillian,
and the dead girl, Hetta, and his growing political ambitions.
Already it was a warm August morning and the sun was
hot. Sweat popped out on him and he mopped his face and
brow more than once before spying Grandpa Tom.

"Morning, Tom. Saddle my horse and be quick about it.
I'm riding over to the Barrow and Crenshaw plantations,
and I'm in a powerful big hurry."

"Yassah, Marster, morning to yall. Ain't you riding kind
of early, sah?"

"Not early enough. This blasted sun'll cook me before I
get halfway there."

"Yassah, yassah, I reckon so. Hope you'll find it cooler
before you starts back home."

John Morris Dutton, sitting astride his chestnut bay horse,

threw his head back and laughed. "Now, how'd you know I won't be home soon? Evening or cooler weather, hanh?"

"Nice to see you then, Marster. Nice to see you then."

And as the horse and his rider went trotting down the path to the Big Road, old Grandpa Tom laughed to himself and scratched the bald top of his head.

When Marse John rode away from his house, Vyry and Mammy Sukey were well on their way toward the Big House. At the same time the slave driver, Grimes, who was Marse John's overseer on the plantation, was returning home with six new slaves he had purchased two days before at the slave market in Louisville. They were all field hands, or supposed to be, and they had brought a high price in the market. But Grimes was a little uneasy. He had been on his way since sunup, and since he was already in the swamp bottoms near Marse John's place he hoped to be home soon after breakfast or close around breakfast time. But the youngest of his chattel purchases, a boy in his early teens who was supposedly seventeen but who acted and looked more like fourteen, kept slowing down the journey by falling on the ground and tugging at the line of rope on which the six were strung. Grimes prodded him on with his horse whip by hitting him a lick or two. Both times the boy got up and staggered forward only to drop again in a half-hour or three-quarters of an hour's time. The sun was hot, and they had not had much water, but Grimes was beginning to suspect that the boy was not just suffering from heat and fatigue, he was sick. The auctioneer had cheated him and sold him a sick slave in the lot. He swore softly under his breath, and then yelled, "Hey you, there! Move along there now! You act like you got lice falling off you. We ain't got all day."

Uneasy as he was, he rode along lazily on his old gray nag not wanting to push the horse too hard. He was tired sitting in the saddle, and the butts of his pistols rubbed against his flesh uncomfortably. The Negroes were glum. When they first started out they talked among themselves. Each night when they stopped to make camp, they had sung their mournful songs while sitting in the darkness before lying down to sleep. Grimes kept them tied together even at night for fear of a runaway, and he hardly dared doze despite the loaded pistols he was wearing. In the morning light the boy's eyes looked glazed and sick. Jack, the big brawny slave standing six feet in his bare feet, put his hand on the boy's forehead as if to determine whether he had fever. Two of the others, Ben and Rizzer, gave the child their water, and he drank thirstily, but he would not eat anything. He vomited once and cried out during the night in his sleep.

Grimes looked up at the early morning sky where buzzards circled high above the trees, and he wished he were already home.

The six slaves, all male, were naked to the waist. Their one piece of clothing was a pair of ragged and faded cotton breeches cut off at the knees and tied around their waists with small ropecord. To this was attached the long piece of rope stringing them together in single file. Their bare legs and feet moved carefully through the swampy ground and the thickets of briers and weeds, heedless of scratches or cuts, while their quick eyes were ever watchful for snakes. Around their faces and feet buzzed flies, gnats, and mosquitoes, which they constantly tried to brush away with their manacled hands. Sweat glistened on all the bodies but the boy's. He looked dry and parched and his thin body was bony. Across his face was a long scar like a cut, and across his back and shoulders a huge welt, which had healed, still stood out prominently. The boy groaned constantly, making a wheezing and delirious sound that was first a moan then a whine mixed with a high-pitched, babbling, sing-song cry. Annoyed by this, Grimes started to hit him again, and thought better of it. They couldn't have much farther to go.

Grimes was a short, thick-set man, his shoulders big and round like a barrel and his heavy thighs like the broad flanks of a big boar with short, stocky legs and short but powerful arms. His watery blue eyes were as small as pig eyes, and when he was angry they turned a fiery red, though not exactly the same red as his thin carrot-colored hair and the dull red freckles that peppered his face and mottled his neck and arms. Even his upper lip and stubby chin were covered with a day's growth of red bristles which also stuck out of his nostrils and ears. His squinting eyes darted right and left, watching carefully for every turn of the road, and keeping the Negroes well in front of him. He was chewing tobacco and when he spat he stained the creases around his mouth and dropped dabs of the brown juice on his blue cotton-linsey shirt. His collar was open enough to show the red bristles on his chest, for the perspiration rolled off him, and where his cotton breeches were stuck in his fine leather boots they were soaking wet to the skin. He used his boots to nudge his nag and urge the beast along. When a horse has trotted nearly a hundred miles without much fancy attention a little easy nudge is in order. Of course, he never did have a good horse. John Morris Dutton kept all the fine thoroughbreds for hunting and carriage pulling and riding, while he gave Grimes all the nags and mules for work horses. Grimes did not think this was exactly right, but then what can you expect from a nigger-loving man like Dutton when it comes to treating poor white people right?

Now his wife's different. She's a lady, Missy Salina Dutton is, a fine, good lady. She nurses the sick far and wide, white and black. She knows how to handle niggers and keep a big establishment; how to set a fine table, and act morally decent like a first-class lady. She's a real Christian woman, a Bible-reading, honest-dealing, high-quality lady who knows and acts the difference between niggers and white people. She ain't no nigger-loving namby-pamby like that s.o.b. pretty boy she's married to. She knows how to lay the law down to niggers and keep her business to herself. Deep down in their hearts, a lot of people might feel sorry for the way her husband mistreats her, carrying on with nigger wenches, and even stooping so low as to raise whole families by them, shaming a good wife and a decent white woman of Quality. Not that she ever gives a sign like she knows about his goings-on. She is always strictly business-like and matter-of-fact. She acts so unconcerned you have to admire her for her guts. Of course people know and folks can't help talking about it, anyhow. Then too, it wouldn't be so bad if she wasn't so all-fired good-looking, but she is a beautiful woman. He sometimes wished his Jane Ellen had the kind of quality looks Missy Salina Dutton had. Of course Janey has had a hard time. She come from the pine barrens and her folks is awful poor, so poor they eat dirt, and sometimes, like right now while Janey is expecting (this'll be number eight), she craves dirt like her Maw done before her and that's why she eats so much snuff. But Janey was once real nice-looking too, before all these younguns, and when her blonde hair was real light colored and not so stringy as it is now, and she wasn't so careless, like walking around in a dirty dress with her feet stomp barefooted like she come in the world. But they is one sure thing, by God, she is a true, good wife and she don't have no nigger-loving husband like that trashy John Morris Dutton.

Most folks would never guess how he longed some day to have a farm of his own. He knew darn well how to run a farm, and he wouldn't be running off all the time leaving the work to somebody else. A lot of people think running a farm and handling nigras is nothing, but that ain't so; it's hard work. Managing a farm and keeping a pack of evil, black slaves in line ain't no child's play, but he knew how to do it. That's what he told Mister Dutton when he hired him, and he, Ed Grimes, was tough and hard enough a man to prove it. Of course you got a lot of things against you, things to contend with like the weather, for an instance. Rain slows the work down and niggers always hollering, "more rain, more rest." You got to keep a firm hand on niggers, else they won't hit a lick of the snake. Half the time they make out like they sick and got the rheumatiz or the whooping cough or just plain misery, and half the time they is just putting on. You can't pay them no mind, because they are the biggest liars God ever made—that is, if God made them. Sometimes it seems like a fact for certain that niggers is the work of the devil, and cursed by God. They is evil, and they is ignorant, and the blacker they is the more evil; lazy, trifling liars, every one of them. The Marster, Mister Dutton, indulges niggers cause he thinks they are helpless and childish, and they ain't got no mind, but the truth is they is just plain evil and stubborn and hard-headed. Best thing to keep a nigger working and jumping is a good bull whip. All you got to do is flick that whip, and believe you me, they jumps. I ought to know. And Missy Salina knows, too, you can't give niggers no rope, do and they'll hang you, give em an inch and they'll take a mile. You can't let up on a niggah if you wanta be a good driver, and that's what I am, a first class A-number-one good driver.

Vyry and Mammy Sukey walked into the backyard of the Big House just in time to see a big commotion. All the house servants and yard hands were crowded around Mister Grimes, the overseer, who had brought six slaves into the backyard and was cutting the rope and unlocking the chains holding them together. Big Missy Salina was standing in the back door of the Big House. Mammy Sukey turned to Vyry and said, "Go ask Aunt Sally for a washpan so's you can wash your footses fore you goes inside." And just at that moment when Vyry ran to obey, the sick black boy fell sprawling face down in the dust. Mammy Sukey pushed forward into the group around Grimes, and then her eyes widened in horror. She yelled, "Lord, have mercy, all you niggers get back! Send for Granny Ticey fast and tell Missy get the doctor quick. I clare fore God this nigger's got the plague."

Vyry pushed open the back door to the one-room, lean-to kitchenhouse and saw Aunt Sally bending over the brick oven in the large fireplace chimney where she did all of Marster's cooking. For a minute Vyry stood there in the hot kitchen inhaling the smell of biscuits still baking, of fried ham with the smell still hanging on the air, and bubbling coffee. It seemed a long time since she and Mammy Sukey had eaten.

"Shucks, child, you scared me so I like to blistered myself with this here coffeepot. What you doing here?"

"I come to stay in the Big House with Miss Lillyum, and Mammy Sukey say give me a pot, please ma'am, so I can wash my footses fore I mess up Big Missy's pretty clean house, and they's a nigger outen there laying on the ground, Mammy say he got the plague . . ."

All her words came out in the rush of one breath. Aunt Sally stood looking through her for another long minute before she seemed to understand about the washpan the child was seeking.

"Got the plague? Oh, my Lord have mercy! Look-a-yonder hanging on the back porch and get that water bucket. You can set out there and wash yourself. I gotta see what's going on outside."

Vyry took the wooden bucket and went to the rain barrel to get water. But all that first day she could scarcely understand what was going on outside or inside. First, Big Ben and Rizzer moved the sick boy to one of the empty slave cabins where Big Missy kept all her medicines and where sick slaves went when they were bad off enough to need the doctor or stay on their pallets and need nursing, and then, as Mammy Sukey said, they had better be sick enough to die and prove it. Granny Ticey and Mammy Sukey took charge because Big Missy said she wasn't fooling with no niggers who had the plague, and she shooed all the rest of the slaves, including Aunt Sally, back to their work. When Big Ben and Rizzer saw that the sick boy was dying they stayed to help the two old women. Twenty-four hours later Ben and Rizzer dug a fresh grave. By their second evening that first new grave was filled. The dead boy was put naked into a feed sack, and then into a pine box in which he was hastily buried. Lime was spread liberally inside the grave, over, and around it.

That first night away from Mammy Sukey, lying on a strange pallet at the foot of Miss Lillian's bed, Vyry trembled for a long time before she could go to sleep. All day long she had gone back and forth from the kitchen to the springhouse, back to pull the dinner bell, then to gather eggs, to help feed the chickens, to fetch Miss Lillian a glass of water, and everything she had done and said was wrong. Twice Big Missy slapped her in the mouth with the back of her hand, and once Vyry barely escaped the foot of her mistress kicking her. Once she yelled to the startled child, "You stupid bastard, if you break airy one of my china dishes, I'll break your face."

If Vyry's first day was confusing, because Mammy Sukey was too busy to get her off to a good start in the Big House, it was increasingly confusing in the days that followed. Big Missy, Aunt Sally, and Caline kept explaining what to do next, and before many hours had passed Vyry sensed that her days here were not going to be what she had thought. There was no more time for mud pies. Miss Lillian was studying book lessons after breakfast. While Caline combed and brushed Miss Lillian's hair into curls Vyry stood by and she said, "Can I have curls, too?"

But Miss Lillian laughingly said, "Niggers don't wear curls, do they Caline?" And Caline watching Vyry's stricken face said, "Naw Missy, they sure don't."

Toward the end of the third day Vyry slipped away from the Big House twice to find Mammy Sukey, and twice she was sent back to her work and threatened with a whipping. Vyry told Aunt Sally she would rather die than catch a whipping. But the next day, fearing something she could only sense, she could not stay away, and she tried again to speak through the barred door of the cabin where Mammy Sukey still was. But the old woman's voice was now tired and troubled and she spoke a final admonition to the child:

"Gone back to the Big House, child, don't come here no more unlessen Aunt Sally sends you. Be good, and mind your manners like I told you and let Aunt Sally see after you . . ." and the familiar voice the child loved trailed off weakly.

That was the day Vyry forgot to empty Miss Lillian's chamber pot. Every morning when Caline and Jim, the houseboy, emptied slop jars, Vyry was told to empty Miss Lillian's little china chamber pot and see that it was washed outdoors and dried in the sun and brought in before bedtime and put under Miss Lillian's bed, but in her distress over being separated from Mammy Sukey, whom she dared not believe was sick, she forgot the chamber pot. That night when she heard Big Missy calling her from her supper in the kitchen with Aunt Sally she jumped up like she was shot. Trembling with fear of the whipping she knew she was going to get she stood before Big Missy, who was standing in the doorway of the kitchen and holding the pot of stale pee in her hand. Instead of whipping her, she threw the acrid contents of the pot in Vyry's face and said, "There, you lazy nigger, that'll teach you to keep your mind on what you're doing. Don't you let me have to tell you another time about this pot or I'll half-kill you, do you hear me?"

"Yas'm."

Early the next morning Vyry started toward the forbidden cabin again. When she saw them bringing out the stiff dead body of Mammy Sukey she began screaming and crying as if she could never stop. She cried all day, but after that evening when she knew Mammy Sukey would never take her down the Big Road any more she hushed her tears and determined not to cry any more.

For five days there was a new grave every day. But Vyry bent her back to Big Missy's hatred and struggled hard to please her. She lost track of the days and she could not know she had been there two weeks when she broke one of Missy's china dishes. This time she knew Big Missy was going to whip her. Vyry saw Big Missy standing with the leather strap in her hands, and she looked up impassive and resigned, then she clasped her hands tightly, bowed her head and closed her eyes, tensely waiting for the first terrible lick, but Missy Salina laughed and said, "Do you think I'm going to hurt myself whipping you? Open your eyes and come here to me." Too startled to feel relieved, Vyry looked up and saw her mistress holding a closet door open. She hooked the strap to a nail, then, snatching up Vyry, she crossed her hands and caught them securely with the strap. Vyry's toes barely touched the floor of the closet. Suddenly Big Missy slammed the door behind her and left Vyry hanging by her hands there in the darkness. Terribly frightened, the child did not whimper. At first she was terrified in the dark, but after such a long time, with her arm-pits hurting so bad, she lost consciousness of everything and did not know how long she hung there in torture.

Two weeks after his early morning encounter with his wife,
Marse John was returning home. Riding along the edge of
his vast home properties he was savoring the pleasant air of
a bright September morning. His mind was not on the pedi-
greed hunting hounds he bought from Barrow, nor the good
whiskey he drank with Crenshaw. His neighbors were coming to his house for a hunting party as soon as the weather
was cold enough. That would mark the beginning of his
political campaign. Things ought to stack up in his favor
as a candidate from Terrell County for the legislature. He
expected to win hands down since he owned Terrell County
and most of what was left of Lee County, too. His drivers
were already his deputy sheriffs. Law and order in the county
were gradually taking shape under his hands with political
organization as his ultimate goal. He owned enough slaves
to give him a large number of votes. For every five slaves
he could count three votes. The only trouble was it took so
much time, and he needed more time to spend covering the
state. Rural traveling wasn't fun, and the weather determined
everything. This trip had not been extended enough to visit
his lands in Bainbridge and Newton counties for these bordered the Alabama line on one side, and the Florida line on another end. He would like to go more often traveling out of the
state, but Salina never wanted to go anywhere except Augusta
and Savannah. Once, before he was married, he spent a carnival season in New Orleans; pretty nearly spent the winter
there. He surely enjoyed the lavish balls and gay social affairs
in that exotic city. He even toyed with the idea of setting up
one of those colored gals who had taken his fancy at the
Quadroon balls. My God, but they were pretty! Only very rich
white men were sought for them; they were bred only for the
purpose of being some white man's mistress. But he decided it
was foolish, a waste of good money, and too far from home to
be convenient. Besides, at that time, he still had Hetta. Anyway, when he came home to Georgia, he came to God's country, and no other place on earth could be half so fine.

Here on his plantation between the Flint and Chattahoochee
rivers was the land he remembered as a boy, where he had
grown to manhood. What good times he had in these very
woods when he was just a slip of a lad and his father took him
coon hunting at night with the hounds, slaves, patter-rollers,
and all! He laughed loudly just remembering.

Once they were coming along this same stretch of swamp-

land with a pack of dogs hot on the scent of a possum or coon
or something, and they ran smack-dab through the tangled
briars and sticky thickets of vines following the yelping dogs
who were barking up a helluva lot of noise. His father, excited,
kept edging the dogs on, calling them by name, Queenie and
Bessie, while they moaned and hollered, leading them into the
thickest and deepest part of the woods. There the dogs barked
like bedlam, the hunters hollered, "She's treed him." And they
gathered around a big live oak tree. It was midnight and no
moon, and they almost ran into the tree before his father
flashed his lantern, and he, a young boy, stood gaping with the
rest of the party, a tattered and tired bunch, with his father
still breathing hard from running, when suddenly there was
a dead hush. The light flickered at the base of the huge tree.
The dogs tucked their tails, whined, and drew back. Against
the dark bark of the tree stood a very large and glittering
rooster. He appeared to be all of two feet high. His red and
green and black feathers were gleaming like satin. His cox-
comb was a bright, bristling red. But his eyes were fantastic.
They looked like the eyes of a human being. He was wide-
eyed and unblinking, and stared back at them unruffled, calm,
and steadily. Finally his father said in a tired voice, "Call
off your dogs, boys, let's go home." Disappointed, he said,
"But why, Poppa? Where's our game? We ain't got no coon
yet."

"Ain't no game, son, leastwise not tonight. When did you
ever see a chicken this far from roost this time of night?"

And the wide-eyed slave boys shook their heads and whispered among themselves.

"Sho ain't no coon!'

". . . and sho ain't no possum!"

". . . and it sho ain't no rooster neither."

Yes, this was his land, and this was home. His mother's
holdings and his father's father's land had become his. They
made him one of the seven richest planters in the center of
Georgia. They kept him on the go so much he had to trust
most of the running of the plantations to his drivers, even
though Salina accused him of leaving the home place in her
hands. He couldn't be in two or three places at the same
time. On one plantation alone, the last time he had it sur-
veyed, he owned three thousand acres. In addition to the
rivers, his broad fertile lands in the river valleys were also
watered by the Kinchafoonee and the Muckalee creeks. It
was here in the marshy thickets and lush swamps of many

meandering streams and treacherous bogs that a number of slaves had tried to run away to freedom. Most of them were caught by the patter-rollers and brought back for a flogging, in order to teach them a lesson and set an example for the others. Once when he was a half-grown boy he had gone on a searching party after a runaway slave. They gave the hounds the scent of his clothes. It sickened him now to remember. Flogging wasn't necessary that time because the dogs tore the fellow to pieces. Even now he could see the hideous bloody sight. His father was fighting mad. Runaway or no runaway, slaves cost money and mangling expensive property didn't please him one little bit, no sir-ee!

Sometimes Grimes overstepped his authority now, but they really had to depend upon him. He had a reputation of knowing how to handle nigras. Perhaps Salina was correct when she accused her husband of being a weak disciplinarian and not firm enough with his slaves. He preferred to leave the stern punishing of all his black labor in Grimes's hands as long as he didn't go too far.

Like an ancient lord in a great feudal, medieval castle surrounded by water and inaccessible except by a drawbridge over a moat (before one entered the fortified dwelling), he lived in a most inaccessible section of Georgia—deep in the forest, miles from the cities, and impossible distances to travel on foot. It was fully a half-day's journey from the old Wagon Road, where the stage coaches once traveled the Big Road, to the long oak-lined avenues leading up to the stately white manor of his own Shady Oaks. When he turned off the Wagon Road he had to travel ten or twelve miles on this narrow road that was overhung with great live oaks and towering virgin pine trees that touched the sky. From the live oak trees hung the weird gray veils of Spanish moss waving wildly in the wind, and trailing like gray tresses of an old woman's hair, lost from the head of some ghost in the wilderness. Often during daylight hours the sky was completely obscured by an archway of these trees. Here in the stillness of the forest one was cut off from reality and lost in a fantastic world of jungle. In this world of half-darkness and half-light he had often felt as though eyes were watching him.

After the twelve miles the road led along the path of the Kinchafoonee Creek where the swampy woods were full of cypress, so dense and dank and dark that it seemed as if the sky were overcast and a shadow hung over the day, sending a shiver creeping along his spine in the eerie atmosphere. Though the summer was waning, the air was fragrant with exotic sub-tropical flowers mingling with the pungent smell of pine. The colorful pink and orange bougainvillea and the royal purple wisteria hung in thick grape-like and trumpeting clusters. They grew in wild profusion, while the undergrowth was tangled with blue morning glory vines and running bushes of the climbing Cherokee rose. Yellow flickers, blue jays, thrashers, kildeers, brown wrens, speckled field larks, and scissor tails darted back and forth through the brush and through the trees, screeching with merriment, while here and there a chattering school of crows made their caw-caw noise. Gradually the swampy woods disappeared and Marse John came at last to his broad fields which were under cultivation on both sides of the road. Now the cotton was white with harvest, and as always his slaves were working in the fields, filling long croker sacks with the fluffy yield.

On his way to the house he passed the cemetery, the family plot where his parents and his grandparents were buried, where he too, in time, would be laid beside them. Fresh mounds of earth drew his quick attention and he got down off his horse to investigate. Six new graves in two short weeks? Name of God, who could they be? The rough wooden boards told him they were slaves but only two bore names, Granny Ticey and Mammy Sukey! From the plentiful sprinkling of lime he knew very well the deaths were due to something contagious.

Sorrowful now, he remounted and went to the house where such a stillness seemed unnatural. Chickens pecking around the back kitchen house and well were a familiar sight. Curtains were drawn against the heat and he was relieved to have his daughter Lillian run to meet him. She whispered in his ear, "Oh, Poppa, come quick, Vyry's hanging by her thumbs in the closet and I do believe she's dead."

He lost no time running up the stairs where Salina sat in her room with a basket of mending in her lap as though nothing were unusual, but when she saw him bound for the closet she jumped up. Quickly he caught the child, Vyry, whose feet barely touched the floor, and he saw she was only in a dead faint.

"What you trying to do, Salina, kill her?"

"Yes. I reckon that's what I oughta do. Kill her and all other yellow bastards like her. Killing's too good for her."

"Well, don't you try it again, d'ye hear me? Don't you

dare try it again! She's nothing but a child, but someday she'll be grown-up and worth much as a slave. Then you'll be sorry."

"Humph! Are you talking to me? I'll never be sorry. Never, d'ye hear? How much do you expect me to put up with? Here in this very house with my own dear little children. And my friends mortifying me with shame! Telling me she looks like Lillian's twin. Don't you dare threaten me, John Morris Dutton, don't you dare threaten me. So far as killing her, I ain't even hurt her. I oughta kill her, but I ain't got the strength to kill a tough nigra bastard like her."

Flee as a bird to your mountain,
Ye who are weary of sin.
Go to the clear flowing fountain,
Where you may wash and be clean.

3   *"Flee as a bird to your mountain"*

"Flee as a bird to your mountain!" Vyry was singing her
favorite hymn, and, although at ten years of age her alto
voice was still timid and small, it promised to be as rich and
dark as Aunt Sally's. Then the whole valley would fill up
with her song. Her bare feet moved swiftly across Baptist
Hill while her heart clamored after the morning. Her faded
blue linsey dress made her look like a ragamuffin and her
sandy hair was wrapped tightly in rags. In one hand she
held the feed bucket for the chickens. She stood on the
hill and watched the sunrise and saw the ribbons of mist
hanging over the valley, all over Marse John's plantation in
a sweep of rich, green fields and trees and the land dotted
with cabins and houses, barns and other farm buildings as
far as her eyes could see. This was her favorite spot in the
early morning, but oh, how she wished she were going some

place. She wished herself out where the fields ended, where
the wagon road was winding, and the Central of Georgia
Railroad was puffing like a tiny black fly speck along the
tracks. If she were only free as a bird, free as the mourning
doves on the wing and circling high overhead in the sky,
racing beyond Marse John's plantation and his squawking
chickens, it would be wonderful to go winging away on such
a golden morning. She would like to go far beyond Aunt
Sally's voice calling her back to her morning chores of picking up chips, feeding chickens, finding that setting dominicker
hen, drawing water from the well, brushing up the backyard,
fetching butter and milk and cream from the springhouse,
brushing flies from the breakfast table, washing dishes, and
waiting on Miss Lillian. Somebody was always asking her,
"Gal, ain't your mammy got nothing else for you to do?"

"Vyreeeeeeee! Oh, you Vyree! Gal, don't you hear me
calling you? You better make haste and come here to me.
I don't wanta hasta come after you. You make haste now,
you hear me Vyree?" and Vyry heard Aunt Sally's voice
only faintly in the distance, but she came running down the
hillside to her morning's work on the plantation. She scooped
up the setting hen and ran with it tucked under her arm
while she wondered how she could explain to Aunt Sally
what took her so long on Baptist Hill.

Aunt Sally was firm, but Aunt Sally was kind and Vyry
loved her very much. Ever since that time Marse John came
home and rescued her from Big Missy, Vyry had lived with
Aunt Sally. She slept in her cabin at night and worked in the
kitchen with her during most of the day. She ran into the
kitchen now almost breathless and with the chicken still
under her arm.

"Get that dominicker outa here, gal, is you crazy?"

Vyry hastily dropped the squawking hen outside the kitchen
door. The kitchen was separated from the Big House by only
a few yards of boardwalk under foot and a lean-to shelter
overhead. Like the house, the kitchen was made of bricks
that were baked Georgia clay, and the same slaves who had
made the bricks cut the oak timbers which trimmed the
handsome mansion of Marse John. Vyry was accustomed,
now, to the big brick fireplace with its brick oven where
Aunt Sally did all the cooking. The big iron pots swung
out on long iron handles. At first they were too heavy for
Vyry to lift but gradually she was learning, first with the
heavy lids and smaller pots, but Aunt Sally did not allow

her to touch them while they were hot or even stir their
contents over the open fire. There was a long wooden table
in the middle of the room where Aunt Sally prepared biscuits,
pies, meats, and cakes. Aunt Sally's dough board and rolling
pin and bread trough were all carved by hand from hard
oak or walnut or hickory and they were almost as heavy
as the pots. At seven, Vyry could not lift them, but now at
ten she could lift the rolling pin and biscuit board with ease.

Along one side of the room there were cupboards with
locks on them. In the morning Big Missy came out with a
bunch of keys and opened the cupboards and took out the
things she wanted Aunt Sally to cook and then she locked
the cupboards again. In one pantry Big Missy kept under
lock and key her jars of preserves and jellies, pickles and
relishes, canned fruits and vegetables. All her precious china
and glass were kept in the Big House and even washed by
Caline under Big Missy's watchful eye. In the smokehouse
hung the wonderfully cured and smoked hams, shoulders,
and middlings. There was a big trough hewn from one huge
log, and in this trough the fresh meat was first salted after
the hogs had been butchered and the meat had been washed.
Big Missy held the keys to the smokehouse as well as the
cane mill, with the homemade syrup and sorghum molasses,
and the springhouse where the butter and milk and cream
and clabber and eggs and all leftover foods were kept. In
the summertime Big Missy supervised all her household of
female help in canning and preserving. There were countless
rows of jars of fruit and vegetables which were raised in
abundance on the plantation and gathered by the slaves from
the nearby woods where berries, grapes, cherries, plums,
and apples grew in wild profusion. There was more than
enough food in Marster's larder, but in the hands of Big
Missy, and under her watchful eyes, none of this passed into
the cabins and stomachs of her slaves unless they stole it.

The well was not far from the house and only a few steps
from the kitchen. When Vyry was seven she was too little
to lift the wooden bucket brim-full of water, but now she
could also carry pails and pans of water into the kitchen.
This was one of her first tasks in the morning, to draw fresh
water.

Naturally, Vyry was learning to cook by watching Aunt
Sally. Aunt Sally showed her how to do everything the way
she did it and how to please the Marster's family. In the
morning when the milk was brought in from the barns so

much was brought to the Big House for the family use, and so much was taken to the plantation cook who prepared the midday meal for the hands in the fields. This was measured under close supervision and often the animal stock received more than the slaves. Under the watchful eye of Aunt Sally, Vyry learned to churn. The child would watch eagerly and delightedly to see the first pat of butter form around the paddle. Aunt Sally showed her how to put the milk in crocks, how to separate the heavy cream from the milk, make cottage cheese and clabber, and how to add warm water when you were in a hurry to make the butter come fast. But the beaten biscuits and spoon bread, fried chicken, hot waffles and light bread, light puddings, fruit duffs, fruit cakes, huckleberry pies, roast turkeys and geese, and the wild game and bird pies that Aunt Sally cooked gave her the name of being one of the best cooks in Lee County and even in the state of Georgia. When Marse John was at home the house was always full of company. Vyry soon learned what Aunt Sally meant when she complained of being too tired at night to sleep.

Mammy Sukey had said that Aunt Sally would look after Vyry, and now, after three years, her words were still fresh in Vyry's memory. Aunt Sally's loving care was that of a mother hen clucking over one biddy. After that terrible time of sleeping in the Big House, Vyry found Aunt Sally's cabin the next best thing to the cabin she had shared with Mammy Sukey, despite the fact that it was bare and rough and at night, lying on her pallet, she could peep through the holes in the top of the roof to look at the stars. When it rained they were careful to put cans and pots to catch the water, and not to let themselves get soaked in the wet places, but it had an open fireplace and most times they were warm, especially after Aunt Sally hung quilts over the rough, shuttered window and the door.

At night when they closed that door it was like going off into another world that was grand and good. Vyry was so devoted to Aunt Sally she would never have told anyone how often she saw her steal great panfuls of white folks' grub, and how many pockets she had in her skirts and her bosom where she hid biscuits and cakes and pie, even though Big Missy had threatened more than once to have Aunt Sally strung up and given a good beating if she ever caught her stealing. Once safe in the cabin they would fill their stomachs full of good food, tittering over the thought of how many different kinds of fits Big Missy would have if she knew how she had been outsmarted. Half whispering and giggling, Aunt Sally would pull out of her apron pockets and in her bosom and they would eat hot biscuits from Big Missy's supper table. "She'd die a unnatural death if she knowed I'm eating her biscuits. Liables to string me up and whup me. Humph! I ain't cooking nothing I can't eat myself." Then Aunt Sally would undo all the rags wrapped tightly around Vyry's hair and comb the sandy hair into curls delighting the little girl's heart beyond measure although her grave little face peered at herself through a cracked old glass seeing bluish-gray eyes that dared twinkle only the slightest bit.

Most of all Vyry loved the stories Aunt Sally would tell about who she was and where she came from, and what life was like, and how to live in the Big House and get along with Big Missy:

"My Maw come here from South Ca-lina and that's where I was borned at. She came here way back when Marse John's Grandpappy and his Pappy first come to Georgy and settled in this here wilderness. Wasn't nothing but Injuns and woods and vicious wild animals here then. I wasn't nothing but a teensy-weensy youngun, too little to do nothing but hang round my Mammy's dress-tail. Every morning she brung me with her to Marster's kitchen to fix vittles for Marse John's Pappy's family. That was when Injuns was sho-nuff bad in Georgy and wasn't no white folks safe outen they doors without they guns. Marse John's Pappy fout in the Revolution-Freedom war with Gen'l George Washington and when he come here to Georgy they give him a bounty for being sitch another good soldier. Fore the war he live in Virginy where his folks come from and then they come to Georgy. First off they live in Savanny. That's where Big Missy come from, but when the New-nited States Government passed a territory law, Georgy opened up this here back country to soldiers to settle, I dis-remember when, but that's when Marse John's Pappy come to Lee County to the Land drawing, and they been a-prospering all the time ever since. And that's how long I been living in Marse John's kitchen."

"How long I been here?" Vyry's question tickled Aunt Sally and her fat sides shook with her laughter. "You just now come in the world, that's how long you been here. You was borned in one of these very cabins on this very place. You was borned in the hot summertime when the corn was all tasseled and the cotton bolls was green and you come here before the stars fell. I seen the stars fall outen the sky with my naked eyes. They fell with a long tail of fire and they fell that very fall before you was borned. Your Mammy died just before the panic struck and Marse John couldn't get nothing for the cotton. That was right after your Mammy died. I thought the world was coming to an end when the stars fell outen the sky. And when the panic come they run the Injuns outen Georgy with guns and they fit and fout and fit all over these here swamps clean down in Alabamy and them Floyda swamps fore them Injuns give up for surrender. Ain't been no passel of time, nohow, seem like just yestiddy and Sis Hetta, your Mammy, was walking round here. Granny Ticey was the granny for you and Miss Lillyum, and I members just as good how they wasn't no time fore we seen how white you was with that there sandy hair and Hetta a right jet black woman. Marse John turn right red when he seen you, and Big Missy she went to have one of her crying and storming fits and throwing things and then they say they got to take you away from Jake and Hetta else Jake gwine kill you. That's how come they give you to Mammy Sukey and that's how come you is in the Big House now."

"But Aunt Sally, I don't see how come that make Big Missy hate me so bad. I ain't done nothing."

"I knows you ain't, child, and she knows you ain't done nothing neither, but she mad with your Mammy and your Pappy, and she mad with Marster 'cause they done accused him of being your Daddy. Now I reckon I ain't got no business telling you, but since you asked me, you keep it to yourself, and stay outen her way. That's all you does. Stay outen her way."

No matter how tired Aunt Sally was at night, she never failed on Big Meeting Nights to go to hear Brother Ezekiel preach. As often as she went, she would take Vyry to the Rising Glory Baptist Church deep in the swamps and a long way from the Big House. They had to walk a long distance across the plantation but Vyry was never tired, she was too excited with the prospect of hearing Brother Ezekiel preach and joining in the singing. There was wonderful and high-spirited singing, such as Vyry remembered long afterward, and she tried to remember and sing the songs they sang such as "Steal away" and "I got shoes" and "I'm going to sit at the Welcome Table" and such jubilant melodies as

"Religion is a fortune I really do believe" and "The old sheep knows the road but the young lambs must find the Way." Brother Ezekiel nearly always chose his text from the Old Testament, dwelling upon the great leaders of the Hebrew people: the prophets, the kings, the judges, and the men whom God had used to lead their people. His favorite and most prominent figure was Moses and the story of his leading the children of Israel out of Egypt, out of the House of Bondage, to a vision of the Promised Land:

"They was ordered by the king to make bricks out of straw."

"Oh, yeah."

"And then they was commanded to make bricks out of nothing."

"Oh, yeah."

"Hear me this evening, children. They made the Hebrew children bend beneath the lash."

"Oh, yeah. Amen, bless God."

"And they ordered the midwives to kill the new-born boy-child on the birthing pots."

"Oh, yeah."

"Well now, listen to me. God didn't like it. No siree! He didn't like it one little bit. No siree!

"And he let it go on just as long as he was ables to stand it. And then he say he can't stand it no more.

"And Moses was born to some poor persecuted Hebrew slaves."

"Yes, he was."

"And his mammy saved him and hid him for three months. Yes, she did, bless God, cause she knowed God had him for a purpose.

"And she made a little basket and stuck him in the swampy water where the king's daughter come to bathe in the cool of the evening. And listen to me preaching this evening. I wants to tell you she took him in the Big House, yes she done it, she done that very thing.

"She took him in Pharaoh's house, that cruel slave owner what was persecuting God's children, what God didn't like, what God didn't have to stand. And God seen fit to use Moses, yes, he sho-nuff used him. And when he called him he said, 'Son, I wants you to go down yonder and tell that cruel hard-hearted slave marster to let my peoples go. And tell him I won't take "No" for an answer. Tell him I say I done run clean outen patience. And you tell him I am the God what Am and Always was and Always will Be. And I'm gettin awful tired of his foolishness. Tell him all I gotta do is snap my fingers and he won't have no water to drink. And all I gotta do is stretch out my rod over the land and make suffering the bedfellow of every living man. I can heal the pain and I can kill the sorrow. You tell him I say be quick about it. And let my peoples go.' "

Brother Ezekiel grew eloquent as he told the biblical story, but his voice softened to a whisper either from strain or fear as he admonished his flock to have faith in God and He would send them a Moses, a deliverer to free His people and prove to the world what the Bible says about a servant being worthy of his hire.

At first Vyry listened with wonder, and gradually she began to understand why Aunt Sally made her solemnly promise, under the terrible threat of never taking her again, never to repeat to anyone what she had heard at the Rising Glory Church, and furthermore not to ask so many questions, because little girls were made to be seen and not heard.

Always the meetings were held deep in the swampy woods, seldom on bright moonlight nights when the moon was full. For a long time Vyry did not understand that these meetings served a double purpose. She enjoyed hearing Brother Ezekiel preach, and most of all she enjoyed joining in the singing. Aunt Sally had promised her mysteriously that when she was older and had her "womanhood" she could be baptized by Brother Ezekiel. She concluded that the reason for the secret meetings had something to do with later mysteries and that nobody must tell a word to the white folks on pain of death itself just because white folks were naturally mean and hateful and hated all poor colored folks who could not help themselves anyhow.

One evening after supper when Aunt Sally had cooked a special meal, Marse John came out to the kitchen to tell her how much he enjoyed it. Aunt Sally grinned and said, "Thank you kindly, Marster, I'm sho glad you did." She caught up one end of her apron and wiped her hands on it, still beaming in Marse John's face.

"Yes, indeed, Sally, that was one of the best meals I have ever eaten, and you surely have cooked many a meal in this house. Let's see now, you were cooking when I was a boy."

"That's right, sir, I sho was."

"Well, that's good. Tell me, how are Sam and Big Boy? I heard something about Sam having a little trouble with Mister Grimes."

Aunt Sally's bottom lip dropped and quivered a little.

"Ain't heerd tell nothing bout it, Marster, ain't heerd tell one God's blessed word."

"Well, I wouldn't worry about it if I were you. Sam was always a good boy. Just tell him to try and stay in line and obey Mister Grimes and everything will be all right."

"Yassuh, yassuh, I sho will. And Marster, just one minute. They's a favor I wants to ask you if I is allowed."

"Why certainly, Sally, what is it?"

"I'd like to have a pass to your other plantation come Sunday if you will let me go. I has to pass through town and I needs a pass and I wants to go early if you says it's all right with you. I has a sick cousin over there."

"Well, I guess you can. I'll write you out a pass. Anybody else going with you?"

"Nossuh, I reckons not, cep'n Vyry."

"Oh, good! Of course you'll take her along. As long as she's with you she's in good hands. You'll be home before nine o'clock, I suppose?"

"Oh yassuh. Yassuh I sho will. This here old niggah gwine be laying on her pallet fore curfew time, I promises you." Marse John chuckled and went out, picking his teeth with an ivory toothpick.

Vyry was delighted to be going to the Rising Glory Baptist Church to hear Brother Ezekiel preach about God, and the Hebrew children, and the Moses who was going to set them free. But she could not understand the troubled look on Aunt Sally's face, nor the great hurry that made her walk so fast. Long before they left Marse John's other plantation and were on their way deep into the woods toward the secret meeting place in the swamps, Vyry was so tired she felt she would drop. She would not have been nearly so tired if Aunt Sally had been laughing and talking pleasantly as usual, but she kept muttering to herself and ignoring all of Vyry's questions.

At last when they reached the place, Vyry knew that this was no ordinary Sunday meeting. Aunt Sally's Sam and Big Boy were there and some of the other slaves they knew from Marse John's nearby plantation, but there were several strangers including a white man and a free black man from the village. They had some papers which they were reading and explaining to all the slaves gathered there. At first Vyry did not pay much attention because she could not understand what the papers were, or what they were saying, or even why everybody seemed so upset. She remembered seeing two slaves down on the bank of the creek, and now she looked off in the other direction and there were two more who were watching and evidently listening for any sound from the guards who patrolled the nearby plantations or, worse still, for the hounds that the guards often used.

Soon Vyry discovered that some of the trouble had to do with Aunt Sally's boy, Sam, and some words he had with Grimes, who struck him with his whip, and then pulled his gun on him. There had also been a runaway slave whom the guards had caught, but he was not even claimed by his master because the dogs had mangled him to death and torn his body to pieces. Some of the papers were new laws and revisions of the Black Code tightening the control of master over slave, and the papers the free man was reading were papers that had been first smuggled into Georgia, and then into his hands. They contained words and messages from black and white people in the North where there was talk against slavery, and where, as Aunt Sally hastened to explain to Vyry, there were a lot of people called 'litionists who were friends to the black slave. Some of the papers were official orders from the governor of Georgia and they concerned movements of black free men as well as slaves. Aunt Sally said she had seen papers like those before although she couldn't read them.

"One time they posted a sign with an Injun head on it, and it said that Injun had the smallpox and everybody keep away from him; and another time the poster read how it was agin Georgy law (still is) for nary nother piece of paper, pencil, pen, writing papers, books, newspapers or print things to get in black hands, slave or free. And they called on all the God-fearing white folks of Georgy to arrest anybody what they catch with these here papers, like what a man named David Walker had done writ a long time ago, and what they say was stirring up unrestlessness and trouble mongst all us slaves. That was a long time fore you was borned. I wonder what kinda new trouble is us got now?"

That evening in the deep swamps Vyry sat listening so intently and tensely she hardly noticed the aggravating bugs, flies, and mosquitoes that were always singing around their heads, stinging and biting through their clothes. The talk sounded like a plan for a plot or an uprising but all of it was confusing to Vyry's young ears, though she felt the tension of time so taut that it was standing still. It was dusk-dark when they first gathered and this, in itself, was a crime. There were more than seven slaves together and a white man and a free man with them and this was an offense with the serious punishment of flogging or prison or both, and if death just happened to take place in the course of the punishment it would be just one of those accidents that ended with another dead nigger. Vyry kept looking at the white man and sometimes she caught herself staring with her mouth hanging open. Who was he and why was he so interested in seeing black folks free he would risk his death? He was saying, "Well, will you do it? Do you really want to be free, or are you afraid?" He was saying to Sam and Big Boy and Caline and May Liza that they were human beings with a right to freedom. "You are just as good as your masters and you will remain in bondage no longer than you are willing to fight and stop enduring all this inhuman treatment. Slaves are rising, all over the South they are rising up and there are other free men who are willing to help you. There are plenty of white people up North who will help you to escape, even give you money, and will protect you at the risk of their lives."

But now a startling answer came forth from one of the oldest slaves on Marse John's plantation, Uncle Joe:

"That's foolish talk you talking, boy, foolish and dangerous, too. Here you is ain't dry behind your ears and here you come talking bout how us gwine be free. Does you know how many hundreds and hundreds of years we's been slaves? Does you know how long since the white man brung us here from Affiky to this here America? You know how come? Well, you know what God told Ham, don't you? You know what we is, don't you? Just hewers of wood and drawers of water, that's what we is. That's our punishment for being black. Yall can swell up, swell on up if you want to, like a dead dog, until you bust. I knows what you think I is, but I'm telling you now bout getting free. You might be willing to die cause you ain't gotta die, and you might be willing to get whipped, but I ain't fixing to say die, and I ain't fixing to get whipped. Sho, us is uprising, niggers uprising all the time and look what happening. Ain't none of them uprising yet went free. Tell me one time they come free, I'm asking you? Just tell one time. You know when us gwine free? I can tell you cause I knows. Us gwine go free when the Good Lord say so and not before, when He come riding in His chariot bringing a Moses with Him. If He means for me to go free, I'm gwine go free one of these days. Me and Esau and Plato and Tom is the oldest on the place and we knows what it is to feel the lash and bend under the whip. Lord knows I'd like to be ables to go wheresomever I wants to go, do what I wants to do, have my own farm, raise my own taters and cotton and corn, and be my own marster, man, and boss like you is, but I knows the Lord's will gwine be, and I'm waiting on the Lord. And I ain't jumping out like that poor boy got chawed to pieces by the dogs. What us gwine do, meantime? Meantimes us pray, that's what. Meantimes us pray."

But all the slaves did not feel as Uncle Joe felt. Big Boy, Sam, and the younger ones were willing to listen to the free black man and the white man suggesting a fight for freedom. You could see the anger in their faces and the frustration. Vyry did not understand very well what was going on, nor why Aunt Sally muttered under her breath after Uncle Joe finished speaking.

But there were other things to divert her mind as much as the meetings at Rising Glory Church in the woods. There were those happy hours after work on late summer afternoons when she was free to play with the other slave children before the cabin doors until bedtime.

From the time Vyry began to live with Aunt Sally she spent less and less time with Miss Lillian and this seemed to distress both children. Vyry had no more time in the day to play games with Miss Lillian and so the young Missy in the Big House frequently stole away to the Quarters to play with the slave children in the late afternoon and early twilight hours:

> Steal Miz Liza, steal Liza Jane.
> Steal Miz Liza, steal Liza Jane.
>
> That old man ain't got no wife,
> Steal Liza Jane.
> Can't get a wife to save his life,
> Steal Liza Jane.

They played "Go in and out the window" and "Hold up the gates as high as the sky, Let King George's horses pass by," and their laughter rang out wide with

> Las night, night before,
> Twenty-four robbers at my door.
> I got up and let them in,

Hit 'em on the head with a rolling pin.
All hid?

But Miss Lillian's favorite game was

Here comes a gentleman just from Spain,
To court, to court, your daughter Jane.
My daughter Jane she is too young,
To be controlled by any one.
Oh, let her be old,
Oh, let her be young.
It is her duty,
And it must be done.
Stand back, stand back,
You sassy man,
And choose the fairest
In the land.
The fairest one that I can see,
Is come pretty maiden and walk with me.

And they always chose Miss Lillian to be the pretty maiden
and the fairest in the land. But one evening in the midst of
the laughter and fun, the old black people sitting in their door-
ways, smoking and watching the young ones play, Big Missy
came down mad as a hornet and snatched Miss Lillian away.
"You come home, you hear me. You're a young lady and
you getting too big to play with niggers." And Miss Lillian,
broken with tears and misery, allowed herself to be dragged
along.

And then the games had lost their fun for Vyry as well as
the other children, even when they played Vyry's favorite
game and let her be the main one:

Baptize Peter, baptize Paul,
Baptize yeller gal, head and all.

Vyry liked that game best because she secretly looked forward
to the real baptizing Brother Ezekiel held in the swamp creek
every spring, and Aunt Sally said she, Vyry, should be baptized when she got her womanhood.

"What's womanhood?"

"You wait and see. I can't tell you now."

But on the shocking day when Vyry ran scared and bleeding to Aunt Sally, she spoke soothingly to the ten-year-old
little girl:

"Don't be scared! It ain't nothing but your womanhood.
You wants that, don't you?"

"What's womanhood?"

"It's what makes you a woman. Makes you different from a no-good man. It's what makes you grow up to have younguns and be a sho-nuff mammy all your own. Man can't have no youngun. Takes a sho-nuff woman. A man ain't got the strength to have younguns. He too puny-fied. Man ain't nothing but trouble, just breath and britches and trouble. Don't let him feel all over you, now, don't let a no-good man touch you, else he'll big you up sho-nuff.

"My Maw say that us colored folks knows what we knows now fore us come here from Affiky and that wisdom be your business with your womanhood: bout not letting your foots touch ground barefooted when your womanhood is on you. They useta hang up the young gals in the swinging trees and take them off way way from everybody else and they don't take no bazing with water and they don't let they footses straddle the rows in the fields less the crops will shrivel up and die. Just like a woman big with younguns don't touch no fresh meat at hog-killing time, less they wants to lose the meat; don't can no green vittles, less they wants them to spile. You gotta be careful when your womanhood is on you."

For one thing, Vyry was glad: Womanhood meant baptizing, and come spring to the swamp woods and the creeks when they would rise and all the swollen streams flow down into the river, Brother Zeke would baptize her.

Don't pay no tenshun to what the guinea hen say,
Cause the guinea hen cackle before she lay . . .

4   *Brother Zeke: "I am a poor way-faring
    stranger"*

"Ain't that that nigger preacher?"
   "Where?"
   "Running yonder through the field."
   "I don't see nobody."
   "I'd take a shot at him if the light was good, but they's a
haze and it's so foggy I can't see straight."
   "Yeah. It is a bad light."
   "I coulda sworn I seen something moving out there."
   "Where?"
   "Over yonder by that there biggest haystack."
   "What you see ain't nothing but a scarecrow flapping his
coattail wings."
   "Seem like I do, but I disremember airy scarecrow before."
   "Les-us go examine that there scarecrow."
   "Zamine a scarecrow for what? Is you losing your mind?"

"Just so. Let's go look."

"Now you see. It ain't nothing but a scarecrow like I told you: a scarecrow with a old rusty frocktail coat on."

"I swear I ain't never seen them arms flapping like that before."

"Well you can see ain't nothing but sticks holding up that there coat."

"I reckon I sees good as you."

And grumbling they went away while the black man lying under the haystack nearby watched them through the prongs of an up-right pitching fork until they were gone, and after waiting awhile, he took his coat off the scarecrow and disappeared into the fine mist of the morning.

Brother Zeke had important business. Such important business often had to coincide with his disappearance. Most times he came and went unnoticed. He could write his own pass: *This nigger preacher belongs to me. He has my consent to go to town and visit his sick nigras on my place. J. M. Dutton.* Most times he didn't have to show the pass. He just wrote it and kept it in case of emergencies. Traveling in the early morning or late at night from one plantation to the other, through the swamp woods and up the river branches, nobody took notice of him since he seemed to belong everywhere and know everybody. Then, too, most times he was alone. But not all the time. Sometimes Brother Zeke had somebody else with him. Those were the dangerous and important times. Even when he was careful not to be seen with anybody else, it was very important business and he had to avoid suspicion. His trembling and fearful companion was his responsibility and Brother Zeke never got nervous. As he constantly reassured such a frightened creature, "Efen you'll trust the good living God and me, we'll see you through."

Every time he made one of these trips he figured this might be the last one. But he kept going and coming under the very eyes of the guards and patter-rollers. "What folks doesn't know can't hurt em."

Brother Zeke never talked to anybody about his occasional sallies forth to see the world. He was a singing and preaching man but wasn't much for gossip. Sometimes early in the morning or about dusk-dark a person might spot him sitting on the roadside whittling a stick, or kneeling by the creek, or over a small fire skinning and cooking a catfish for his food. He might even swap a few words with white and black alike or be humming a tune and whistling bird calls, but next thing a person knew, the fire was out and the man had vanished.

He was ever so good with the sick. A sick child in the Quarters or even in the Big House would always laugh at the funny stories Brother Zeke could tell. He was a funny man with children all the time. Vyry loved Brother Zeke. He spent time explaining puzzling things to her when nobody else had time to pay her any attention. He soothed her fears, quoted Bible verses to her, and told funny stories about the spider and the cat, the wise donkey and the silly man, but best of all she loved to hear him sing:

> I am a poor way-faring stranger,
> I'm tossed in this wide world alone.
> No hope have I for tomorrow,
> I'm trying to make heaven my home.
> Sometimes I am tossed and driven, Lord,
> Sometimes I don't know where to roam.
> I've heard of a city called heaven,
> I've started to make it my home.

Oh, my poor Nelly Gray,
They have taken you away,
And I'll never see my darling any more . . .
One night I went to see her,
But she's gone, the neighbors say
The white man bound her with his chain.
They have taken her to Georgia,
To wear her life away,
As she toils in the cotton and the cane.

5   Grimes: "Cotton is king!"

Weather had a lot to do with the life of a black slave, whether
the sun was beating down hotly over his head, whether it
rained, whether it was dry and dusty, or whether the winter
wind came out of the northeast, bitter and cold, and bringing
chills and fevers and lingering coughs. There were sharp con-
trasts in this Georgia back country where magnolias, crepe
myrtles, and palm trees flourished. The winter months were
times of great privation among the slaves. They never had
clothes warm enough to keep out the wet cold. The field hands
were worse off than the house servants.
Vyry was fortunate to be in the Big House, where the fires

were burning in the iron grates and the kitchen was always a nice, comfortable place in winter. When she and Aunt Sally went out into the night after supper they had only a short distance to walk to the cabins built of logs and chinked with clay, only down the lane from the Marster's mansion. Consequently, they did not suffer from the cold. It was generally in November, however, when Grimes bought shoes for the field hands, and frequently they were suffering with frost-bitten feet before they received shoes. Those who could, wrapped their feet in rags or burlap torn from ragged croker sacks which they carried to the fields in cotton-picking time, but even so, there was hardly a winter when someone did not lose a toe because it had frozen and later came off.

Vyry was especially fortunate in winter, for she not only had shoes, but also stockings, to keep her feet and legs warm. Long dresses of calico and linsey kept her comfortable, with an extra apron of blue gingham check around her waist and a shawl to throw over her head and around her shoulders against the damp chill of the night air.

Winter was also a time of much sickness. In summer there was very little illness on the plantation, but in winter there were constant coughs and sneezes, chills and fevers, sometimes deadly pneumonia. Some winters were worse than others; winters when the slaves seemed to sense, with some superstitious fear, that the wind out of the northeast brought plague and death with it. Those were the winters when their numbers were dwindled by death. In the spring there would be new faces among them, for Marster would send Grimes to buy replacements.

As Vyry grew older she began to realize that even in the midst of plenty in the Big House there was want in the Quarters, and while Marster and Big Missy were feasting and rejoicing there was misery among the suffering slaves. Always, too, there were the poor whites, po buckra, who lived back in the pine barrens and on the rocky hills. They suffered more than the black slaves for there was no one to provide them with the rations of corn meal and salt pork which was the daily lot of the slaves, and therefore the black people were taught by their owners to have contempt for this "poor white trash." These po buckra were always coming around in the winter knocking on the kitchen door and telling Aunt Sally that Marster said they could have corn to make bread for their hungry young. The slaves, however, complained that a peck of meal was not enough to feed seven to ten people for a week. Their sorghum always gave out before the cane was ripe and ready for new syrup-making. The fatback got rancid in the summertime, what was left of it, and weevils and worms got in the meal.

Grimes, the overseer, lived in circumstances not much better than the slaves. His house was slightly better than the Negro Quarter houses on the plantation, and his wife, Janey, was only an indifferent housekeeper. When he woke at daylight to that first early morning stillness, before all their brats started hollering and the confusion of the house in disarray began to unnerve him, he generally lay in bed awhile, thinking about the business of the day. If it were summer, he wished he could go fishing. If it were winter, he wished he could go hunting. He had some good hunting dogs, dogs he loved, and they gave him some real good times, best fun he ever had, but most days, he didn't have time to fish or hunt. His job of driving niggers kept him on the run. It was first one thing, then another, till his patience at the end of a day was almost gone. He worked from sunup till sundown, and he never seemed to have anything. He was so dog-tired at night when he went to bed he jumped in his sleep. First thing in the morning, count the things to do that day: get a team of boys tearing up trees in bottom land to clear a new field; mend the nigra houses that were always falling down, or mend the corn cribs and smokehouses that needed fortifying and buttressing; plow a field and get it ready for planting; or cultivate corn and cotton and peas; summertime haying and wintertime feeding, autumn harvest and spring planting. Rainy days he fumed because the work was getting behind. Sundays he tried to sleep.

Four o'clock in the morning, when the guards and patter-rollers were going home to sleep, the big bell in the plantation yard was their last duty. It awakened the plantation slaves to work. It also got Grimes out of bed. Generally he worked one or two hours before he came back home to eat a hearty breakfast of grits and salt meat and grease with eggs and biscuits and coffee. He would get things started in the fields with the wagons and the mules going full force before he could stop to eat. He didn't trust the slaves to work well unless he was around most of the day. But he was bound to have trouble keeping up with them because he couldn't be in several places at the same time.

In the summertime he hired a number of white workers on the plantation, skilled workers and artisans. Sometimes he hired extra black hands too, but in this part of the country there was only one free black man, a blacksmith with his own shop, and Grimes didn't like to have him on the place unless absolutely necessary. Free niggers meant more trouble than slaves. He preferred white laborers when the black hands were few or when he needed a petty boss to oversee a job of carpentering. Naturally he chose the poor whites in the near-by communities. Some of these people were his own kin, and some of them were even poor relations of Marse John. Grimes regarded them as decent and respectable enough. They were hard workers, proud, and independent. Not that they got anywhere. Most of the time they were down on their luck. The dirt farms they owned did not pay. They pooled labor among themselves to build a house, to harvest a crop, to dig a well, or to mend a barn. But many winters found them coming to Marse John to beg bread and corn, and in the spring they came to borrow money and seed to get them started on a new crop. In the summer they were always begging for work. When times got really hard, they suffered greatly, and things went from bad to worse.

These white people did not work well with slaves. Each group regarded the other contemptuously and felt that the other was his inferior. This only made one more headache for Grimes in the summertime. Summer was always the busiest time of the year. The rain fell seldom; sometimes there was dry weather for two months, which meant more work days. Winter was always a dull time. Spring and fall were unpredictable insofar as weather was concerned; there were sometimes whole weeks when the slaves could not go into the fields, but this almost never happened in the summertime. Grimes tried to harvest two crops before the summer was completely over. Harvest time began in August, lasted throughout September and October and well into November. By the end of November harvest was over, which meant he had the job of getting the utmost work out of the slaves in the summertime. When there was conflict between the poor whites and the black slaves over the necessary work it was Grimes's problem. The poor whites hated both the slaver and the slaves, for they reasoned that the cotton planter and the slave kept bread out of their mouths. They even envied their own kin who always had bread and lived securely in their Big Houses. The slaves claimed that the poor whites were lazy and wanted the easy jobs, shifting the hard work on them, while the whites got wages and the slaves got none. Sometimes the poor white

worker brought his family with him—women and children—
but they only came for the midday meal of collards or peas
and cornbread. While the black women and children worked
in the fields, only the white men worked—leaving their women
and children in the wagons. These poor white children often
had swollen bellies and many of these people died of pellagra
and dysentery, and some of them ate the red clay. Their
measly little farms where the land was no good hardly ever
brought them a good crop. They lived back in the piney woods
and they were always throwing taunts and filthy epithets at
the black slaves who taunted them back again as "Ignunt, and
worthless, and lowdown, thievish, sickly looking trash." This
conflict always seemed to amuse the planters like Marse
John, who never failed to dole out food and clothing to these
people, but let the drivers and the sheriff keep the peace. Most
times the driver was the sheriff.

Although Grimes had been poor white trash in Georgia,
and had grown up in the environs of Marse John's plantation,
he longed to improve his lot and rise above his beginnings.
When he became a man he left the state and worked at odd
jobs on small farms and plantations in neighboring states
before he became a driver, or overseer. This was not his first
job as an overseer, but it was the first job he had successfully
held for such a long time in Georgia. He came back to
Georgia to seek a wife from his own people and he married
a woman from "Cracker country," or the pine barrens of
Georgia. She could neither read nor write and she had no
dealings with black slaves in any fraternal fashion. She told
her husband, "I hate niggers worsener poisonous rattlesnake.
We'uns is poor, but thank God, we'uns is white."

Early one hot summer morning one of the patter-rollers
called Grimes before sunup to tell him that the main smokehouse on the place had been broken into. Grimes rushed out
to find one of his best hound dogs running around in a circle
as if he were going mad and about to die. Grimes was shocked
to see his dog foaming at the mouth and howling in pain.
Obviously there was only one thing to do, shoot the dog. He
did not have time to examine the dog more closely, but Bob,
a patter-roller, took time to see if he could determine what
had happened. They concluded the dog was poisoned, that
somebody had fed him powdered glass that cut his insides to
pieces. Such a good watchdog had evidently witnessed the
smokehouse incident. Angered beyond telling, Grimes said,
"If I could only find the nigger that done it, I'd kill him." But

he didn't know whom to kill and when he looked at his fine dog lying dead, his dog whom he dearly prized, tears stood in his eyes.

Big Missy was just sitting down to breakfast, cross and fretful as usual. May Liza was running back and forth waiting on the table already heavily laden with grits and eggs and ham with red-eye gravy, biscuits and jellies and butter and cream and sugar and coffee when Mr. Grimes suddenly appeared at the back door, his hat in his hand, asking to see Big Missy. Marster was not at home. He had gone to Milledgeville on particular political business. Grimes was so disturbed that he blurted out his business in the full hearing of the house servants:

"Niggers done broke open the smokehouse and steal the best meat and what they left, the field rats is covering up the damage."

"Can't you find out what niggers done it?"

"Ma'am I can try, but you know they ain't telling on theyself, and the damage is done."

"Just the same, call all the fields hands in the yard, and threaten them with a beating. If you let them get away with such as this they'll run all over us. You got to get some discipline in them. That's what we pay you for, you know?"

"Yas'm. I can try." And he did try. He tried hard to find the culprits. Every field hand was called up to the Big House and they were lined up in the backyard. Grimes was short of guards to search the slaves' cabins, and it took an awful long time to search the whole place; meanwhile work was waiting. He had three white guards helping him, other than members of his own family. Those three white guards patrolled the plantation at night to see that the slaves kept the curfew, and they wanted their sleep in the morning. He dared not trust the black slaves, even though in a pinch he did use them to lead bloodhounds, to tie up a black for a beating, or else help carry a strange runaway slave to the county seat in Dawson. But a thing like this, "All these black bastards is in cahoots." So he really was in a fix. He hated to send for Marster or have him come and find the meat was stolen, knowing how many hogs they had killed at hog-killing time. But that night, after wearily searching the place over and over, and threatening to beat every nigger involved and shoot the ringleader, in the face of the tight-lipped silence and the stony eyes of the Negroes, Grimes, more desperate and frightened than usual, was forced to write Marse John. He discussed the matter with

Big Missy, and the eavesdropping house servants heard him reading the letter next morning:

> Dear Sir:
> As you know, last fall or rather winter, we killed 65 or 6700 pouns of fat pork—50 hogs at one killing 14 or 15 beeves weighing 4000 besides others at or about the same time and 6 or 8 mutton to dry and we have had two workmen with a little grand daughter Lucy Moore and I have sold 8 pieces of bacon. The beef is all consumed and out of 300 pieces of bacon we have perhaps 75 or 80 pieces. There are 45 negroes who are eating from our field provisions and 6 or 7 of them is too small to consume much meat. We have 25 negroes to feed from the smoke house and corn crib. They consume 7 bushels of meal a week and 3 and a half midlings of meat and my wife has their provisions cooked under her own eye. The house servants and children eat from the yard and take a part from the rest including 3 and a half bushels of milk. For twelve o'clock dinner we cook more turnips and collards and peas than any family I ever know and yet my negroes are complaining in the neighborhood they don't get enough to eat. If so, I can't help it, for I am at my best, but they have now come to the place they have stolen it. They have stolen a great deal, how much I don't know. They have torn up rock underpinning and taken off locks and smokehouse keys. I procured false keys but I am at a loss to know what to do. I am unable to know what disposition they have made of it. Some we found in their possession but that was a mighty little. I hope you will come home soon.
>
> Your friend in the faithful performance
of my duty,
ED GRIMES

A week later, almost to the day, one of Grimes's children became sick and in a matter of hours, despite all the doctor could do, the child was dead. The doctor was unable to diagnose the cause of the child's death and examination after death revealed no poison, nothing wrong except an apparent death from natural causes. This, Grimes refused to believe.

As if he had not had enough trouble, his wife was at the same time expecting another child and a week after their little girl was stricken and died, his wife miscarried and lost the child weeks before it was due to be born. It seemed almost a miracle that his wife did not die, too. Now Grimes was both grim and evil. The slaves kept out of his way as much as possible, and worked desperately hard in the fields. They never let him catch them looking at him. When he came around them they were tight-lipped and stony faced. He was no less taciturn, speaking only when absolutely necessary.

To cap the climax, one morning he went outside his house

and found one of the dogs digging after something under his steps. The dog howled and pawed frantically. Grimes stood without speaking and watched the dog. Finally the dog found what he was seeking. At first it appeared to be a doll. Grimes took the thing and saw it was a fetish made with some of the clothes from the child who had died. The clothes were streaked with blood and despite the fact that the dog clawed and tore the thing, he could see that the face, which had been buried in the soft clay, had been painted chalk white and marked to resemble his little girl as much as if her picture had been painted. A short while later Grimes stood outside the back door of the Big House with the repulsive object in his hands, shaking in fright. Breakfast was being served and Vyry, who knew that Grimes's wife was still sick in bed, wondered what he was doing at the Big House this time of morning. He asked to see Big Missy. When she came to the door he showed her the object and at first her eyes widened in horror. Then she gave a hollow laugh and said, "Why, Mister Grimes, I never would have thought you was superstitious."

"No, ma'am, I ain't, but these niggers is up to something awful. If I knowed who 'twas I'd strangle them with my bare hands, but this kind of stuff ain't nothing but evil witchcraft and black magic. I reckon I can't fight this kind of stuff. This here is hoodoo!"

"Nonsense. Pay it no attention, and I tell you it will all blow over."

"I done lost my youngun, and I done lost my dog. I lost my unborn baby and my wife still sick a-bed. I ain't never been scared of nigras, but if airy nother thing happens, I'm quitting without no further notice."

"That's just what they want you to do. Get scared and leave. I thought you was a man. Go home and comfort your wife. Don't breathe a word of this to her, and keep a stiff upper lip before the nigras and they'll stop their devilment."

But it was a dejected Grimes who went home to his wife. When he saw he could get nothing out of the slaves, he sent them to the fields where they were hoeing cotton and corn. The middle of the summertime was usually a good time of the year if the wagons didn't break down. Most of the slaves were healthy in the summertime, and since the days were longer they could stay in the fields many more hours. They stopped in the middle of the day to empty the dinner buckets that were brought to them in the fields. They were allowed fifteen to twenty minutes to eat and drink a dipper of water.

The water boys carried buckets of water with dippers up and down the rows all during the morning and afternoon, but it wasn't good to drink very much water in the heat. You might get waterlogged or have stomach cramps. Sometimes Grimes had them cultivating cotton, corn, peas, and sugar cane all at the same time. Only the men and larger boys could drive the mules and the plows, but all the women and children could hoe and chop cotton and keep the weeds away. Grimes found his hands full with more work than he had men and plows enough to do.

Things were going along in a kind of humdrum way and the afternoon heat blanketed them. Old Grandpa Tom, who kept Marster's stables, was dozing in the shade. Suddenly he was rudely awakened by Grimes, who was in great distress because one of the wagons had broken down and the overworked mule drawing the wagon fell dead in his tracks under the blazing heat. Grimes demanded that Grandpa Tom bring out two of Marster's best thoroughbred horses for him to use in the emergency. One horse could take somebody to town to bring the blacksmith from the village so that the wagon axle could be fixed, and the other horse could take the mule's place in the field. Grandpa Tom said, "No. I dassent let Marster's good horses be mules in the field and run hard in the hot sun. You'll work them to death, then I'll be blessed out and blamed for it."

"Nigger, don't you tell me, no."

"I has to, Mister Grimes, less Marster say so."

"Your Marster's not here, and you know it. I'm in his place, and you'd better obey me and be quick about it if you know what's good for you. Now make haste and do what I say and don't argue with me."

But Grandpa Tom still hesitated and refused to bring out the horses. Grimes grabbed him by the scruff of his neck and flung him out in the yard flat on his face in the dust. Grandpa Tom said nothing and make no effort to move. Then in a frenzy of anger Grimes took his bull whip, which he always carried, and cut across the old slave's back with such vigor the ragged shirt on his back quickly tore in two and the blood came streaming out. Grandpa Tom screamed in agony, but this only made Grimes lay on with greater fury and he could not have told anyone how many times he cut into the old Negro's quivering flesh with that whip before he came to himself.

When Aunt Sally and Vyry heard Grandpa Tom hollering

and screaming to God for mercy they ran out to see what was the matter. He was making the most awful sounds Vyry had ever heard, pitiful and weak and so terrible they did not sound human. When Grimes was exhausted and almost breathless he stopped. He pulled out a big colored square of grimy cloth and wiped the sweat from his beef-red face. Then he walked over to the huddled and trembling lump of flesh and deliberately kicked him. When he saw him still trembling and moaning, he put his whip in his left hand, then took his right hand and reached in his belt, pulled out his pistol and shot him once. He held his pistol cocked as if to shoot again then, evidently thinking about it, he kicked him once more turning him over with his boot. Then he walked toward the stables to get those horses.

The flies gathered quickly and began buzzing around Grandpa Tom. Vyry ran to him and tried fanning the flies from his deeply lacerated and bleeding back. His old cotton shirt was sticking in shreds to a tortured pulp of flesh. Vyry knew that he must die if he were not already dead. He was too old to stand a beating like that. Aunt Sally hissed at her, "Get away, get away, fore you gets the same thing." Aunt Sally grabbed Vyry and led her back to the kitchen. But Vyry saw the unshed tears in Aunt Sally's eyes now spilling over on her wrinkled brown cheeks. She was praying in whispers, "Lord, when is you gone send us that Moses? How long, Jesus, how long?" Grandpa Tom was blood kin to Aunt Sally.

A few hours later, after the mutilated body had been washed with loving care, they put a black linsey suit on Grandpa Tom and laid him out on a cooling board. The next evening, after dusk, all the slaves gathered around the pine coffin they had made for him and Brother Ezekiel led them in his song, "I am a poor way-faring stranger." Afterwards he prayed and said, "ashes to ashes, and dust to dust" and the rude coffin was lowered into a hole dug in the Georgia clay, sprinkled with lime, and covered again with clay. Then darkness came on quickly, and another day was done.

I'm gwine sit at the welcome table,
Some of these days!

6   *Marse John's dinner party*

Vyry could always tell when Aunt Sally was out of sorts and
did not want to be bothered. It made no difference whether
she was busy with preparations for a feast or troubled in mind
about something going wrong. In the seven summers Vyry had
worked and lived with Aunt Sally lots of things went wrong.
In the morning the sun welcomed another day, but in the
evening one never knew what trouble the sun would put to
rest. Vyry often understood what Aunt Sally meant when
she said, "Bad luck to laugh too much in the morning. You
liables to cry before bedtime."

Anytime Vyry went into the kitchen early in the morning
and heard Aunt Sally singing it was a true sign of trouble.
Aunt Sally loved to sing at the Rising Glory meetings and
sometimes she seemed to enjoy singing in the evenings when
her work was done and she sat in the doorway of her cabin,
especially on hot summer nights fanning herself with a big

palmetto leaf. But singing in the kitchen of the Big House
early in the morning was rare. Most of the time when a tune
came to her mind she hummed it softly to herself over the
biscuit board where she was kneading bread. Then Vyry
would strain her ears to listen, to catch the thread of the tune
and follow it in her mind. But when Aunt Sally was deeply
troubled, she opened her mouth and raised a real wailing song
over her cooking. Her voice was dark and rich and because
of her ample girth she was capable of great volume, while the
melody always poured out sweet and strong:

> I been buked and I been scorned,
> Lord, I been buked and I been scorned,
> Lord, I been buked and I been scorned,
> I been talked about sho's you borned.

When Vyry would try to suggest tactfully that she was singing
rather loudly. she would sing louder; and if Caline and May
Liza came out to say Big Missy heard her or try to hush her
singing, she would tell them crossly, "Leave me be. Don't
care if the white folks is sleep, and don't care what they say."
And she went on singing her mad-mood song,

> But I ain't gwine a-lay my religion down
> Lord, I ain't gwine a-lay my religion down
> I ain't gwine a-lay my religion down, Lord
> Untell I wears a heavenly crown.

Vyry always loved to hear her sing, but the songs often puzzled
her before she grew to associate them with Aunt Sally's mood
and mind, her anger and resentment that she could voice in
no other way. But some of the songs were frightening. They
made Vyry want to cry. She did not like to hear Aunt Sally
sing,

> Before this time another year,
> I may be dead and gone.
> Be in some lonesome graveyard bed,
> O, Lord have mercy, Lord, how long?

Nobody dared go near Aunt Sally when she sang that song,
not even Marse John or Big Missy. She was likely to pick up
her rolling pin and run you away with, "Go way from me.
Do I'll brain ya." Vyry had grown so accustomed to Aunt
Sally she could not imagine what her life would be without
her. She prayed fervently that Aunt Sally would not die like

her own mother, Hetta, and Mammy Sukey had done. That would leave her all alone in the world.

One of the largest dinner parties Vyry remembered in the Big House was a big political celebration for Marse John. Some of his friends were coming from the state legislature, even a congressman from Washington was expected, and planter friends from seven counties. Vyry was a big girl now, and could do anything Aunt Sally wanted, but there was extra help for the feast. Jake's gal, Lucy, was also going to help. Caline and May Liza were in charge of washing all Big Missy's fine crystal, claret and sauterne glasses and water goblets and all the different things you needed in order to serve whiskey and brandy. Sam, the carriage driver, was also butler and in charge of fixing drinks for Marse John's perpetually drinking company. He would stand resplendent in his fine black swallowtail coat and scarlet vest and gold buttons and open the heavily carved oaken door and announce the guests, and he would also keep the trays of glasses in a steady trot without spilling a drop.

The preparations in the kitchen seemed endless. Aunt Sally was making patty shells to fill with creamed chicken. Vyry and Lucy cleaned oyster forks and polished silver trays and salt cellars and toothpick holders and carried boxes of candles for Big Missy to count for the gleaming chandeliers and wall sconces. There must have been thousands of the homemade wax lights because the whole place was shining, from the gleaming wood and red velvet portieres and scarlet carpets to the brass fixtures and the rose and teakwood furniture. There were game and mutton to be served with all their attendant sauces and jellies and special pickles and conserves. Sometimes, when there were so many underfoot Aunt Sally could hardly turn, she would lift her big cooking spoon out of a scalding hot mixture and brandishing it in the air like a sword, she would scream and say, "Scat!" and everybody scatted.

Big Missy was flushed with the excitement. She loved company and liked nothing better, as Aunt Sally said, than "putting on airs." She rarely had had an opportunity like this to remind many that she had been to the manor born and came from the elite of Savannah. Living here in the backwoods of Georgia had been a sore trial which she regarded as nothing less than a sacrifice her marriage had demanded. Perhaps now that John was coming up in the political world their social life would be greatly expanded. She might get to go to Milledgeville more often, to Macon and Athens and Augusta and even home to Savannah for the winter balls. In addition to super-intending the house-cleaning down to the most minute and immaculate detail, Caline had piles of linen and laces as her responsibility. The finest silver and linen and china and crystal hardly seemed adequate, now that the occasion loomed upon them, "But there's no time to buy more, now!" brooded Salina. Besides she had her own clothes to think about, three new dresses, one a very brilliant plum satin with bugle beads and tucks and flounces trimmed with tiny pink satin rosebuds with embroidered green leaves, fitting closely through the bodice and falling behind in a regal train. In addition she had a scarlet crêpe de chine with an accordion pleated bertha collar and a back panel floating from the waist and gathered around the bottom of a hoopskirt. The showpiece, however, was a bottle-green velvet with waist, collar, and leg-of-mutton sleeves embroidered with seed pearls and rhinestones. With it she would wear gutta-percha combs with jeweled and rib-boned tops and a touch of delicate plumes.

Some of her guests would be in the house for an entire week. She hoped nothing would go wrong with the running of the place in that time. She could always trust Grimes, but you could never tell what ornery nigras would do at the very worst possible time. And she simply could not do so many exhausting things and be at her radiant best each evening. They were going to have a hunt breakfast and then journey (by way of the hunt of course) to the next plantation of Crenshaw and Barrow for the afternoon. There was a gala cotillion planned and an evening soirée after another large dinner party. It would really usher in the social season that continued through the winter, with Christmas festivities as the highest point.

One of her greatest problems was making sure she had the appropriate jewelry for each of the evening costumes and whether she could wear the emerald brooch, diamond neck-lace, sapphire bracelet, and ruby earrings to match without seeming too garish. "Why, this can decide our social future for the rest of our natural born lives." Not to think, of course, of what it would mean for John's political chances. But she was not dreaming yet of the governor's mansion.

Aunt Sally was told a month ahead to begin preparations by baking cakes, some to be soaked in rum and others to be stored with wine, and brandy poured over them frequently. Her fruit and rum cakes were always properly aged. She must cook turkey, young roast pig, a side of mutton, chicken fried, as well as creamed in patty shells, and guinea hen. She must bake for the moment at hand spoon bread, biscuits, waffles, corn sticks, muffins, and light bread, with a generous amount of buckwheats for breakfast. There would be damson preserves, fig preserves, watermelon rind conserve and pickles, elderberry wine for the ladies and lots of whiskey and brandy for the men. For vegetables there were jars of snap-beans and baby-green butterbeans, corn, and okra, tomatoes, and Jerusalem artichokes. The usual homemade chow-chow and hot mustard pickles were generally not offered to company unless, remembering how good they were at the Dutton place, the guests especially requested them. Marmalade made of lemons, oranges, and walnuts vied with tomato conserve. And, of course, there was always an abundance of baked hams and geese and wild game. A week before the party began, Aunt Sally complained at night that her feet hurt and she and Vyry hardly felt like eating the hot buttered biscuit and damson preserves that she had wrapped in a rag and stuck in her bosom.

Vyry kept wondering how she could see and hear the festivities way back in the kitchen, and she wanted to see the company arrive and see how they looked. Aunt Sally told her to step outside the back door and stand in the dark under the big oak tree and watch them come up to the door.

As each black barouche drawn by four horses stopped before the mansion, the great ladies and gentlemen alighted and entered, the light of the flickering candles sweeping beyond the open door where Sam stood proudly ushering in the guests. Luckily, Vyry and May Liza and Lucy were needed back and forth for duties in both house and kitchen, so Vyry caught snatches of conversation, too. What she did not hear, the other servants heard and rehashed afterwards in the kitchen and the cabins. Nobody was too interested in what the white ladies were talking about, but the men were different. They discussed the news and the crops and the weather, their slaves, and the politics of the county, the state, and the nation. It was this conversation that the slaves wanted to hear. It was for this they kept their eyes and ears open and their mouths closed. As Aunt Sally said, "When the womens goes in the bedrooms and the other parlors to whisper and titter over a trifling bit of nothing, then the serious talk among the men begins."

"Well, Jeb," said Marse John, "how's crops down your way?"

"Well, now, I reckon I can't complain. When you take into consideration the miserable weather we've been having down in my neck of the woods, I'd say crops are good. We've already sold five hundred bales of cotton and my nigras are still picking in the fields. But you remember how cold it was in the spring and how dry it was all summer, and then just at harvest time it started raining so terrible and even as early in the fall as September we had that right cold spell, so I didn't rightly think we'd have a crop at all, but I've got one and a fine one. Corn as fine as any in the country, more than enough to feed all my mules and nigras through the winter. I'll have corn to sell. I've got my hay-feed for my mules and thoroughbreds already put away. We've been planting peas, too, and despite the dry weather we had wonderful luck with the gardens. I reckon I can't complain. How's yours?"

"Well, I haven't been to my other places yet, but I've heard from my drivers, and each one says I'll find the best crop at his place. You know how it is, every driver doing his best to outdo the others in handling the nigras and bringing up a good crop. I haven't had much trouble this year, but a lot of my nigras have been sick and sometimes last winter as many as eight and ten a day were out of the fields, laid up and couldn't work, or *wouldn't* work, I don't know which. But if the luck I've had here is any indication, it looks like a pretty fair year to me. You talk about corn, I know I've got a fine crop of corn, and my cotton is bringing the best price in ten years. Remember way back there in the panic when cotton was way down to nothing and everything you had to buy, including boot blacking to mark the sacks, was sky-high? Well, I just do declare if it hadna been for my good drivers, I reckon we would have come near starving. But this year has been good, a mighty good year I'll say. How about you, Lee?"

"I'm not in a position to say, just yet. We haven't finished cutting oats, the rye is hauled in, and we're planting peas, too. Oughta be through in a coupla days, but I'm mighty short of hands. I hired old Cab from Bynum two days last week for his and his mule's feed, but the nigger didn't do one good day's work. I can't put any confidence in my nigras for steady work anytime I'm absent from the place. I haven't been able to find a driver tough enough to put the fear of God in the nigras and hold them down. To give you an example, I just

bought a nigra boy named Hal for three hundred and
twenty-five dollars. He's about forty-five years old and looks
like he oughta be able to do a good day's work. I told my
driver to put him to work in the low ground, and for him to
cultivate forty acres of cotton and corn after he clears the
land, and then to help run the wagon. But the very first day
the nigra come up sick. I found out I've been cheated and
he's suffering with running of the reins!"

Marse John broke in to say, "I've got a nigra here just like
that myself. Name is Jake, and he has been one of my best
stud niggers. Had been planning to sell him, but kept putting
it off. Now he's got running of the reins." Then Lee continued,
"Last January all my nigras took down with awful bad colds
and whooping cough and fevers. I thought they'd cough their
insides out before spring when they suddenly got well. By
that time they had used up more tar syrup and horehound
and rock candy and good whiskey than they're worth. I'll be
lucky if I don't have to buy food."

"Speaking of provisions . . ."

Just then, Sam, who had been standing listening for a-
while, walked into the room smiling and resplendent in his
butler's uniform, and said, "Dinner is served."

At dinner the talk invariably got around to politics. After
dinner, over brandy and cigars, with the ladies once more
out of earshot, the men began congratulating John Morris
Dutton on his recent election to the state legislature and
joking with him over his political future.

"Well, John, do you know enough Blackstone to back up
your speeches and resolutions on the floor?"

Marse John laughed and looked at his cigar. He was cautious among these men for they represented some of the most
brilliant minds in the Georgia House of Representatives. Most
of them were around his age and, like himself, had inherited
their roles. He had been bound to go into politics as his
father had done before him and his grandfather on his
mother's side. In Virginia and South Carolina as well as in
Georgia, he came from a distinguished line of public figures
and political tycoons. Some of his guests had been at Oglethorpe with him and, like him, had been members of the
Demosthenians. Some of them had gone East for further
education at Harvard, Princeton, or Yale. Clark Graves had
a New England background with a law degree from Harvard;
Allen Crenshaw was a magistrate on the State Supreme
Court; Smith Ambers Barrow was an industrial wizard; Mal-

colm Ezra Winston was a scholar of such repute that his
political comments were regarded for their literary expression as well as for their content. Jebusite Hendrix and Porter
Lee Butler, Marse John's nearest planter neighbors, were,
like himself, descendants of pioneer families in Georgia. It
behooved him in such company to think before speaking what
law was indeed derived from reading Blackstone. He had
tried to keep an eye on his plantations with a good working
basis between himself and overseers whom he felt he could
trust. And after building himself a place to live, it was no
wonder that, in keeping with the tradition of the Georgia
country squire, he too should become absorbed in that favorite
of southern pastimes, politics. With his vast holdings in the
county he had only to organize his constituents, most of
them either directly in his pay or living on his land. The
election was a mere formality; of course he had won. His
guests tonight, together with himself, were the richest planters
in central Georgia and they controlled, both politically and
financially, a third of the state.

"If you mean what kind of politician I'm going to be with
my homespun Blackstone, I'll tell you. I intend to know the
law, yes, and know whereof I speak, but I also mean to
know it in a practical sense. And the main thing, it seems
to me, is to know the people. I believe I know the good
people of this sovereign state of Georgia. I am sure I know
my constituents and I believe I know what they want."

"Yes," said Judge Ezra Winston, "but it is no longer just
the law of Georgia that we are confronted with today. Those
confounded idiots and abolitionists are trying to make a
different Constitution out of the document written by Jefferson and Hamilton and amended by our governing bodies.
I'm reminded of our illustrious Thomas Cobb when he said
that they are trying to build a fire that we can only ex-
tinguish in the blood of war. Especially since this past year's
new compromise over Missouri, I'm afraid we are in for
some more battles on the national issues and for the protection of our natural rights here in the state of Georgia."

"Such as?"

"Such as our sacred way of life, our agricultural system,
classic culture, with the natural divisions of mankind into
servile and genteel races. Even now, gentlemen, I believe
it is quite clear that Congressmen Stephens and Toombs
are at work on a document stating our complete position
here in the state of Georgia."

Crenshaw had been listening thoughtfully while picking his teeth, and now he spoke up, "This revision of the Missouri Compromise seems to point up two facts, first, that anti-slavery sentiment is growing in the North and they want to spread it into the territories, and that more stringent laws regarding the restrictions of slaves and free nigras are absolutely necessary. According to the various rumors I hear, there have been several reports in South Carolina and Virginia of attempts by slaves at insurrection, even some word of that kind of trouble here. By the way, I heard through one of the lower courts just this past week about two slave cooks who have been arrested for poisoning three in their master's families."

The men alerted themselves and spoke quickly, "Where?"

"I think here in Lee County, though I'm not sure it wasn't Wilkes."

Later in the evening when Marse John was preparing for bed he heard his wife say, "I really think you've got to do something about Sally, sell her or something; she's really getting too temperamental, and those patty shells! She nearly ruined them with salt. For a moment I thought they weren't fit to eat."

And Marse John, with the words of Judge Crenshaw concerning the poison murders still ringing in his ears, said nothing, silently assenting.

7   *Cook in the Big House*

Early in the spring of 1851 a fairly well-developed plot for an uprising among the slaves of Lee County, with the assistance of free Negroes and white abolitionists, became known to the High Sheriff of the county. How the news began to leak out and through what sources could not be determined by most Negroes. In the first place, the slaves on Marse John's plantation were not fully informed as to what nature the plot took nor how an uprising could take place. Brother Zeke was so troubled that he confided to his flock at their regular meeting place at the Rising Glory Church that it must be a false rumor since no definite plans had ever come to his knowledge. It was first suspected, however, by the guards or patter-rollers and the drivers, who claimed that the Negroes were unusually hard to manage. And the neighboring whites claimed there were unusual movements in town among strange whites and in the county among free Negroes. At first the planters were not suspicious and hardly dared believe the piece-meal information they received. Why would their slaves want to do such a thing?

As Big Missy said to Marse John, "They are all well treated, and we love them and take good care of them just like a part of our family. When they are sick we nurse them back to health. We feed and clothe them and teach them the Christian religion. Our nigras are good and wouldn't try such a thing unless some criminal minds aided and abetted them, like abolitionists and free niggers from outside the state." Such monstrous activities were beyond the wildest imaginations of their good and happy childlike slaves!

Nevertheless, if there was such ingratitude lurking among them, after all the money that had been spent on food and clothes and doctor bills, the owners must be realistic and resort to drastic methods to counteract such activity. They must not wait too long to listen to reason. Hastily and secretly, Marse John and his planter friends gathered with this purpose. There they decided, as their drivers had suggested, that the first thing was to seek out the culprits and see that they were punished to the full extent of the law, chiefly by hanging. Thus they would make an example of them and put the fear of God in the rest of the slaves. Second, they must clamp down harder on the movements of all blacks, enforce the curfew laws and all of the Black Code, thereby rigorously maintaining control over their property, both land and chattel slaves. Finally, but not least, they must seek out all abolitionists guilty of giving aid and comfort to the black enemies of the Georgia people, and either force them out of the state or deal with them so harshly that they would willingly leave. As for the free Negroes, all of them should be called in for questioning and under threat of revoking their papers, forcing them back into slavery, they should be made to leave the state. Meanwhile, the planters should continue to question trusted slaves for any information and should keep watch for any signs of the development of the plot or for any unusual movements of the slaves. The guards and patter-rollers were ordered to search the slave cabins to make sure no weapons or firearms of any kind came into the possession of any black person, slave or free.

May Liza and Caline told Vyry and Lucy and Aunt Sally, "Marster and Big Missy done taking to whisper and shush all the time."

"We act like we don't see nothing and don't hear nothing neither."

If any Negroes were caught in the woods or in the swamps they always said, "We's looking for greens and herbs for medicine and teas."

Many slaves, like Aunt Sally, had gardens around their cabins with collards growing almost into the door. These they cultivated when they did not go to the fields. But the tension was growing so they were forbidden any free activity. Marse John like his other planter friends redoubled his guards and patter-rollers and changed the curfew from nine o'clock to first dark or about one hour after sundown.

The growing tension exploded when the two Negro women accused of having killed their master and his mother by poisoning his food were convicted of murder and sentenced to be hanged. Like Aunt Sally and Vyry and Lucy, they worked in the kitchen of their Marster's Big House. When they were brought to the county jail for trial one afternoon it was quickly decided that they were guilty and had confessed the crime so that nothing was left but to hang them as soon as a judge could set the time and a hangman nearby could be summoned to do the deed.

This episode created a great disturbance among both planters and slaves. Among the planters' families there was unmistakable panic, and among the slaves there was great fear. Mutual distrust hung in the air between blacks and whites. In addition to the recent increase of guards on his place, Marse John, at the request of Grimes, purchased three additional bloodhounds for his plantation.

One of the murders had been committed several months before the second crime and the women were not at first suspected, but when the master died, a doctor confirmed suspicions expressed earlier when the man's mother died. The news traveled fast, and long before the date of the hanging had been set, the crime was common knowledge in every household.

The darkest day in Vyry's young life came without warning. Big Missy and Marse John had arranged to sell Aunt Sally. She would go first to Savannah and then by boat to New Orleans, where she would go on the auction block and be sold to the highest bidder. The morning she was ordered to go, she and Vyry went as usual to the kitchen. Big Missy came out in the kitchen after breakfast and told Aunt Sally to get her things together; there was a wagon in the back-yard waiting to take her to Savannah. Now Aunt Sally was

ready. She had her head-rag on and she had tied in a bundle
the few things she had in the world including the few rags
of clothes she wore. She had spread out one of her big
aprons and tied them in it. Now she carried it in her arms.
Tears were running down her fat black cheeks and she could
not control her trembling lips. Vyry stood dazed and numb.
Even when Aunt Sally hugged and kissed her, Vyry did not
cry. She could not believe this was real, that she would be
forced apart from Aunt Sally, that Aunt Sally was leaving
and going somewhere. She heard Aunt Sally saying, "Goodbye, honey, don't yall forget to pray. Pray to God to send
His chilluns a Moses, pray to Jesus to have mercy on us
poor suffering chilluns. Goodbye, honey, don't you forget
Aunt Sally and don't forget to pray. Aunt Sally know she
ain't never gwine see yall no more in this here sinful world,
but I'm gwine be waiting for you on the other side where
there ain't gwine be no more auction block. Goodbye,
honey-child, goodbye."

Even then Vyry's eyes were dry. But then she saw poor
old Aunt Sally clinging to Sam and Big Boy. She heard her
sobbing pitifully, "Oh, Lord, when is you gwine send us that
Moses? When you gwine set us peoples free? Jesus, how long?
Marster, how long? They is taking all I got in the world from
me, they is sending me way down yonder to that cruel auction block! Oh, Lord, how long is we gotta pray?" They were
pulling her away but stumbling along crying and muttering
she kept saying, "Oh, Lord, have mercy!"

Then Vyry found herself shaking like a leaf in a whirl-
wind. Salt tears were running in her mouth, and her short,
sharp finger nails were digging in the palms of her hands.
Suddenly she decided she would go with Aunt Sally, and just
then Big Missy slapped her so hard she saw stars and when
she saw straight again Aunt Sally was gone.

The first woman who came in from the fields to cook in
the Big House did not suit anybody. Her food did not please
Marse John and he said so, complaining and cursing at the
same time. He grew more and more petulant at each meal,
and Big Missy railed at him, "You are so cross and peevish
you act like a child!" And he would swear, "Damn you, I was
a fool! Had a good cook, been cooking ever since I was a
boy, and I let you persuade me to sell her, damn you, don't
you talk to me." To make it worse the house servants swore
all-out war with the woman and would not help her do any-

thing. She had never worked in the kitchen and knew nothing about where to find anything. She was confused by all the house servants whispering and muttering around her, even within earshot of the white folks. Caline said, "House servants and field hands just don't mix. I ain't no yard nigger myself and I don't have nothing to do with yard niggers. First place, they stinks!"

Vyry was still grieving over the loss of Aunt Sally, but she also resented the woman, and did no more than absolutely necessary to help her. Finally, Big Missy Salina admitted that the woman would have to go.

Then there was a brief interim when Big Missy tried several other women. After the field woman, an older woman from a nearby plantation was sold to Marse John and recommended as an excellent cook, but she ran away within twenty-four hours. They caught her, but Big Missy and Marster decided not to keep her but sent her back, instead, to her former master. The third woman was sickly and she coughed over the pots. In less than a month she grew so much worse that before they realized her trouble she was dead, dying one night on her own pallet after having cooked supper and worked all day. Vyry took her place in the emergency. Thus began her life as cook in the Big House. She always dated the time back to Aunt Sally's going away. Vyry knew the work thoroughly, having been accustomed to the kitchen from childhood. She had worked seven years under Aunt Sally and she not only had learned all she knew from her, but she cooked exactly like Aunt Sally. Although Marse John was immediately pleased with the food, he thought she was too young to be entrusted with the responsibility of chief cook, and that the work would be too hard for her. When he said this to Missy Salina she decided at once that Vyry should be the cook. Vyry did not care. She had really had to do all the heavy work with the other women anyway, and she was glad to get the kitchen once more to herself. For a short time she was troubled with Big Missy coming into the kitchen, opening the pots to see what was in them, and giving shrill nervous orders which Vyry generally disregarded. After a terrible steaming burn Big Missy ceased to trouble Vyry, much to the girl's relief. The house servants were again satisfied, and the usual atmosphere of an uneasy peace seemed to descend once more over the household.

One morning Vyry was busy with the breakfast dishes when

Big Missy came into the kitchen and said, "Vyry, there's a free nigger down at the stables shoeing Marster's horses. I guess you'd best take him a mouthful of something to eat. But mind, you'd better not give him anything fresh. See if you can't find some leftovers. Claims he's hungry and can't work. I don't see howcome he needs anything before dinnertime. He's only been working since six o'clock." Vyry said, "Yes'm. I'll see after him." Big Missy went off grumbling about free niggers being nothing but trouble, "and you mark my words, John'll be sorry for bringing him on this place."

Vyry finished her dishes and when she was ready to start dinner she fixed a plate of food and took it to the hired blacksmith. Rarely, indeed, did a free Negro come on the place to work. The overseers were afraid of the trouble free Negroes might make among the slaves, but there had not been a blacksmith on the place for a long time, so this man had been brought in from the nearby village where he owned his own smithy.

He was so busy working he did not hear Vyry's light step behind him, and when he turned and looked up, her milk-white face startled him. She was five and a half feet tall with her sandy hair roped high on her head. Her cold, bluish-gray eyes looked out without emotion. Her mouth was tight in a straight, hard line. He quickly recovered when he saw she wore the cheap calico and sack clothes of a slave.

"First off, I thought you was the young Missus. You look just like her."

"I'm a slave all right," snapped Vyry. "Here's your food. I ain't got no time for swapping gossip."

Then he stood up straight. He made no move to take the food, but giving her a long look said, "Ain't no hurry, is there? Or do they *pay* you to work so fast? I just wanted to know what might be your name?"

"Ain't got no name," said Vyry, and putting the food down on the ground she turned to walk away from him. But he was too quick for her. He jumped before her and caught her by the arm, "Easy, gal, I mean no harm. Bide a bit, and tell me who's your man?"

"You know who ain't, I reckon, and I'll thank you to turn me loose."

"Too good for a black man, hanh? I reckon the white folks got they eyes on you themselves."

"Don't know about that. I ain't had no trouble so far, and I ain't looking for none from black nor white."

He snickered. "Ain't feeding you saltpeter, hanh, to keep a good cook cooking?"

Vyry spoke out angrily, "Nigger, make haste and turn me loose!"

At that he narrowed his eyes and moved his hand.

"I may be a nigger, but I'm still a free man, and that's more'n you can say, Miss Stuck-up, with your ass on your shoulder. If you would marriage with me, I'd buy your freedom!" With that he turned to one side, looked her full in the eye, tossed back his massive black head, sparked his eyes, flashed his pearl-white teeth, and jingled the coins in his pocket. The word "freedom" caught her up short, and giving him a quick questioning glance she sized him up from head to toe. He had the strong, hard, muscular body that went with his trade and his shoulders were as big as a barrel. Black as a spade and stockily built, he looked like a powerful giant. There was just enough animal magnetism in him to trouble Vyry, and he was never more magnetic than now while she paused to weigh his words.

"You ain't got enough gold to buy me with what you jingling in your jeans." She said this half-scornfully, but she did not move now that she was perfectly free to go.

"I got a thousand gold pieces and a thousand silver pieces and I don't carry them in my jeans. I reckon they'll buy your freedom, or do you think you're worth more than that?"

"Show me your money first, and talk to me later."

"Why I got to show you? Can you buy, or can you sell?" Scornfully he chided her,

> White man got the eye for gold,
> And nigger man do what he told.

She continued just as pertly. "Then I gotta be getting back to my cooking. When you speaks to Marster bout buying my freedom so's I can marriage with you, I'll gossip with you then, till times gets better."

Lil piece of wheat bread,
Lil piece of pie,
Gwine have that yaller gal,
Or else I'll die.

8   Randall Ware

Randall Ware was a free man because he was born free. He
was black as the Ace of Spades because nothing but the
blood of black men coursed through his veins. He knew the
trade of blacksmith when he came to Georgia and to Lee
County with a sack of gold, enough to register himself as
a free man, enough to guarantee the payment of his yearly
taxes as a free man, and enough to buy himself a stake of
land through the confidence and assistance of his white
guardian, Randall Wheelwright. Of course, he would have
stayed in Virginia where there were other relatives who were
free and artisans, but Randall Wheelwright had persuaded
him to come to Georgia. And Ware felt a closeness to this
white man whom he respected so highly he had even taken
his given name instead of the foreign name with which he

had been christened in the Islands. Between these two men there was mutual and implicit trust.

Randall Wheelwright was a staunch Quaker whose ancestors had given material assistance to the cause of American freedom during the Revolutionary War. He was, therefore, entitled to draw in the land lottery of 1852 held in Lee County in the state of Georgia. He was an old man when he finally settled in Georgia, but he lived long enough to help young Randall Ware establish himself and find other white friends who could help him in need. Moreover, he willed this young black friend much of his property. Thus, Randall Ware came into possession of the two hundred and two and a half acres of land that Wheelwright had originally owned. They seemed nothing but woods and marsh land. He inherited this by a legally drawn will and the proper papers were duly recorded in the County Courthouse by the Clerk of the Court. It made Randall Ware a rich free Negro who was closely watched by the planters of Lee County. With some of his money he bought the land where his smithy stood, and next to it he had a grist mill where poor white farmers came in large numbers to have their corn ground into meal. He built the structure which housed his anvil and the nearby stalls for horses which were brought to him for shoes.

Another factor that had drawn Randall Ware to Randall Wheelwright was the latter's strong abolitionist views. As a Quaker his religious views were regarded as far too independent for the southern community, but his abolitionist views were hated even more. He and old Bob Qualls had frequently been suspected of helping slaves escape to freedom and even daring to buy slaves on the auction block and, after purchasing them, giving them their freedom. Randall Wheelwright was an immaculate and dapper little gentleman with brown hair and shrewd but kind and twinkling hazel eyes. He wore a Van Dyke beard and carried a gold-headed cane. He was built sparely and delicately. Old man Bob Qualls, on the other hand, a big heavily built man, was frequently unkempt, chewed tobacco, and talked with a Carolina drawl. His abolitionist views, however, were just as strong as Wheelwright's; moreover, he had been a soldier and had fought in both Indian and Mexican wars, so he, too, had a claim to land in the lottery. These two men had an interesting association with Randall Ware and their coming to Georgia near the middle of the century had both meaning and purpose.

As a free man in Georgia, Randall Ware had his troubles. The law was strict in the surveillance of all blacks, and the free black man was only slightly better off than the slaves. His movements were proscribed and all his actions defined. His legal status was flimsy because he must always have a white guardian. This white guardian must be a property owner of some means, and technically, the free man was attached to the land of his white guardian in much the same manner of a serf or slave. His status was also similar to that of an indentured servant whose time was not his own. He had the same difficulty in owning firearms as a slave or an Indian, but he could own property and had some legal rights that neither slaves nor Indians possessed. Every year he was forced to renew his free papers by paying an exorbitant tax which increased annually. These free papers must always be found on his person and when he traveled from place to place he must buy a permit and register in each county he entered so that his movements could always be checked. If, for any reason, he could not produce the yearly assessment for his papers, they could be taken from him and his freedom revoked. If he were arrested and charged with a crime or held under suspicion, his freedom was also questioned and endangered and he could be thrown into jail without redress unless he could speedily produce a white friend in the county.

Randall Ware was a literate man. He understood printed materials, could read and write and figure his own accounts, and he had read much abolitionist material. When he came to Georgia he understood what both Randall Wheelwright and Bob Qualls represented as Quakers and abolitionists and he knew that he was of invaluable assistance to them and to all runaway slaves on the underground railroad. Brother Zeke was an important contact who must never be placed in jeopardy. No matter what time of night he brought a trembling runaway to the smithy, Randall Ware must hide him or get him to Wheelwright and Qualls without suspicion. Thus far, things had worked well. Thus far, he, Randall Ware, had encountered no real difficulty, even here in the backwoods of Georgia, until he saw the white face of the slave girl, Vyry.

For the first time in his mature life he felt the hot blood of desire for a special woman burn his flesh. It was the first time that such a physical desire had ever been uppermost in his mind. He felt he must have her for his own, and he

knew nothing in the world could make her more willing to
be his than the promise and fulfillment of her freedom. No
matter what a white planter said, every slave craved freedom,
and nobody knew this better than Randall Ware.

Vyry at fifteen was, nevertheless, not merely the chattel
slave of John Morris Dutton, but obviously she was linked by
blood to his household. Randall Ware reckoned that her
resemblance to the young Missy and to Marse John was no
little coincidence. She was their own blood kin, but tied to
slavery by a black mother, he was sure. She would not be
easy to buy. He had ways of learning, however, by the grape-
vine of the underground railroad whether her master would
sell Vyry, who was now his cook in his Big House. He also
knew that as a mulatto, by Georgia law she could be free
to marry a free man with her master's consent, that is, if
she could get that consent. There was also the possibility
that she could be smuggled out to freedom. But he wanted
her here in Georgia, and he wanted her to be legally bound to
no one but him. He had enough to buy her, that ought to be
all there was to it. He reassured himself that he could be
confident that gold would buy anything on the market. His
money had always been powerful enough to buy anything
he wanted. Surely it would be powerful enough to buy the
object of his heart's dearest desire.

Meanwhile, Vyry was troubled with strange emotions.
She could not get the black face of the free man out of her
mind. She still felt the casual touch of his hand on her arm.
Above all she was fascinated with his talk of freedom, of
buying her freedom, of making her free to marriage with
him. He told her he had money. Did he have enough? Was
he telling the truth? Was he playing and spoofing with her?
Did he mean what he said? Who was he, anyway?

With great caution she casually inquired about the blacksmith. She knew his name was Randall Ware, and she knew
he owned a blacksmith's shop in the village. But she still did
not know all she wanted to about this free black man. How
old was he? Did he have another gal or woman of his own?
Rumor was a witness that he had plenty of money, that he
had a rich white guardian, and that he was one of those smart
niggers with letters in his head. A nigger with book learning?
A nigger with money and a nigger free on top of all of this?
Was she dreaming? Was such a thing ever heard of in Georgia?
*Maybe he can teach me how to read and write and cipher
on my hands.* But it was the idea of freedom and the proposi-

tion he had raised in connection with that miraculous idea that fascinated her most. She turned it over in her mind idly, as a child turns over a new play-toy. She tried to imagine what it meant to be free. She had never before entertained the faintest idea or hope of freedom, except some dream of an answer to prayer, when God would suddenly appear and send a deliverer like Moses, and set free all the people who were in bondage such as she. She had heard tell that once in a great while a master had been known to set a slave free for saving his life, but not once in her own short life had she ever heard of such a thing happening where she lived. She had never thought of anything else except accepting her lot as a slave, obeying her master and mistress and working hard. She had been resigned. She had never before thought about freedom.

Now the idea of being free began to take hold of her and to work up and down and through her like milk churning to make butter. All day long she thought of nothing but Randall Ware and freedom. At night she dreamed confused dreams in which she struggled to be free while something struggled against her to keep her in chains. Once she dreamed she saw a beautiful door and she tried to enter it, because someone told her the name of the door was Freedom, but the door was locked and although she kept trying the lock and turning the golden knob, it would not open. Then she beat against it with her fists and butted it with her head, but she only made hollow noises and it would not open. Then she saw a black man standing by the door. He held a golden key dangling from a dazzling chain, and he was smiling at her and promising to open the door, but his face kept changing into strange faces. When she woke up crying, she remembered that the door was still locked, even in her dreams, and that he had backed away from her, tantalizing her with that key. She begged and begged him, but he would not give it to her and backed away until he disappeared.

If her dreams and her thoughts were confusing, the talk around her was even more dismaying. She sensed what she did not have to be told: that Big Missy would put up a terrible fight against letting her be sold to a free black man or letting her have freedom in any way. Big Missy hated free Negroes worse than she hated Vyry. Marse John might want to do the right thing if she spoke to him alone but he was so mixed up and so indecisive and unpredictable that he might not be able to make his decision alone. He might make the mistake of asking Big Missy and then no telling what would happen. Even when she gambled against hope that maybe he wouldn't tell Big Missy, she remembered that he liked her cooking. Maybe he would not like her to have her freedom, either. Added to all this anxiety, she suddenly learned from Caline that Randall Ware was busy trying to get slaves to rise up and that sometimes he even slipped into the fields and talked to the field hands. She was very worried that something might happen to him before he had done anything about buying her freedom. She discovered that talk and gossip were strange things. Talk had feet and could walk and gossip had wings and could fly. She heard whispers and she was afraid they would grow as big as men, and she felt the wings of gossip threatening to sting and to smother her. It buzzed around her and flew against her and her words came back upon her to settle motionless in the air. The house servants confided to her that Randall Ware was telling Sam and Big Boy and many field hands that he knew a way they could all be free. As if all this were not enough, Big Missy kept throwing out broad hints and remarks about free black biggity niggers stirring up trouble amongst our good hard working niggers. When she finally came out and questioned Vyry sharply and asked her if she knew anything about the trouble that was being stirred up amongst all the niggers in the county, Vyry answered, "Lord, no Missy, I ain't heard tell of nothing," and "Yes'm, when I does I sure will let you know."

Whippoorwill!
Whippoorwill!
Whippoorwill!
  Bobwhite, Bobwhite
  Can you come out tonight?
Whippoorwill!
Whippoorwill!
Whippoorwill!

9   Springtime is sallet time

One very dark night when the moon was new, Vyry was
sitting in the door of the cabin that once was Aunt Sally's
and now was hers. She was combing her hair, and humming
a tune. It was unusually warm for spring and felt more like
summer. Crickets and cicadas were droning their night music;
fireflies flickered; a few crows and magpies made quarrelsome
noises and occasionally a cow mooed or a cow bell rang in
the distance. Vyry's hair was now long enough for her to sit
on it and it was a long and tiring job to arrange it. According
to the instructions of Aunt Sally she caught rainwater in a
barrel to wash it, and took pains not to use the lye-potash
homemade soap used to wash clothes. She still braided the

long locks of hair and coiled the braids around her head, tying them with black rags and fastening them close to her head with two precious gutta-percha hairpins Miss Lillian had given her, sneaked out under the nose of Big Missy. Sometimes in the kitchen she was obliged to tie up her hair in a head-rag, but at night she liked to sit and take her time and feel the night air blow through the mass of pent-up hair. The patter-roller had passed her cabin and completed his rounds of the Quarters, and now with his hound dog and his gun he was making for the Big Road some distance from the plantation.

Suddenly she heard the faint call of a whippoorwill. The bird cried three times, then stopped. It was a clear, distinct call, and seemed to come from a distance of more than a mile. In a few minutes she heard the sound again three times without stopping and then again there was silence. This time she was sure the bird was much closer. Now she waited tensely to hear the bird's call for the third time, for then she could be sure it was a sign and not a bird at all. This was the well-known bird call that had always been a sign among the Negro slaves. The next time the bird cried, it startled her, for she was sure that the cry came from the back of her own cabin, only a few yards away. With trembling fingers she hastily coiled her hair around her head and ran behind the cabin.

Once there, she had taken only a few steps in the darkness toward the open fields before she bumped into Randall Ware. Instantly, without speaking, his arms went around her and he kissed her hard on the mouth. When she pushed him away and pulled free of his arms she was trembling violently, and her heart beat so fiercely that for a moment she could not speak. Weakly she fell on the ground and he dropped down beside her.

"What you doing here?" she whispered. "You wants to get us both in bad trouble?"

"I had to see you. Don't you want to hear how I'm trying to buy your freedom, or don't you want to marriage with me?"

"You ain't go to Marster, by yourself, is you?"

"I dassent. I sent a man."

"Who?"

"A white man. One I could trust."

"What he say?"

"Say he don't want to sell. He like your cooking and you

been trained to cook here and to suit his taste and you honest. But I know with all this new trouble stirring up he's bound to think it over. Said he'd think it over. Meantimes, I want you to trust me . . ."

"Trust you how?"

"Marry me. Marry me now. I promise you I'll buy your freedom if it's the last thing I do. It won't be long, I'm sure, but I can't wait. I want you for my woman now."

"When you buy my freedom, then I marriage with you, and not before! And I'll tell you like the monkey say to the parrot when they was fighting over the brush-broom, them's my final words of dust you eating, Mr. Coon!"

A week later Vyry was picking herbs and greens and gathering roots in the swamp woods when she was suddenly startled to look up and see Grimes and one of the patter-rollers with him. They had their guns tucked under their arms and one hound dog with them and they were watching her. It was Sunday afternoon and not at all near sundown, but the sight of them gave her a pang of fear. *Look like that same old patter-roller passed my cabin the other night. Wonder what does they want?* She had a basket made of palmetto strips and it was already over half full of various herbs, greens, and potent roots. She quickly covered over a few mushrooms she had found earlier. It was poisonous mushrooms that had killed the master of the two women convicted of murder and scheduled to hang. *Must I quit or keep on like they ain't here or I ain't seed them or wait for them to speak to me first?* They soon gave her no choice. Slowly they ambled over to her. The dog was hot and his tongue hung dripping with saliva, but he did not bristle in anger. Instead he stood quietly while the men spoke. Grimes spoke first, "What you doing here by yourself in the swamp woods, Vyry and what you want with them weeds?"

"Them ain't no weeds, Mister Grimes. Them is greens to cook to eat, and yerbs and roots to cure all kinds of miseries what ails you."

The patter-roller said, "Tell us what you may call 'em and what you makes from them."

"Well sir, this here is my greens. I got some creasy and some pusley, and some poke sallet. I parboils them and cooks them with wild onions and salt meat and they makes good eating with corn pone. Now that there is mullein. I takes mullein and pinetop and salt and I does different nother things with different ones. Mullein bath is good for the feets and legs to stop swelling and heart dropsy. I also uses it for teas. This here is barefoot root. I cooks it down and adds pyo lard and salt and makes a salve for the rheumatiz. May-apple root is good to work the bowels and black halls and cherry root makes a good tea to strengthen the appetite. Them there is Jerusalem oats for worms. Mosten everybody knows that." She looked from one to the other but their faces were expressionless. The dog sat panting at their feet. "Now this here pusley is fine for dysentery and just like ripe pomegranate hulls it'll stop the bowels from running off, too. Tansy tea, and red shank, and hazel roots, them is all good for womanhood troubles. They tells me the tea from tansy'll keep a gal from getting big, and hazel root boiled down with alum stones is good for a woman's body what's falling, and red shank is always good. Penny-royal make a good tea just like peppermint do, and Samson snake root is mighty good for cramps and pains in the belly. I reckon, beings you is mens, you knows about John the Conqueror. I uses Jimson weeds and red-oak bark like I do my salt and mustard poultices, and you knows elderberry and poke berry is good for making wine. Course I ain't got room for nuff to make wine. Now gentlemen, that's what I does with my *weeds!*"

"You sure you ain't got no pizen in there, has you?"

"Nossah, I ain't fooling with no pizen. Course I can't tell what's pizen from what ain't pizen. I just knows the good roots. I ain't never knowed the bad roots."

Sally, come up! Oh Sally go down!
Oh, Sally come twist your heel around,
The old man he's gone to town,
Oh, Sally come down the middle.

10 *Wedding in the Big House and love in the cornfields*

"Johnny, your sister is the prettiest girl I've seen in many a moon!"

"Thanks, Kevin. I guess she's all right, if you like her type."

"She's sweet too."

Johnny turned to look at his friend more closely. Then, a bit reluctantly, he said, "Yes, she does have a pretty even disposition. Gets it from my father. He's the sunny, optimistic type."

"I don't think your father likes me."

"Nonsense. He's just a hunting, fishing, political man, an outdoors type. I think sometimes he distrusts studious people. But if my mother likes you, Dad's opinion won't matter a bit. La Mere is the strong mind around here."

"Yes, I've sensed that. You are a lot like her yourself, aren't you?"

Johnny stood with his black tie and white starched collar

in his hand and glanced in the bedroom mirror at the reflection of his friend Kevin. The two men were strikingly different. Johnny Dutton had the dark coloring of his mother, even darker. His shoulders were broad and under his white, pleated, and ruffled shirt he carried them proudly. His fleshy lips were cynical and he had a way of slightly parting them to show his beautiful teeth as though he were an animal baring his fangs.

Kevin was slightly smaller. His hair was auburn and his nose freckled. His blue eyes were sometimes merry, other times serious and unfathomable. They were always soft, however, and the corners of his mouth never curled in the cynical twist of his friend's.

Now as they silently took each other's measure, opposite thoughts ran through their heads. Johnny spoke first.

"Well, Kevin MacDougall, it surely doesn't take you long to figure out people. I hope I am like my mother. I love her strong-willed character, her good judgment, and her depth of feeling, to say nothing of her tenacity of purpose. She's a woman who belongs to the times of King Arthur. She might even be like Spenser's Una. She's a noble lady, my mother, and I adore every inch of her proud and haughty self."

"You're lucky, Johnny. My mother died when I was born. They say I'm like her. Not like my father at all, who you know is a colonel in the army. I hate the military, soldiers, war, and all that kind of thing . . ."

"And I love it! You know, that's the one thing I'm excited about now, waiting to get my appointment to West Point. And, I tell you, Kevin, I just couldn't bear to be disappointed."

"You won't be. But I don't envy you. Give me books and music, and a lovely girl like your sister, and my life will be complete. I ask no greater happiness."

"Gosh, you are sweet on Lillian, aren't you? Suppose she doesn't like you and La Mere doesn't take to you?"

"I'm not worried about the first. I know your sister doesn't dislike me; I'm sure we are already attracted to each other. I can sense it. And as for your mother, I'm dedicated to be her slave until she approves of me. And what about that Fanny Crenshaw I met last night? She kept fluttering her eyelashes at you."

"Oh, Fanny? We grew up together; when we were children I was always teasing her, pulling her hair, racing her on her pony, threatening to scare her or frightening her with the dogs. She can't be liking me now!"

"I think she does." Kevin spoke quietly but in such a serious tone that Johnny was caught up sharply. He looked a full minute into the unsmiling face of his friend, but then he shrugged his shoulders and laughed, "More's the pity. I'm off for West Point in the fall, and after that who knows? I'm itching for adventure, excitement, anything but the boring life of these backwoods saddled with a wife and responsibility."

Now they were putting on their long tail-coats, and rushing out to meet the guests arriving for the evening's party.

The young girls were dawdling together in Lillian's bedroom, podering their faces and fussing with their hair, gossiping about the news in the country valley, and sizing up the boys. Five of Lillian's best friends from around the county were enjoying her hospitality: Fanny Crenshaw, a green-eyed red-head, her nearest neighbor; Addie Barrow, a small dark-eyed little dynamo with a spitfire temper; Belle, the parson's daughter, poor as the proverbial church-mouse but highly respected and with more brains than all of the other girls put together; Hilma, the doctor's daughter, who was, it was rumored, one-fourth Cherokee Indian, and finally Mildred Butler, whom the girls did not like but tolerated because of her twin brother, Milton, who went everywhere with her. Mildred was as rich as any girl in Lee County and she was also a snob and a bore. She was what Fanny called a damper on everybody else's good spirits. There was no question but that Fanny was the leader of the group and all the girls vied to be Fanny's "best friend."

"Lillian, darling, where did you find him? You've been keeping secrets from us, now haven't you?" Lillian colored and answered with annoyance, "I don't know what you're talking about, Addie. Kevin is my brother's friend. My father says he looks awfully old. I think he must be nearly thirty."

"That's old for Johnny, too, isn't it?"

"Not when you know Johnny. He's always been old for his age." Fanny tossed her head and said, "Johnny's ageless. He belongs with everybody, young and old."

"Is he really going off to West Point and *more* military school?"

"I think so. Papa's proud that Johnny wants to be an army officer. Says it is in the genuine southern tradition of a gentleman."

"Humph, I'd think after graduating from Marietta that

he'd want to be something else. All they ever do over there is drill, drill, drill!"

"Well, Millie, if you last through all that drilling, you're bound to love it, I guess."

"That's not what Jeb Hendrix Junior says. He hates it and he had to drill, too."

"He's going to Oglethorpe, isn't he?"

"Yes. You know he's always got his head in a book. Politics and economics—that's what he likes."

"Well, take all that serious talk away from the Winston boys because they're all dandies and even if they are all going to be lawyers and follow in their father's footsteps, they never bore you with books. They love a good time, and so do I!"

And laughingly the girls began tripping downstairs to find their beaux, to set their nets, and lay their charming traps.

Kevin MacDougall was courting Lillian before she realized it. Everybody understood what was happening before she did. Every Sunday afternoon young people came calling in buggies and carriages. Although Big Missy considered Kevin a little old for Lillian, this nevertheless gave her a good excuse to keep the house full of other young ladies and gentlemen. As usual, Marse John was last to realize what was happening and was caught up short when this young Scotch-Irish schoolteacher began asserting his intentions.

The young Missy was fascinated by this man who courted her with books of love poetry, reading Shakespeare and Burns and Keats under the shade of a big live oak. But her father suspected such unmanly activities and wondered what Johnny saw in such an unlikely fellow. Big Missy thought it was quite romantic and said so. She had completely fallen prey to the flattering attentions and compliments of the determined Kevin.

Vyry watched Miss Lillian's beaux and callers with great interest. There was talk that pretty soon Miss Lillian would be getting married and having her wedding, then going away from the plantation as a young bride on her honeymoon before settling permanently, and all before the long summer would end.

Spring gave way to summer. At first the heat was intense only in the day and at its worst at noon. Then, as the summer proceeded, the heat began an hour earlier, gradually intensifying at eleven, then at ten, until by eight o'clock the sun was scorching and relentless. From noon till three in the afternoon the heat was blistering, and finally they felt the heat early in the morning shortly after sunup, and it lasted until an hour or more after sundown. Then the earth began to cool gradually. The night breezes were pleasant with the scent of Cape jessamine and wild honeysuckle vines. Throughout the early evening the earth was like a fire banked with ashes; it was nearly midnight before there was real relief. These were the evenings when slaves sat before their cabin doors fanning with wide palmetto leaves, and children played ring games. Working days were long now and the nights were very short.

It was also the season of love. Big Missy laid in a big supply of ipecac, ergot, and saltpeter to control the passionate natures of house servants. "I don't care what the field niggers do, but I'm not having niggers acting like dogs around me!"

Vyry remembered the warnings of Aunt Sally and she was careful what she ate around Big Missy. She felt sorry for Lucy who could scarcely spend a day without being fed either ipecac or saltpeter, especially when canning and preserving had to be done.

When the nights were hottest and sleep did not come quickly to restless bodies, the slaves often took their pallets outside and slept under the stars. The young bloods, scornful of pallets, made their beds in the cornfields. Everywhere in nature they could watch the season of mating. Spring was the beginning, like the first blush of a budding rose. Summer was the fulfillment, the ripening of perfect fruit and the opening of the full-blown flower.

Vyry was now in her sixteenth summer. During the day she was working in a steaming hot kitchen and jumping to the orders of Big Missy. There was not much time for thinking, and she was glad because thinking was so confusing. She did not like to remember all the painful things, and with no time to think, she had even less time to daydream her hopeless, unreal dreams of freedom. If she kept her mind on the present work at hand, she could keep busy without dreaming or thinking. Thus life went on without anything changing her world or changing her life as a cook in the Big House. She dreaded the nights when she called out in her sleep after Mammy Sukey or Aunt Sally or remembered the way Grandpa Tom had died. She preferred to think now of Miss Lillian, who was going to be married this summer. Try as she could not to think, she continued to think painfully of Randall Ware, that free man. She fought his image in her mind, but she could not forget his arms of steel and his kiss of fire. He disturbed her more and more, and she wished she had never seen him nor heard him talk of freedom, "Marriage with me and I will buy your freedom." But summer is more a time for feeling than for thinking, because thinking is always confusing and only the strange emotions you cannot understand are real and powerful. She was all mixed up in her head and even more confused in her heart. She could not understand the despair in her mind and heart that fought with the craving in her body and the yearning in her soul. Sometimes at night she found herself straining her ears for the triple call of a single whippoorwill.

That summer Marse John sent Grimes to buy a dozen new slaves. Big Missy grumbled because they cost a small fortune. One of the young boys, it was soon learned, was simpleminded or touched in the head. He tried to do what he was told. He was docile and obedient, but he could not be trusted with any big responsibility. He hung around the yard and the house doing errands and anything he was told. If anyone asked him about himself, where he was from, what he could remember about his folks, his mind was a blank, even though he was a big boy. He seldom laughed or cried. Vyry felt very sorry for him and sometimes she gave him stolen tidbits to eat. He felt her mute love and sympathy and hung around the kitchen door, eager to do anything to please her. If Grimes cursed him and threatened to beat him, the boy would simply stare at him. If Big Missy yelled at him, he would only shake his head from side to side and look at her. Both Grimes and Big Missy found him maddening. Nobody could understand such a wooden head. He made no effort to run away. He would curl up anywhere and go to sleep—in a barn, on a doorstep, against hay or cornshucks, and all day long he was sleepy and yawning. Big Missy said, "He's just a dunce, stupid and lazy." Marse John was annoyed that Grimes had made such a bad bargain. But to Vyry there was no mystery. This child was just another slave who had been kicked around like a dog all his life, from one plantation to another, from pillar to post, until now he acted more like a dumb, driven animal than a human being.

One Sunday afternoon Miss Lillian was sitting on the

veranda with her dinner guests. Her friends had been laughing and talking, teasing her and Kevin. She was blushing and trying uneasily to answer their taunts when suddenly she felt ill. At first she thought her stays were too tight. In the midst of a large burst of laughter she suddenly felt a rumble of air bursting loudly from her stomach and she could not refrain from a huge fit of belching. She was embarrassed because everyone became silent and she could not stop the air from rushing forth. Addie said, "Are you ill?" and then poor Lillian burst into tears and ran into the house. This awkwardness lasted for a few minutes until some of the girls rose to leave.

For days Lillian was sensitive over the incident. She told her mother she was too embarrassed and could never show her face again. "Nonsense," said her father, "forget it." But her mother sympathized with her daughter in her anguish. Genteel, well-bred southern ladies were above such human frailty. May Liza and Caline whispered with Vyry and Lucy over it and snickered over the whole thing as a joke. As the weekend approached and thoughts of her returning company upset Miss Lillian so much, her mother began to scheme to rid the girl of such embarrassment. Marse John said, "Aren't you making a mountain out of a molehill? Forget it, I say, forget it."

But not Big Missy. She was not usually a foolish woman, but where Miss Lillian's pride was concerned something had to be done. She sent for the new dumb-wit boy, Willie. She told him what she wanted him to do. Willie had already demonstrated that he would do anything he was told. He was a good and harmless boy, just a dunce.

On Sunday when the crowd gathered as usual most of the guests had either forgotten the incident or assumed that Miss Lillian was ill and had quickly recovered. Suddenly in the midst of the jokes and laughter, Willie appeared. He came around the side of the house and stood looking blankly at the young people on the veranda, who in turn stared at him. He stood for such a long time with that faraway look in his eyes and his mouth hanging open that finally young Marster John accosted him with, "What do you want, Willie?" Willie stammered and looked at him and then from one face to the other. Finally he stuttered out his message, "Evening to yall. I come around here to take that fart on myself what Miss Lillian farted last week."

"Boy, what did you say?"

"I says I come around here to take that fart on myself what Miss Lillian farted last week."

And with that same blankness in his eyes he turned and ambled away. Now for the second time, Miss Lillian did not know whether to turn and run away or cry or try to laugh it off. There was nothing more Big Missy could do about Willie. He did exactly what he was told to do always. What could you expect from such a dumb-wit boy?

Kevin and Lillian were going to be married in late June. Preparations were already underway and going at a great pace when Lucy ran afoul of Big Missy because of her pet parrot. Big Missy was entertaining a very important visitor from Milledgeville when Jake's Lucy displeased her so much that Vyry wondered how things could continue thus until the wedding.

Lucy was always a sullen child and now that she was grown up and working in the Big House she often seemed to drag at her work and not move with a willing heart. Lucy was tall and seemed big and strapping, but she was not really as strong as she looked. Big Missy hollered at her most of the time, and the girl would often start and jump like a scared rabbit. Lucy always seemed to be lingering around when there was much conversation, and it became patently clear that she was always listening to what other people were saying. They assumed that she was just idling and dawdling at her work. Vyry did not feel free to advise Lucy or tell her how to avoid Big Missy's wrath, as she had learned to do from childhood, because there had never been any real feeling of kinship between Vyry and Lucy as there had been between Aunt Sally and Vyry. They were too close in age and too inarticulate about their mutual sisterhood.

Every morning Big Missy would bring her pet parrot out to the kitchen. Caline and May Liza said the parrot was supposed to be a kind of watch dog and counseled Vyry and Lucy to be careful what they said in earshot of the parrot because it knew a few curse words and would start its screeching noise at the least provocation. At night after supper the parrot went back into the Big House. One night when there were guests and Big Missy had nagged Lucy all day, Lucy felt sullen and mean as she served supper. She had just come out to the kitchen to sit down for a minute when May Liza came out and told Lucy Big Missy wanted her for something else. Lucy, cross and irritable, impulsively turned to May Liza and said, "Go tell Old Missy I says to kiss the monkey's ass!" May Liza's eyes popped. Vyry turned to speak and saw Big Missy standing in the doorway. The parrot let out his screeching noise, and Lucy, not yet aware of her Mistress standing in the door, slapped the parrot from his perch saying, "Shut up, you hellion!" Then turning, she saw Big Missy. The three slaves stood stricken with fear. Vyry wrung her hands on her apron and looked at the clay-brick floor. May Liza still had her hand over her mouth. Poor Lucy, beside herself with fear, was shaking, her face working without sounds, her eyes popping in dread. Big Missy first looked coldly at Vyry, who felt her gaze go over her like so much swift lightning, seeing at one glance the worn and slightly soiled checked blue and white apron, the long skirt hiding her shoes, the white poker face, and only a twitching of the muscles around her tight lips. Big Missy seemed to ignore May Liza; instead she moved quickly toward Lucy. With her bare hands she struck her swiftly on both cheeks, first one and then the other. She slapped as hard as she could, at the same time saying, "You impudent good for nothing sassy black wench, I'll teach you to remember your place!" And the parrot began whistling and laughing and screeching with merriment. Big Missy, now beside herself with anger, grabbed her bird and flung it out into the night where the parrot continued to mumble a jumbled disturbance.

But that was not the end of it. Big Missy went back to her guests after first ordering May Liza and Lucy to bring more coffee. After supper, when the slaves came up for prayers, they stood outside and sang spirituals for Big Missy's guests and then she read her favorite passage from Paul's Letter to the Colossians:

> Servants, obey in all things your masters according to the flesh; not with eyeservice, as men pleasers; but in singleness of heart, fearing God: and whatsoever ye do, do it heartily, as to the Lord, and not unto men; Knowing that of the Lord ye shall receive the reward of the inheritance; for ye serve the Lord Christ. But he that doeth wrong shall receive for the wrong which he hath done: and there is no respect of persons.

Then the slaves went back to their Quarters and Grimes was summoned for his regular report of the day. This particular evening, May Liza, by pure accident, heard Big Missy tell Mr. Grimes that she wanted him to see to it that as soon as her guests left the following morning, Lucy was to be tied up and given a good whipping with the lash. He promised her that it would be done without fail.

The next morning Lucy could not be found. She had disappeared during the night. Grimes came to the back door and told Big Missy he would take the dogs and go after her.

"She's more than likely hiding in the swamps nearby and the hounds can scent her out in a little while."

But Big Missy demurred. "I don't want her killed or mangled by the dogs. We don't want her dead on our hands. That just means another nigger slave dead, though God knows she's not worth much. My husband is complaining now that too many of our slaves are either dying or unfit for work and the price of slaves is going up sky-high. We paid four thousand dollars for that last group. A good worker is hard to buy. Bring her back, but don't let the dogs get at her. They might tear her limb from limb." Mr. Grimes went away, but Vyry did not think he looked too pleased.

They did find Lucy and they brought her back, her hands tied behind her and Grimes pushing her ahead of him on the end of a rope. He threw her down in the backyard while some of the slave boys struggled hard to keep the dogs on their chains. Vyry was sure the dogs had been given something of Lucy's clothes to smell and had picked up her scent in the swamp woods. Grimes knocked hard on the back door and told a slave to fetch Big Missy. His boots were muddy and he dared not enter the house. He had his whip doubled back and caught up in his hands. Vyry knew he was itching to use it, but waiting for Big Missy's say-so to go ahead. Meanwhile Lucy blubbered with spasms of fear and Vyry's heart beat painfully.

When Big Missy came out she and Grimes had a whispered conversation between them. Vyry strained her ears, but she could not make out what they were saying. Lucy looked as if she were having fits. She was twitching all over and foaming at the mouth, but they had her tied securely and she could not have gotten away even if the dogs had not been there. The slave boys from the yard were lounging around with solemn expressions on their faces and a few of the smallest children from the Quarters idled up to the house and out of sheer curiosity peeped around the corners of the house and the barns. Big Missy went inside the house and did not come back. Suddenly Grimes went into action.

Vyry saw Grimes giving orders to the boys and they began to tie Lucy to stakes in the ground with the ropes, but Vyry could not figure out what they were going to do with her. They were tying her legs as well as her arms, and now they had driven a steel spike into the ground and tied the rope that bound her legs to the spike. Grimes now whispered something to one of the white guards and he went off for something. Then Vyry saw them building a small fire while Grimes was still giving orders. The Negro boys who had been holding the hounds had taken them away and returned. According to Grimes's directions they squatted on the ground and prepared to hold Lucy's head down with their hands. Meanwhile the guard had come back with something in his hands.

Vyry was watching from the kitchen and her whole body began tightening like a drum. She was sure that if Big Missy had slapped her at that moment she would have felt no pain, only this creeping numbness in her flesh. Suddenly Vyry saw the guard stoop over the fire and with a pair of tongs lift a red hot piece of iron no bigger than a small piece of coke from the fire. Vyry gasped in horror. Now they had the hot iron firmly grasped in the tongs and they were going toward Lucy. The slave boys began to tremble in terror and loudly they pleaded, "Mister Grimes I feels awful sick to my stomach!"

"Well, damn you, go on, you ain't no help nohow!" and he stooped to hold Lucy down himself.

Vyry did not see them when they actually branded the girl. She did not hear the hissing sound of the iron on the sizzling flesh. Her heart thumped in her so loudly that her eardrums throbbed so painfully that it was as if thunder were all around her and everything went black and red before her in a whirling wheel of fire and blood and darkness so that she dropped in a dead faint on the dirt and brick floor while somewhere back in her consciousness there was the terrible bellowing sound like a young bull or calf crying out in pain. When Vyry came to herself later, she did not know how long she had lain there, nor how much later it was. Caline was throwing cold water in her face, and May Liza was muttering, "Lord have mercy, do Jesus!"

Slowly returning to reality, Vyry remembered and she got up to see if Lucy were still lying outside in the yard, or if perhaps she had had another bad dream. Not a black head could be seen in the yard except Lucy's and she was writhing in agony and still tied down with the ropes. Blood was streaming from her face, which was puffed to twice its natural size and too bloody to be recognized. Nobody seemed to know where Grimes had gone, but far off in the swamp woods they could hear the hounds yelping and crying, so they figured that perhaps he had gone hunting wild game.

The mammoth preparations for the wedding were exciting Big Missy beyond measure. None of the house slaves could please her, and she even brought in extra women to spin and weave and sew. They made piles of lovely soft nainsook lingerie for Miss Lillian's trousseau. The wedding dress was of imported embroidered white silk with a beautiful lace veil. The slip was of white boux de chine and crinoline, sewn over three wide hoops. Her orange blossoms were real and her buttoned white shoes were of satin and kid. It was Caline who helped her dress. "She will smother in that corset, I do believe."

Vyry thought she had never seen anything in her life more beautiful than Miss Lillian on her wedding day. Her eyes and hair were shining and her clothes were so beautiful, of such soft, silken, shimmering stuff that she was really an unbelievable vision. All the house-servants and old slaves around the place came up to wish her happiness before the ceremony started because afterwards there would be no time. Vyry had to stop her busy preparations in the kitchen where she was creaming chicken for patty shells, to say goodbye to Miss Lillian.

"Oh Vyry, wish me luck and happiness!" And there was the same excitement in Miss Lillian's face that Vyry had known in her playmate when they were little girls.

"I do, Miss Lillian. God knows I do. I wish you all the luck in the world, and I just know you will be happy. You just got to be, ain't no reason why you shouldn't be."

Lillian looked at the solemn face of Vyry who sounded so old to be so young, and then she reached down and pulled an orange blossom out of the fresh, untouched bouquet and handed it to Vyry. Then laughing happily she ran out of her room to meet the wedding party in the yard, to marry Kevin, and begin her life's journey as a married lady.

The wedding was over for Big Missy when the bride and groom stepped into their barouche under a shower of rice with the old shoes flung after the carriage and the old tin pans tied to the wheels. But for Vyry the wedding was not over when the guests departed. There was still a mountain of dishes. Every bone in her body ached with fatigue, and she could not yet see the end. For her the wedding day was not a happy one. It was full of back-breaking work and the terrible stress of hurry-hurry-hurry, get this done and then do this, get that done and then do this, do this, do that and that and this, and never, never, never say you are too tired. You must not stop because you can't go on, but you must go on because you can't stop. And at the end of the day she could not tell whether her head ached because she was tired, or her heart ached from unhappiness, or it was her feet that felt so bad. But she was more tired than she could remember ever having been before in her whole life. She set her lips grimly and she persevered through the long day. She worked down the mountain of orders, prepared the mountains of food, heard the shrill cackling noises of the women's voices, saw in a fog the steadily moving figures of May Liza and Caline and Lucy. Sweat popped out and dribbled down her nose into her mouth and off her chin.

Lucy's face was still sore, although it was no longer puffed from the swelling and inflammation. When it was a running sore and Lucy had ached with fever, Vyry thought Lucy would not only be forced to bed but that the thing might kill her. But Lucy could only talk of the horrible pain and the ugly mark it had left on her face—the mark of "R" for runaway. But she had stumbled on through pain and sullenness. She had worked until she staggered, until her glassy eyes looked dull and witless and her shaking fingers steadied themselves under some strange rigid control from within. Never had Vyry felt sorrier for anyone.

Beads of perspiration stood on the foreheads of Caline and May Liza, and they scarcely had time to wipe away the fine line of water over their upper lips with the edges of their apron hems. The June heat was bad anyway; most of the guests were fanning or being fanned. Caline kept wondering and muttering how Miss Lillian was standing it in that tight corset. But evidently the stays never crossed Miss Lillian's mind, for she came through all the wedding in fine fettle, and as Lucy whispered afterward, "left all this work here behind for us niggers."

Vyry dragged herself home to her cabin thinking she would fall on her pallet and drop off to sleep at once from complete exhaustion. Instead she sat in her doorway watching the moon rise high in the heavens, still too tired to take off her clothes. Out of the night there came the sudden call of a distant whippoorwill.

Eating goober peas.

11 Fourth of July celebration

Lee County was planning a hanging on the Fourth of July,
when the two women convicted of murder would be made a
public example. A gallows was built in the county prison
yard where all the public could witness the execution, and a
holiday was chosen because it was the best time for all the
people. Every able-bodied slave in the county was, by order
of his master, forced to attend the hanging.

Fourth of July was always barbecue day in Georgia, a day
for political speeches and all kinds of festive celebrations.
This year the barbecue would be held on the courthouse
grounds. Various planters' families would carry baskets of
dinner to spread around on the grass under the trees like a
picnic. Vyry was busy preparing lunches and baskets for all
those going from Marse John's family. The plantation cook
was in charge of dinner for the field hands. Big Missy and
Marse John had generously ordered extra rum and tobacco
for the slaves and they were going to make a barrel of sweet-

ened water for the slave children. Vyry told Caline and May Liza, "It makes me sick to my stomach every time I thinks about it. How you reckon we will swallow over a hanging?"

On the appointed day, however, the huge milling crowd generated an explosive excitement. The courthouse was decorated with bunting and small flags and there were lots of benches placed out under the trees. Large stands were erected so that people could sit and look over the fence into the prison yard where the hanging was going to be. The gallows was ready, made of new pine lumber with heavy new rope and a trap set in full view of everyone. Up in the trees were perched a number of poor whites, chiefly boys and young men who heckled the crowd, calling out obscenities and insulting jokes. Vyry sat in a dull stupor with the other members of Marse John's household retinue. Although they arrived early, around ten o'clock in the morning, they found others who had been there long before, some since sunrise. The country wagons kept rolling into town from all parts of the county until after twelve o'clock. Some of the white women, wives of poor dirt farmers, were in their best bonnets, but many of the planter families were represented by the men only. Vyry looked out at the motley throng of people clothed in bright checkered colors. There were hawkers in their colored shirts, red suspenders and gaiters, with lots of baubles to attract the children whose parents could afford to buy. There were scattered groups around different activities. In one group she could see a cock-fight, another had a gander pulling; men fighting were gouging eyes for a prize. Lots of horse-trading was going on over odds and ends of junk and even a small auction took place on the courthouse steps. Now and then she saw slave traders moving among the crowds, whispering bargains into the ears of slave owners.

Seated on the rude benches many people were eating goober peas, and the old toothless women smacked their lips over various tid-bits and gorged their under-lips with sweet snuff. Most of the white people seemed to be enjoying themselves in the holiday atmosphere and were in high, laughing spirits. With the exception of small black children who could not comprehend the day's doings, the Negroes were for the most part silent. They sat stiff and stolid, their faces morose, their bodies tensed. Grimes, and his guards, like all other drivers, were very busy checking their crowd and keeping their slaves herded together. They made it impossible for them to escape because they kept each group ringed with armed guards.

Firecrackers were popping from early dawn. Most of the fireworks were homemade from saltpeter and black gunpowder, but there were rumors that after the hanging there would be a big display of new and store-bought fireworks in harmony with the patriotic nature of the day.

It was a churning crowd; noisy and raucous and partly under forced control, there was nevertheless a current of tension running through the subdued mass of people. There were women in huge bell-bottomed and hoop-ringed skirts and close-fitting bonnets. There were dandies in tight-fitting pants and high hats. The slaves wore their usual homespun and linsey; some with straw hats flopping in the air as they walked; many of the women wore red head-rags; the children were barefoot, wearing a ragged shift and nothing else; old men wielded canes as weapons of protection. All the socializing was confined within each group. They did not mix. The poor whites clustered together. The rich planter families sat alone. The Negro slaves were huddled under the watchful eyes of overseers and guards. What small camaraderie existed was within each separate unit. There was absolutely no bantering back and forth.

Exactly on the stroke of twelve noon the judge came out in his black robes and with him the preacher, also in black robes, and the two women prisoners in chains between their guards. They appeared on a high platform in the prison yard. With them also were county officials. The hangman sat like a hawk, perched on a stool, also wearing the blackest black.

Judge Winston presided. The whole affair was a formal occasion. After addressing the dignitaries and the crowd he said, "We are gathered here on this eightieth anniversary of the birth of our great country to celebrate another milestone in our history. We are also gathered to perform a painful duty in the course of justice and before all men. A very fine program has been prepared for your edification, and an eminent theologian has consented to bring us the sermon for this occasion. Before he begins to speak, however, we will be favored with a musical selection by a local *artiste* who will sing for us, 'Flee as a bird to your mountain.' "

This was a song Vyry loved but the plaintive minor notes and words fell on deaf ears like so much gravel on rock or slate or tin. Her personal agony had begun. She could not bear to look at the women in shackles nor at the gallows or the hangman, much less the preacher with his oily face, or the judge in his official robes of justice. Now he was introducing the speaker. Vyry promptly forgot his name, but as long as she lived she knew she would never forget the sermon of that preacher.

"I open the Book of Holy Scriptures to the Fourth Book of Moses called Numbers and I choose for my text the words of that eternal law concerning M-U-R-D-E-R!" (He thundered the word so loudly that it reverberated into the distance like an echo.)

" 'WHOSO KILLETH ANY PERSON, THE MURDERER SHALL BE PUT TO DEATH . . .' This is the eternal word of God, and God cannot lie: the murderer shall surely be put to death.

"I want to direct my few remarks to three separate groups. I want first to speak to the planters who are masters of African slaves: My friends, I speak to you leading farmers of Lee County as your humble servant. I admonish you in the name of the Lord and the fear of God to *guard your property with your lives!* Remember, your slaves are your sacred property. They are committed to you as a sacred trust from God. Read in His Holy Word where he tells you that your bondservants are yours and you are responsible for them. You are morally obligated to teach them right from wrong. You must constantly tell them the awful consequences of evil doing and the heavenly rewards for obedience and faithful service. God does everything well and for a purpose. Since the beginning of civilized man there have been slaves and masters and there always will be. Slavery is a natural and righteous state. It is the civilizing principle of all great societies. Yours is the God-given right to admonish your slave in the fear of the Lord; to punish him when he does wrong and to teach him of the heavenly rewards after death that God has in store for him when he is your faithful, humble, and obedient servant. The Christianizing of the black heathen is your sacred duty. He was brought to these great shores for a Christian purpose. It is your duty to see that that great and sacred purpose is fulfilled; that the savage becomes a docile, faithful, humble, and obedient servant."

Vyry could not help but think how differently Brother Zeke preached at the Rising Glory Baptist Church. But she did not want to miss a word.

"And now, I turn to you black slaves. You are fortunate to have found Christian masters and to be cared for by these wonderful gentlemen. They protect and feed and clothe and shelter you. You must reward them with faithful service and strict obedience. You must obey the laws of Moses when he says, Thou shalt not kill, thou shalt not steal, thou shalt not lie! Do you know what these commandments mean? Do you know what will happen when you kill, when you steal, and when you lie? I will tell you. God says He is a God who will never forget the disobedient. He will punish you and your children and your children's children, all your little black pickaninnies down to the third and fourth generations, but He will have mercy on them that keep His commandments and obey Him.

"When you steal from your Master's crib . . . When you steal from your Master's smokehouse . . . When you steal from your Master's table . . . God sees you and God does not forget. God sees you and God will surely punish you.

"So, niggers, stop stealing! Stop stealing from your masters. Stop stealing and stop lying! And woe be unto him that is a murderer! The murderer shall surely be put to death.

"And remember what the word of God says to you slaves: Servants, obey in all things your masters.

"God meant for you to have masters.

"God meant for you to be slaves.

"God meant for you to be humble, obedient, honest, truthful and God-fearing servants of your earthly masters."

If his words were having effect on his black listeners, you could not tell from looking at them. Vyry looked around her, and like her own poker face, saw her expression mirrored in her fellow sufferers. Not a slave turned a hair. Now the preacher began to work himself up into a frenzy:

"And finally, I speak to you, you awful sinners, you guilty of the terrible sin of murder! I turn to you in the name of God and I beg you to repent. Repent before it is too late. Prepare to meet your maker. May God look down into your evil black hearts and make the devil unfasten his hold on your souls, before you burn forever in that eternal hellfire and brimstone prepared from the beginning of the world for such as you. God is a just and righteous God. God is an awful, jealous God. God is a God of vengeance, but God will also have mercy on you black sinners. So I beg you to confess your sins and repent while there is still time. You cannot be spared the punishment for your awful crimes, but for your sins, God alone will have mercy on you. That you could be so ungrateful, so evil and blackhearted and lowdown; that you could commit crimes so enormous against your best friends on earth, against your masters, your dearest protectors, your Christian benefactors and your kind guardians, that you should take their lives is a terrible thing. But terrible as it is, I implore you not to go into eternal hell and brimstone to burn forever in the pit of the devil's hellfire without saying you are sorry. Say you are sorry. Don't commit your souls to eternal damnation without repentance. Just say one time you are sorry and beg God to have mercy on you. Do you have nothing but hearts of stone? Are you nothing but cunning serpents? Are you nothing but ugly black beasts proud of your abomination and your sin? God look into your evil black hearts and God will be sorry that you have got to die for being murderers beyond the pale of redemption. And may God have mercy on your lowdown souls."

But the worst of the day remained: the ordeal of the two women. As the time approached and the hangman moved to take his perch, the tension in the people grew so great it was unbearable. A youth perched in one of the tallest trees shouted, "Kill the black bitches! Hurry and kill 'em. That's what we come here for!" The crowd murmured as the ugly suspense mounted.

One of the women was stony faced and silent. When they unfastened her chains and led her up the steps to the gallows, her lips were set and her face was grim, but she said nothing. She did not even answer the words of the preacher nor the jailers nor the questions of the curious who heckled her. Without any black cap or covering over her face and head, the noose was fastened around her neck and tightened and she was throttled with her eyes popping and bulging and her tongue forced out and hanging in plain view of the crowd. This completely unnerved the other woman and she became hysterical. She screamed and jerked herself and sobbed and kicked against her jailers and struggled against the strong arms of the guards. "Ain't done nothing to be sorry for. Ain't sorry. Ain't sorry for nothing. Ain't done nothing to be sorry for. Ain't, I tells you. Ain't. Ain't done nothing."

There were some who declared that they actually heard the women's necks pop as they fell through the trap, but this might have been a gross exaggeration. Under the stress of the moment one could hear almost anything. Vyry was shaking and shuddering and her teeth were clattering in her head. She put her face in her hands and prayed. Bedlam broke loose. Black children screamed and cried; women fainted, but on the faces of some of the men and boys there was an unnatural look, neither human nor sane, a look of pleasurable excitement, a naked look of thrills born from cruel terror.

There were long shadows when the guards and drivers began herding the slaves into the wagons. It was late afternoon, but hours before darkness. It would hardly be dark when they reached home, but there were lanterns and torches lit. The planters and their families had gone in barouche and carriage. Some of the drivers and their guards rode horseback, but the slaves were seated in tightly locked wagons. The long drive home was a silent ride. Some of the women were still nauseated, and since there was no top over them, they tried to hold their heads over the wagon sides and relieve themselves. All of them were shaken and disturbed. Whatever the motive had been in the minds of their masters to put on this monstrous show, one thing had been surely accomplished. The Negroes were frightened and sickened out of their wits. Vyry was in one of the three crowded wagons going back to Marse John's plantation, but like every other slave, she was alone with her own terrifying thoughts.

Once they had driven into the yard and gotten out of the wagons, Grimes and his guards began checking them by names and cabin. Suddenly it flashed into Vyry's mind that she had not seen Lucy all day. When Grimes called Lucy, Caline spoke up quickly, "She sick. She in her cabin on her pallet, sick. Last night she say she ain't go today cause she sick."

"Who give her permission to stay home?"

"I don't know, sir; I disremembers her telling me that."

"Go there, Bob," speaking to one of the guards, "look in her cabin; make sure she's sick an laying on her pallet."

The guard went. Evidently he saw a head under some rags, and a body on a pallet, for he came back and reported to Grimes's satisfaction.

But the next morning they discovered that the head was a dummy. Lucy was gone. How long she had been gone, nobody knew. Whether she had had two nights and a day to get a good head start up the northern road was neither here nor there. Grimes took a posse of men and bloodhounds and went after her. But this time they did not bring her back. She had gone too far, and they could not find a trace.

Deep River,
My home is over Jordan.
Deep River, Lord,
I want to cross over into Campground.

12   She has the letter "R" branded
on her face

Vyry exulted in the freedom of Lucy, but she kept her exultation to herself. She did not even confide in Caline and May
Liza and they did not confide in her. Brother Zeke was absent,
but no slave mentioned this as a coincidence and the white
folks did not notice. Vyry did discover, however, that Caline
and May Liza knew much more than they had disclosed. Lucy
told no one of her plans, but now that she had gone they
remembered her strange actions in those last days. She had
practiced covering the scar on her face with a mixture of
yellow ochre, red clay, and charcoal, until it had blended into
her skin. They thought she was merely trying to cover the ugly
mark on her face.

Grimes was harassed and nonplussed. Everyone was disturbed over Lucy's disappearance. Marse John and Big Missy talked about the problem over breakfast:

"The whole trouble is that the confounded Yankees won't abide by the law. Even when we advertise our missing slaves they won't send them back and they won't give them to our law officers who go after them and go to all the trouble of finding them. Instead they aid and abet them in running away and then teach them their false doctrine about slavery being wrong and they have a right to be free because they are human beings. All the time they know they are our personal property, bought with our own money, a pretty penny I tell you, they cost too much now; just look what we have lost on just this girl alone."

But they decided, anyway, to advertise in the papers for Lucy's capture, all the Georgia papers from Augusta to Athens and Savannah, to Milledgeville, as well as the New Orleans *Picayune*. Grimes insisted that they should also advertise in the Carolinas and Virginia and as far north as Maryland, because he believed she had gone North, aided by the abolitionists and underground railway, headed toward freedom in Canada. Every means available was considered and even the slaves knew by heart how the ad in the paper was worded:

REWARD: $500 DOLLARS FOR THE CAPTURE AND RETURN OF A SLAVE GIRL, AGE ABOUT EIGHTEEN. TALL AND BLACK. SHE ANSWERS TO THE NAME OF LUCY AND BELONGS TO JOHN MORRIS DUTTON OF LEE COUNTY, GEORGIA. GENEROUS REWARD ALSO OFFERED FOR ANY INFORMATION LEADING TO GIRL'S WHEREABOUTS. SHE HAS THE LETTER "R" BRANDED ON HER FACE.

Jimmy crack corn and I don't care,
Jimmy crack corn and I don't care,
Jimmy crack corn and I don't care,
My marster's gone away!

13 Harvest time

The blistering summer heat hastened the harvest. Cotton and
corn and cane grew fast and ripened all during July. It was
the usual hot, dry summer with long days and parching skies
relieved by brief humid nights. This was a summer Vyry
would never forget. She lay often in the arms of Randall Ware
after that first time of shock. She could not remember, when
the summer was over, how many nights they had lain under
the stars and he had made love to her in the cornfields; nor
could she speak in knowing ways of the hot young blood of
passion that flowed between them, fumbling and simmering
like a fever in her flesh. She ceased to struggle against him,
for she was certain when he was near there would be no
frightening dreams in the night to shake her awake on her
pallet screaming after Mammy Sukey and crying after Aunt
Sally. She drowned the sorrow and the horror of Grandpa

Tom, and the branding of Lucy, and the ordeal of those women at the hanging in the sharp sweetness of his love plunging through her flesh. Everything in the distant past died. Time and the present went far away. All the painful knots inside melted. She lost their remembrance and a blank went over her mind while her thinking was softly padded with a velvet blackness that admitted nothing into her consciousness rocking back and forth. She could not explain to herself why she had finally lost all resolution and given in to the fiercely passionate but tender embraces of this black magnet, nor why she pushed back into a corner of her mind the idea of freedom and the marriage that was to come after, and let herself be carried along with feelings that matched the summertime. She did not tell him that in his arms she found such comfort, nor would she willingly admit her heart hungered after this love he offered her and she in turn could give; he was just as inarticulate.

Big Missy was supervising her annual canning and preserving and jelly making. She was breaking in a girl in Lucy's place to work for the first time in the Big House. Vyry soon discovered the girl was silly, but as usual she minded her own business and tended her cooking. Everytime Big Missy told the girl to do something, she would grin and giggle and say, "Yes'm, Missy, yes'm." Vyry told May Liza, "She forever showing Old Missy her teeths. I get sick and tired of her grinning and bowing and scraping in Big Missy's face. Ain't doing her nary speck of good, and I reckon she'll soon find that out."

Everyday when they had finished cooking fruit and vegetables and Big Missy sent the girl into the pantry and cupboards to put jars that were cooled and fastened on the shelves, she would prepare a big dose of medicine for the girl to take when she came back out after everything was put away. The stupid girl did not understand and Vyry would not explain. Big Missy would say, "Open your mouth like a good girl . . ." and, thrusting a spoon full of ipecac down the girl's throat, purred with satisfaction, "That's a girl! Good girl!" And the girl would grin and say, "Yes'm, Missy," and swallowed the nasty stuff. Soon she would begin heaving and her eyes would wall and roll all the whites around, then she would begin retching and run to the door to vomit. Big Missy would watch closely and then follow the girl to the door to see what she spat out. This went on for three days until the silly girl could hardly keep anything in her stomach at all. By the end of a week she was so weak and sick she would begin crying when Big Missy would start toward her with the ipecac. "Don't need no hipecac, Missy, please don't give me none! I ain't sick from nothing but that hipecac! Please, Missy, please, ma'am don't give me no more." But Old Missy was insistent and adamant. Finally in desperation the girl turned to the silent Vyry. "How come she give me that nasty tasting stuff what makes me so sick to my stomach I hast to puke?" Vyry looked at the girl and without cracking a smile, said, "She wants to see if you eating her 'zerves and jams and jellies, and that's her way for making sure you ain't tasted none." The wretched girl then burst into tears, "I ain't stealing nothing. My stomach too sick to stand one mouthful of vittles. What kind of she-devil can that old woman be?"

"I reckon if you keeps on grinning in her face you'll find out soon enough. Don't never grin in that white woman's face. She don't know what you mean. I was borned here, and I been here all my life, and you don't see me grinning bout nothing, now does you? Well they ain't nothing here to grin about, that's how come I ain't grinning."

August came and the slaves were busy picking cotton. The heat was so intense that the field hands in the middle of the day said they felt like they were breathing air from a red-hot oven. It was so stultifying, so stifling and suffocating, that both Big Missy and Marse John went to the coast in Savannah for a vacation. Grimes was in complete charge of the plantation. The slaves proceeded to harass him grievously. They had deep-seated grievances against him, and they knew a dozen ways to dawdle and try his patience without actually giving him anything he could put his hands on to punish them. If he beat them to make them work they would lie down and not work at all. He expected every able-bodied child and woman slave to pick a hundred pounds of cotton in a day, from sunup to sunset; the men were expected to pick two hundred pounds. He also had carpentry work to oversee. Almost all the slave houses were falling down; the crib always needed patching and bolstering or reinforcing. If he managed to line up the work the first of the week so that he had enough hands picking cotton in the fields, and hired men working on the houses, then the wagons would break down or the mules would balk. Every summer he had to contend with sick, broken down, worn out mules, and not enough hands. This was no exception. After he had put every hand in the field he was still short. He looked around in desperation, wiping perspiration, and fighting the heat, while trying to find more help. The house servants were not under his jurisdiction except for policing purposes of the patter-rollers. Their work was considerably less now, because the Big House was practically empty. He would have gladly put them to work in the fields, but he did not believe either Big Missy or Marse John would countenance working their help in the fields, and he never knew when they might unexpectedly return. Then he thought about two old slaves who were past working any more, Uncle Plato and Uncle Esau. They were both so old they walked with a stick and their heads were as hoary as the top of a hill on a frosty autumn morning. Marse John had plainly told them and told Mr. Grimes that they were not to go into the fields any more. They sat around the cabin doors smoking their corncob pipes, taking the young children in their arms and telling stories of their youth and early manhood. Suddenly on this August day, at the end of his wits for help, Grimes ordered them to get in the fields and help pick cotton. At first they thought he was joking. They slapped their thighs and laughed, and told him they wished they could fill a bag the way they once could fill a croker sack, but they had gotten too old. Grimes cursed, and when he swore they knew he was angry and not joking, and when he ordered them the second time, remembering Grandpa Tom, they hobbled up from their comfortable seats in the shade and tried to obey him by going into the cotton fields. When the slaves in the fields saw them, they thought they had come out of their own ambitious desire and they waved them back from a distance. Then in quavering voices the old men told them that Mr. Grimes had demanded their labor and they were trying to obey. Then three of the younger slaves went to Grimes at the corner of a field. They took off their torn straw hats and held them in their hands. Then they asked him to let them pick extra for the old men instead of keeping them in the fields. "And who will pick for *you*, you insolent, stupid sons of bitches?" Silently they turned their hats in their hands and went away. In less than an hour in the blazing sun the two old men had collapsed in the fields, overcome by the heat and unaccustomed exertion. Quickly their fellow sufferers took them bodily out of the scorching heat, carried them again into the shade, brought water for them to drink, and washed their faces. Grimes, angered, and yet helpless in his rage, ordered them to leave the old fellows and get back to work. Then he told the old men to go in one of the empty houses and get out of the way. The hired white carpenters and their Negro slave apprentices were busy repairing the houses in the Quarters, but some were not worth repairing and some had not been lived in recently. These abandoned houses were falling down and it was into one of these that Uncle Plato and Esau went for refuge. They must have fallen asleep because afterwards no one could explain what happened and nobody was willing to believe that Grimes was not telling the truth when he said their trouble was merely an accident. There was a big mix-up over whether he actually ordered his guards to burn that particular house or another. Anyway they threw a drum of coal oil on the rickety shack and saturated it, then they lighted it.

When the flames flared up the two old Negroes screamed for help and cried to God for mercy, but when they saw their fate was hopeless they began to pray. When the house servants saw the blaze in the distance they ran with buckets from the well and rain barrels and from the spring but the dried thatch and wooden shingles burned like paper and there was no hope for rescue. The white carpenters stopped their work. They got off the top of the old cabins and came and stood at a distance watching the crackling fire and listening to the commotion. The black slaves in the fields were demoralized and could not work, but they dared not let Grimes see them leaving. Instead they cried and worked and muttered prayers, hissing each curious black child back in the line of cotton rows and away from the fire. Inside the burning shack they could barely hear the voices of the old men praying.

Finally the great cloud of smoke cleared away. There was no wind, not even a breeze, and as the fire burned, the stench and heat were almost unbearable: flesh mingled with coal oil, and fire added to the August sun. But that night the rain fell for the first time in nearly two months. Even before dark the thunder rolled, and lightning flashed, and the clouds broke loose as if all the elements had opened. All night the storm raged and the rain poured. Next morning on the spot where the shanty had burned with Uncle Plato and Uncle Esau inside nothing appeared but a big puddle of black water with charred bits of bone and log. Even the ashes were mingled with water. On top of the black water were the greasy spots of oil. But there was no smell of human flesh, smoke, or fire, nothing but a black hole of water left on a charred bit of earth.

The first day of September was still hot and summery, but Marse John and Big Missy returned to the plantation. And then, as Vyry put it, all hell broke loose. Marse John was incensed over the "accidental" deaths of Uncle Plato and Uncle Esau. First, he deeply resented the fact that Grimes was always ignoring his orders. Second, he complained that too many slaves had died under Grimes and he was just destroying his property, to say nothing of creating such ill will among the slaves that they were getting sullen and he could not get enough work out of them. Big Missy argued that Uncle Plato and Uncle Esau were no longer assets to Marse John. "They wouldn't work, or maybe as you say, they couldn't work, yet they were still eating and wearing clothes and needing shelter and a doctor's care. Nobody would buy them because they were too old. Maybe it is just better this way."

But Marse John continued to argue. "What did he gain by killing them? I told him not to send them to the fields. I don't believe it was any accident. My father never believed in selling slaves when they got too old to work; they could always live in peace and die on the place. I've got a good mind to prose-cute him for killing my slaves and not carrying out my orders."

"Now I know you are joking. Where would you prosecute him and how? I thought you said he is the sheriff's deputy? He's the best overseer in the county, and you know it. He knows how to handle nigras, and a good driver is hard to find. You'd better leave him alone."

"One of these days he's going to make me so mad I'm going out and tell him to get off my place in twenty-four hours and nobody can do anything about it!"

Big Missy smirked and said nothing.

"I guess she knows," Caline said, "his say-so don't amount to nothing."

At last the cotton was all picked, ginned, and baled. Now Grimes had the Negroes harvesting corn and cane. He kept them busy and drove them with unbelievable fury. The harvest was heavy and Marse John would make a pretty penny. The summer heat had abated and the languorous twilights were gone. September ended with brisk mornings, and October brought early frost. The field hands were digging sweet potatoes and storing them in hills covered with dry pine-needle straw. As fast as the fields were emptied and the ground permitted, Grimes turned the men loose with the plows to turn up the corn stalks. While the harvesting continued they were already sowing the winter crops, and the work went along without a hitch. Marse John was pleased and he gave Grimes money to buy shoes for all the hands. When they got their shoes they would make syrup from the cane juice and sorghum and then they would have a taffy pulling. It would be lay-by time. They rushed with the work because now there would be a brief period of rest and this lightened their spirits. In the midst of the harvest there was a big party and Marse John generously handed out tobacco as a bonus for such a good crop. From the syrup, secretly they made corn likker and a mash which would be ready for drinking at Christmas time.

In the midst of all this hullabaloo, and just as the autumn days began to spend the last gold of the old year, Vyry discovered that she was "big." May Liza and Caline confirmed her suspicions when she complained that she did not feel like herself and she knew something was wrong. Never would she forget the way Caline muttered, "As many coon-bloods been laying out all over the cornfields all night long and all summer long, risking they death of cold in the dew from midnight till sunup, Lord knows how many gals is done been bigged. They just ain't no telling!"

There's a star in the East
on Christmas morn,
Rise up shepherds and foller,
It'll lead to the place
where the Savior's born,
Rise up shepherds and foller.

14   *"There's a star in the East on Christmas morn"*

Christmas time on the plantation was always the happiest time of the year. Harvest time was over. The molasses had been made. Marster's corn was in his crib and the slaves' new corn meal had been ground. Lye hominy and sauerkraut were packed away in big jars and stone or clay crocks. Elderberry, blackberry, poke weed and dandelion, black cherry and scuppernong, muscatine and wild plum, crab apple and persimmon, all had been picked and made into jars of jelly, jam, preserves, and kegs of wine. There were persimmon beer and home-made corn likker, and a fermented home brew for future use. Despite Big Missy's clever vigilance with her ipecac, some of those jars of jelly and preserves and peach brandy had inevitably gone out of the pantry window into the waiting fingers of black hands. What the slaves could not conveniently steal, they begged and made for themselves. Many of the delicacies that they loved were free for the taking in the woods. Who did not know how to mix the dark brown sugar or black cane molasses or sorghum with various fruits and berries to make the good wine and brew the beer and whiskey from the corn or rye that every clever finger learned early how to snatch and hide? When the frost turned the leaves and the wind blew them from the trees, it was time to go into the woods and gather nuts, hickory nuts and black walnuts, and chinkapinks. There were always more pecans on the place than could be eaten and the hogs rooted out the rotting ones. If Marster had not given them a goober patch, they had patches of goober peas around their cabins anyway. Sometimes there were whole fields of these wonderful peanuts. Like the industrious squirrels around them they scrupulously gathered the wild harvest and wrapped them in rags, laying-by their knick-knacks for the long winter nights. When the autumn haze ended and the chilling winter winds descended upon them it was time to hunt the possum and to catch a coon. No feast during the Christmas holidays would be good without a possum and a coon. Of course, Vyry said, "You got to know how to cook it, or it ain't no good. You got to boil that wild taste out with red-hot pepper and strong vinegar made out of sour apple peelings and plenty salt. You got to boil it one water and then take it out and boil it in another water, and you got to soak the blood out first over night and clean it real good so you gits all the blood out and you got to scrape all the hair left from the least bit of hide and then you got to roast it a long, slow time until you poured all that fat grease off and roast sweet potatoes soft and sugary, and if that stuff don't make you hit your mama till she holler and make you slobber all over yourself, they's something wrong with you and the almighty God didn't make you at the right time of the year. Marster, he like foxes, but what good is a fox when you can't eat him? Make sense to catch varmints stealing chickens, foxes and wolves, for that matter, and it's good to catch an old black bear, or a ferocity vicious bobcat, and nasty old varmint like a weasel when he come sneaking around, but when you hunting for meat and you wants fresh meat, kill the rabbit and the coon, kill the squirrel and the possum and I'll sho-nuff be satisfied."

If the slave did not kill his meat, he wasn't likely to eat fresh meat, although at hog-killing time they were given the tubs of chitterlings, the liver and the lights, and sometimes even the feet. After a very good harvest Marster might let them have a young shoat to barbecue, especially at Christmas time. Marse John was generous to a fault and always gave plenty of cheap rum and gallons of cheap whiskey to wash the special Christmas goodies down.

Big Missy had a taste for wild game too, but it was quail and pheasant, wild turkey and wild ducks, and occasionally the big fat bucks that came out of their own woods for wonderful roasts of venison. The Negroes were not allowed to kill these and if they made a mistake and accidentally killed birds or deer they had better not be caught eating it. Vyry had learned from Aunt Sally how to lard quail with salt fat pork and how to cook potted pheasant in cream, to roast and stuff turkey and geese and ducks, but she knew also the penalty for even tasting such morsels if Big Missy found out about it. Sometimes, however, half a turkey or goose was stolen from the springhouse, after some expert had carefully picked the lock. Most of the time, however, they did not worry about Big Missy's game as long as they could get enough of what they could put into their hands while foraging through the woods. By some uncanny and unknown reason real white flour came from somewhere for Christmas, and eggs were hoarded from a stray nest for egg bread instead of plain corn pone, but real butter cake and meat and fruit pies were seldom found in a slave cabin. Sometimes on Christmas they tasted snacks of real goodies such as these as part of their Christmas. On Christmas morning all the field hands stood outside the Big House shouting, "Christmas gift, Christmas gift, Marster." Then, and only then, did they taste fresh citrus fruit. Every slave child on the place received an orange, hard Christmas candy, and sometimes ginger cake. There were snuff and chewing tobacco for the women, whiskey and rum for the men. Sometimes there were new clothes, but generally the shoes were given out in November before Thanksgiving.

On Christmas morning there was always a warm and congenial relationship between the Big House and the slave Quarters. If it was cold, and very often it was not, the slaves huddled in rags and shawls around their heads and shoulders, and Marse John would open his front door and come out on the veranda. His guests and family and poor white kin, who were always welcomed in the house at Christmas time, came out with him and gathered round to hear his annual Christmas speech to the slaves. He thanked them for such a good crop and working so hard and faithfully, said it was good to have them all together, and good to enjoy Christmas together when they all had been so good. He talked about the meaning of Christmas—"When I was a boy on this place at Christmas time, seems only yesterday . . ." He got sentimental about his father and mother, and he told a "darkey" joke or two, and then he wished them a merry Christmas, ordered whiskey and rum for everyone, handed out their gifts of candy and oranges and snuff and tobacco, and asked them to sing a song, please, for him and his family and all their guests. Then they sang their own moving Christmas carols, "Wasn't that a mighty day when Jesus Christ was born" and "Go tell it on the Mountain that Jesus Christ is born" and the especially haunting melody that everybody loved:

> There's a star in the East on Christmas morn,
> Rise up shepherds and foller,
> It'll lead to the place where the Savior's born,
> Rise up shepherds and foller.

Then Marse John and all his white family and their friends would wipe their weeping eyes and blow their running noses and go inside to the good Christmas breakfast of fried chicken and waffles and steaming black coffee with fresh clotted cream. And the slaves, happy with the rest that came with the season, went back to their cabins, certain that for one day of the year at least they would have enough to eat. They could hardly wait for night and the banjo parties to begin. On Marse John's plantation, Christmas was always an occasion and all during the holidays there were dancing parties and dinners with lots of wonderful food and plenty of the finest liquor. Marse John and Big Missy became celebrated for their fine turkeys and English fruit cakes and puddings, duffs full of sherry and brandy, excellent sillabub and eggnog, all prepared by their well-trained servants, who cooked and served their Marster's fare with a flourish.

But for Vyry, Christmas meant as much hard work as any other time of the year. Of course, she had her chance to get whatever she wanted to eat simply by slipping and hiding grub in her apron and skirt pockets as she had watched Aunt Sally do. But this Christmas she had no appetite for Marster's delicious food, none for the gaiety of the parties in the Big House nor for the banjo singing and dancing in the Quarters, nor for anything the Christmas season meant. Randall Ware could no longer console her. She was already his and she had no freedom either. Now they would have a child in the spring and this child would not be free either. This child would belong to Marster. Desperately she pressed Randall Ware to do something about her freedom. He tried to satisfy her by having Brother Ezekiel "marriage" them in the way the slaves called it, "Jump the broom," but this was not all Vyry wanted. She wanted to be free, and more than that now, she wanted freedom for her unborn child. A number of her fellow slaves were jumping the broom that Christmas. For them it was simple, so she reasoned. They were already slaves on Marster's plantation or on his "other plantation" or from the plantations nearby, and their children were naturally doomed to be slaves. But Vyry sensed, more than Randall Ware seemed to care, that this child of a free father should be free. Randall Ware brought her gifts of food and game, but she was indifferent. He declared that he would buy her at the first opportunity, but that he must buy her through some white man and Marse John would not think of selling her to him. Laws governing slave marriage to free Negroes were very strict in Lee County. Randall Ware contended that he must bide his time. One wrong move now could mean disaster for both of them.

Finally in desperation, Vyry decided to go to Marse John and ask his permission for her to marry Randall Ware. She planned to go when Big Missy was not around to influence his decision. She would go in the midst of this Christmas season while his heart was softened and his generosity at its height, when he would be mellow with brandy and whiskey, and everything seemed to be going right on his plantation, and therefore with his world. She picked a night when the slaves were having a big party and all around one could hear the fiddlers and the banjo picker singing, "Oh, Sally come up, Oh, Sally come down, Oh, Sally come down the middle," while all the others joined in the singing and you could hear one voice louder than the others calling the rounds of the dancing.

"Evening to yall, Marster," Vyry spoke from the doorway, fumbling with her apron in her hands.

Marse John, startled, turned from his desk where he was wrestling with bills for merchandise and accounts with his drivers. He nearly let his book fall when he saw Vyry. This white-looking, thin-lipped girl always managed to make him feel ill at ease. But he spoke in such a condescending tone and his usual patronizing fashion, that she would never have known how much she disconcerted him.

"Why, good evening, Vyry. Why aren't you over at the party dancing and having a good time?"

"Don't feel like it, Marster. I ain't in no shape for dancing."

"Why, what's the trouble?" Her eyes were on the floor before her, and she did not look at him when he spoke. "Are you sick, or is something the matter?"

"Yessuh. They is something the matter. I don't know as you'd call it trouble, but in a way, I's sick and in a way I ain't, and it's sho-nuff trouble for me."

Marse John turned all the way around in his chair now to face Vyry. He looked her over warily, and then he said in an offhand fashion, "Well, if you don't tell me the trouble, I can't help you. What do you want me to do about it?"

She lifted her eyes then, and looked him squarely in the eye. "Marster, I wants your permission for me to get marriaged."

"Oh, is that all," and he seemed relieved, "I thought it was something serious. You mean you're going to have a baby?"

"Yessuh, that's what I means. I'm big all right, and I wants to get marriaged."

"Well, now that's no trouble, lots of gals are getting married around here everyday, how do you say, jumping the broom?" And he laughed, but she did not crack a smile and she remained silent. Between them there arose a silent question, but Vyry waited for him to speak first.

"By the way, who do you want to marry? Is it one of my boys around here or a boy from a plantation somewhere around here?"

"It ain't needer one."

"Well, if it's none of my nigra boys and none around here, who could it be? You don't mean some of these overseers or guards have been getting fresh with you, do you?"

"No sir." She looked up again and through narrowed eyelids with her face still solemn she said, "It ain't none of your boys around here, and it ain't no white man neither. This here man's black, *but he free*." If she had shot him, he could not have been more deeply shocked. His face turned pale as death and he looked as if he had surely seen a ghost. For a full moment that seemed very long he could not trust himself to speak. Vyry looked at him and waited.

"You mean you're asking me to give you permission to marry a free-issue nigger?"

"Yessuh, I is. He ain't a slave cause he borned free."

"Do you know what that means?"

"I reckon so, Marster, I reckon I does."

"Why don't you ask me for your freedom and be done with it?" Now he spat out the words with such fury that Vyry jumped as if he had hit her.

"Marster, is you mad cause I asked you to let me marriage with my child's own daddy?"

Now, red with anger, he stood up and came close to her, leaving only a step or two between them, and his voice moderated to a low but urgent tone while his hands were raised as if in self-defense:

"You should have thought of this before you got a free-issue nigger to get a child by. Getting a child by you don't make him own you nor own the child. I own you, and I own your unborn child. When you ask me to let you marry a free-issue nigra you ask me by the law of the state of Georgia to set you, a mulatto woman, free, and that's a mighty lot to ask. There's a big difference between asking to get married and asking to be set free. Why, I never heard of such in all my life!"

She drew back from him in fear as if he had hit her, or might decide to do so. Suddenly she burst into tears and looking up at him again with the tears on her face she spoke cuttingly, "Marster, does you think it's a sin for me to want to be free?"

Her words were knifing him like a two-edged sword. He opened his mouth and his lower jaw sagged. A dull red moved again over his face and mottled the blood through his skin. Again the silence between them crackled with tension they could feel. But he was master of his situation, and he knew it. He did not intend to let that mastery get away from him. But now he tried another tactic. He deliberately moved back to his desk, and half sitting upon it, he crossed one leg and folded his arms. Then he looked steadily at her.

"So. That is what you wanted in the first place. And what do you think it would be like for you to be free? And where do you think you would go? Who would take care of you, feed you, and clothe you, and shelter you, and protect you? What do you think it would be like to be free?"

She knew he expected her to say she didn't know. She started to speak the sober thought in her mind—that her husband would do these things for her—but she knew he would consider her impudent so she thought better of it and held her peace. When she did not answer him, he went on, "Do you think you would be better off free than you are working for me? Look all around you at the poor white people who are free. You don't want to be like *them,* now do you? What is it you call them, 'po buckra'? They are free, free and white; but what have they got? Not a pot to piss in. Every blessed thing they get they're knocking on my door for it. Can't feed their pot-bellied younguns; always dying of dysentery and pellagra; eating clay cause they're always hungry; and never got a crop fit for anything; no cotton to sell, and can't get started in the spring unless I help them. Do you think you would be better off if you were like them? And being black and free! Why, my God, that's just like being a hunted animal running all the time! All over the South now they're talking about making free-issue niggers take masters and become slaves. They're not that much better off now anyway. Suppose that happened to your free-issue nigger and you fell into the hands of a cruel master? Does anybody bother you here? Aren't you free to come and go as you please?"

Again she did not answer. He was watching her as he talked, and seeing the growing bitterness in her face, her tight lips, her jaws working grimly as she occasionally bit her lips and twisted her hands, he tried still another tactic.

"I've often thought about setting you free."

She looked up now at this, and he thought he caught the faintest gleam of hope in her surprised eyes.

"But here in Georgia it's very hard to manumit a slave, you know what I mean—set you free. I don't have the right to break the law. I would have to have you taken out of this state and carried to a state like Kentucky or Maryland where the law permits a man to set his slave free if he wants to. Here in Georgia manumission is only permitted as a great reward for saving a white person's life and sometimes, in great exceptions when a slave has been very faithful, on the death of his master he may be set free. When I die you will surely be free. It's already in my will."

Now the scorn in her face was quite apparent to him. He knew she did not believe him, and he was withered before her scorn. He had no additional weapon with which to fight such scorn and he was forced to drop his eyes and hang his head. But when she still said nothing, he quickly brought this painful conference to an end.

"Now that is all, I'll have to ask you to leave. I was working on my accounts and I'm very busy tonight. You'll have to excuse me."

Dismissed, she turned with drooping shoulders and went out without saying another word. But now her hope was shriveled and dead within her. Her beautiful dream of freedom again seemed forever lost.

Sitting alone in her cabin door with her own bitter thoughts, she heard music. In her mind there was the bitter music of an acid little jingle she had heard the slaves often sing among themselves:

> My old marster clared to me
> That when he died, he'd set me free
> He lived so long and got so bald
> He give out the notion of dying at all.

Over and over the bitter jingle kept recurring to her, but the music she heard floating out on the balmy December air was another Christmas carol also in keeping with the season and her thoughts:

> Oh, Mary, what you going to name your newborn baby?
> What you going to name that pretty little boy?

Oh, Freedom, Oh, Freedom
Oh, Freedom over me,
And before I'll be a slave
I'll be buried in my grave
And go home to my Lawd and be free.

15   Freedom is a secret word I dare not say

As the time drew near for the birth of her child, Vyry wondered to Caline and Mary Liza who would be the "granny,"
for there was no longer anyone on the plantation who followed "Granny" Ticey, but Caline told her that she and
May Liza would help her, and she was not to worry. Vyry
dared not ask Big Missy for a doctor. She knew Big Missy
was mad about the child anyway. She must have told Marse
John that he ought to send her away, because he came out
to the kitchen one morning to see Vyry and to reassure her
that everything would be all right.

"Don't worry if Missy Salina is cross. She means no harm,
that's just her way of worrying."

Vyry answered him almost defiantly, "She got no call to
worry about me. I reckon I'll be all right."

"Sure you will. I told you that, didn't I?"

But he didn't linger long. Vyry wondered how her heart within her could continue in the same old way. For now she lived with no will and no dream. She felt that her life was taking on the pattern of doom. She worked and stayed on her feet as usual. She cried and swallowed her salt tears, and then dried her face and straightened her back.

And Caline and May Liza were as good as their word. They were there when the time came. Caline was there to hold her knees and help her to bear down with the birth pains.

"Tain't no use in your hollering. You just sucking up the baby and sucking in air. Make you just that much longer."

So Vyry bit her lips and never made another whimper.

She looked at her boy-child and loved him as any mother would.

She prayed, as she had promised Aunt Sally, for a Moses to come so her son would not always be a slave. No one could say the boy was the "spitten image" of either Randall Ware or Vyry, for he was neither black like his father nor milky-white like his mother. He was brown, at first a creamy brown that promised to be the color of shelled walnuts and pecans. His hair was also different. Vyry's sandy hair was silky straight except when it was wet; then, damp with perspiration, or soaked in rain water, it hung in tendrils that threatened to curl. Randall Ware's hair was black like his face, only it seemed blacker, and it grew tightly against his head, responding to a comb with difficulty, just like the beard on his face that was thick and tangly. Their child's hair was crinkly and darkest brown, soft and curly and growing sparsely on his head. It would never grow as tightly as his father's and never be so silky as his mother's, but it went with his soft brown skin and black shoebutton eyes. He was a small wiry baby, all legs and arms. Vyry could not help smiling at him even through her frequent tears. He was her son, but what could he know of this world into which he had come? His father was proud, proud as a peacock spreading his brilliant plumage over the whole barnyard. But how could he be so proud? How could he feel pride when he could only slip in to see them, when their very hours together were clandestine and dangerous? How could he boast of a son who was not free?

"Some day," said Randall Ware, "he will be free."

But Vyry no longer shared his hope that he could buy their freedom. All her life she had been a slave and perhaps all her life she would remain a slave. Unless, unless there was a miracle and a Moses truly came.

They named the child Jim. His father called him James Ware. On the plantation he was Vyry's Jim. When he was a toddler he would hang around her feet in the kitchen of the Big House. Big Missy did not bother him and Marse John strictly avoided him. Vyry kept him with her everywhere she turned. His father made a cradle for him and she placed it where she could watch him during the day. At night he slept at arm's reach. But she could see he would never be like his mother. His bright eyes wandered and his quick fingers nervously explored and his ears were alert to all day and night sounds. He would never be quiet and serious and wear a poker face. He was his father's son, and his mother wondered if she would ever understand him.

That summer, after her son was born, Vyry was seventeen years old. She was now a woman and both her childhood and adolescent years were swept completely behind her. She lived from day to day with no hope. Even the days had lost their color. Life was the same as always, drab and hopeless, with always a slender undercurent of a nameless fear. Whatever happened could not be good. Only evil could happen, and more evil, and it was this evil that peopled all her fear. Nevertheless she began to unburden herself as Aunt Sally had by lifting her voice in song. She was surprised to hear the dark rich voice of Aunt Sally come out of her throat. She was surprised to discover how much she enjoyed singing and what a relief she felt when she sang. The days always went faster singing.

Before she was twenty she had two more children and one of them was dead, dead before it was born and there was no grief within her nor tears to shed. That was one who would never be a slave. She accepted death and the fate of her unborn child as she had come to accept her life. She was dull to all feeling and nothing seemed new. The same years were passing without hope. The same seasons were arriving on the heels of each other. From Randall Ware she asked nothing any more, and she expected nothing. He was like everything else around her and everybody else she accepted. He was part of the scenery. There was no joy in her life. There never had been, and she wondered if there ever would be.

Her third baby was a girl; a doll baby with the same bright, beady eyes as her brother, the same high brown skin, the same soft curly hair. But she was too quiet like her mother. She seldom cried. Her eyes never wandered and her fingers did not stray. She was as small as a minnow and they named her Minna.

Strangely enough, Randall Ware never warmed as much to the girl as he had to the boy. He touched her timidly, he kissed her, but his beard tickled and made her tighten up her tiny face to cry. He scarcely saw his family in daylight. He came between the patter-roller's runs. Always he seemed like a stranger to Minna, but his arms were always ready for Jim, who was just learning to know his father when life suddenly changed for all of them.

Vyry did not understand politics and she did not know how to read. But Randall Ware could read and write and somewhere underground he had his finger on the pulse of the nation. News traveled slowly in the backwoods and news meant nothing to a slave. Marse John read the papers that came from Athens and Augusta and Savannah and even papers from Richmond and Montgomery and from the North and Big Missy began expressing herself openly about her hostile views toward northeners. Much had happened during the past seven or eight years that meant nothing to Vyry. She knew that important men often visited Marse John. They came from Milledgeville, from the legislature, and they talked about politics. This meant nothing to Vyry until suddenly Caline and May Liza noticed that the white folks were no longer talking about Georgia and what the people of Georgia wanted. They were talking about the West and the North and the South. Vyry remembered Aunt Sally's saying that the white folks had been stirred up over the Indians in Georgia the same way, and when Vyry was a child she had heard them talk about Texas and the Mexicans, but none of it stayed with her. It went in one ear and out the other. Now they talked about slavery a lot, always defending their rights, and they talked about the hated abolitionists about whom Vyry remembered hearing first from Aunt Sally. When she timidly asked Randall Ware what "abolitionists" meant, he began to talk again about freedom for the slaves and all the colored people. This was a boring subject to Vyry, so she asked no more about it. "Why work myself up all over again about freedom? Freedom is a secret word I dare not say."

But Randall Ware was really getting stirred up again. He was excited, tremendously excited, and he could not help but spread the contagion of his excitement. The neighboring planters now came more frequently to see Marse John, who in turn frequently went on long and extended trips. Sometimes they took him much farther than Milledgeville, and sometimes he even went out of the state.

Big Missy and Mr. Grimes still kept a tight watch on the slaves but there seemed less terror and less cruel treatment. Of course Grimes drove the field hands as hard as ever, but now they seemed to smell danger that was no longer a personal danger. Something seemed to threaten master and slave alike, something as sinister as the plot which the masters had feared but which never exploded; something that reared its head like a copperhead snake and that might suddenly strike without warning.

This was the thing that excited Randall Ware. Meanwhile his own position became more dangerous and more insecure. There were loud, open threats against the free black man, and the threat to his freedom which Marse John had intimated the Christmas before Jim was born now returned to haunt Vyry's fearful heart. There was no question about it, her life was bound up with this black man's life as tightly as Marse John claimed her life for his own. Whatever affected both surely affected her. Randall Ware was not unaware of the open threats to free black men. At first he laughed at them. Now he was taking those threats seriously and told Vyry that Georgia was considering a law to regulate free men. He told her that any time now he might be forced to leave.

"Before I'll take a master and become a slave, I'll die trying to stay free."

Vyry said nothing, but she thought many things about freedom that she did not say. What she thought was tied with what she felt and what moved through her heart was without words.

One morning May Liza and Caline overheard Big Missy say to Marse John, "It's dangerous having that free-issue nigger hanging around here. I'm sure he's coming to see her regular. I told you the first time he came on the place there would be trouble."

"But there is no trouble. He just comes to see Vyry. I've had him watched, and I'm keeping a tight watch on him now, night and day. He just comes here to see his wife and children. All nigra boys do that."

"His wife and children? Humph! If they were really his wife and children you couldn't keep them here."

"Why not? I own them."

"Yes, I reckon you do, but it's dangerous just the same. She's a half-white bastard and you know it, and he's free."

"Well, what about that?"

"According to law, they're free anyway."

"She's not free unless I consent to the marriage and I never gave it."

"Then why do you say, 'wife and children'?"

"Oh, you know how you speak of all the nigras that way. It doesn't mean anything legal, you know. The law only applies to white people. They're my property. I own her and her children, too."

"Something has got to be done about them, I warn you. It's getting dangerous. It's getting entirely too dangerous."

Randall Ware undertook to explain to Vyry the major events in the country, but she did not listen well. He seemed to get discouraged because it was all so foreign to her, like another world. And she was listless and unconcerned. Only when he told her that people were getting upset all over the country about poor colored people in the South did she open her ears.

"Why? What they care about poor colored peoples? Why they get upset over us?"

"I've told you for a long time that we've got friends up North. People who want to see us free: free colored people and abolitionists and other white people who believe all human beings have a right to be free. The white man down here is getting fat and rich on colored people, and now he wants to spread slavery all over the country."

"You mean white folks getting rich on *cotton*. Us slaves just make they cotton. I reckon I always figgers wrong. I figger white folks has slaves everywheres."

"That's where you're wrong. I guess you know cotton don't grow everywhere. It grows down here bettern' it do up North. This here is real cotton country where cotton is king, and cotton is making these white folks sho-nuff rich."

"Well then, how come they so upset?"

"The richer they get, the more slaves they buy, the more money they get for cotton, the more they worries."

"I sure don't see how come."

"Everybody else don't think like they think. Some folks say that slavery's wrong."

"What can they do about it?"

"Nothing much, I reckon, except talk."

"Well, talk don't mean nothing. Talk don't get you nowhere. Don't pay no attention to what the guinea hen say, cause the guinea hen cackle before she lay."

My way's cloudy
Lawdy, my way's cloudy . . .

16   *Get a man to buy my time out*

Shortly after breakfast one morning a stranger appeared at
the plantation. He came to transact urgent business with
Marse John. During this uneasy time of the late fifties, there
was a growing tension between the Negroes and the master's
family, even in the Big House. Caline declared she could tell
from his smell that he was there to trade slaves, to buy and
sell. Just such a man came, she said, when Aunt Sally was
sold. What was Marse John fixing to do?

Vyry felt her heart stand still when she saw the man. The
slaves were not able to learn anything by eavesdropping.
Marse John and Big Missy did their talking behind closed
doors, and they even whispered to this white stranger. He
stayed in the Big House for several days.

The house servants quailed before his gaze. May Liza
said, "He makes me feel like I'm walking around naked."

He paid no attention whatsoever to the slaves outside the
Big House; he scarcely seemed to see the field hands or even
notice the cabins in which they lived. Vyry caught him star-

ing one day at her little Jim, who was now more than three years old. Suddenly her heart began to thump.

Then, as mysteriously and suddenly as he had come, the stranger disappeared. He walked away with his black traveling satchel swinging by his side, and no black man was the wiser for his visit. They did not know why he came.

Randall Ware was also busier than usual. He was prospering to such an extent that he had begun to think of expanding and buying more land. Sometimes he disappeared from his smithy and there were many nights when he did not come to visit Vyry. Sometimes he explained his absences to Vyry and sometimes he did not. While he was away on one of his frequent trips, absenting himself from his smithy and from Vyry, she faced a real crisis.

The stranger reappeared. This time there was no secret. He had come to arrange a private auction for Marse John. Caline and May Liza were so frightened they came to Vyry with their eyes nearly popping out of their heads. Big Missy Salina had set her heart on selling Vyry, but Marster would not give his consent. They were sure, however, that eventually she would have her way. She had gone ahead with her plans for an auction on the place this Saturday and already this was the middle of the week. "What are you going to do?" they asked Vyry.

Oddly enough, Vyry did not feel disturbed. Knowing what was going to happen calmed her. Gravely, she thanked Caline and May Liza for having brought her this news, but she could not say what she would do because she did not know. That day in the kitchen her work flagged and time hung on her hands like leaden weights. Once during the evening meal she decided to go into the Big House and take a good look at the stranger. She stood behind the dining room portieres and measured the strength of her adversary. Dressed in a black suit with a white shirt and black string tie he looked on the surface like any other ordinary white man on business. He was mousy looking and fawn colored. His watery, light eyes were hard and his face was expressionless; he ate and drank with relish. Vyry noticed that Big Missy seemed especially anxious to please him and she was offering him her best claret. Marse John was silent, morose, and even sullen. He would stare into space with his fork half-way up to his mouth, push his plate away from him, and drop his head as if he were alone and seriously thinking about something.

As soon as the evening meal was over and Vyry was free to leave the kitchen, she took her children and set out across the plantation to find Brother Ezekiel. She prayed he would be at home. It was early fall and the dew dampened the night air. Jim walked beside her and Minna lay asleep in her arms. Over her head and around her shoulders she had thrown an old black shawl. It was light and warm, one she had made herself, guaranteed to protect her from dampness. Her mind was in a ferment. Brother Ezekiel was the only slave she knew on the place who could read and write. Since he was the preacher nothing was thought about it. Maybe the white folks did not know. She was sure he could help her and she believed she could trust him. Although she was not afraid, she felt tense and uneasy. Everytime she heard a bird cry or one of the dogs bark, she would stand rigid. The moon was half full and moonlight scattered itself obligingly across her path. The shadows were peopled in her mind's eye with strangers who watched her. She thought of Aunt Sally and her daily admonition to pray and trust God. She thought idly of Randall Ware and wondered where he was.

Brother Ezekiel was sitting in the door of his cabin, whittling a stick and singing a song:

> I want to die easy, when I die
> I want to die easy, when I die
> Shout salvation as I fly
> I want to die easy, when I die
> I want to die easy, when I die

He glanced up when he saw Vyry.

"Howdy, child, how you making out, and why you come so far with them younguns just to see an old man?"

"I'm just tolable, Brother Zeke, and I comes to see you cause I'm in deep troubles."

"Set here a spell and rest yourself. Then you tells me your troubles."

"I'm scared Marse John gwine sell me away from here."
Brother Ezekiel looked shocked.

"Naw, child. He can't. I don't even believe he wants to."

"He might not want to, but she wants to."

"Oh."

"She's been hating me ever since the day I was borned."

"I figgers since you has the younguns things is better for you."

"Things is worser. They daddy is a free man."

"Does the white folks know that?"

"I told them."

"But is they bothering him? That's gwine on now four-five years. Do he still come to see you?"

"Yassah, he come in the night and leave before day in the morning."

"He hasta slip?"

"Yassah."

"Do he know they might sell you? He got money. Maybe he buy you."

"That's what he say when we marriage: 'Marriage with me and I buys your freedom,' but Marse John say he don't wanta sell."

"But now, you say he willing to sell?"

"He ain't willing yet, but she making him willing."

"But he say he ain't selling when your free man try to buy?"

"That's what he say then."

"Well, if he bound to sell, he might as well sell where your free man can buy."

"Not if Ole Miss can help it."

"She ain't gotta know."

"How us gwine do that?"

"A white man can buy you with a nigger man's money."

"Where the white man us can trust?"

"Leave that to your free man."

"He ain't come lately, so I come to get you to write a letter."

"Why sho, child, what you want me to say?"

"Just tell him I says to get a man to buy my time out, Saddy."

"That's fine, that's true and fine. I do it now, right-a-way."

"And sign my name."

"Naw. No name be better."

"Well, I reckon so."

"You got to pick somebody to fetch your letter. Right now I can't go."

"That's all right. I can figger that out."

"You needs a pass. Maybe I better write that pass."

"Yassah. If he have a pass, ain't nobody can kick."

On her way home. Vyry decided to send the dumb-wit boy. His movements were scarcely restricted since he made no effort to go anywhere, and he was devoted to her. Next morning, Vyry asked him, "Does you know my free man, Randall Ware?"

"Yes'm. Ain't he got a shop and grist mill?"

"Does you know his house?"

"I knows his shop, yes'm."

"If he ain't there, stay until he come. Don't give his letter to nobody excepten himself."

"Yes'm."

"Here your pass."

"I never needs no pass."

"Take it for fear you does."

The pass that Brother Ezekiel had written read, *This nigger is my slave. He has my consent to go to town. John Morris Dutton.* Willie put one piece of paper in one ragged pocket and the other piece in the other in order not to mix them, since he could not read what he carried.

"Letter in this here pocket, and pass in this-a-one."

"Mind, you try to get back before dark."

"Yes'm."

Willie saw only one white man who stopped him, and he was a stranger. Willie took out the piece of paper from one pocket and let him read. The stranger smiled, folded the paper, and gave it back to Willie.

It was late afternoon when he saw Randall Ware. He gave him the paper from his other pocket. Then something was wrong. Randall Ware asked him, "Do you have another paper?"

"Yassah. I has a pass."

"Let me see it."

The boy hesitated but he gave him the other note.

Randall Ware read the paper and looked at it for a long moment. He read, "Get a man to buy my time out, Saddy, V." Then he looked at the boy again and said, "This is my letter. Did anybody else see this?" The boy shook his head from side to side and said, "Nossah, nossah."

"Are you sure? It's very important for me to know."

"Well, sir, since you ask me, one white mister stopped me, but I give him the pass."

"Which is the pass?"

"You has it, sir, you can read it, can't you?"

"Yes, I can read. Go home, tell Vyry I got her message. Here's the pass. Show it to anybody who stops you."

And the dumb-wit boy, Willie, went back to the plantation.

On Saturday nothing happened. A lot of horses and buggies brought visitors to the plantation for the auction. Vyry had had no further word from Randall Ware, and she did not know if he had gotten a white man to buy her or what he would do. One thing she knew, he could not come himself. That morning she gathered her children in her arms and prayed because praying was all she knew to do. After that she felt a little better, but in the kitchen she worked with her heart in her mouth, expecting to be summoned at any moment. Marse John said nothing to her about putting her up for sale at auction, yet she kept hoping and expecting that he would. He did not.

After breakfast, when the dishes had been cleared away and washed, and Vyry was on the verge of preparing dinner, Big Missy came in the kitchen and told her to take her children and go down to one of the barns where all the other house servants were going. Vyry took her children and went to the barn. May Liza, Caline, Sam, Uncle Joe, Jim, the houseboy, the new kitchen girl, Katie, and a few of the stable boys were there, and the dumb-wit boy, Willie. Sure enough, here again was the stranger. He was talking privately to the various callers who had come on horseback or in buggies that morning. Vyry searched the white faces, wondering if she could read in any face a sign of the man for whom she was looking, but she could not detect such a face.

As each female slave was put on the block she was either stripped to the waist or wholly naked while the auctioneer recited her worth. Nobody seemed interested until Vyry was offered for sale. Her children cried when she was put up alone. The bidding picked up until it was clear that an old white man lounging in a corner with a mop of white hair and standing quite apart from the others continued to bid higher for her than anyone else.

Then the bidding abruptly stopped. Vyry was told to dress again. Nobody was sold but the dumb boy, Willie. He was sold for less than a hundred dollars, which was a pittance as slave prices went. Vyry saw that he would be taken away again and she was filled with distress. For a moment she forgot her own situation in pity for him. But, as usual, he displayed no emotion. He did not seem surprised at anything. At noon, the auction over, he gathered his few rags and, whistling a broken tune, went along amiably enough, wandering again on an unknown witless way.

In that great gitting-up morning
Fare you well, fare you well
In that great gitting-up morning
Fare you well, fare you well
There's a better day a-coming
Fare you well, fare you well
There's a better day a-coming
Fare you well, fare you well.

17   Put on men's clothes and a man's old cap

Early in the next week Randall Ware came to visit Vyry. He came as usual, at night, after the regular run of the patter-roller. Vyry was listening for the second call of the whippoorwill when suddenly she heard the crackling sound of a shot distinctly ring out in the autumn night. When Randall Ware reached her cabin he was bleeding profusely, although the bullet had only grazed his arm.

"It's only a scratch," he said, but she was shaking with fear.

He was also somewhat shaken and truly alarmed despite his attempted bravado. While she washed and dressed the flesh wound, they talked.

"This means I got to go."

"Go where?"

"Go away from here; get out of Georgia, maybe get clean outen the South."

Vyry began to cry.

"Don't cry. I can take you with me, if you've got the will to go."

"What you mean?"

"I mean run away."

"How I'm gwine run away with two children?"

"Leave them here."

"Leave my younguns? Is you done lost your senses?"

"Naw. If you'll just trust me and do like I say, you'll get your babies back again, but you can't run far with them pulling on you."

"If I leave my children, I'll never see them no more in this life. Sho's you born to die, I'll never see them no more."

"Do you want to be free?"

"You know I wants my freedom, but I ain't leaving my younguns."

"I keep telling you they'll be safe. Leave them like I say, and you'll get your freedom and your babies."

"Naw. Big Missy'll sell them. She'll sell 'em sho's you born. I knows that woman. She hates me worser than poison."

"She won't do no such thing. They too young to bring a price. I got plans to see they are taken care of. We'll have them again as soon as we get out the South and out of danger."

"What kinda plans you got now?"

"If I can just get you to Maryland, there's a woman there to take you straight into Canady. I know the road all the way to Maryland. I know every underground stop."

"Underground? Underground where?"

"Underground railroad. Don't you know the secret road slaves use to escape up North? Lucy went that way, and if you do like I say, as milk white-skinned as you are anyhow, you won't have a speck of trouble."

"What kinda plans you got for my younguns?"

"I'm begging you to trust me; believe me when I say they'll be safe. And we won't lose them. You will surely see them again."

"I knows I is, cause I ain't leaving them."

"All right, you be stubborn and stay here. They'll be worse off here with you than they'll be if you do like I say. And anyways they just ain't no ifs and buts about it, I gotta go. If they catch me again out here they liable to kill me. This

here bullet tonight ain't nothing but a warning. I thought
you wanted your freedom. I wants you and the younguns with
me but if you ain't coming . . ."

"What you want me to do?"

"Wait till Friday night. Don't tell nobody nothing; but
start getting ready tomorrow. Put on men's clothes, a pair
of britches and a coat, and a man's old cap. Be sure you
dress good and warm, and dress the younguns too. Dress
them good and warm and give the baby a sugar tit. Then
lie down till midnight. Wait till you see the moon riding
straight up overhead and then leave. Be sure you leave the
younguns. They'll be sleeping and they won't know when
you leave. Then make it to the swamp. But don't walk the
log across the creek. You know where the lowest part of
the water is?"

She nodded her head for yes.

"Wade through the low water. That'll kill the scent of
your tracks, cause bloodhounds lose the scent in the water,
and they won't come across."

"Bloodhounds?" Her eyes widened.

"Well, when they miss you, they liable to sic the dogs on
you. You know that as well as I do. That's why I say leave
by midnight and come by yourself. There'll be somebody
waiting for you on the other side of the creek."

"Don't you reckon they can pick up my scent across the
crick quick as they do here?"

"If you do like I say, you'll be a long ways off when they
start to look for you."

"I don't like it. I don't like it, at all. Supposen something
go wrong?"

"Something's already done gone wrong."

"What you mean?"

"That boy you sent that note by mixed it with the pass.
That's how come they wouldn't sell. They knowed I had a
man set to buy you."

"Was the man there?"

"Of course he was. I got old man Bob Qualls, but I reckon
they getting on to him, his buying slaves and setting them
free, and they suspecting he's a abolitionist, too."

"You think that's how come they wouldn't sell?"

"I told him not to let nobody outbid him, don't care how
high they go, and I know he done what I said, but before
they would sell to him, they quit."

"Stead of me, they sold the boy."

"That's what I'm talking about. That's what I know. They watching me. They been watching me, and now they may be watching you. I gotta go. You can see tonight how come I gotta go, but I don't wanta leave you here."

"I wants to go with you. I wants to go bad."

"Do like I say and I won't have to slip here no more."

"What I'm gwine do with Jim and Minna?"

"Leave them to me. Do like I say. I'll meet you Friday night, and mind, don't you fail to come alone!"

Friday was a rainy day. It rained all day until nearly ten o'clock that night and the ground was soaked and muddy. Vyry was tense and desperate. She was so jumpy and nervous and so fearful she could scarcely control herself. She seemed to sense, however, that this night might be the last break she could make for freedom. Everything else had failed. If once her little family became separated they might never be together again. She knew how slave families were constantly sold one by one to different masters in faraway places. If Randall Ware were caught or killed here Marse John could claim his property, all his land as well as the family he owned. He could even say her free man was a slave and belonged to him. When the rain poured down all day she began to give up hope of going, but at last it ended and the moon came out again quite clear and bright in the sky.

Her baby, Minna, was teething. She was feverish and fretful; cried easily, and was wakeful. Vyry nursed her and gave her water, but she slept fitfully until late in the night. Vyry would look at Minna and her heart would turn over in loving anguish at the thought of leaving a helpless nursing baby. After the rain ceased and the moon came out, she felt it was getting late, so she put on her clothes to go. She had so much under the breeches they felt tight. They were very unfamiliar anyway since she had borrowed them without asking anyone's permission. Suddenly the baby slept. She stood and looked at her children a long time, and then she stood in the door of her cabin and watched the moon climb high in the sky. Just as she turned to kiss the children once more goodbye, Jim woke up. He wanted to get up and she helped him, but when he saw her strange clothes he whimpered drowsily and asked her where she was going. She answered him, "Nowhere," so he went back to sleep.

The moon went in and out of the clouds in the sky, weaving back and forth through darkness into light. She still hesitated.

Each time the baby cried out in her fretful sleep, Vyry winced as if someone had touched her. She turned again to the door and seeing the moon moving across the top of the sky, sailing through the middle, she steeled her inner resolve, and then taking the knapsack she had prepared with food and water, she started from the cabin. This time Minna cried loudly and Jim opened his eyes wide. Vyry trembled in desperation. She grabbed the baby and told Jim to get up, too. He was so sleepy he could not move fast, but since he was already dressed in all his clothes she only paused long enough to wrap the baby again. Then, with the baby in her arms and Jim pulling on her stuffed pantsleg, she started out to make it to the swamp.

Whenever it had rained as much as it had rained that day, the packed clay around the quarters was thick and gooey. Every step Vyry and Jim took, they could feel the mud sucking their feet down and fighting them as they withdrew their feet from its elastic hold. Jim was so sleepy and so little and so scared of the night that he whimpered and whined and cried with each step. The baby still slept fitfully while Vyry pressed her way doggedly to the swamps. She knew Randall Ware would be angry. "But I couldn't leave my children; I just couldn't. I knows if I leave my baby she will die."

They were leaving a tell-tale trail of footsteps behind them with no accompanying rain to wash away the tracks. She heard hoot owls, night noises of small creatures—birds and insects, a distant dog's baying at the moon, but no whippoor-will. They had gone no more than a mile and she had nearly three-quarters of a mile to go farther, when day began to break and roosters began to crow for morning. Desperately, Vyry tried to hurry. The baby sucked on the sugar tit and slept quietly, but poor Jim was still stumbling along, crying and whimpering and whining to himself. At last they were in sight of the swamps. Feeling sorry for little Jim she decided to rest a few minutes before trying to wade the creek. She would have to take both her children in her arms and then balance them on her hips with the small knapsack slung across her back in order to wade the creek. She sat down on an old log, meaning to rest only a few minutes.

The morning was foggy and over the creek the fog hung like a thick gray cloud, but despite its density she began to discern figures moving. A bad spasm clutched her stomach instinctively. She tensed her body with the sure intuition that she was not only being watched but that the watchful figures would soon surround her. Impassively she saw the patter-roller and guards, together with Grimes, emerge from the shadows and walk toward her. Fervently she prayed that Randall Ware was no longer waiting for her across the creek, but had gone on his way. As for herself, she was too tired and bleak to care. Exhausted and hopeless she sat and waited for the men who surrounded her to capture her and her children. She could not have run one step if her very life had depended on it. Despite everything, she felt glad the children were still with her and they were safe. She looked into little Minna's sleeping face and smiled, and she patted Jim's hand softly to reassure him of her nearness. Then she pulled him closer to her in a warm embrace.

> I look up at the stars,
> and I look at my scars,
> and I look at my children
> and I wonder . . .

18   Seventy-five lashes on her naked back

That morning going back to the plantation everything around her seemed unreal. The fog lifted slowly and through the misty morning she moved steadily toward what she knew would be her punishment. The children were not alarmed, and for that she was glad. Little Jim trotted homeward without a whimper while the baby sleeping in her arms was soundless. Grimes and his men did not speak to her but she knew that they were ruthless and there would be no compassion. It was a well-known fact that if a slave ran away and was caught in the act, flogging was the punishment. She could expect a whipping. She did not let herself think ahead beyond each step. Once she thought about Marse John. Perhaps he would interfere and not let them beat her. But she knew this was not possible because he was never at home whenever anything happened. He had been gone three days and might be gone two or three more; supposedly, he had gone to town on business. Maybe they can put it off until he comes home. No, she also knew better than that. Big Missy would want to get this over with before Marster's return. It was always easier for Miss Salina to explain things later and justify them most after they had occurred. Vyry was not at all surprised, therefore, when Grimes took her children from her on entering Marster's backyard. He led her to the whipping post not far from the wet fields where the field hands were not working this morning because the ground was too wet.

Two of Grimes's men tied her hands together as if she were folding them to pray, and then stretched them high above her head. They tied her to the post so that her feet were tied together and crossed above the ground. It seemed as if she were hanging on the post in mid-air, her feet stretched as far as they could stretch without touching the earth beneath her and her hands stretched as far above her head without reaching beyond the post. Her body was naked to the waist, and she braced herself to bear the lash of the whip upon her naked flesh.

Grimes did not choose to beat her. One of the guards who was generally hired to whip slaves was now ready to flog Vyry.

He took the whip in his hands. It was a raw-hide coach-whip used to spur the horses. He twirled it up high over his head, and when he came down with it he wrapped it all the way around her body and cut neatly into her breast and across her back all at the same time with one motion while the whip was a-singing in the air. It cut the air and her flesh and cried "zing" and Vyry saw stars that were red and black and silver, and there were a thousand of those stars in the midnight sky and her head felt as if it would split open and the whip cut her like a red-hot poke iron or a knife that was razor sharp and cut both ways. The whip burned like fire and cut the blood out of her and stung like red-hot pins sticking in her flesh while her head was reeling and whirling. It hurt so badly she felt as if her flesh were a single molten flame, and before she could catch her breath and brace herself again, he had wrapped the whip around her the second time. When she heard the whip go "zing" the second time and felt the stars rocking in her head, she opened her mouth to scream, but her throat was too dry to holler and she gritted her teeth and smashed her head hard against the post in order to steel herself once more to bear the pain. When he wrapped her all around with the whip the third time she thought she heard a roaring noise like thunder rumbling and a forest of trees falling in a flood. Everything went black; she was caught up in the blackness of a storm. She was whirling around in a cutting, fiery wind while the fire was burning her flesh like a tormenting fever and she kept sinking down in the fire and fighting the blackness until every light went out like a candle and she fainted.

She never did know how many lashes he gave her, whether he cut her the required seventy-five times as he was told to do, or whether he quit short of that number, thinking she was already dead and further beating was useless.

When she came to she heard a buzzing in her ears and everything still looked black though it wasn't yet evening. It must have been afternoon but there was no sunlight. Somebody had cut her loose from the post and left her huddled in a heap on the ground at the bottom of the whipping post. At first she thought it was night because all she could see looked black. She looked at her hands and her arms and she pulled at the shreds of rags on her legs and all her flesh looked black. She was as black as a man's hat and she was black like that all over. She looked around her on the ground and saw blood splattered and clotted around her while something glistened white like salt. Although her mind was still dazed she knew now why her back was still on fire and she felt as if she were lying on a bed of red-hot needles and iron. It was the salt somebody had thrown on her bleeding raw back. She was too weak to move. She wondered why she was still living, because they must have meant to kill her. "Why has God let me live?" *All the black people must be scared to come and get me till it is black dark. Maybe they think I'm dead. Lawd, have mercy, Jesus! Send somebody to get me soon, please Jesus!* The flies were making the buzzing sound and she felt her body throbbing in a rhythm with the flies. Fever parched her lips and eyes and her bruised hands and ran through her brutalized flesh.

After dark the other house servants came and got her and took her to her cabin. Caline and May Liza poured warm oil on her back and washed it free of salt. Then they put her on a soft pallet of rags and let her sleep. When the fever had parched its course through Vyry and the raw bruises began to form healing scars, the cloud in her mind began to lift. She could remember deep waves and complete inundation in the dark waters that threatened to take her under. She could not remember her own children and when they were brought to her she did not know them. Once she thought she saw Marse John standing over her and thought she heard him cursing terrible oaths, but even his face was vague in her memory. Caline and May Liza brought her hot broth to drink and coaxed her to swallow but she did not know them either or remember what they had done. After three days the fever seemed to be leaving her and her mind began to clear. She was too weak to speak above a whisper, and when she was able to examine herself she saw where one of the lashes had left a loose flap of flesh over her breast like a tuck in a dress. It healed that way.

II *"Mine eyes have seen the Glory"*

THE CIVIL WAR YEARS

Mine eyes have seen the glory of the
coming of the Lord.

19 *"John Brown's body lies a-mouldering in the grave"*

John Morris Dutton was fifty-seven years old and he had been in the House of Representatives of the Georgia Legislature for fifteen years. During those years he watched several developments in Georgia which coincided with his personal life and interests. First, he watched the elevation of three of Georgia's greatest statesmen: Alexander Stephens, Robert Toombs, and Howell Cobb. Although he could not claim these men as his closest friends and cronies, he had more than a speaking acquaintance with them, and his deep admiration of their policies, personalities, and philosophies was well known. Second, he was in total agreement with their belief that Georgia and the pro-slavery South should gird on its armor and enter the throes of a political battle in order to preserve their sacred states' rights. Georgia's property rights and fundamental religious beliefs as free men and citizens in a free country were being threatened by the unconstitutional actions of that Anti-Slavery party now coming into power in the North. It behooved every loyal southerner to battle this party to its just and certain death. Third, there were many changes at home on his plantation. At least a half-dozen of his slaves had died or disappeared during those stormy years of the fifties when he was very busy in Milledgeville. Sometimes he blamed his wife, Missy Salina, and their zealous overseer, Ed Grimes, for this deplorable state of affairs. Often he blamed himself. With these exceptions, however, he was fairly content with his personal life. His son, Johnny, was doing well at West Point. His daughter, Lillian, was married and had two children, Robert and Susan. She and her husband, Kevin, made their home in Milledgeville at Oglethorpe University and he saw them frequently. Once he had seriously thought of running for the Senate. The Senate was a natural stepping-stone to Washington. Howell Cobb had gone from the Senate to Washington, and Dutton had thought in time he would do the same. Now all that was changed.

He was riding home from Montgomery, Alabama. He was ending a long journey on the Central of Georgia Railroad and he was weary in body and mind. Sam would meet him at the station and then there would be a long jostling ride through the swamp woods on the old wagon road. They would be lucky to get home before dark and in time for supper. Vyry would have a good meal ready and Salina would be eager to know the news. He felt half-hearted in spirit, not burning with the same enthusiasm with which he had left home. Perhaps it was a natural reaction to feel let down after so much excitement. This was his third long journey out of the state in the past six months. No wonder his body felt weary to the bone. Last year during the summer he had attended two conventions, both Democratic. The first one was held in the North, where the South felt insulted and infuriated with the compromising tactics used to discourage slavery in the territories. The second was held in Baltimore, where loyal southerners took a bold stand against those radical anti-slavery northerners and nominated Breckinridge as their states' rights candidate. Splitting the Democratic party was, of course, disastrous, and for the first time since its origin a brief eight years before, the Anti-Slavery party of Radical Republicans won the national elections.

In four short years people learned much about their successful candidate. Ever since Fremont was defeated in 1856 and the controversy over slavery and states' rights had verged on secession this man, who was a tool of the Republicans, kept breathing thunder against the slave states. They really heard more about him during his debate with Stephen Douglas, who finally made a poor candidate for the northern Democrats. In 1857 the South won a moral victory with the Dred Scott case, but then came 1858 and that threatening speech of Seward's about the rising of an "irrepressible conflict" and the dire imminence of a social revolution. It was still 1858 when Abraham Lincoln, the candidate, declared that the country could not remain half slave and half free but would have to be one or the other. As John Dutton told his wife, Salina, at the time, "The northern abolitionists and free-soilers have finally got themselves a man. They say he is from the poor people—a backwoodsman of low origin from Kentucky. He has been first one thing and then another. I believe I heard once he made his living splitting rails, and just lately has been a lawyer of sorts who got himself elected to the Illinois Legislature. He is obviously nothing but a willing tool for those northern radicals."

Then came elections and the Republicans won with Abraham Lincoln. South Carolina saw the handwriting on the wall and immediately seceded from the Union, but in Georgia they waited, chiefly on the advice of Howell Cobb, who was still in Washington. But on January 19 when the legislature met, Georgia seceded. Now during the month of February in Montgomery, Alabama, seven southern states formed the Confederate States of America: South Carolina, Alabama, Mississippi, Georgia, Louisiana, Florida, and Texas. Jefferson Davis and Alexander Stephens, both good men, were elected to lead the new southern nation. *We couldn't have chosen better men. Salina will be pleased.* Both Alex Stephens and Howell Cobb like Robert Toombs had honored them with a visit to the plantation. The South would be in good hands. This was the trip he had just made, and the historic events he had witnessed.

Now he looked out at the sky appprehensively. From the time he left Alabama it had been raining steadily. The rain was turning to sleet and the temperature was rapidly falling. He looked forward to his home-coming with a warm supper, a hot bath before bed, and a stiff toddy. He felt a cold coming on and the weather was surely getting worse. The train was stopping at Dawson. He looked out and was relieved when he saw Sam, right on time.

"Hello Sam! Good to see you."

"Evening sir, glad to see you too. Kinda nasty out and Missy been wondering would you be late."

"No, looks like we're right on time."

"I'll take your bag, sir."

"Never mind. I can manage. Just anxious to be getting on. Sky looks bad. See if we can't make it home before dark."

"Yessir. I sure hope so, sir."

Darkness was coming on fast, and the cold rain was slowly freezing. They started out with the horses moving in a quick trot until Sam paced them faster and then they were racing at a clip.

Marse John, warm in his carriage robes, was dozing when he suddenly felt a sharp jolt as though they had struck a large rock in the road and the horses had stumbled. He looked out and saw the horses rearing. He heard them neighing nervously and just at that moment he was thrown forward as the carriage rose in the air and fell over on its side. In a whirling split second he saw Sam thrown from his high coachman's seat. The harness snapped and the frightened horses ran off leaving their master and his coachman on the old wagon road with the cold February night rapidly closing on them.

For a long moment Marse John felt stunned, then he tried to get out of the carriage, but his right leg was doubled back under him and when he tried to move, the sharp pain sickened him and sweat popped from his forehead. He saw he was pinned inside while the carriage lay on its side. He could see Sam lying still on the icy road, but when he called to him, Sam did not answer.

When the harnessed horses trotted into the stable of Marse John's plantation a general alarm was sounded throughout the Big House. Big Missy quickly ordered Jim, the houseboy, and Grimes to fetch old Doc, while a wagon and another carriage with fresh horses were quickly harnessed for the rescue. Darkness had now fallen and the winter night was frigid. In the Big House the fireplaces were blazing with cheerful fires. Supper was waiting and Vyry tried to keep the food hot without burning it in the midst of all this excitement and impending gloom. Big Missy wanted to join the searching party but the servants in the Big House persuaded her against such foolhardiness.

The hours seemed much longer than the time actually elapsed before the party returned. Sam's cold body lay stiff in the wagon with his neck broken, but Marse John was still conscious and they lifted him into the house after warming him first against the chill of the night with a stiff shot of brandy.

Supper was very late for they kept it waiting while Doc examined Marster's leg and found it broken in two places. Big Missy agreed with the doctor that her husband would be better off downstairs, so they put him to bed in the room where he often worked over his accounting books and legislative papers. The room had a huge fireplace, books, a desk, and family portraits. It was comfortable, warm, and familiar, and here it was hoped he could make a speedy recovery as pleasantly as possible.

Vyry carried supper to the Marster, once he was as comfortable as they could make him, and she was startled at the sight of him in repose with the legs in splints and his huge hulk of flesh dominating the room in this strange fashion. He lay on a large black-leather couch with an improvised feather bed under him and pillows piled up to elevate his leonine head. He looked paler than usual, his graying blond hair faded or washed out, but his blue eyes were sharp as ever and his mouth had a twisted smile. When she had placed the tray of food on a table within his arm's reach, she looked up to find his eyes on her face. Her eyes dropped and she stepped backward toward the open door. He looked up at the pictures over the mantel and flanking the sides of the fireplace before he spoke to her, "See that man up there, Vyry? He was my grandfather, and on both sides of him are my parents, my mother and father."

The portrait over the mantel showed a man in colonial dress with a powdered wig. His face was stern and his mouth was a thin straight line, but his eyes looked kind and they seemed to be staring down upon the occupants of the room. The faces on either side were younger and were in full-length portraits. The man looked a dandy with his high hat in his hand. The lady was dressed in a full-length ruffled hoop skirt with an open parasol held over her shoulder. Her bodice had a priscilla collar crisscrossed in a fichu. Vyry studied them curiously, wondering why he was telling her this, while he went on talking:

"Every time I look at them I think they are telling me to uphold the honor of this house. I have inherited their responsibility just as my son will inherit the honor of this house when I am dead."

Vyry thought of Miss Lillian, who was more devoted to her father than Johnny, who worshipped his mother, but she said nothing.

"He must be a little tipsy from all that brandy," she thought, and sure enough, looking at him, she saw his eyes swimming and his head nodding. She heard Big Missy coming down the hall and she hastened back to her kitchen.

We shall meet but we shall miss him,
There will be one vacant chair
We shall linger to caress him,
When we breathe our evening prayer.

20   *This pot is boiling over and the fat is in the fire*

On March 4, 1861, Abraham Lincoln was inaugurated the sixteenth President of the United States. On that same day in Montgomery, and for the first time, the Confederate flag of seven stars and three bars on a field of gray was unfurled and hung on the Capitol of the Confederacy. Marse John had been confined to his library for two weeks, and he was chafing with enforced confinement. He could see that his swollen leg was slightly inflamed. He listened quietly enough to Big Missy, who was reading the newspapers to him, and he was delighted to hear in a letter from Lillian that she was bringing the children for a nice long visit, but he confided to old Doc that he was about to go out of his mind with inaction.

"I can't remember ever being sick in bed a day in my life."

"Well, you can sit up in a chair, and rest yourself from the bed to the chair, but you're going to be in this room a long while."

"How long, Doc, two more weeks?"

"At least. Maybe more or less, I can't tell right now."

"When will you know?"

"Well, barring accidents, if this inflammation only continues and doesn't spread, if the fever doesn't get too high, or you contract pneumonia, and the bone continues to knit properly and fast, you could be on crutches in six weeks."

"Six weeks! You must be out of your mind. I'll die first!"

"Let's hope not, but that's a limited possibility."

Then he changed the subject.

"You notice these black frosts we're having here in March? Had one this morning. Wouldn't be surprised if they didn't hold up spring planting quite awhile, don't you think?"

Marse John did not answer. He was muttering and fuming while old Doc was closing his bag and preparing to leave. The doctor glanced at him and then spoke again. "Just wouldn't be surprised when your hands can get on with spring plowing, not with all these black frosts." And he shut his bag and went out.

By the middle of March, however, Marse John was suffering from a great deal more pain in his leg. Miss Lillian was home with her two young children and she was trying to tempt her father's appetite with special dishes and tidbits such as custards and calf's-foot jelly and other delicacies. Instead of eating he was drinking more heavily, and as his temper grew worse and his cursing grew more vociferous, his horrified family left him more and more to the strict care of the servants. The doctor still refused to admit any worry over the growing amount of inflammation and swelling and the possibility that the leg might be gangrenous. He suggested rather tentatively and timidly the possibility of amputation. Marse John's reaction to this was such a wrathful explosion that old Doc retreated without further discussion:

"Amputate? You mean cut off my leg? Are you out of your mind? Why, I would die of the very pain. What will you use, a hatchet or an axe? I saw a poor fellow lose his leg like that once. The howling wretch was full of whiskey too, but it didn't dull his senses one whit and he died in a matter of hours."

One day without warning, a delegation of seven men from the Georgia Assembly descended in a body upon their colleague. Big Missy thought this was sure to cheer him and make him more like his flippant self, but his cohorts were either too jolly or too morose and their visit put such a strain on his weakened sensibilities that late in the afternoon when they departed, after much liquid refreshment, he subsided into a gloomy silence and drank himself into a stupor.

He had too much time to think. First, he reflected on the state of affairs of his beloved Georgia and the whole Southland. Big Missy read the news to him and he chafed with the way things were going. He hated the name of Lincoln. As for his slaves, when he thought of how Sam had died that night, how Aunt Sally and Vyry had cooked so many years in his kitchen, he concluded that if the northern radicals only knew and understood his nigra slaves the way he did, they would not carry on such foolishness about *containing* slavery and not letting it spread to the territories.

"They must take us for big fools if they thought we would stay in their Union and let them control congress and dictate to us against our interests. If it has come to war, then let it come. But they are nothing but cowards and they won't dare fight us. They know we would whip them so fast it would be pathetic. The Bible is a witness to the benefits of slavery. The Church defends our system and the Constitution protects it. I don't see where they have a leg to stand on, but I wish I were out of this bed."

In the ensuing days he was less coherent. His leg was steadily growing worse and his temperature rose higher at night. In the morning he always seemed better. Old Miss would find him wet with perspiration and sleeping after a restless night of tossing with fever.

Jim, the houseboy, and Caline, now growing more aged but still active and haughty, were given the difficult task of nursing Marse John. Vyry carried his meals to him and May Liza cleaned his room. At first Missy Salina read the daily mail and newspapers to him, but after those first four weeks she realized he wasn't listening. Alexander Stephens delivered an important speech in her beloved Savannah on March 21, 1861, and his words were inspiring to her, especially when he said, "The new Southern Nation is founded upon the great truth that the Negro is not equal to the white man; subordination to the superior race is his natural and moral condition." But when she tried to read the speech in the newspapers to her husband he was too sick to pay any attention.

Marster loved his good old jamaica,
His good old jamaica, his good old jamaica,
Marster loved his good old jamaica
Down in Georgia Land.

21   *The Vernal Equinox of 1861*

Spring came late to Georgia in 1861. Cold rain, black, killing frosts, and temperatures as low as freezing delayed the usual spring plowing and spring planting. With Marse John ill in bed and the 1860 crop still bulging in the barns, nobody seemed to worry too much about the weather. The field hands were glad to have rest, and so was Grimes. He offered to help Missy Salina as soon as he saw how it was with Marse John. She gravely thanked him for his offer, but said, "There's nothing you can do that you haven't already done." Grimes had little faith in old Doc, but then he was the only doctor they had used around the plantation for all these years, and surely now he would do his best for the master.

It was Missy Salina who first noticed the turn for the worse in Marse John. He continued to call for whiskey and he was steadily drinking more and more. When his eyes began to glaze she thought it was from too much liquor; but his mind, too, seemed to wander. And then she noticed the peculiar

odor that subtly began to cling to the room. She ordered May
Liza and Jim to use more carbolic acid in the scrubbing and
cleaning water which afforded a high degree of disinfectant.
At first she thought the odor was due to the fever and liquor
but gradually she realized it was coming from his badly
swollen and inflamed leg, which now clearly showed signs of
gangrene. For the first time, fearful about this turn of events,
Missy Salina took old Doc aside.

"I think he's getting worse, Doctor. Is he going to die?"

The doctor looked at her for a long moment, as though he
were trying to assess the amount of hysteria she could gen-
erate. She looked strong and tough enough, but then you can
never tell about a woman, so he looked off and let his eyes
wander in the distance.

"Ma'am, that's something a doctor never knows. You know
life and death are in the hands of our God."

"Yes, I know that. I shouldn't have said die, but I mean
is he going to get well?"

The doctor did not smile nor did he have a quick answer
ready for her, but he was determined to dismiss her fears at
this stage in her husband's illness.

"It's a possibility, but not a certain fact. He has a strong
constitution and he has already withstood the worst, I think.
He has had a lot of laudable pus which I think is good, if only
the gangrene doesn't take a firm hold. I suggested amputation,
but you remember he wouldn't hear of it."

"Maybe we should go ahead with amputation anyway."

"Not without his consent. And every day we wait may lessen
his chances to survive amputation."

Missy Salina carried such a solemn and sanctimonious
expression into Marse John's sickroom, he quickly read her
face. She approached the difficult subject as tactfully as she
knew how.

"Why won't you let Doc amputate that leg? Can't you see
it won't be much use to you like that?"

"Damn you, no! When did you ever hear of anybody my
age recovering from amputation? Or is it, that I'm not dying
fast enough for you? Don't count on my death, Salina! I
may live yet to stand over your open grave."

"You ought to be ashamed of yourself talking like that!
You ought to pray and stop cursing everybody out when all
we are trying to do is help you. Do you want me to read to
you from the Bible?"

"Hell, no. Why should you start something now you never

have done before? And get out of here, standing over me like a vulture. I'm tired of your sham piety and all your pretenses about your concern for me. Your solicitude would be touching if it weren't so false. Get on out, get out I say!" And when she hesitated, he picked up a book and hurled it after her. Startled at his action, and considerably shaken over his condition, she ran from the room. Tearfully she reported this scene to Miss Lillian, who was awfully upset and kept saying, "Poor papa, poor papa!" And that very day they sent a telegram to young Marster Johnny in West Point.

According to the field hands and the old slaves in the Quarters, Marse John was dying "hard." They declared they could hear him yelling and cursing in the night, and indeed, Jim, the houseboy, admitted he found it hard to hold him down on his bed when the fever was raging at night, the liquor no longer having any effect, and the pain in the gangrenous and rotting leg driving the master out of his mind.

In the morning when Caline and May Liza entered the place to straighten and clean the room the odor made them hold their breath. Old Missy and young Missy scarcely went farther than the door, sometimes to speak if he were affable and conscious, but mostly to see what further changes had taken place in him. They prayed that the liquor and the opiates the doctor administered would sink him into a dying stupor but he raged through these until too exhausted to do more than lie and mumble in his troubled sleep which was also broken with pain.

At the full moon Brother Zeke told Vyry that he doubted the master could live another two weeks. "When the new moon come, he be gone." The weather was changing and as the folks in the Quarters muttered, "March come in like a lion, she going out like a lamb." In the night Vyry heard the honking of geese flying north, and in the swamp woods she saw the spring flowers blooming. Under the pines on Baptist Hill there were dogtooth violets, sheep sorrel, and may hops, and in the barns the cows were calving. The winter weather had broken and the long stormy weeks were ending.

Vyry could tell by the untouched tray that Marster was getting weaker. Except for liquids he took little nourishment, had no appetite, and lost interest in what was going on around him. He made a great effort to rouse himself when his small grandchildren came to his door to speak to him, or Lillian brought him a vase of spring flowers. Now his days were divided into three periods. Early in the morning he slept hard, sometimes not rousing or opening his eyes until noonday. Afternoon was his best time. The fever was at low ebb, he drank water and whiskey, often let himself be shaved and washed, and carried on a little conversation with Jim, but now he was growing more listless in the afternoons and noticing those about him in the room less and less. As the darkness drew on and the fever began to rise to interminable heights he began to rave and scream. Then began the unbearable hours. In those first days of April almost nobody in the Big House closed their eyes at night except the small children. The doctor now gave sedatives to Missy Salina and Miss Lillian so that they, too, slept late in the mornings.

One afternoon, a few days before the new moon, Vyry was surprised to have the Marster recognize her when she carried his tray. There was little on it except clear hot broth and coffee and soda crackers, but he showed no inclination to eat. She could see that he had wasted away to nothing since that first night when they had brought him into this room. His eyes were sunken in his head and they glittered strangely. His hands were unsteady and they pushed the cover alternately back and forth, sometimes plucking at the coverlets or pulling them closer. She was surprised when he spoke to her.

"So you're still here, hanh? And you not afraid to come in here, hanh?"

Startled at his hoarse voice, her eyes widened, but she did not speak, only nodded and shook her head in agreement.

"Think I forgot what I told you? I promised to set you free when I die, didn't I? Got it in my will, right here!" And he patted the books and papers beside his bed. "But I ain't dead yet!" And he rose up from the couch as though he would strike her, so that she hurriedly backed out of the room, but as she fled down the hall to the kitchen she could still hear him saying, "You ain't free till I die, and I ain't dead yet!"

That night he died. Early in the evening they heard him screaming and hollering in pain as usual, but shortly around midnight his howling stopped. Jim, the houseboy, was with him at the end, but he decided to say nothing to Big Missy until morning, that is, unless she came down to inquire, and she did not come down until morning. It was May Liza, Caline, and Jim who washed the dead body and dressed him for burial, while Missy Salina began to put into operation the elaborate plans she had made weeks in advance for her husband's funeral.

Southrons, hear your country call you
U^r! t worse than death befall you!
To arms! To arms! To arms! in Dixie!
ALBERT PIKE—1861

22   *Don't make them come and get you! Volunteer!*

When young Marster Johnny first heard of his father's accident he did not have the slightest idea that it would prove
fatal. When he received his mother's first telegram, he was still
loath to go home, but when her final message came that his
father was dead he knew he had to go home at once. He had
never especially admired his father but he respected his position. There was only one matter about his father's death that
disturbed his thoughts, whether his mother would expect him
to come home and run the plantation. This he did not want
to do. Things were happening in the East and when he graduated in June he would be a commissioned officer in the army.
He wanted nothing to interfere with that appointment.

Kevin MacDougall came to his wife and children before
young Marster Johnny arrived from school. He found the two
mistresses in deep sorrow and planning the costumes of

mourning. Even the children must wear black armbands for their grandfather. Kevin had never felt that Marse John especially liked him, but he had been able to maintain good relationships with all his wife's people. In a way, he was secretly relieved when he heard that his father-in-law had passed. He missed his wife and children and needed them at home. He steeled himself, however, for the ordeal of the long obsequies, and tried to think of comforting words to say to his wife, Lillian, whom he truly adored.

The final rites for John Dutton occupied a week. His coffin was sealed and remained shut in the legislature, the church, his house, and at the graveside. Big Missy regretted this necessity, but she realized it was physically impossible to do otherwise. There were two sermons and three speeches eulogizing the dead legislator. The music was supplied by a black-robed choir singing hymns, a group of slaves singing spirituals, a white soloist who sang the perennial favorite, "Flee as a bird to your mountain" and a black fiddler who played plaintive notes at the grave.

Big Missy ran the gamut of her emotions at her husband's death. She told all the servants and neighbors who came to call, the friends and distinguished legislators, "My husband has suffered so greatly, I rejoice that he is out of his pain and misery even though death has taken my companion of twenty-five years." She maintained her stoic poise and the dignity demanded of her in the public eye, and wept only before her children and grandchildren. She was annoyed with Lillian, who sobbed audibly during all the services. She was proud of Johnny, who wore his dress uniform as a West Pointer, and she was even pleased with Kevin because of his tender devotion to his wife and small children. At the graveside she faltered only once. There swept back over her mind all the memories of her youth and early marriage, her wedding journey to this backwoods place, her children's births and the childhood, the acute embarrassment she felt over her husband's attachment to a nigger woman, the bastards he had brought in his house to rear as servants, the distinguished career he had carved out for himself in the state house of Georgia, and now this lingering death that had reduced his big handsome body to a bony frame. She bit back her sobs and stifled her tears, for they were not for him but entirely for herself. She was not so stupid as not to realize that she was burying a large part of her life now that her married life had ended, and she would leave this grave with the new status of a widow-woman. But when Johnny wondered about running the place, she laughed. "Your father never gave this plantation a passing thought. Mister Grimes, the overseer, and I have always run this plantation. I guess we can continue."

Johnny was proud of his capable mother and along with admiration he felt a surge of relief that the tiresome job of being a farmer was not required of him.

John Morris Dutton was buried in the same family plot where his parents lay buried and where many of his slaves were also interred. Over the master's grave, however, was a significant monument. It was chiseled of marble and rose high enough to be discerned from the road. There was space in that grave lot for six more bodies.

The April sun was shining when the preacher said his last words over Marse John and as the mourners turned away from the grave, relatives, friends, and slaves, they could hear the mockingbirds making merry in the trees. Even as they turned away, the Winston boys startled young Marster Johnny and Kevin MacDougall with the news that the guns of Charleston, South Carolina, had fired on the Federal flag at Fort Sumter, and Abraham Lincoln, President of the United States of America, had declared the seceded states of the Confederacy to be in a state of rebellion which must be put down if the Union were to be preserved. He had called for seventy-five thousand volunteers and a state of war now existed between the Federal Union and the Confederacy. Johnny's face—especially his eyes—lighted up when he heard the news, but Kevin, more cautious and unwilling to believe such news, asked, "Are you sure?"

"Of course I'm sure. My father received a telegram from Montgomery this morning, and I would have told you then, but I promised not to say anything to you all about it until after the funeral. Now what are you going to do?"

Johnny hastened to speak. "My mind is already made up. I would enlist immediately because I intend to fight for our Cause, but I've got to go back to school and get my commission first. Kevin, what will you do?"

"I honestly don't know. You know how I hate the thought of war but I won't be called a traitor to our Cause nor a coward. I'll probably fight, but I've got to get myself together and think about it first."

When the subject came up at the dinner table, Big Missy Salina was shocked with the news and she remembered her husband's words. "John said they wouldn't fight, that they are cowards."

Johnny said, "It's not written they'll fight long. They don't have the fighting spirit, and that shows they are cowards."

But Miss Lillian was terribly distressed. "First papa, and then this! Oh, Kevin, you don't have to go, do you?"

Johnny's lips curled as he looked at her. "What kind of southerner are you? Is that your patriotism?"

Lillian wept and said, "But I don't *feel* patriotic."

"Nonsense," said their mother, "we will all do our patriotic duty and fight for the Cause however we are called upon to serve."

The death of Marse John set up a chain of mixed emotions and reactions in Vyry. On his very last day of life he had taunted her with the promise of her freedom, something he knew she wanted more than anything else in the world. If he had really emancipated her in his will, would Big Missy free her? She knew better than to believe it. According to Aunt Sally and all the stories she had heard around the plantation from Mammy Sukey and other slaves, Marse John was her natural father. She was as much his child as Miss Lillian and she looked as much like him. But she was also his slave as her mother had been before her, and now her children were slaves. When she saw Miss Lillian weeping in grief over the death of her father, Vyry felt no sympathetic emotion. He had never once acknowledged her as his child and she had no tears to shed for him. True enough, he had never been as cruel to her as Big Missy, but neither had he ever showed her any parental love. Her condition was peculiar; her color was a badge of shame and her children, like herself, were bound in servitude to the household of John Morris Dutton. He did not prevent the guards from whipping her, he would not give her permission to marry, and now in stone-cold death she knew he had taunted her with the promise of freedom. She could not help recalling with bitterness his speech that first night about the honor of his house.

There were almost as many guests in the house for the funeral as there had been for the wedding. Big Missy Salina's folks came from Savannah and all Marse John's relatives came from far and near, mostly poor kinfolk. This meant Vyry was cooking whole sides of beef and hams and baking pies and cakes. She worked her worry down, for that was what Marse John's death brought to her, a new measure of worry.

It was late when she lay down on her own pallet and then she could not sleep. Her babies were sleeping beside her, but she was wakeful, too tired to sleep, and brooding over many troubled thoughts. She thought she heard a bird cry, but then she wondered if she had only imagined it. It seemed too faint and distant for her to be sure. Fully another fifteen minutes passed before she heard the whippoorwill much closer. She jumped up and threw a shawl around her shoulders against the night dew, then she waited almost breathless for another cry from the bird. Sure enough, soon she could detect the low, shrill cry of a whippoorwill behind her cabin and she quickly moved in her bare feet around the side of the shanty. There crouched a boy whom she had never seen before, and when he stood up he was as tall as a man. He was dressed in dirty rags but his eyes were keen and in the darkness they searched her face for the answers he needed before he gave her his message. He had a written note but neither he nor she could read it. He told her, "A man brung it from the North this morning, say get it here by night." Then he was gone as quickly as he had come.

Vyry felt sure that this was a note from her free man, Randall Ware, but she was unable to read a word. She was fascinated by the piece of paper and she turned it over and over before she thrust it inside her bosom to keep it until Brother Ezekiel could read it to her. A thousand hopes sprang suddenly to birth. Perhaps this time she would escape. After all Lucy tried twice before she succeeded and Vyry was willing to try more than twice if she thought she could ever succeed. Perhaps he had another plan to help her. But the next afternoon her hopes died when she learned the contents of the note. The door to freedom was still closed in her face and she did not know the magic password to open the door. Brother Ezekiel read, "There's going to be a war to set the black slaves free. When the war is over I will come and get you. Wait for me." Vyry burst into bitter, angry tears of disappointment. "A war to set us niggers free? What kind of crazy talk is that?"

Hurrah! Hurrah! for Southern rights,
Hurrah! Hurrah for the Bonnie Blue Flag
that bears a single star!

23   We'll be back home before breakfast is over

The news that war had been declared between the South and the North changed nothing on the plantation insofar as the usual routine was concerned. Mister Grimes was late with spring planting, but once they were started, the field hands seemed to work as well if not better than usual. Big Missy was looking forward to young Marster Johnny's graduation from West Point, his new commission, and his return to Georgia. Ever since her husband's accident, the news had been more confusing. He had always been her chief source of information. He brought the papers home, his mail always included papers and letters, and he was always personally in touch with events in the state. Now all this had changed. Even before he died, some of the papers had ceased coming, but he was too sick to notice. She had been too occupied with the day-to-day tasks of his illness and death to notice very much or care. Now she chafed when the day brought no news. She was almost as excited as her son that at last the sectional conflict was in the open. There would be no more compromises and there could be no more evasion. The South would soon show the world how well she could defend her rights, and there was no question but that she would prove the victor because Right was on her side. *Don't the Bible and the Constitution and the Church say "Yes" to Slavery? Who is that enemy of the South in the White House who dares to go against the Bible, the Constitution, and the Church? It is just the same as trying to fight God. As for the nigger slaves, the less they know what is going on, the better.*

If the reading of Marster's will ever took place, Vyry never knew. May Liza and Caline whispered with her and Jim, the houseboy, about Marse John's promise to emancipate his faithful slaves at his death. While speculating on the possibility, there were some days when they were sure he had made no will. Other days they felt certain that he had made it, but without mention of his slaves. And still at other times they concluded that even if he had, Big Missy either knew nothing about it or didn't intend to mention it. Sometimes they laughed at the grim joke the dead man had played on them. Other days they reasoned such speculation was a waste of time since it could come to nothing. They could always depend on Missy Salina to keep a tight hold on her slaves.

There were times, nevertheless, when Vyry hugged to her heart the news of the war and the implications of her free man's note. *A war to set the niggers free? Humph! White folks sho don't think so. But wouldn't that be fine, if it was only true?* The only trouble about this was that nothing like a war was going on anywhere near them. All they could hear was preparation, that word "Preparation." "Big Missy making Big Preparation!"

Johnny came home in June with the rank of captain in the United States Army, but he quickly announced he was going to fight for Georgia in the army of the Confederate States of America. His fond mother had never been more proud. At the same time he informed her that a great army general named Robert E. Lee had refused Lincoln's bid to lead the Union Army and instead would fight for Virginia and the Confederacy.

"He's the man who got that crazy John Brown, you remember the one they hanged for treason at Harpers Ferry in Virginia. Lee is the greatest general in the whole country. The South is bound to win under his leadership, and I mean win soon!"

Johnny was bubbling over with enthusiasm and he was anxious to go to the war so the fighting could soon be over. His enthusiasm was only matched by his mother's. Lillian had gone home with her husband and children to Milledgeville so that all through the hot summer her family heard no more of Kevin's plans for the war. There really wasn't any need to hurry. Only one battle was fought throughout the summer and the South won at Manassas Junction. "Of course we won; we're going to whip those damn Yankees so fast, before you can say Jack Robinson! We'll be back home before breakfast is over."

July 1861 came and the capitol of the Confederacy was moved from Montgomery to Richmond but young Johnny had not yet gone off to join the rebel forces. Preparations were going forward. He chose the cavalry for many reasons. It was automatically an outfit for the aristocratic class only. Every volunteer must furnish his own horse, and a horse that could withstand battle-fire must be a trained horse and a thoroughbred. The Dutton stables contained at least a dozen such. His uniform must be made at home, and he needed more than one: one for dress and one for the battlefield. His outfit would also carry sabers and this he had inherited. He would need riding boots and breeches, a soft colonel's cap, and his own gun which could fit into his belt.

Such slow preparations, however, irritated young Marster Johnny. His mother assured him there was no hurry. There were no battles, but he reminded her that there had already been the battle of Manassas and that if he did not hurry the war would be over before he could get in it. He found the countryside dull. All the sentimental women and girls who were sending off their sweethearts and brothers and husbands to war got on his nerves with their tears. Women were gathering in groups throughout their county sewing uniforms for their gallant young men. All the Negro house servants were pressed into service. Vyry and May Liza and Caline were ordered to spin thread on the spinning wheel, to card cotton, to weave cloth on the loom, and then to cut and sew for the young Marster's uniform of gray. Big Missy was the proud possessor of a real sewing machine and her slaves furnished the power to tread it while she supervised the work. Big Missy remarked that they were especially fortunate to be able to produce cotton clothes from the stalk in the field to their backs. "Just think," she said, "once the cotton is ginned we have nothing to do but card it and spin it, to weave it and dye it and then cut the cloth into patterns. In this modern age we are able to follow all this procedure so much easier than ever before because we have our own gin and spinning wheel and our own sewing machine!"

Young Marster Johnny Dutton had a dress uniform of light blue pants and a gray coat to match his soft colonel's cap. His riding breeches and blouson were made entirely of gray cotton, while his heavy coat of gray woolen material was also a product of the wool from sheep grown on the Dutton plantation.

At the end of August, while Johnny was still waiting at home, Lillian wrote about the strange reaction of her husband, Kevin, to the war:

> Frankly, Kevin is not just uninterested in the war effort, and making no immediate plans to go, but he seems downright opposed to it. You know how he has always felt about war. He says that no matter who wins the battle nothing will be solved by the war, that a lot of people will be killed for nothing and though many things may be changed at the end of the war, the fundamental issues will not change. While we are fighting for our rights, the people up North think we are revolting against the Federal Government, which I suppose we are, in order to get our rights. He thinks Secession is an ugly word. He says he has studied history and that all wars are a form of revolution like the American Revolution and the French Revolution, and that fratricidal war is the worst of all. In any case now it doesn't look as if he is going to volunteer. He says if he has to go he will wait for conscription before he chooses to leave his wife and children and go to what may mean death.

Big Missy was appalled and young Johnny cursed Kevin under his breath, clenched his teeth, and would have torn the letter into fragments if his mother had not taken it from his hands.

"I'm not surprised at his reaction. He's a teacher with a book mind. He's not a farmer with slaves, and he doesn't feel he has any property to lose. But *I* will answer this, and mind you, he will go and go of his own free will. We will not have the disgrace of a *coward* in this family."

"Yes, but mother, the longer he delays the worse will be his place in the army. He's not a trained soldier anyway, although he can ride well and could get into the cavalry if he would go into the same outfit with me. We have horses a-plenty, and Lillian could come home here and bring the children to stay with you until the war is over and he comes home again. After all, it can't be long. The best brains in the army are on the southern side—all the generals and officers—and I don't know what those Yankees plan to do for leadership anyway. They really don't have anybody. We not only have the best officers but we also have forts and ammunition, too. Before they can manufacture more, we'll be occupying the city of Washington. As Honorable Toombs says, 'I'll call the roll of my slaves in New York.' "

Big Missy managed to have all her family at home for Christmas, and during the holidays she persuaded Kevin to join the Confederate Army. Reluctantly he consented, but he refused the offer of a horse and would not join the cavalry with Johnny. Instead he decided to try his luck with the infantry. Johnny was disgusted.

"That's the worst outfit you can join. Don't you know that the infantry is the least protected unit of the army? When you go into battle you will be fighting on foot, at the worst maybe hand to hand, and even with bayonets. Doesn't that make you think twice about the cavalry?"

But Kevin was not a swashbuckling professional soldier like Johnny and he was not going into the army for glory and excitement nor for the great adventure he suspected Johnny was expecting, and he told him so.

"You talk like war is a great adventure and we are sallying forth like great white knights in armor to rescue damsels in distress and slay the wicked dragon who is terrifying the people. I think you are going to find that it's a life and death matter and a lot of people are going to be killed without reason. Almost anybody who goes into battle is sure to be killed."

"Yes, but you sound scared. I don't think war is a party or some kind of picnic, but it is a game, and you learn to play the game according to the rules. Your first rule is to learn to protect yourself while you advance the Cause of your side and at the same time kill the enemy."

Kevin smiled wryly. "That's the grim part I don't like. I know no man who is my enemy and I have no desire to kill a man even in self-defense to protect my skin. I don't think I am a coward either, but I just don't believe in the war."

Big Missy's eyes looked shocked and she spoke in a tone of disbelief, "You mean you are against us?"

"No, the whole truth is I'm not against anybody, and I don't believe in any war."

On a bright sunshiny morning in January 1862 young Marster Johnny was ready to leave for the war. Big Missy's preparations were finally completed, and the whole plantation gathered to bid him Godspeed and say goodbye. The field hands were summoned to the backyard where Grimes ordered them to line up and pass before their young Marster and speak their names as they passed him. There were many of Marster's field hands whose names were unknown even to the house servants such as Vyry. Johnny had suggested to his mother that it might be a good thing to take an accounting of how many hands were now on the place, male and female, and to maintain extra precautions to keep them working, for their labor would mean much to the war effort.

"We can't fight a war without food and supplies. The Confederacy needs money, guns, soldiers, and labor. As long as you can keep this plantation running in good order you will be contributing to the war effort by providing for many things our new nation needs."

Big Missy was mindful of this and she thought his words were sound and practical. Now they stood on the ground outside the back door while Grimes brought up the slaves. Vyry, Caline, May Liza, and Jim, the houseboy, watched with interest as black men, women, and children came forward. Vyry listened to their names in a daze of wonder that there were so many despite the winter sickness and death that always thinned their ranks.

"My name's Mandy. Howdy, sir!"

Johnny spoke to each of them in turn: Babe, Lige, Luke, and Cindy; Sugar Baby, Custer, Bo-Griggs, Moe, Molley, Crowley, and Caesar; Cressy, Dangles, Witchie, Heziah, Socie, Long, Ressie, and Dude; Toots, Han, Roscoe, Buster, Steffer, and Wincie; Jonah, High, Hiram, and Clothie; Kallie, Buddy, Bella, Osum, Riggs, and Toddle; Rupert, Reuben, Rufus, Doll Baby, Sweetie, Comus, Dooley, Ridgeman, Cootie, and Bowlie. While they bowed and curtsied and the children shyly grabbed their shifts and twisted their faces, Big Missy and Mister Grimes counted forty-six field hands that morning. Then they listened to Johnny's farewell speech:

"I think all of you understand why I am going off to war. This is my home just as it is yours and I am going to fight to keep it that way. Every man, woman, and child, every master, and every slave is called upon to do his duty now in this war. If you remain faithful and obedient servants under the prudent direction of my mother and Mister Grimes, you will be rewarded. When the war is over we will set you free. If you protect the lives and property of your master and your master's family we will give every mother's son of you a parcel of land. Now, goodbye, and let us pray for a speedy end to war."

Vyry listened flabbergasted to his promise of freedom, and she glanced at Big Missy Salina to see how such news affected her. Whatever she thought, she looked composed as usual and did not turn a hair. At the first mention of freedom there arose a feeble yell but it went down quickly when Grimes and Big Missy ordered them to sing the new southern rallying song, "I wish I was in Dixie, hooray!"

Johnny knew that his departure from home did not mean that he was going straight to the battlefields. In Georgia the troops were still forming and organization was painfully slow. As a West Pointer he was needed to train the raw recruits who had volunteered in such vast numbers as patriotic answer to President Jefferson Davis's first call for volunteers. But Johnny's hopes were high that he would see action in this war between the states and when the slaves were finished singing "Dixie" he got on his father's favorite chestnut bay horse. Accompanied by Jim, the houseboy, as his body-servant, he rode down through an avenue of live oaks to the old wagon road and cantered off to join the Confederate Army where he hoped to win the war.

I wish I was in the land of cotton,
Old times dar am not forgotten,
Look away! Look away! Look away!
Dixie Land.
In Dixie Land whar I was born in,
Early on one frosty mornin
Look away! Look away! Look away!
Dixie Land.
Den I wish I was in Dixie, Hooray! Hooray!
In Dixie Land I'll take my stand
To lib and die in Dixie
Away, away, away down South in Dixie.
Away, away, away down South in Dixie.

24   *They made us sing "Dixie"*

The South was winning the war in 1862. The morale of the
Union Army was disturbingly low. Lee was out-maneuvering
and out-thinking the Union generals, and his strategy, military
victories, and commanding personality were raising the morale
of the southern people to a high peak of jubilation. This year
the war was gathering momentum and moving along much
faster than in those last six months of 1861. In the beginning
the South defended outposts on the Mississippi River and
river tributaries, and in 1862 the war was continuing along
this western front. The battles of Pea Ridge and Shiloh, hard
fought with disputed victories, raised the hopes of all southerners that the war, although bloody, would not be long. In
1861 no battles touched Georgia soil, but she was gathering
her sons from every part of the state and sending them into
battle. She was also building defenses at home and trying to

strengthen her war economy with necessary industry and finance. The people willingly bought bonds, and four munitions factories rose on Georgia soil. They were located at Augusta, Atlanta, Columbus, and Macon.

One morning during the first spring days of 1862 Big Missy was startled by a caller who wore the gray uniform of a Confederate officer. He was beautifully turned out in gray with brass buttons and gold braid, and at first the sight of such an important visitor slightly awed the loyal rebel, Missy Salina.

"Come in, sir, do come in. We've finished breakfast but one of the girls will bring you some refreshment. Would you like coffee, wine, or whiskey?"

"Just cold well-water, Madam, and I do thank you for your thoughtfulness. My name is Smith, and I am colonel in charge of Ordnance in this vicinity, that is, what Ordnance we have been able to command. You understand that the Confederacy must manufacture guns and other ammunition in order to keep a continuous supply line to our battlefields and before the large supply which our forts afforded has diminished or been completely exhausted."

"Yes, I can understand that, but what can I do to help?"

"We need labor, ma'am, and that is what I have come here to ask you to contribute. If you could spare about a dozen or more of your able-bodied hands we would be willing to pay you, and our government would be much obliged to you now and in the future. You understand that we would feed and sleep this help until such time in the future when we have won the war and can return them safe and sound to your establishment here."

"Well, sir, we are here to do anything and everything we can do to help our Nation win the war. My late husband served in the state legislature and you can be sure he would have given his all for the Cause of the Sovereign State of Georgia. Even now, my son, a West Point graduate, is training troops for the war, that is, if the war is not over before they are trained."

"Do you mean, Madam, that you are single-handedly managing this large establishment yourself?"

"Well, yes, but you must understand, I have a very capable overseer. He has been with us for many years and is entirely trustworthy. He has had much experience and knows how to handle the nigras. I am actually doing no more now than when my late husband was alive and had to be away so much attending to political business."

Colonel Smith listened sympathetically to Missy Salina, but his admiration was quite apparent.

"Madam, I must confess my deep admiration for such a loyal lady. I tell you our greatest asset in this war is our great southern womanhood with the wonderful support you are giving us at home. You have remarkable courage, Madam, and I salute you as I would a fellow officer in our cherished Confederate States of America."

Big Missy beamed, but in the meantime she pulled on the parlor bell cord and summoned May Liza.

"Liza, find a pickaninny and send for Mister Grimes to come here at once."

May Liza went to the kitchen back door and started hollering down in the Quarters.

Grimes was resting. He had put out his morning's gang of workers and was considering whether it was worth his trouble to start them in a new cotton field. Cotton from year before last was still waiting in Dawson to be shipped to Savannah. Last he heard, the damn blockade was taking more and more effect and cotton wasn't moving from Savannah at all. He wanted to get in the war, but neither his wife nor Missy Salina wanted him to go. They needed him at home. The law said for every twenty niggers there had to be a white guard, patter-roller, or overseer. That meant he had to stay here as long as there were slaves to oversee which meant he was out of the war for the duration. Now here he sat under a sour apple tree whittling a stick. He saw the child and heard her hollering after him, "Make haste and come quick, Missy want you." And he thought, "Now what-in-hell she wants me to do now?"

In the course of six months Grimes made three round trips with work gangs for the munitions works in Macon. The slaves had to be shackled in iron and heavily guarded for the journey, but despite all precautions taken before they left the plantation, despite Grimes's watchful eye, there were steady disappearances and breaks for freedom. After they arrived in Macon and were put to work the numbers continued to dwindle for various reasons. The work was different and more dangerous than any work they had ever done. Making the gunpowder was not so bad as soldering the guns. This work was hot, hotter than Georgia sun, and so they worked stripped naked to the waist with noise and fire as their constant companions. If a slave were not careful, unskilled and unaccustomed as he was to such work, he might lose a hand and then he was no longer good for the job. Moreover the work was desperate work, for the Confederates always felt they were working against time and the war must be won in a hurry. Grimes assured the perspiring poor-white foremen, who were harassed to speed up operations in the factory, that "niggers are used to the lash. If you don't beat them they won't work." So the slaves who were impressed into service in the munitions works also worked under the lash. Some of the unhappy slaves heard through underground rumors that the Union Army was fighting the slave owners and many of them took desperate chances and made a break for freedom with the hope of reaching the Union Army lines. When they did not make it, they were shot in the attempt. If they made it, they were gone to freedom and the work gang was short.

Grimes and Missy Salina were disgusted when they heard how many of their workers either got away, were mutilated, or shot in the attempt to escape. Being disgusted did not help and brought no remedy. Finally they decided to advertise in all the Georgia papers, and they offered rewards for the return of any or all five slaves known to have escaped:

> $50 REWARD: Ran away on the night of Sunday last, the 25th inst., five NEGROES engaged in cutting wood in Bibb County for the Macon Munitions Manufacturing Company. Cootie is about thirty-five years of age, about five feet seven inches high, and of a gingerbread color.
>
> Osum is about thirty years of age, about six feet high, very black, thick lips, and has a feminine voice.
>
> Jonah is about twenty-eight years of age, five feet six inches high, yellow and quite stout.
>
> Hiram is twenty-five years of age, nearly six feet high, black, and speaks in a low tone.
>
> Roscoe is forty-five years old, six feet high, of gingerbread color, and inclined to stoop while walking. A reward of ten dollars apiece will be paid for each one of the above, if delivered either to Mr. Ed Grimes at Dutton's Plantation in Terrell County or to Mr. O. A. West at the Macon Munitions Manufacturing Company.
>
> > Signed by President Crenshaw and his Agent
> > of the Macon Munitions Manufacturing Company.

Just before the battle, Mother,
I am thinking most of you.
While upon the field we're watching
With the enemy in view.
Comrades brave are round me lying,
Filled with thoughts of home and God.
For well they know that on the morrow
Some will sleep beneath the sod.

25   *Chickamauga—River of Death*

On July 18, 1862, "Fighting Joe" Wheeler was named in command of the cavalry of the Army of Tennessee by General Bragg. Johnny Dutton, tired of long inaction as an instructor and chafing at the bit in his longing for excitement on the battle front, quickly joined the rapidly forming brigade of his fellow West Pointer. Wheeler was young, only twenty-six, and he was already known to be one of the most intrepid fighters in the West.

The far western front of military action moved from the Mississippi River to the junction point of three other rivers where the Cumberland River moved east and west, where the Ohio became the Tennessee, and where the Alabama and Chattahoochee rivers divided Georgia from Alabama. This involved three southern states at the southernmost tip of the Appalachians, the northeastern corner of Alabama, the southern border of Tennessee, and the northwestern corner of Georgia. Control of the strategic rivers here meant that the northern armies of the Cumberland and the Tennessee could invade the state of Georgia and thereby cut the Confederacy in two. Here, too, lay a network of the most important southern railroads which were necessary for the moving of supplies of either army. Control of the Chattanooga and Nashville Railroad, the Atlantic and Western Railroad, and the Memphis and Chattanooga Railroad became an absolute necessity toward the winning of the war. Along the Cumberland River and through the mountainous passes known as Gaps the Federal forces attempted to make their first real thrusts into the heart of the South and the Confederacy. But the Union Armies were stalemated toward this objective throughout the year of 1862. Only after the victories of 1863 did this thrust receive concerted attention and massive action. Two major victories for the Union Army opened this possibility, for in the summer of 1863 the tide was swiftly turning the winning of the war away from the South. General Robert E. Lee had limped away from Gettysburg nursing the wounds of his badly whipped Army of Northern Virginia. They had failed in their second attempt to invade northern territory. Lincoln was annoyed because as was usually true his generals did not follow through this advantageous victory and they let Lee get away. Almost at the same time in July, General Ulysses S. Grant had run the gauntlet of Confederate gunboats in the Mississippi and broken the long siege of Vicksburg. Now there remained in the West only one more obstacle to the strategy of the Union Army and its slowly evolving pattern for victory.

When the Confederate Armies lost the battles of Gettysburg and Vicksburg, the southern generals began concentrating their attention on the last strategic center of the whole Confederacy. This was the western front centered in Chattanooga bordering on a small tributary of the Tennessee River, West Chickamauga Creek, which the Indians had named the River of Death. General Joe Wheeler moved up his cavalry units to this mountainous position and began to flank the left end of General Bragg's Army. Johnny Dutton watched this mountainous country turn golden from Indian summer into early fall while he waited here for serious military action.

They were bringing up the big guns for battle. All day long the wagons were rolling, the roads across the mountain were criss-crossed with men and horses and heavy artillery. Johnny could see from his position in Pigeon's Gap how the September sunshine dappled through the thickly grown trees while all the wide open spaces and fields around the dozen farm houses were golden yellow. It was a sunny primrose scene that lay before him like a picture painted by a sundrunken artist. In the heavily timbered areas there was an impeding undergrowth of tangled vines and brush not unlike the thickly growing vines and flowers that grew in his native section. Everything here was dry, however, dry as tinder, and ready to blaze into burning bonfires at the slightest touch of flame. Where he lived, on the other hand, the land was damp and marshy. There it was all low ground and wet swampland with the rich alluvial soil in the river valleys of the Flint and Chattahoochee. Here the little stream known as West Chickamauga Creek that meandered through the mountain was shallow enough to wade across. This was hilly, mountainous, and treacherous country, hard to move across and impervious as roads for animals, wagons, or men. These mountains were natural battlements and fortifications. They obstructed the view for the people in the valleys below, but on the mountaintop the view was wonderful. Johnny could look across Missionary Ridge and Lookout Mountain yonder in Tennessee, then back again across Sand Mountain and Raccoon Mountain in Alabama, while here on the south bank of this West Chickamauga Creek he was guarding the northern gate into his beloved Georgia. And the vistas were breathtaking. It was as if he stood on top of the world astride his beautiful horse, riding the crest of the sky like a young sun god, Phaeton, with the rays of the sun highlighting his brown hair, and the earth spread before him in the low valleys like a golden brown and clay-red bordered carpet. The people in the plains looked like tiny black and red insects scurrying back and forth for food and drawing up their lines for ant battles. Even the shiny black rails of the railroad trains chugging and puffing into Chattanooga were toy tracks, and seemed of no importance from this immense distance. Those railroads criss-crossing through the mountainous terrain were the supply lines, however, for General Bragg's and General Rosecrans' armies and they went east to South Carolina and Virginia, west to St. Louis, Missouri, north to Illinois and Ohio, and south to Alabama and Georgia.

Johnny was twenty-two, and he had found the whole meaning of his life in this war. He had come through Antietam and three subsequent raiding parties with Wheeler without so much as a scratch. He had led such a charmed battle life that he felt himself almost invulnerable. He was accustomed to the din of battle, to the smoke and fire, the terrible noises of the horses and guns. In fact, the flashing guns exhilarated him and he felt the blood racing hot in his face. He came alive on the battlefield. He always kept a cool head, and he was alert in all his movements. In a way, he felt himself unusually fortunate. He was born into a class of men who naturally took the role of leadership in this war. As an aristocrat he had been schooled from childhood for military combat. As a graduate of West Point his colonelcy had been literally assured. He was a rich southerner so it was natural that his sword and his horse felt easy in his hands. His body-servant, Jim, looked after all his menial and physical necessities. His horse, Beauty, had withstood the baptism of fire on the battlefield and seemed undisturbed by the thundering guns belching fire and black smoke. Aside from his mother he had no sentimental attachments to distract him from his duty and the business of this war. He could handle his Colt 44 with unusual skill and effectiveness. He was savage when it came to killing the enemy. He had neither mercy nor compunction. The Confederacy must be maintained, the southern states must secure their complete and unquestioned independence from the tyranny of the hatred Federal, radical government in Washington.

During the night the battle lines were formed, and on the morning of September 19, 1863, the fighting began. With a signal from Wheeler's cavalry they moved forward in a rush with all of Bragg's Army plus steadily appearing reinforcements, slowly encircling Rosecrans' men and almost from the beginning forcing them back. At noon there was a lull, but in the afternoon the fighting began again in earnest, and for an hour it was the most bloody and ghastly that Johnny had thus far seen. Despite the overwhelming numbers on the Confederate side and their improved position the whole day passed with no special advantge gained, and that night both armies slept on a blood-drenched battlefield.

In the morning his usual battle elation returned. During the night Longstreet had come up with heavy reinforcements and the courage of all the men was renewed. Johnny found his horse, Beauty, ready and waiting and he rode forward thrilled by the Confederate colors that went before them. He heard the stirring sound of the drummers and the bugle corps, and he rode with the conviction that victory must reward such a righteous Cause.

At first when he heard the sudden neighing of his horse he thought it must be elsewhere. He felt the horse tremble under him, so he gripped the reins tighter, but simultaneously he felt his beast give way to the ground under him while a sudden tearing pain burst through his right shoulder and the upper part of his back. The pain was both a knife and a fire and bewilderment numbed him while he tried to collect his faculties. Slowly he realized as other horses rushed past him that both he and his horse had met with an accident. He was hit and Beauty was also hurt. Somehow, he did not quite understand how he managed it, he waited until the heavy rush of men and horses had passed by him, and in a deathlike stillness he found his feet and got off his horse. His beautiful animal was suffering and obviously a leg was broken. He must shoot him at once and get him out of his misery. Placing the gun at the most vulnerable part of the beast's head, he closed his eyes and shot him. The horse gave one convulsion and lay still. Now Johnny's emotions were fourfold. He felt his eyes sting with tears he dare not shed for his dead horse. He felt chagrin and disappointment to be left behind the battle. He was revolted when he looked at the carnage around him. There were dead men sitting upright with eyes staring at him. For the first time in his life he felt fear for his fate. How long must he wait here before the ambulance wagon could find him? How badly was he hurt? He felt a fullness in his chest and a choking of phlegm in his throat, but when he felt obliged to clear his throat and spit he saw his sputum threaded and colored with blood. The tearing pain, once it had sizzled through him, had just as suddenly subsided. He tried to rest himself against the body of his dead horse, and thus be still and protect his wound as long as possible.

Night was falling when they found him. He was unconscious and having a nightmare for he called in his sleep to his horse and he thought he heard men screaming, "Chickamauga!" When the next day broke he was in the Hunt House, improvised as a hospital near the battlefield. That morning when Johnny awoke he had a long wait before he saw the doctor for there were many hundreds of men in worse shape that he, and their improvised cots and litters were all over the place. He heard, as he had heard on the battlefield, the groans and the labored breathing of the dying, but he was also amazed to see how quickly the townspeople from nearby Ringgold were rallying to the aid of their wounded.

Johnny had a bullet in his lung and the doctor told him he could not get it out.

"Will it kill me?"

"Might. Might not. It's hard to say about a thing like this. Your wound will heal outside, and as long as you lie quiet you'll be all right. Guess you noticed you've been spitting and coughing blood, but not as much as at first. Well, you just might be all right unless there's a hole inside and it keeps on bleeding. Sorta like old-fashioned consumption, or galloping consumption; you know if you have a bad hemorrhage you might go like that," and he snapped his fingers, "then again it depends on your constitution."

"Can I go home?"

"After a few days, yes, I don't know why not. Have you got a way to travel and somebody to go with you? You couldn't go alone, you understand?"

"I've got my body-servant with me, Jim. But I guess he'll have to scout around and find a wagon. He's still got a horse. Mine was hurt in the battle and I had to shoot him."

"A wagon would be fine. You could lie flat. You might have some discomfiture going over these mountainous roads but not much I hope. By the way, where is home?"

"Southwest Georgia, about thirty-five miles from the Alabama line and about thirty-five miles from the Florida line."

"That's pretty country. It will do you good to go home. Just breathing that air might be better than medicine, and it surely would be better than staying here."

The doctor looked around at the bloody scene of miserable men.

Jim hovered around the hospital but he kept his eyes and ears open. Without Johnny's knowledge he slipped in and out of the Union lines more than once. He offered his services to the Yankees but when they discovered his connections and his mission they urged him to go back and wait for a more opportune time when his knowledge of Confederate movements would serve them best. Twice he thought he caught a glimpse of Brother Ezekiel but on both occasions Brother Zeke made no attempt to recognize him.

He was trying to buy the use of a wagon to get young Marster Johnny home to his mother. It was nearly two years since he had gone to war. Times had changed. Jim was no longer willing to remain in the Dutton house as a slave. He had seen the war from the Confederate side and gradually he realized that his own chances for freedom lay with the Union Army. He knew that Abe Lincoln had already declared for the second time that all slaves living in the States of the Rebellion were free, but he also knew for a fact that none of these slaves were set free from their masters. On the roads at night, however, there were crowds of Negroes fleeing from the plantations, hiding in the woods and swamps and mountains while gangs of them were guerrillas in the country and camping on the roadsides and in the foothills. Some of them made it to the Union lines. Some of them were destitute and suffering from exposure, privation, sickness, and hunger with no place to turn for help. Jim was forty years old. He doubted that he would make a soldier. All he knew how to do were the menial tasks of a domestic servant. The guns terrified him but he wanted to help in the struggle for black freedom, and he wanted to be free. *Marster Johnny dying and he can't get home by hisself. I'll carry him home to his Maw where he can die in peace, but I sho ain't staying there.* If Jim had been a field hand, such a delicate conflict would not have disturbed him. He would have felt no ties to the Dutton household, but he had nursed the old man and he had watched the children grow. Contemptuous as he was of Big Missy he was nevertheless tied to a strange code of honor, duty, and noblesse oblige which he could not have explained. So he was taking Johnny home. He found a wagon after some difficulty, but six weeks had passed since the battle of Chickamauga when he found himself on the road with Johnny lying flat in the wagon.

Oh I was born in Mobile town,
A-working on the Levee.
All day I rolled the cotton down,
A-working on the Levee.

I've been working on the railroad,
All the live-long day.
I've been working on the railroad,
To pass the time away.
Don't you hear the whistle blowing?
Rise up so early in the morn.
Can't you hear the captain calling?
Dinah, blow your horn!

26   Can you forge?

Randall Ware was walking up a dusty road barefooted. Foot-sore and weary, he was longing for a place to stop and rest, a chance to soak himself in a big wooden tub or tank of water, and wishing, too, for some work along the way to replenish his dwindling stock of gold. Three times he had already met the rebuffs of northern white villagers. Once, when he knocked on a back door, the woman screamed and her husband came running with his shotgun. Another time, the dogs ran him away, and once when he was taken in, he slipped away in the night following his unerring instinct that told him he was not among friends, but they were merely detaining him until they could turn him over to the slave-catchers. He learned to be wary.

A little white boy sitting on a fence was watching him intently. He was barefoot, too, and had on a faded and ragged pair of blue cotton pants held up with sagging suspenders. His short-sleeved shirt had only one button and his old straw hat sat back on his fiery red hair, while his face was mottled with freckles like a child with the measles. His blue eyes were friendly when he spoke.

"Howdy, who are you?"

"Howdy yourself. I'm a stranger man. I'm tired and I'm hungry and I'm looking for work. Where's your father?"

"Are you the same color all over?"

"Are you?"

"I guess."

"Well, so am I. Didn't you never see a black man before?"

"Naw."

"Well, you see one now. I asked you for your father."

"I'll call him."

The man looked as surprised to see Randall Ware as the boy. But he gave him work. And the woman gave him food to eat in the barn. He stayed there and slept in the barn for a week before moving on. For five days the boy followed him around. They made friends, and when he left the youngster held out his hand to say goodbye. But Randall Ware did not like farm work. He was not really a hired man, but he could do most things from chopping and hauling wood to cutting corn stalks and picking cotton. He liked work in the small towns best when he could work at a livery stable shoeing horses. Twice he ventured into the big cities. In Ohio he was tempted to stay in the city of Cincinnati where work was plentiful and he could make more than ten dollars a month, even sometimes as much as a dollar a day. He did stay six months, and then he went wandering through the surrounding Ohio country before going back to Cincinnati for another half-year of odd jobs.

He was in Ohio when the war came. The Union sentiment there was very strong and all the people talked about putting down the Rebellion. He heard many snatches of conversation while he was shoeing horses. Much of what he heard startled him and he came up with strange conclusions.

"Anything those southern rebels don't like they declare on their sacred honor is wrong, and then they start hunting Scripture to prove their interpretation is the only one that can be morally right."

"They're so all-fired twisted in their thinking, they don't know right from wrong."

"Wa'al now I'll tell you, I think it's mostly a war for the

naygurs, and I say let the naygurs do the fighting and let the naygurs do the dying. It's a rich man's war, and a poor man's fight, and I don't fancy dying for the naygur."

Randall Ware discovered the painful fact that in the North his status was little better than in the slave-South. He felt free to walk the streets and that was all. He was an experienced blacksmith with his own smithy in Georgia, but here he was lucky if he worked for a journeyman's wages, and then mostly at odd jobs. He longed for his own anvil, to hear the ring of his hammer and watch the sparks fly around him while he forged. But he had been forced to leave because of the hated system and now he wondered who in the country hated colored people more, the slavers, the poor whites, or those northern white people who were not abolitionists.

One good thing about a blacksmith, he kept remembering, *he can always make his own tools.* He managed to hang on to his bellows even when he knew he could not carry most of his tools with him. His hammer was too big. But then he could always make pinchers, and files and the crowbar tool he used for leverage. It was not easy to adjust to another man's hammer, but it wasn't impossible. And he had hardly needed his forging tools because most of the time he was just shoeing horses.

Hearing that the Union Army headquarters in the West were at Cairo, Illinois he made his way back to the Missouri River and across to St. Louis, then back to East St. Louis and up to Cairo, working all the while at his trade. He was about to leave and head back toward Cincinnati, disappointed because his services as a soldier were rejected by the Union Army, when he heard that the Army was looking for common laborers as well as skilled blacksmiths to work on the railroads leading from Alabama into Tennessee. Blacksmiths were greatly needed as well as sawmill workers to make rails and crossties and repair the roads. General Dodge was recruiting workers, but Randall Ware did not know where to find Dodge. When he inquired, he was given sundry directions, many misleading, but he had found a purpose. Now perhaps there would be a place for him in this conflict. He was determined to find Dodge.

General Dodge was an engineer and a professional railroad man. He had been hired by General U. S. Grant, who was now in command of all the Union Armies in the West, to repair the road from Stevenson, Alabama, into Chattanooga, Tennessee. Although there were blacksmith shops along the way, they were in the hands of the enemy, and all the saw-mills likewise were on enemy property. He was, therefore, forced to set up shop in the field and fight his way through the countryside. He captured the necessary shops and some-times took the men working. If they objected to working for the Union, they were automatically prisoners anyway. These shops had to be brought up to the lines for their protection and this made long, slow, and complicated work.

Many of the workers available were runaway slaves eager to work for Uncle Sam's armies but often not skilled. They could cut down trees, saw wood, and split logs, but most of them were not equipped for the more important jobs.

Randall Ware caught up with Dodge's army camp after five days of traveling from Missouri. While he was traveling through southern territory he had to be as careful as he was when he was running from Georgia. Negroes falling in the hands of the Confederates were frequently killed since the rebels would take no Negroes as prisoners.

"Halt! Who goes there?"

Randall Ware had been watching the soldier walking sentry duty for a long time before he approached the camp. He sat in the tall grass and chewed the sour stalks of sheep sorrel, trying to make up his mind whether to go forward. He thought of St. Louis when he first heard about the war and went there to enlist. He thought about his feelings when he heard the Union Army didn't want nigger soldiers. He heard they were turning them back to the slave-catchers in some places, holding them as contraband of war in others, or putting them to work, but not in uniform. He didn't want anybody treating him like dirt. But he did want to get into this war for freedom.

"Halt! I say, who goes there?"

"Open up, soldier, for Shady. I'm one of Old Ride-up's Boys."

The soldier, nonplussed at first, watched Randall Ware rise up from the tall grass and then rested his gun. The black man moving toward him was ragged and dusty. His feet were bare and the thick hair on his face and head were only slightly darker than his skin. He had a croker sack tied with rope which he carried on his back, and to the soldier's amazement the sack was full of iron tools. The broad back of this Shady was wide as a barn door and under thick beetle brows his eyes peered with a cool and searching gaze at the soldier.

"What you want, Shady?"

"Wanta see the boss-man. Who's in command here?"

"General G. M. Dodge is in command here, but you better have urgent business to see the general."

"Take me to him, soldier, and let him decide how urgent my business is."

He found the General eating his supper in a tent which served as his temporary headquarters.

"What do you want, Shady?"

"Sir, I come all the way from Missouri, mostly crawling on my hands and knees, to get here and offer my services to you."

"What can you do?"

"I'm a blacksmith, sir, had my own smithy before the war but the rebels ran me away."

"Can you forge?"

"Sir, I just told you I had my own anvil. You wanta see me forge?"

"You can show us bright and early in the morning. Now tell the quartermaster to find you a place to sleep and have the cook feed you. You look as if you did crawl all the way!"

"Thankye sir. I'll prove myself in the morning."

And he did. Happily he watched the sparks fly from the anvil while he lifted his powerful hammer and beat the red hot iron, forging the metal into rails. At last he was in the war doing what he liked best, and striking a powerful blow for the freedom of the blacks.

I have seen Him in the watchfires of a hundred circling
    camps,
They have builded Him an altar in the evening dews
    and damps;
I can read His righteous sentence by the dim and
    flaring lamps,
His day is marching on.

27   *Down with the shackle and up with the star!*

Randall Ware was warming himself over a campfire. It was
November 1863 and the night air blowing from the tops of
Lookout Mountain and Missionary Ridge could chill him to
the bone. All over the Union camp there were knots of men
hovering over fires. Casting their eyes up the mountain sides
in the distance they could see the campfires of the enemy.
Randall Ware's thoughts, however, were not on the enemy,
even though he knew that General Grant's Army was be-
sieged here in Chattanooga, and had been ever since Bragg
had forced Rosecrans to retreat from Chickamauga in September. The blacksmith's mind went back to other days and
places he had known during the five years he had been absent
from his anvil in Dawson, Georgia. He thought fleetingly of
Vyry, but he did not allow himself to dwell long on the

face of a woman who had changed his fortunes and made him flee for his life.

Just before he was forced to leave Terrell County, he had thought his fortunes were moving up as fast as once could hope, in a place where no black man really had any form of security. But when his guardian, Randall Wheelwright, died, and old man Qualls was under much suspicion as an abolitionist, in case of any direct contact with the law or some hostile planter, he would have had no redress. Any day he could expect his status to change from free man to slave or prisoner or both. He still had his free papers, however, and although his movements were proscribed, he decided that night when his arm was grazed with a bullet that he must leave. He had hoped that Vyry would follow him, but he also knew how attached she was to her babies, and he could well realize that morning in the swamps when she did not appear that she had not obeyed his instructions after all.

And now, after going North, he was back in the South again. Grimly he remembered how carefully he had picked his way out of the South, traveling as a fugitive slave through the underground railway even though he was a free man. There were days and nights when he lay hiding in a friend's barn or breathless under a haystack, when he dared not walk the streets of a strange southern town in daylight without taking the chance of running afoul of the law.

Now in the deepening night, as he stood over the campfire, companions joined him. Randall Ware, listening to these men, was moved to murmur only a few words. He spoke softly but passionately and he said, "I don't know what you thinking, and I don't know how you feeling. You are white folks, and my people are black, but I tell you I believe God means for my people to go free. When this war is over we gonna be free, just like Old Ride-up say, we gonna be forever free. We fighting this war to be free. We working and we dying just like everybody else. We doing all in our power in this war so we can go free."

Nearby was another knot of men laughing over a game of cards. Detached from the rest was a group of colored workers assigned to the work detail of the camp. Now they were yelling out in the night, "What you got to put in the pot? . . . Roll them bones, boys, seven come eleven . . . Roll them bones!"

If de Debble do not ketch
Jeff Davis, dat infernal wretch,
And roast and frigazee dat rebble,
What is the use of any Debble?

28   Shall be forever free

"Mama, do you see where Abraham Lincoln has set all the
slaves free?"

"He can't tell me what to do with my property. He's not
my president, anyway. Mr. Jefferson Davis is my president,
and what's more, he's a southern gentleman and not like that
boor in Washington. Ape Lincoln ought to be his name."

"He sure is an ugly man. But you know Kevin has always
said this war is going to be the end of slavery and all the
niggers will be free when it's over."

"Don't tell me what your schoolteacher husband says. He
sounds like a lot of these peace-talking white trash who don't
know what they're talking about. Georgia crackers don't
care whether we lose our slaves or not, just as long as they
save their necks. Haven't you heard President Davis say
time and again that the whole thing is a question of superior

white people and inferior black people? Even the northern
white people know that gorilla Lincoln is wrong. They don't
like him nor what he's doing to the South any more than
we do. Look at that big mess they had in New York just last
summer when he tried to draft soldiers . . . Where is Susan?"

"She's in the kitchen, I think, with Vyry, or out in the yard
playing with the children from the Quarters."

"Well, you ought to know where she is all the time. I
guess she's all right, but you can't always trust niggers and
I never did trust Vyry . . . What was I saying?"

"You were talking about the draft riots last summer in
New York."

"Oh, yes, well, anybody can tell who the slaves' friends are
from that. Nobody but good southern white people would
nurse and take care of slaves like we do. You see they burned
and shot and hanged all those New York niggers just to show
Lincoln how they hate the war, just massacred them!"

"Mama, do you think I should French-seam this?"

"If you make the stitches fine enough so they'll hold, unless you're going to stitch on the machine."

"I can't pedal that thing. I'd rather do it on my hand and
Susan won't break the stitches loose the way Bobby might."

"Well, French-seam it then."

"Did anybody go to town for the mail?"

"Already sent this week and there wasn't none. Why, you
looking for a letter again from Kevin? I thought you just
got one from him last week."

"I did, but we haven't heard from Johnny in a long time,
now. Thought we might be hearing how he is since he must
be up there where they fought the battle around Tennessee."

"I guess no news is good news. Johnny always could take
care of himself. I hear we won that battle, Chickamauga,
and if anything was wrong with Johnny we would be bound
to hear something. I reckon Jim would come and tell us."

"Or the Winston boys. Aren't they with him?"

"They're in Wheeler's cavalry, yes, but you never can tell
whether they're together. I did feel a little uneasy at the time
of the battle, but my mind tells me he's alive and I feel
sure of that."

On the road from Chickamauga, Jim encountered few
difficulties but he was delayed time and again for different
reasons. Johnny could not rest too well when they were moving, even though Jim had made a bed for him, and together

with what the hospital had managed to furnish, and neighbors from the nearby town, he was as comfortable as possible. But the jolting of the wagon on the road kept a steady trickle of blood on his lips. At night he kept his gun near and Jim kept watch. Ordinarily they would have made the journey in a week or ten days at the most, even around the mountains near Atlanta, but they could not follow the river, which was the quickest way, because the Feds were all along the river. At night it was cold and there were frequent heavy frosts, so that they waited in the morning, until well into the day, before they could move southward on their way. Jim just hoped they wouldn't run into much rain. It was November now, and the winter always began with a cold rain. Although the wagon was covered, rain would be real bad for young Marster Johnny. And frostbite was another mortal danger they could well expect. Neither had good shoes. Jim's were paper soled and Johnny's soles were worn so thin they no longer seemed like leather and there were no shoes to be had for love nor money. Jim tried to buy shoes and blankets but he couldn't buy either.

Fortunately they were not hungry. Along the way all through Georgia there was plenty to eat. "Not the finest, mind you," said Jim to young Johnny, "but it'll keep body and soul together till we get home."

Sweet potatoes and corn were in all the barns and people gave freely for the asking. Sweet potatoes made good eating when Jim made a fire and roasted them. Once or twice he caught a rabbit and another time a friendly white woman in a town brought hot chicken soup out to Johnny's wagon and gave them an extra chicken to carry. All along the way Johnny was among friends, and although Jim was frequently questioned as to his destination and who owned him, young Marster Johnny was his protection.

When they passed through the cities and towns like Macon and Milledgeville they found the people were short on things like salt and coffee and nobody had white wheat bread or flour to make any. Along the countryside there was catfish in the streams and Jim was a handy fisherman and hunter, but there was no substitute for salt. "Food just don't taste right without salt," said Johnny.

But now Jim was getting worried. After ten days they still had a third of the way to go and he felt Johnny was weaker and getting a little feverish, but almost always after a good night's rest he seemed better. "I gotta get him to his Maw fast. Don't want him to die out here and folks think I killed him. Lord, do let me make it home!"

Caline was sweeping dust off the front veranda when she thought she saw them coming. She ran in the house hollering, "Missy, make haste and come quick, I believe my soul I sees a wagon coming."

Big Missy threw a shawl around her shoulders first but Miss Lillian ran out without any wrap. Vyry had gone down to the springhouse and when she heard the commotion she ran, too.

Missy Salina was shocked to see a ghost of her Johnny, but she bit her lip and then smiled before she hugged and kissed him. Lillian began to sniffle, but Big Missy ordered Jim and Caline to get help quickly and to get Marster Johnny upstairs. They put him in his own bed, and he groaned with a sigh of relief to lie on fresh clean sheets in a warm house with the smell of good food steaming hot on a tray and the promise of salt.

Big Missy wasn't short of anything on the plantation except help. As she confided to Johnny, "Only twenty field hands are left on the place out of that forty-five we counted the day you first went away. Twenty went to Macon to work in the munitions works and five of them got away from there and five more ran away from here."

"Grimes couldn't catch them?"

"Claims he didn't have enough help. All the patter-rollers and guards have now gone to the war, leaving only him to do everything. But you shouldn't be talking so much. Doc says you must lie still. I'm going now, Johnny, so you can rest. Pull the cord on the bell if you want anything. I'm going down and see about fixing something nice for your supper." He smiled up at her and she kissed him. "Now you just lie there and go to sleep." And weary Johnny was only too glad to do just that.

Johnny was home only three days when Fanny Crenshaw came to call. Shyly she presented herself one morning at the front door. She was dressed in her riding habit and May Liza let her inside and ushered her in one of the parlors. Big Missy Salina was surprised but more than pleased to learn the meaning of her call. "I hear Johnny's home wounded, Mrs. Dutton. I wonder if I might see him?"

"Why, bless you, Fanny, you know you can. I'll go up-stairs first and see if he's presentable."

Big Missy fussed over Johnny and fluffed up his pillows. She brushed his hair and then went down to send Fanny upstairs.

Fanny stood in the doorway momentarily trying to get her composure and yet blushing when she saw a wan Johnny smiling up at her from his pillows.

"Hello, Johnny, I see the conquering hero has come home!"

"Not conqueror yet, Fanny, but it's good to be home. Come on in and have a seat." She drew a chair close to the bed and sat down.

"I was just riding and I happened to be passing this way. I heard you were home and ill and I thought I'd stop by and see how you are."

Johnny listened to her elaborate lie, knowing well she would have to ride miles out of her way to come to this place. Feeling his pulse quicken with gratitude that she had, he controlled his voice to say, "Nice neighborly thing to do, I must say."

She thought she detected the old sarcasm in his voice and she blushed and looked away, but looking back he caught her eye and she saw the unmistakable twinkle.

"Oh, I don't know about that," she said carelessly, "but seriously, Johnny, how's the war going?"

"At this particular moment, Fanny, I don't know, but we won at Chickamauga and that kept the Yankees from invading our state. Of course, that was over two months ago and I don't know too much about our progress since."

"I guess you miss your regiment."

"I certainly do. I hate lying here uselessly."

"But you've done your part so gallantly and you deserve to rest."

"Well, I don't have much choice," he remarked drily, "but tell me about yourself. What does a lovely young lady like you do to keep herself busy in this backwoods while a war is going on?"

"Oh, I help mother and do what I can around the place. You know our help is scarce and most of the niggers have run away."

"My mother told me."

"And I roll bandages, and sew packets for the soldiers, and . . ." Her voice trailed away and she fiddled with her riding crop, looking down at her hands. Johnny waited.

"Oh, Johnny, the war has spoiled everything! All our good times are gone and it's so horribly lonesome!" She burst out with this abruptly, then covered her face with her hands, dropping the crop on the floor. Johnny watched her and felt a small twinge of compassion for her distress. Fanny had grown into a lovely young lady, but all the fiery excitement and tempestuousness of her nature seemed held firmly under control, much as her horses submitted to the bit. If things had been normal they might have married. Suddenly, he felt old, the war had made him a man, and in his young manhood he felt cut down like a flower of the field, while Fanny felt that the war had taken life with it and left her behind. He struggled to think of something to say to her but couldn't.

Now she had control of herself again. She dropped her hands and forced a smile through what looked like tears gathering in her eyes. "What am I doing? Thinking only of myself, and here you lie wounded from the war! If I can't cheer you up, I certainly don't need to share my despair." She laughed and put out her hand. Swiftly he covered it with his own in a reassuring grasp while he smiled at her. But the language of his touch had a meaning all its own and, startled by that meaning, she suddenly stood up. Johnny felt awkward and said nothing.

"I'm going now, Johnny. But I'll come back soon, if you'll let me."

"Please do, Fanny. I'll be looking forward to that pleasure."

She stared for a moment into his eyes and saw reflected there in his grave face the same dawning awareness of what she had felt with his hand on hers, then without speaking again she picked up her riding crop and walked quickly out of the room.

The first few days after Johnny came home, Jim hung around the kitchen of the Big House talking to Vyry. He was tired and tense and he felt he could not settle down again into the routine of the plantation.

"So much taking place on the Big Road it makes you want to see what's gwine on. I seen a lot, lot of suffering, lot of fighting and them big guns nearly scared me to death. I done a lot of different things round the Confederate camp, like barbering and toting water for the soldiers to drink and bathe in, and cutting wood. That is, when I wasn't looking after Marster Johnny. He gwine die, and I don't wanta be here to see it. They say he was mighty brave on the battlefield and I know his Maw is that proud of him, but I seen what they was fighting for and I knows he fought against me and you and all us colored peoples."

"How come you think he gwine die?"

"Army doctor good as told me so. Said get him home fast, cause anytime he have one of them big hemorrhaging spells he gwine go before you can say Jack Robinson."

"He lucky he ain't had it on the road. All that far ways you come in the wagon."

"Yeah, that's what I know. Look like he saving hisself for something, and he determine to make it home. He got a constituency like iron, the doctor say, and he got a will stronger than iron. He made like his Maw."

"I ain't never liked him and I know he ain't never liked me, but I feels sorry for him now."

"Why, cause he dying?"

"Well-er he young and he ain't had no time for living and he wasted in a war for the wrong things. Here, I got some goober peas roasting. You want some?"

"Sho do. I'll just sit out here on the back steps and eat em whilst theys hot."

When Fanny came again to visit Johnny she had the carriage hitched up and brought her mother. She also brought Johnny home-made wine, fresh huckleberries put down in sugar, and pressed chicken jelly she had made herself. And she was wearing a beautiful dress which was years old.

"Gosh, Fanny, I never thought you could cook. You're so pretty, I always figured pretty girls were light-headed and just ornamental."

"I know what you thought!" she said, wagging her finger playfully at him. "How do you feel? I brought a cribbage board." At this, he actually laughed. "I feel better. And you are a tonic. I think I'll be up and around soon if things keep on like this."

No one was buoyed up higher with false hopes than Johnny's mother. When Fanny came and Salina heard Johhny laugh, her heart lifted. He had been lying there quietly staring out at the November sky. This handsome son who was the apple of her eye was too young to die. "Please, God, please let him get well."

During the last week of November Johnny came downstairs with the help of Jim and Grimes. He wanted to sit on the veranda but Big Missy said the wind was too strong even though the sun was warm. He insisted and they bundled him up in wraps and blankets and scarves and let him have his way. He was sitting outside when Fanny came and she was cheered immeasurably to see him sitting up.

"You must feel good, like your old self."

"I do, better than I have felt in a long time."

"Well, you mustn't overdo it. We can't have you taking a setback."

"Yes ma'am. Thankye ma'am," he teased and she laughed.

He went inside the house after a short time, vigorously protesting, but he stayed downstairs all day and Fanny did not go home until nearly dusk. When she left she brushed his lips with a brief kiss, and then he caught her by the wrist and held it in such a grip she flinched.

"Oh, Fanny," he whispered. "I dare not tell you all my heart would have you know."

She nodded, fighting back the easy tears, and whispering over and over, "I know. I know," even after she had run outside the house.

Missy Salina believed firmly to the end that he would have been all right, that he was getting better, that he would have gotten well if the dismaying news from the battlefront had not come just then. The Yankees were fighting at Chattanooga and breaking Bragg's siege. One day's battle was over when they heard the news and all the words were disastrous. In the night she heard Johnny coughing, and she got up and ran into his room. There, when she had made a light, she saw the blood streaming from his lips in great gulps every time the tearing cough would wrack his frame. She screamed for help and sent for Doc. But all night long he bled. And there was nothing they could do.

Early in the morning when Fanny came the house servants had cleaned the bloody bed and Johnny lay flat and wasted and gasping for each breath. She took one look and saw all the pity and pain and the hopeless love in his dying eyes and she fell across the bed sobbing all her bitter frustration and dying hope. He tried to speak her name and clinging to his hand she sobbed out all the endearments she had kept so long to herself.

They buried Johnny in a driving autumn rain with rivulets of water running through the Georgia clay heaped up beside his grave. Big Missy and Miss Lillian and Fanny, all in their deepest black with veils covering their stricken faces, stood in the downpour, uncaring, scarcely knowing that the umbrellas held over their heads were dripping little streams around their feet. This was Big Missy's blackest hour and she complained, "I feel like something has got my heart in an iron grip and is squeezing the very breath out of me." She could not eat or sleep and her body sagged with an aching burden her spirit could not bear.

Goodbye Marster Jeff, Goodbye Mister Stephens
'Scuse this niggah for takin his leavins.
'Spect pretty soon you'll hear Uncle Abram's
Coming, coming. Hail! Mighty Day!
Goodbye hard work wid never any pay.
I'se gwine up North where the good folks say
That white wheat bread and a dollar a day
Is coming, coming. Hail! Mighty Day!

29   Mister Lincoln is our Moses

Jim, the houseboy, was grinning in Randall Ware's face and saying, "Howdy!"

Randall Ware said, "Howdy yourself," before he recognized him. Then he broke into a broad laugh and slapped Jim on the back.

"Where'd you come from?"

"I come from home. But I could ask you the same thing. What you doing here?"

"Man, I been here in Uncle Sam's army, leastwise in General Dodge's work army since way back yonder in Tennessee. How'd you get here?"

"I just walked off. I come here first with young Marster Johnny, but he got hit with a bullet in his lungs when they fought at Chickamauga. You member that?"

"Yeah, I was in Missouri or Alabama. I disremember which."

"Well, I stayed with him and took him back home to his Maw where he died. But I wanted to stay here so bad that when I got there I couldn't make up my mind to stay in that place no more. I guess they was burying him when I just walked off. Didn't nobody pay me no mind. Things getting kinda slack anyways. Grimes ain't got no patter-rollers. All of them is in the war. Big Missy she so outa her mind with grief over Marster Johnny I don't think she knowed nothing else, so-o, I just walked off."

Randall Ware looked off in space and then without looking Jim in the face said softly, "Did you see Vyry?"

"Yep, and your babies too. They fine. They just fine. Them younguns is growing like weeds."

"Brother Zeke is here."

"Say he is, where?"

"In the hospital. He so sick I don't believe he'll make it."

"Say he is! I sure hate to hear that. I seen him once behind the Confederate lines but he make out like he don't know me. I felt bad, but I say to myself maybe he got a reason."

"He was a spy. That's why he didn't say nothing to you. He was scared you mighta give him away to the rebs."

"He oughta knowed better than that."

"Well, you might not meant no harm, but you wouldn't never know what you say might be meaning to them."

"Can I see him?"

"I reckon so. They let me see him yestiddy."

Brother Ezekiel was a very sick man, and when Jim saw him he felt Randall Ware was right. He seemed to be dying. But he was very glad to see them.

"I was just laying here praising the Lawd. I thank God I done see the year of Jubilee. Now, like Simeon, I can pray 'Lord lettest now Thy servant depart in peace.' I knows all my peoples going free someday. Mister Lincoln is our Moses and God done told him to make old Pharaoh set my people free."

"Yeah," said Randall Ware, "but old Pharaoh ain't never done no such thing yet."

"Well, he gonna, he ain't listen to God nor Moses the first time, but when the angel of death come by he let em all go."

"Is they anything we can do for you? Anything you want."

"Naw. I'm all right. I reckon my time ain't long, but I ain't grieving bout nothing now.

One of these mornings bright and fair
I'm gwine take my wings and try the air."

And when he died, it was Jim and Randall Ware who dug his grave and begged the army preacher to read the Bible and pray and say a few words over him. He would be buried here in the winter camp of the Union Army.

"How old do you think he is?" the army preacher asked Jim and Randall Ware, but they shook their heads.

"I reckon he might be nigh on to a hundred," said Randall Ware. "My wife, Vyry, said he was a grown man when her Maw died, and now she's a grown woman. Every since she can remember he was an old man."

"That's funny," said Jim, "but he never seemed old to me."

"That's cause he could get around so spry and he walked so many far places."

"He was a good man."

Randall Ware said to Jim, "You know I coulda gone East with General Grant. They need blacksmiths all over in this war."

"Yeah, but I reckon I knows why you didn't."

"Why?"

"Well, some of these days Mister Sherman gonna cut loose through Georgia, and I reckon you'd rather follow him."

Randall Ware grinned. "Yeah, I got me a shop and a grist mill, a anvil waiting for just my own individual hand."

"Yeah, and them babies what Vyry's got down there waiting for you, hanh?"

"Yeah, and them babies."

Many are the hearts that are weary tonight,
Wishing for the war to cease.
Many are the hearts that are looking for the right,
To see the dawn of peace.

30   Action at Olustee

As the year 1863 came to a close a bleak atmosphere settled
over the whole South. The Confederacy had been struck a
mortal blow. Some said that the beginning of the end came
at Gettysburg when Lee's second attempt to invade the North
failed. Others believed that Vicksburg was the crucial turning point when the Federals gained control of the Mississippi
River. "The Father of Waters goes again unvexed to the
sea," as Abraham Lincoln expressed it. Still there were others
who considered the five colorful and amazing battles fought
in the Tennessee Mountains as equally decisive, for they broke
through the gates to Georgia and Virginia and made the subsequent strategy of the "Anaconda" possible for the Federals.
In any case, 1863 marked a turning of the tide in the winning
of the war by the Union forces. It was clearly decisive in a

psychological sense. The morale of the North was lifted. The despondency of the South was increased.

That year was also a high water mark in the lives of the slaves, for the word seeped through to every hamlet and village that Abraham Lincoln had issued a proclamation emancipating the slaves. Whether there was clearly a correlation between the military victories and the Emancipation Proclamation was hard to say. Slavery had always been considered a moral issue in the North, especially by the abolitionists, but the North as a whole was repugnant to the idea that slavery was a real issue in the war. The South protested loudly that it was not. The South declared that the Almighty Dollar was the northern issue but that slavery was not an economic or political issue in the war since slaves were their personal property and the slave states had a right to reject any political proposal that conflicted with their sectional interests. But the more vociferous the protestations on both sides the more obvious it became that slavery *was* the issue.

Now that the slaves, themselves, had sensed this fact, the year 1863 saw a wholesale disappearance of the black people from the southern plantations. Thousands of them were fleeing to the protection of the Union armies. They left the hoe in the field. They left the making of the guns and gunpowder in the factories. They fled from the Confederate fortifications and breastworks for the southern army. The whole work force of the southern states went on a general strike. And what the black slaves had done for the Confederacy under bondage they now did for the Union free of charge, for there was little pay or compensation they could gain from anything they did. It was enough to be free. Freedom from chattel bondage filled the Negro people with exultation with praise to God, and thanks to Mr. Lincoln, the Moses who had come. For. Mr. Lincoln had certainly changed his mind about the black man.

If 1863 marked a turning point insofar as changing concepts and attitudes toward slavery and the black slave, it was no less the revolutionary point in the war insofar as the weapons and the technological aspects of the war were concerned. In 1861 and 1862 until well into 1863 the soldier in the field, especially the infantry soldier and the cavalryman, fought much as Napoleon had fought the war in 1812 against the Russians. But now with the invention of the Minié ball, the repeating rifle, and the longer projectiles, which doubled their former distance, trench warfare had become an absolute necessity.

The navy underwent an even more remarkable change. General Grant had already witnessed at Vicksburg in July 1863 this amazing revolution from the old wooden sail ships to the new iron-clad gunboats. The guns on the boats turned on turrets and the ramming power of these new and faster vessels was amazing. They were moving under the power of steam and the old days of fighting with wooden sail ships were gone forever.

The North had more money, more factories, and more manpower to put these new inventions and methods into use while the South had been depleted of what ammunition, money, and manpower she had possessed at the beginning of the war. Thousands of her bravest sons had died on the battlefields. Many more thousands were dying of diseases that were now epidemic and making death rampant in the South because of increasing deprivation.

Christmas of 1863 passed on the plantation without the usual gaiety. Big Missy was still grieving over the loss of her only son. Vyry tried to help Miss Lillian make Christmas pleasant for the children, but there were no parties. Over the heads of the southern household there hung the fear of the Union Army invading Georgia in the spring. Both armies had gone into hibernation. But the Yankees were camping outside the state of Georgia with nothing to hinder their coming through in spring. True enough, General Johnston was there and the word came down daily that he was going to hold the Yankees and even push them back.

Big Missy's fundamental faith in the Confederacy had never wavered. Although she now felt martyred in the loss of Johnny, this did not disturb her implicit faith in President Jefferson Davis and his conduct of the war. She was somewhat bewildered by the actions of Governor Brown, who declared he wanted no Georgia boys taking part in battle actions outside the state, and yet she could partially understand that they needed protection at home, for after all Georgia must come first. But she also disliked the way he criticized the President of the Confederacy in general. The South must all stand together in order to win the war.

Six weeks after the new year, 1864, had begun, Big Missy said, "Here's a letter, Lillian, from Kevin for you. See what he's saying." Kevin had gone with the infantry to protect the southern border of the state. He wrote home regularly and

Lillian lived for his letters. Her fingers trembled in haste as she opened the envelope.

"February 7 1864—In the Field—C.S.A. Ocean Pond, Florida.

"My darling wife," he wrote, "I am sitting here counting the days before my time is up and I can come home to you and the children. I have only two more weeks here before I am due for a furlough and my two years in the service will be over. I have no intention of re-enlisting."

"Humph," said Big Missy.

"In the first place it would be useless, and in the second place my heart is not in this war. It never was. I am not cut out to be a soldier and above everything else I want to be with my family and do the work I feel more suited to do."

"That's enough," said Big Missy, "I don't want to hear any more." But when she saw Lillian's stricken face and saw her folding the letter as though forbidden to read any further, she relented.

On February 20, 1864, by some strange quirk or accident of fate, one day before Kevin was due to be mustered out of the infantry a battle took place at Ocean Pond. It was entirely a mistake, never intended, but it happened. The men were suddenly aroused and ordered into battle. It all happened so fast that many of them were facing the enemy before they realized what was happening. Unlike Kevin, who was now about thirty years of age, most of these were young callow boys in their teens who had never smelled battle smoke before. By some poignant touch of fate, they were facing a company of Union soldiers where for the first time a brigade had been formed with both white and colored soldiers. Some of the young white southern boys were startled when they saw the black faces and they began cursing. Strangely enough, Kevin felt no fear nor did he have any sense of disaster nor any emotion of anger. He seemed merely watching things from a distance, objectively, as though he had no place here, and had no part in what was happening. Suddenly he stumbled and looked up in the face of a huge black Negro. The soldier had his bayonet pointed at Kevin but what surprised Kevin most was the look of hatred on the black man's face. Kevin raised his own bayonet to protect himself and strike at the same time. As he plunged it into the Negro's groin, he felt the pain of a stabbing knife in his own abdomen and twisting against it he grabbed the other man's gun while turning loose his own. His assailant fell back with a cry of pain, and Kevin struggled in his own mortal agony to pull the blade out of his stomach. Now in a fiery agony of pain he staggered back toward the rear lines, holding and pressing his wound with both hands and hoping to reach safety and a doctor before he collapsed. His wits remained with him, but the pain of the knife did not lessen and he could feel and see the blood gushing out and running in a stream down his leg and foot. He did not remember how far he was away from help when he fell prostrate and to his surprise heard himself saying, "Oh my God, have mercy on me."

Woe for the homes of the North,
And woe for the seats of the South.
All who felt life's spring in prime,
And were swept by the wind of their place and time.
All lavish hearts, on whichever side,
Of birth urbane or courage high,
Armed them for the stirring wars—
Armed them—some to die.

31   Pensive on her dead gazing

All day long in the Big House they were gay with preparations
for a celebration. Kevin was coming home. The children
were chattering and nobody was minding them. Big Missy
gave orders to Caline and May Liza and Vyry much in the
manner of her old self. The house had been cleaned, the food
was baking, and Miss Lillian was the gayest of all. She had
awakened singing. They were not exactly sure which train
he would come on, nor when he would arrive at the house,
because she had had no further message since his letter, but
Miss Lillian felt certain according to the time he had written
that by this time he would come home.

When the wagon came up from the Big Road nobody was
noticing because it was first dark, and strangers were at the
door before anybody realized there was company. When she
heard the knock, for a moment Miss Lillian felt her heart

thump painfully, but she stood still, while May Liza went to the door. Then Liza was calling Big Missy and Lillian, with her heart in her throat, came running. She did not know he was hurt . . . she could not believe what she saw . . . she began screaming even before she saw him lying in the wagon.

"Lucky, ma'am, he ain't in a coffin. Most of the others was. And them that's lying still on the battlefield will be buried where they lie." But it was Big Missy listening to the words of the soldier speaking, his cap in his hand, his face so sad, and his words so grave. Miss Lillian was screaming and crying and those in the house could not tell whether Kevin was dead or alive. He was still alive, but they could hardly get him in the house for Miss Lillian had thrown herself upon him, hysterical and holding him for dear life, heedless of any wound.

Kevin tried to speak but he could only point to his wound. Inside the house, he tried to explain while they tried to quiet Miss Lillian. The children came to see their father with solemn faces, and seeing the twisted look of pain in his eyes, they too began to cry. For a short while the place was in pandemonium. Big Missy recovered first and firmly began to set the house in order.

The surgeon general had sewn Kevin's wound, but he had warned that the sutures were not strong. Inflammation or blood poisoning could burst the wound open again, hence he must be careful.

"I was determined to make it home," he explained finally.

They got him in bed and sent for the doctor. Old Doc stayed inside the closed room a long time examining and probing the wounded Kevin. Once Kevin cried out aloud, and when the doctor came out he was shaking his head and Big Missy could only bite her lips, while Lillian, who had never ceased her sobbing, now wept silently.

The next three days passed in a gloomy darkness with the pall of death hanging over the house. Not for an hour of the life left to Kevin was he free from the agonizing pain. The suffering was so acute that he literally prayed to die, and when he did, it was his heart that could not bear the strain and simply ceased to beat.

There was a bitter cold wind whistling in the pines on the day they buried him. Lillian, whose tears had flowed incessantly, stood twisting her wet handkerchief in a ball, her shoulders heaving and shuddering like a child, her lips still tonelessly calling her dead husband's name. Death had come three times in three years to the Dutton household, and the whole crushing burden of the war seemed to lie heavily on this one young widow's shoulders. A silence seemed to shroud the whole place. The children moved and spoke in whispers while their mother scarcely noticed them but sat listlessly looking out of the window. Every day she went to visit Kevin's grave.

Caline whispered to Vyry, "How long can this go on?"

And Vyry shook her head. "Lord knows. Only the good Lord knows."

But Big Missy, as stoic as ever in this black hour of grief, despite the fact that she had seen two soldiers in gray come home to die, busied herself with the making of a Confederate flag, gray with bars crossed and studded with stars. Proudly she hung it over the front door that all who came might see the patriotism of her stricken rebel home.

You ain't worth a Confederate nickel!

32   *Confederate specie*

Big Missy was reading the newspapers. The news was old and all the information from the battle front was depressing, but she read each item with varying degrees of interest. She knew that the Yankees were planning to invade Georgia; that their spring offensive would come any day. The torrential rains now criss-crossing Georgia would be more than welcome as a deterrent to the offensive if there were not so much suffering among the people from dangerous fevers and such delay to the farmers and their spring planting. She glanced at a reprint from one of the Virginia papers and she began reading one item with avid interest:

A. S. Buford, Esq., Ch'm. Comm. on Banks
The currency is at a fearful depreciation, and mortifying and alarming as the fact may be, the process of depreciation is rapidly going on. A limit to its decline cannot be assigned, unless there be a prompt termination of the issue of new notes.

Here she looked up from the paper and glanced out the window toward the hill where her dead lay sleeping. After a moment she read on:

> The inquiry admits of a solution which dissipates the apprehension, that the expenses of the war, however large the scale on which it may be conducted, need not subject us to a suspected and depreciated currency, and the Government finally to repudiation and bankruptcy.

"Oh, no," she cried out in alarm, "this must not be!" Now her eyes scanned the page more feverishly. There was no question in her mind but that the loyal southern people would respond to any call for sacrifice.

> It needs only the combined action of the States, their citizens and their banks and other stock companies; and to this they should be impelled by the considerations that supplies will be augmented, prices reduced, and the expenditures of the Government, now at a fabulous amount, reduced to limits which may be contemplated without alarm.

Why doesn't he get to the point and tell us the plan?

> The plan requires a large sum of money, but one within the capacity of the Confederacy, provided the country will yield its assent to the economical and patriotic considerations which back an appeal for an instant and thorough financial reform. The excess of their currency must be admitted to be a fair measure of the ability of a people to contribute to an object of great and pressing necessity.

Suppose, she thought for a fearful moment, *people do not see this?* Her heart throbbed painfully and she fought to overcome the distressful sinking feeling that almost overwhelmed her.

> There will, we are induced to hope, be very little opposition to this plan. All must feel the necessity of reducing the currency and stopping further issues. All feel that this cannot be effected unless a large proportion of the outstanding circulation be gathered in.

Well, she reasoned, *if it is known soon enough, this can be done.*

> This plan for accomplishing the object is the best that we have yet seen, and it has the very great advantage of having received

the endorsement of Mr. Memminger who will recommend it to Congress.

We shall resume this subject at a future day.

When she had finished reading the article, Missy Salina turned to the *Macon Confederate and Telegraph* and read where Congress in agreement with this plan and under the advisement of Secretary Memminger had passed a law on February 17, 1864, requiring the people to turn in their paper currency and buy long-term war bonds at 4 per cent interest. If bills of large denomination, that is, from one hundred dollars up, were not turned in by April 1, 1864, and bonds bought, the holders would suffer a further reduction in their paper currency of at least one third its face value. In the case of small bills of a dollar, two dollars, and five dollars, each would be exchanged at the rate of three old dollars for the purchase of two new dollars.

Missy Salina sat thinking for a few moments. She looked at the present date, and then she called Miss Lillian. Her daughter sat in a stupor as usual. When her blue-gray eyes were not suffused with tears and she was not looking out of the window in the direction of Kevin's grave, she sat staring vacantly at her hands or even at the wall. Now her mother spoke again to her, this time more sharply.

"Get up, Lillian, and put your things on. We're going to town."

Smith Ambers Barrow was the sole banker in the county. He was neighbor and friend to the Dutton family, having known John Morris Dutton from boyhood. Their families had grown more intimate through the years and their associations were bound by business and pleasure. Mr. Barrow was a man of medium height with a middle-aged paunch and a slightly balding head. He had a way of rubbing his palms together when he approached his prospective clients that reminded one of the obsequious manner of an undertaker. Every day at the bank he wore a cut-away suit with striped trousers and a high collar with a cravat. For a man who was an expert with horses and dogs he looked more the part of a banker than sportsman. When he saw the Dutton ladies alighting from their carriage with no coachman to assist them or to tie the reins of their horses to the hitching post, he went outside to meet them and directed one of the hands at the bank to do the necessary chores.

The delicate beauty of Mrs. Lillian MacDougall was in sharp contrast to the haughty bearing of her beautiful mother. Lillian was diffident and fragile looking in her widow's weeds. The black clothing and veil swathed her from head to toe and served to minimize her size and dwarf her personality while at the same time it heightened her blonde and porcelain beauty. Mrs. Salina Dutton, on the other hand, swept through the bank doors with an assurance that only years of capable managing had given her. She was a big woman, but well shaped and with a commanding presence. She extended her black-gloved hand to Banker Barrow.

"Hello, Smith, I've come to change my currency."

"Of course, Salina, step right this way."

Miss Lillian murmured Mr. Barrow's name and extended her hand, but withdrew it quickly when he ignored it and seemed embarrassed when he looked at her. He spoke her name abstractedly, briefly rushing through the formality of a greeting.

"How are you, Lillian, my dear?"

Lillian wanted to say, "But I'm not your 'dear', Mister Barrow." Instead she asked, "How is Addie?"

"She's fine, just fine. Very busy with war work, you know. Doing her patriotic duty."

"I can just imagine," thought Lillian but she lowered her eyes and said nothing.

They were seated on large hard chairs in Mr. Barrow's private office. To Lillian's surprise her mother was not only taking out a large wad of paper money from her hand bag but some other papers as well.

"I want to buy five thousand dollars' worth of bonds, Smith, and I also want to turn these other securities in the form of stocks and cotton investments to help the Confederacy in any way I can."

Smith Barrow's eyes widened but he only murmured, "Of course, Salina," in his most unctuous manner.

"But, Mama," said Lillian, "suppose we lose? We'll lose all those investments, won't we? And you know the very last letter Kevin wrote he said we are not going to . . ."

"Lillian! Please! You know nothing about business, my dear, and I do. We are going to win the war. Every patriotic Georgian knows that, and there'll be no ifs and buts about it. I'm sure poor dear Kevin meant well. After all, he sacrificed his life for the Cause. Surely we can sacrifice a few investments."

"Salina," said Smith Barrow, "I feel it is my duty to warn you that this is a gamble, a patriotic gamble I grant you, but a gamble just the same. Should anything go wrong, you would have placed vast holdings in jeopardy."

Salina Dutton leaned forward and looked Banker Barrow in the eye.

"Do you mean to tell me, Smith Ambers Barrow, that you are so much as daring to hint that the Confederacy will in any way fail to triumph? How can you sit there and doubt when my late husband spent his last working days bringing the Confederacy to birth? When my only son lost his life on the battlefield? When I have only in this past six weeks buried my son-in-law, too, who gave his life for the Cause? Are you telling me my money is more than they, or have they died in vain?"

Mr. Barrow's face began to redden.

"Believe me, Salina, it is only because of John and Johnny and Kevin that I am conscientiously trying to advise you. For their sakes, I would feel I had betrayed their memory and their friendship if I let you place in jeopardy what they have left behind for their loved ones. I honor them and their heroism. They are my sacred and honored dead, too, believe me."

"I appreciate your concern, Smith, but this is what I wish to do, and I do not believe there are any unnecessary risks involved. Thank you just the same."

And drawing on her wraps, she rose haughtily and called to her stricken-faced daughter, "Come, Lillian!"

What does you know bout Marster Lincum?
Marster Lincum be everywhere.
He walk de earth like de Lawd!

33   General Sherman is in Georgia

All during the winter of 1863-1864 the Union Army in the
West dug down deep in its wooden huts on the Tennessee
border of Georgia. General William Tecumseh Sherman was
now in command of all the forces General Grant had left in
the West when he moved East to give battle in Richmond.
Although the two generals had many ideas of war in common, General Sherman was considered far more radical, more
impetuous, and more tempestuous. It was his belief that in a
war the good and the bad suffer alike, and there can be no
ameliorating circumstances where the enemy is concerned.
But it was General Grant who had ordered Sherman to carry
total war into Georgia, to destroy the heart of the Confederacy, and to leave nothing that the southerners could use
to advance their cause when the Union Army had moved out
of the state.

Early in May the gigantic Union Bear began to shake itself awake from long hibernation. The sleeping camp began to stir itself. The Union Forces were ready to strike a mortal blow against Georgia and both Randall Ware and Jim, the houseboy, were in those forces.

What concerned both Randall Ware and Jim, more than the spring thrust of Sherman's three armies into Georgia, was the growing number of runaway slaves who were finding their freedom at the Union lines. Now, whole families were arriving together, those who had been allowed to remain in slavery together. Young mothers with babies wrapped in one rag, old men walking with a stick, young field hands scarred with the whip and the branding iron, some with broken arms or legs encountered while trying to escape. And they had absolutely nothing. They begged the army to feed them, to clothe their bodies, heal their diseases, and let them hang-on.

Jim was now a barber in one of the Union armies, while Randall Ware continued to work with General Grenville Dodge on railroad jobs, for Sherman was tearing up or repairing railroads all along the way. But there were other black people who could do little and thought that freedom meant doing less. When the general or the quartermaster or staff officer asked what they could do, they answered by telling what they used to do for marster.

"You ain't with marster now. Here you can either cut wood or cook, tote water, or work in the commissary. I don't care which. I don't know which."

When Sherman took Atlanta and ordered the city to be evacuated of all its civilian population, Randall Ware contracted fever. Jim was shocked to see this powerful black man suddenly incapacitated. It irritated Randall Ware. One day he felt terrible, had fever, and couldn't hold his head up. The next day he tried to work. When he was asked how he felt, he insisted, "I'm all right." But after two months in Atlanta, he found himself less and less useful and when Sherman left in November, Randall Ware was forced to stay behind.

King Cotton's dead
And Sambo's fled . . .

34   *What's that I smell?*

One morning just after breakfast, Mister Grimes appeared at
the front door. Big Missy was just going out to see him when
he met her halfway. There he stood resplendent in his Confederate uniform of gray and gold.

"Why, Mister Grimes, what's the meaning of this?"

"Ain't nary a nigger left on the place, ma'am. I'm going to
the army, fact of the business is, I'm already enlisted as you
see, and I'm on my way to Macon to defend that city."

"And your wife and family, what about them?"

"They're already on their way to my wife's people up in
the hills."

"They could have stayed here."

"Yes'm. I thought you wouldn't mind, but my wife she
wanted to go home."

"Well, then, all we can do is wish you Godspeed, Mister

Grimes. I know it is your patriotic duty to go. We need all the
soldiers now we can get. But remember, when the war is over
we'll be looking for you to come back. You've got a job here
as long as the place stands."

"Thankye ma'am. I 'preciate that, I really do. Well, ma'am,
goodbye."

"Goodbye, Mister Grimes."

It was hot summertime but there was nothing humming on
the plantation. The Big House ticked like a huge clock that
had suddenly wound down to a slowly deliberate pace. The
war news occupied all Big Missy's waking moments. She or
Miss Lillian hitched up the buggy and went to town once or
twice a week to get the mail and the papers. Even when there
was no mail and the papers repeated the same news, "Sherman
is in Georgia", they sometimes picked tidbits of information
around the station or at the bank or in the cotton shipment
offices that were virtually shut down while idlers stood
around. Sometimes Miss Lillian took her young son, Bobby,
with her. Bobby was nine years old, the same age as Vyry's
Jim, but he was growing old enough to understand what the
war meant. He knew that his grandfather and uncle and
father were all dead because of it and now he was the man
of the house. His mind was alert and although he looked like
his father he had the fire in his personality that his Uncle
Johnny and his grandmother Salina possessed. Day after day
he heard his mother repeat,

"I wish the war would end and all this senseless killing
cease."

"It can't end until we have justice," said Big Missy, "until
we drive out the Yankees who have invaded Georgia."

"And then it won't bring back all our loved ones."

"No, but they will not have died in vain."

"Mama, do you actually think things will ever be the same
again?"

"Why not? I tell you one thing, I never want to live to see
the day when niggers are free and living like white folks."

In the middle of July, Big Missy made up her mind to go to
Andersonville. Her fields were idle and there was not even
one good-sized nigger to hoe the weeds around her door.
Vyry's Jim was big enough but Big Missy declared, "He's a
simple little nigger who just grins and says 'yas'm' and then
won't do a thing." If she hoped ever to make a crop again, to
keep her place looking like anything, or even to recuperate
from her financial losses she would have to have help and

have it fast. Mules were feeding in the fields, cows and horses grazing where the land should be making good crops for harvest. What kind of harvest would they have and who would do the harvesting?

She had read in the papers early in the spring that there was a prison in Andersonville with Yankee prisoners. "Maybe," she thought, "there're some niggers too."

She ordered Vyry to pack food and told Lillian to get the children ready. Then on second thought she decided to take her whole household, Caline, May Liza, Vyry and her children too. She would at least know where they were and not give them the temptation of trying to run off. With Grimes gone, she didn't know what she would do if these niggers suddenly got notions in their heads. She decided to harness a covered wagon as well as a buggy. The journey was about thirty-five miles and it might take them a week altogether. The wagon would give them a place to sleep. It was like a picnic for the children. Miss Lillian, as usual, was impassive and indifferent. "Who'll feed chickens, and hogs, and take care of all the stock while we're gone?"

To solve this problem Big Missy enlisted the aid of both neighboring families, the Barrows and the Crenshaws. She didn't want them to get too curious nor to think she was growing apprehensive, so she said she would be back in a day or two.

Fortunately, the hot summer sun had baked the clay roads hard and, except for kicking up dust now and then, they made good time traveling. After they left town, Big Missy had to ask her way several times, going northeast, but in the early afternoon of the second day their noses could have told them the way. The air smelled as if all the privies in Georgia had been emptied on the wind, and May Liza put her hand over her nose and said,

"Hmmmmm, what's that I smell? It stinks just like a shitpot."

The dismal rank pigsty of the stockade-pen at Andersonville was so repulsive they could not linger near the place. The Yankees were dying by the thousands every day and rotting where they died. Big Missy transacted her business with the jailers and prison officials with greater dispatch than one could have imagined. The answer everywhere to everything was "No." First, there were no black prisoners because there were explicit orders not to feed and keep niggers for exchange. Either put them to work, send them back to their masters, or in the case of injury and battle wounds, shoot them.

The horses fairly flew home and Big Missy only had to say "Gidyap" once or twice.

The trip was tiring because they scarcely stopped for rest and they made it in three and a half days from home and back again. They arrived at the plantation before dark on the fourth day but Vyry would never forget the horror of Andersonville.

Now Big Missy could hardly keep from the household her growing anxiety. What was worse, late in July word came that the Feds and Rebels were fighting a terrible naval battle around Mobile. Sherman was threatening Atlanta and the number of Confederate desertions grew with the battle lists of wounded and dead, outnumbered only by those dying of pestilence.

August came to Georgia and with it the twilight of the Confederacy. The weather was hot and sultry and the atmosphere of the Big House, except for the giggling and laughter of the children, black and white playing together, was one of deepening gloom. Big Missy complained one morning to Miss Lillian, "My head aches so bad I feel like it will split in two." Caline got the camphor smelling-salts bottle and May Liza fixed cold compresses. The spring water was the coldest they had since there had been no ice harvest at the plantation the past year. All day long Big Missy's head ached and throbbed and Miss Lillian was constantly hushing the children's noise: "Sh'sh, your grandmother's head aches and she can't stand all that noise."

On the morning of August 6 the plantation was jarred awake in the early dawn by a booming noise that was louder than a clap of thunder and like nothing they had ever heard before. Vyry could have sworn the earth shook. Caline said, "Jesus have mercy, I believe my soul the world done come to an end!"

In less than an hour the noise began again and this time it continued at intervals of fifteen minutes apart. Big Missy looked at the stricken face of Miss Lillian and said, "What you think in the name of God is going on?"

"I don't know, but if it's what I think it is . . ."

"Well, God's body and soul, what you think it is?"

"Don't get upset, Mama, I think it's the big guns."

"Big guns? Name of God, where?"

"I don't know, but they must be close."

As if to corroborate her fears, Banker Barrow sent word to tell Big Missy the big Yankee guns were firing at a rebel gunboat on the Chattahoochee not more than twenty-five miles away. But Miss Lillian got the message and did not tell her mother, seeing how alarmed she was. Miss Lillian was glad to see the messenger not only because of the mystery of the big guns but because she was worried about her mother. She sent word, "Tell Doc that my mother's not feeling well, has been complaining of her head for two days now, and ask him if he can't get out here sometime today."

All day long the booming noise continued. Sometimes the noise was so shattering that the pictures on the walls would fall and the china in the cupboards shake. Under the stress of heat and noise some of Big Missy's fine crystal tingled and broke. At noon May Liza came down to the kitchen to get a tray of food for Big Missy and a silver pitcher full of cold water for drinking and cold compresses.

"I clare fore God, she scared to death of them guns. Every time one goes 'boom' she jumps and runs back and forth through the house just a farting, poot-poot-poot."

It was Caline who said later in the afternoon to Vyry, "I believe she done lost control of her body, her bladder and her bowels. We just emptying one slop jar after another."

It was late in the afternoon when Doc came and as he entered the house Miss Lillian screamed to Caline and May Liza, "Come quick, Mama's on the pot and I can't get her up."

And the guns boomed on relentlessly.

Old Doc did not want to believe every symptom that told him that Big Missy had suffered a massive stroke. There was nothing to do but keep her in bed, try to keep her clean, bathe her face with cool water, and let her rest.

By midnight she was speechless, but the guns were still tearing their world apart. All night long the guns continued to hammer away. Only the children were put to bed in the Big House. The four women sat up and constantly attended Big Missy. She was sleeping but they felt it was an unnatural sleep. She could not feel any pain and they could not communicate to her. When the earth-shattering guns were not booming, the four whispered to each other through the night.

Miss Lillian said, "Vyry, do you think she's any better?"

"No, Miss Lillian, I don't think she gwine be no better."

Lillian fought back the tears and kept standing over her mother. Sometimes she would speak to her, "Mama! Mama, can you hear me?" But Big Missy did not answer. Toward morning they took turns dozing and each cat-napped while sitting up straight in a chair.

So in the dawning light of August 7 they felt such an unnatural stillness that at first they did not know what it was—for at last the guns were quiet. Big Missy, too, was dead.

The three servants tried to comfort Miss Lillian, who wept silently.

"I'm all alone now, Vyry. I'm all alone."

"You ain't alone, Miss Lillian. You got your babies. We's all still here."

"Oh, Vyry, please don't leave me. I'm all alone now. Please don't leave me." And suddenly she clung to a confused but sympathetic Vyry. But Big Missy Salina would surely have her last wish. She would never live to see niggers free and living like white folks.

Say, darkeys hab you seen de marster
Wid de muffstash on his face
Go long de road sometimes dis mornin
Like he gwine to leab de place?
He seen a smoke, way up de ribber
Whar de Linkum gunboats lay.
He took his hat, an lef berry sudden
An I spec he's run away.
De marster run? Ha, ha!
De darkey stay? Ho, ho!
Hit must be now de kingdom coming
And de year of jubilo!

35   *"We'll hang Jeff Davis from a sour apple tree"*

When the guns were silent on the Chattahoochee River on
August 7, 1864, they marked the end of the naval battle of
Mobile Bay, and the final success there of the Union blockade. The war in the West was rumbling toward its bitter end.
Sherman was nearing Atlanta, and he entered that city after
hard fighting on September 1. The state of Georgia was in
turmoil; the Confederacy was tottering; and the people cried
out first against the enemy invading their land, and then
against the southern government for its manifold failures.
Jefferson Davis was the target of many political foes. The
Governor of Georgia, Joseph Brown, blamed President Davis
as much for the failure of the Confederacy and his conduct
of the war as the people had blamed Lincoln in 1863 for
emancipating the slaves. While Sherman was resting his army
in the evacuated city of Atlanta the rest of the Georgia coun-

tryside heard how he had destroyed their factories and burned their brick buildings and how the ruins of the city were still smoldering.

President Davis decided to come to Georgia and speak to the people in person, with the hope that he could bolster their falling morale and perhaps shame some of the deserters back into the losing Cause before it would be too late. He spoke in Macon and the people flocked to hear him and to applaud his highly rhetorical oratory.

Miss Lillian would have gone to Macon to hear him, but with her mother's death still fresh in her mind, and less than six weeks' lapse of time since then, she had no inclination to go anywhere. She read his speech in the *Macon Confederate and Telegraph*. She wanted Vyry and Caline and May Liza to listen to the speech while she read and she could not understand why they were not genuinely interested in the fortunes of Mr. Jefferson Davis and what that eloquent gentleman had to say. Caline and May Liza promised with straight faces to listen respectfully, but Vyry begged off by saying she had work to do.

Mr. Davis was introduced by former Representative Howell Cobb, who had become a general in the Confederate Army. In his opening remarks President Davis compared the citizens of Georgia to the Russian people in their fight against Napoleon and predicted the same fate awaited Sherman as awaited Napoleon in his retreat from Moscow:

> What though misfortune has befallen our arms from Decatur to Jonesboro, our Cause is not lost. Sherman cannot keep up his long line of communication; and retreat sooner or later he must. And when that day comes, the fate that befell the army of the French Empire and its retreat from Moscow will be re-enacted. Our cavalry and our people will harass and destroy his army as did the cossacks that of Napoleon, and the Yankee General, like him, will escape with only a body guard.

He complimented the women of the Confederacy for their noble spirits of sacrifice and urged all deserters to consider the women and children left in the path of the enemy. He reminded them that the women had never faltered in their loyalty or their sacrifice:

> I know of one who had lost all her sons except one of eight years. She wrote me that she wanted me to reserve a place for him in the ranks.

He urged the young girls to choose for their sweethearts and

husbands the Confederate veterans with an empty sleeve
rather than one who had exploited the Cause and stayed home.

> To the young ladies I would say when choosing between an
> empty sleeve and the man who remained at home and grown
> rich, always take the empty sleeve . . . You have not many men
> between 18 and 45 left . . .

Miss Lillian's eyes brimmed with tears as she thought how
true this was with Johnny and Kevin sleeping with her parents
here on the old home ground. He spoke of the touchy and
difficult subject of prisoner exchange which was complicated
because of the question of slaves:

> Butler, the Beast, with whom no Commissioner of Exchange
> would hold intercourse, has published in the newspapers that if
> we would consent to the exchange of Negroes, all difficulties
> would be removed.

In his closing remarks he pleaded again that the deserters
would return to the army:

> It is not proper of me to speak of the number of men in the
> field, but this I will say, that two-thirds of our men are absent
> —some sick, some wounded, but most of them absent without
> leave.

That both the Virginians and the Georgians thought theirs
was the most deserving front and men should be sent from
one to the other:

> I have been asked to send reinforcements from Virginia to
> Georgia. In Virginia the disparity in numbers is just as great
> as it is in Georgia.

He had but one hope, that deserters would return to their military posts:

> With this we can succeed. If one-half the men now absent without
> leave will return to duty, we can defeat the enemy. With that
> hope I am going to the front. I may not realize this hope, but
> I know there are men there who have looked death in the face
> too often to despond now. Let no one despond. Let no one
> distrust, and remember that if genius is the beau ideal, hope
> is the reality.

Even to a distraught and grieving Miss Lillian it was clear that
President Davis's speech was an admission of defeat, that the

people were losing their will to fight, and that they were being overwhelmed on all fronts by the Yankees.

Sherman did not attempt to keep his communications with Chattanooga, for he recognized the difficulties facing him from Confederate General Hood in Tennessee, and from the cavalry units of Wheeler and Forrest moving through Mississippi and Tennessee and into Georgia. He therefore decided against fighting the gradually diminishing Confederate forces whose annihilation could gain him nothing. Instead, he asked General Grant for permission to push through the countryside living off the land and at the same time destroying all the resources of war remaining for the Confederates' use in Georgia. This was what General Grant had originally asked him to do anyway. Bands of guerrilla fighters were now making last ditch stands in all the outlying wooded sections, along the roads, and at such strategic points as bridges. But these were no deterrents against Sherman in his new method of all-out war against everything in his path. His soldiers were moving in a wide swath of twenty-five to sixty miles, spreading out across the land with special bands of "bummers" who were foraging, pillaging, and burning all along the way. His men were tearing up railroads, heating them to a malleable state and then twisting them around telegraph poles. The people called these Sherman's "hairpins" and calling cards. Never before had Georgians seen such wholesale destruction and utter devastation. He took their cattle and hogs and chickens, their provisions stored against the oncoming winter, their crops barely harvested, ransacked their barns and burned and destroyed their houses as well as their factories, terrifying the country folk as well as leaving them destitute. When the outraged people complained to General Hood and he wrote an official letter of complaint, General Sherman replied, "War is Hell," and those who started it must be made to suffer for it. He explained that he was merely making war, total war, against a completely belligerent people. What was more, he said he intended to make Georgia howl before he was finished.

While Sherman was moving from Macon to Milledgeville to capture the capital city, word reached the plantations around Dawson that he was going next to Andersonville to relieve the Union prisoners incarcerated there, and since this was less than thirty-five miles away, terror gripped the whole community.

One morning late in November, Fanny Crenshaw made a

personal call to the Dutton plantation. Fanny was still wearing black for Johnny, which Lillian could not understand. She had remarked about this fact to her mother, Missy Salina, shortly after Johnny's death, but Big Missy defended Fanny and said she quite understood her feelings. Lillian could hear her mother saying, "After all, if things had been different, Fanny would have been my daughter-in-law. She always did adore Johnny and I don't see why she shouldn't mourn for him if she wants to. She'll always be like a daughter to me." Lillian had always liked Fanny; they had been the best of friends all their lives, but she wasn't certain how any one could be sure that Johnny and Fanny would have married. Fanny had not come often after Johnny's death but now Lillian was very glad to see her.

"I can't stay long. I just came to warn you that Sherman's on his way, and you'd better hide all your valuables and save whatever food and stock you can. They say he is another Attila the Hun and just tearing up the country. Do you think you'll be safe here?"

As usual, Miss Lillian in her uncertain and diffident way didn't know, but she thanked Fanny anyway. "We'll be all right, I guess. You know, I still know how to shoot a gun."

"Yes, but will you if you have to?"

"I hadn't thought about it. But I guess I still could." Fanny left reluctantly, but Miss Lillian let the news about hiding valuables sink in more deeply than fear for their safety.

"I wouldn't want anything to happen to all Mama's nice things," she confided to Vyry. "She'd never forgive me for it."

Vyry looked at Miss Lillian and wondered if she expected Big Missy to rise up out of her grave, but instead of speaking her thoughts she muttered, "I reckon she would turn over in her grave if she thought the Yankees would ever walk in this house."

Caline and May Liza began to gather whatever Miss Lillian decided she wanted to hide. First they took a chest four feet long and about thirty inches deep and filled it with silver and gold plates and jewelry including Big Missy's huge candelabra, massive and ornate, silver tea and coffee pots and water pitchers, dinnerware, both hollow ware and flatware, and all her precious stones which she kept locked in a little casket. They wrapped these in quilts and counterpanes to protect them. They packed china and crystal in barrels; took down the family portraits from the walls and tied them in croker sacks. By dint of much hard labor, since there were no adult males around to help, they dug pits to bury root vegetables and covered them with pine straw. The hardest to hide was the chest. It was Vyry's idea that they put it in a hollow tree trunk or log near the swamp, so they dragged it there and with both young boys helping, managed to hide it in the huge hollow of an old water oak. One bundle they hid in a well-a long time gone dry. Money they hid in the cemetery. "It's not worth much anyway," said Miss Lillian, "Confederate specie." But the hoard of gold pieces left on the place they buried under the planks between the house and the kitchen.

November was a beautiful, golden month that year. Vyry tried to persuade Miss Lillian to sit out on the veranda in the sun and watch the children play, but Miss Lillian was wilted in spirit and energy and she almost made no effort to do anything.

Christmas on the plantation that year would have passed unnoticed but for Vyry's determination to make the children happy. Caline and May Liza admonished her, "What you cooking all that food for? Ain't nobody here but us to eat it." But with Vyry, at Christmas time it was habit to bake cakes and pies and make molasses candy for the children.

Miss Lillian some days was dreamy-eyed and smiling, but most days she was too depressed to notice much of what happened around her. She still took Bobby to town for the mail and the newspapers even though there never were any, but she seemed afraid to go farther. Thus, the last days of 1864 passed without their knowing that Abraham Lincoln was re-elected President of the United States, or that Sherman had sent a telegram from Savannah to Mr. Lincoln offering him the city as a Christmas gift. Meanwhile Sherman had by-passed Dawson and never come near the Dutton plantation.

Hurrah, hurrah, we bring the Jubilee
Hurrah, hurrah, the flag to make you free!

36   A noise like thunder . . . a cloud of dust

January 1, 1865, the Emancipation Proclamation was repeated in Georgia. But the telegraph poles and wires had all been damaged or cut by Sherman's men in their march to Savannah and the sea, so there was no news, and the people in the backwoods knew nothing. The first three or four months passed without any news from the eastern war front and with little news from Tennessee where the last western battles were being fought around Nashville.

Vyry persuaded Caline and May Liza as well as Miss Lillian that they should try to plant some kind of crop.

"What for?" asked May Liza. "Big Missy never could get the last harvest."

"We got to eat," said Vyry, "and we got the younguns to feed. Leastwise Miss Lillian got hern, and I got mine."

Vyry took the initiative, and to the amazement of the whole

household she set the plow in the field and made more than a dozen long furrows in one day. When the other women saw her determination they grudgingly helped her plant corn, collards, pease, okra, mustard and turnip salad, tomato plants, potatoes, and onions. Miss Lillian seemed to pay less attention to what was going on around her as the days passed, but she smiled and gave her approval to their plans.

The first green shoots were in the fields by the middle of May and Vyry looked at their "crop" with pride and pleasure. Life on the plantation was no longer pure drudgery, with every hour one of hard driving labor. Things were not so hard, but an almost deserted farm with no men was not easy either. Vyry's children were growing. Minna was a quiet one, docile, obedient, and easily controlled, but Vyry was having difficulty trying to train Jim to work.

Early one morning, about the third week in May, Vyry was in the kitchen cooking when all the children came running to alarm the house. They could hear a noise like thunder and the sky was black. Caline and May Liza closed the upstairs windows against a possible thunder storm. But as the rumbling noise grew louder and the black sky obscured the sunlight, they heard voices singing with drums and bugles sounding and in a few minutes they saw that the black cloud was dust from the horses' hooves of a great army of men riding and singing:

> Hurrah, hurrah, we bring the jubilee
> Hurrah, hurrah, the flag to make you free
>
> .   .   .   .
>
> While we go marching through Georgia!

They rode up to the steps, and in less than fifteen minutes soldiers and horses were overrunning the place. They came like a crowd of locusts and the noise was so great that suddenly there was bedlam. Miss Lillian had only just finished dressing and, as Caline said, "I don't believe she ever got her shoes buttoned, and her hair was still hanging down her back in one long yellow plait like she went to bed."

The commanding officer, a major-general, came to the front door and knocked. When May Liza saw for the first time the Union blue uniform, she was so flustered and excited she kept curtseying and bobbing up and down saying, "Come in sir, come right in sir, and make yourself at home."

He smiled and said, "Is your mistress home?"

"Yassah, yassah, she'll be down terreckly. Won't you have a seat in the parlor sir? That's where gentlemens generally goes."

"I'll wait here till she comes, thank you."

Miss Lillian came down the long stairs slowly, her skirts trailing, her blue eyes looking more calm than stricken, and only her husky voice sounding a little startled.

"Good morning, sir."

"Good morning, madam, are you the mistress of this place?" Miss Lillian looked around as though expecting Big Missy to answer and then again at the soldier, his hat in his hand.

"Yes. I reckon I am. I'm the only one left."

"The only one left?" He was puzzled.

"Of my family. My mother and my father, my husband and my brother are all out there." And she pointed vaguely toward the cemetery.

He still looked puzzled and seeing his bewilderment he hastened to say with more alertness than usual but with no asperity, "They're dead."

He saw her agitation because she was ringing her hands. Now he fully understood.

"I'm sorry ma'am. How many slaves do you have on the place?"

"Slaves?"

"Yes, servants?"

"Oh, about five, I guess. Vyry and Caline and May Liza and Vyry's children. I think the rest must have all run away."

"Well ma'am, I am ordered to have all your slaves appear in the yard, and in the presence of you and the witnessing soldiers, hear me read the proclamation freeing them from slavery."

"Oh." Her voice trembled only ever so slightly. "Mister Lincoln's proclamation? I told Mama he had set the slaves free." And then she turned toward the cord to ring the parlor bell, but seeing May Liza and Caline standing gaping in the inner door, she called instead.

"Liza, call Vyry and tell her to get her children and you and Caline come out on the porch. This gentleman has something he wants to tell you."

Vyry would never forget the scene of that morning of the front veranda as long as she lived. Miss Lillian stood in the door with her two children, Bob and Susan, and her arms were around their shoulders. Standing beside Vyry were Caline and May Liza, their faces working though they were trying to look solemn while the man read the paper. Vyry scarcely heard a word he said. It was all she could do to keep Jim still because he wanted to dance a jig before the reading was over. Minna stood quietly beside her mother, holding a corner of Vyry's apron in her hand and, like Miss Lillian's children, she stared curiously at the soldiers. Vyry caught snatches of the long document as the man's voice droned on, "Shall be . . . forever free" and she was caught up in a reverie hearing that magic word. Could it be possible that the golden door of freedom had at last swung open? She mused further, watching the long lines of soldiers standing on Marse John's plantation, and still coming in long lines from the big road, and she was thinking, *There must be no end of them.* Her ears caught the words:

> And I hereby enjoin upon the people so declared to be free to abstain from all violence, unless in necessary self-defense; and I recommend to them that, in all cases when allowed, they labor faithfully for reasonable wages.

He was folding the paper before Vyry realized that the tears were running down her face. Then she turned to go back inside to her kitchen and her cooking.

Jim could restrain himself no longer. The ten-year-old little boy grabbed his six-year-old sister and, lifting her in his arms, began to dance his jig and sing,

> You is free, you is free!
> Minna you is free!
> You free as a jaybird setting on a swinging limb.
> Jubilee, you is free!
> Jubilee, you is free!

And Minna, who was puzzled but excited, smiled and tried to catch some of the contagion of her brother's wild spirits. She laughed and clapped her hands and said, "Free? Free? Free?"

When Vyry got back to her kitchen she found it overrun with soldiers. They had eaten her pan of biscuits and the ham she had cooked for breakfast and the big coffee pot was empty. They were, moreover, all over the barnyard catching the chickens and wringing their necks and hollering, "Fried chicken for breakfast! Come and get it! Fried chicken!" And they took a big black wash pot and made a fire under it in the backyard and inside the kitchen they were breaking open the cabinets taking food out and emptying the flour bin and getting out the lard. Vyry stepped back in amazement. "Scuse me ma'am," then seeing she wasn't the young missus they began to beg her to cook some more food, saying they were hungry.

"If yall will just get outa my way, I'll fix some more food."

Perhaps, if she had known what she was saying, and getting herself into that day, she might have gone out of the kitchen and let them have it. But instinctively she ran them out of the kitchen and began to make pans of biscuits and fry chicken. She fried chicken all day long. She stood so long, cooking as fast as they could scald the chickens and pick the feathers off and dress them, that at last she was too numb to feel anything and she lost track of the time and how late the day was getting.

In the meantime the soldiers were ransacking everything. They broke open the smokehouse and emptied it of all hams and shoulders and middlings, the sides of beef, and the dried mutton. They gathered basketfuls of eggs, cleaned out the springhouse of milk and butter and cream and cheese; loaded the corn into wagons, gathered up all the ducks and geese and turkeys and tied them with strings and ropes. Vyry heard a great yell go up when they found Marse John's liquor. They drank up or carted away all the whiskey, brandy, rum, and wine that was left on the place. They turned loose all the horses and ran some away while they hitched others to all the wagons on the place, the carriage, barouche, and buggy. They found two new calves and took these and all others with the cows. They left an old pesky bull in the pasture. They gave the hogs and pigs a merry chase with sticks and they ran through muddy pig sties catching the slippery, slimy, squealing animals, mud, slops and all, in their arms and boxing them into pens. They set the gin house, that was full of cotton, on fire and burned it to the ground. They took molasses and started strewing it all over the place, in and out of the Big House, up and down stairs and through the parlors making trickling streams all over Big Missy's fine scarlet carpets. They yanked down the heavy silk and velvet portieres and broke up half the furniture.

Behind the soldiers came still another motley lot, more than a mile of freed slaves following the army. They had bundles of rags and some had pots and pans and sqawking chickens and other fowl. They were in wagons and on foot, riding mules and driving little oxcarts. There were gray-haired men and women, young mothers with their babies at the breast and streaming lines of children walking. These people were also hungry, and some were sick and diseased with running sores. One poor old gray-haired woman was driving a cart pulled by a team of goats and she had in the cart every possible thing she could carry, such as sacks of seed and meal, squawking chickens, geese, ducks, and a shoat, iron cooking pots and skillets, a wash pot, quilts and croker sacks, and a big tin coffee pot. One of the soldiers observing her said, "Hey, Auntie, where'd you get all this stuff? You look like the children of Israel coming out of Egypt!" The soldiers laughed but the old black woman answered indignantly, "I buyed it."

"You buyed it? Buyed it with what? Worthless Confederate specie?" And they laughed again.

"Nossah. I buyed it with myself. I work for Marster nigh on to fifty years; ever since I been big enough to hold the hoe. I ain't never even much had enough to eat, had to scrounge around for scraps half the time. When we come away to freedom everything turn wrong-side-outwards. I just took what was mine, cause I buyed it with myself."

Somewhere among the motley crowd was Jim, the houseboy. When Caline and May Liza appeared in the kitchen with him, Vyry was flabbergasted.

"Vyry, look who's here," said May Liza, much more gaily than usual, although she had been bubbling over with joy all day.

"And he come to take me away!"

This was the most surprising news of all to Vyry. All these years she had never thought of Jim and May Liza as sweethearts, but they had worked all their lives in the Big House and Jim was a man in his forties. Come to think of it, May Liza had to be near the same age. Caline was much older. Vyry had never known exactly how old Caline was, but when she was a child and Aunt Sally was cooking in the Big House, Caline was a much younger woman than Aunt Sally. Caline was a middle-aged woman now, more than twice the age of Vyry. Vyry was twenty-eight years old, now that freedom had come to her, but she had not let her mind wander past the business of the morning. It was the middle of the afternoon when Jim appeared. May Liza had her few things tied in a bundle and so did Caline.

"Yall ain't gwine now, is you?"

"Yes we is. We's gwine right now," said May Liza, "Jim says our best bet is to follow the army and they'll be all getting away from here by sundown."

"Why don't you come, too, Vyry?" said Jim. "Me and May Liza is getting marriaged today and Caline gwine live with us soon as we can find a place to stay."

"Where yall gwine, and whichaway is the army headed?"

"We's gwine down in Alabamy. The army is headed thataway now. And Vyry, you might as well, cause I seen the last of Randall Ware."

Vyry's heart lurched painfully at the mention of Randall Ware's name. Her voice was unsteady as she answered Jim.

"What you mean, you seen the last of him, and whereabouts was he at?"

"Last I seen he was sick in Atlanta. Too sick to follow Uncle Billy when he came through Georgia marching to the sea. I seen him on a litter. He was wasted until he was too poor to stand on his feets and he had the fever so bad I doubt he coulda lasted another week. They was sending all the sick and wounded back to Chattanooga and I reckon thereabouts is where they brung him. He bound to be in his grave now. You better come with us."

Vyry felt so weak she had to sit down, and then she trembled so for a moment she couldn't speak. When she did find her voice she was surprised to hear herself saying, "Naw. I don't believe he's dead. I feel like he mighta been sick and couldn't get here by now, but he told me to wait here for him until the war was over . . ."

"Well the war's over now. Mister Lincoln's dead and buried. . . ."

"Aw, naw he ain't!"

"Yeah, and Lee had done surrendered to Grant before ever Mister Lincoln got shot."

"Who shot him? The Confederate soldiers?"

"Naw, but it was a southern white man what shot him. He say some kind of gibberish in a foreign tongue bout Mister Lincoln was a tyrant."

"What is that?"

"I think it means a overbearing ruler like a king."

"Lawd, ain't that a pity! I reckon he done it cause Mister Lincum was trying to help the poor colored peoples."

"Yeah, it just like Brother Zeke said that time, Mister Lincoln sure enough the colored peoples' Moses. He make old Pharaoh get up and git!"

"Where you seen Brother Zeke?"

"He died in the Union camp where me and your free man

Randall Ware was before Randall Ware taken sick. I was right there when Brother Zeke died and I helped to bury him."

"Lawd, I sure hates to hear that. He sure was a good man."

"That's just what we says. Now, is you gwine with us?"

"Naw, Jim, I ain't leaving here now. I gotta feeling he ain't dead and I'm duty bound to wait. But I sure hates to see yall go, and I thanks you just the same."

"Wellum we gwine," said Caline. "I been here all my life and I ain't never seen nothing but this here piece of Georgia woods and I'm sick to my stomach of this here place. I wants to travel and see some more of the world before I die. I had me a husband once, Big Boy, but they sold him away and I think they sold him down in Alabamy. Course that was years ago and I don't know where he's at now, living or dead. I ain't got no where to go, but I'm gwine. I'm free, and I ain't staying here no more."

"I ain't heard tell nothing from Randall Ware but once until today. My youngun, Minna, were a young nursing baby when he went away and she nigh on to seven summers old. I got his younguns and I prays to Gawd to see they daddy one more time in this life. I feels like something down deep inside of me would tell me was he dead. I ain't got nowhere to go, neither, but I'm duty bound to wait."

The sun was still high in the sky when Jim and May Liza and Caline left Marse John's plantation and Vyry told them goodbye. She was still working in the kitchen. Miss Lillian and Bob and Susan came in the kitchen where she was cooking, saying they were hungry, and she fed them fried chicken and bread and went to the back door to call Jim and Minna.

"Maw, ain't we gwine with the soldiers?" asked Jim as he stuffed his mouth full of chicken.

"Whoever give you that notion?" asked Vyry.

"Aw Maw, everybody what's anybody is gwine with the soldiers. We's free ain't we? We ain't got to stay here and work no more is we?"

"Yes, son, we's free and we ain't got to stay, but being free doesn't mean we ain't gotta work, and anyhow I promise your daddy I'd wait here for him."

Jim was crestfallen, but slightly mollified with the promise of his own father. He was excited, however, over the prospect of going with the soldiers and secretly he had been getting a bundle of rags together, too, to follow the army.

Vyry really hadn't promised Randall Ware to wait, but she had promised so long in her mind to stay where he could find her that now it did not make sense for her to go. In the first place, where would they go? She knew that sometime in the future, unless Randall Ware was really dead, he would make it back to his blacksmith shop and grist mill in nearby Dawson. He could make money and make a living for them and give her and their children a home. Maybe her children would even learn to read and write, as he could, and cipher on their hands. She wasn't ready to leave the plantation, not yet.

Jim went outside to tell a newly found friend, a man who was among the contraband freedmen, "My Maw says naw, we ain't gwine with the army. She waiting here for us daddy."

"Oh, I see. How long your daddy been gone?"

"I dunno. I can't hardly remember him. I musta been real little."

"And your sister were a baby?"

"Yassah, I reckon so."

Jim was sharing his fried chicken with his new friend, and the man ate awhile and said nothing. But he was still with the children around the back door of the kitchen when Vyry finally quit cooking and made ready to go to her old cabin for the night.

Bow down, dear Land, for thou hast found
release . . .

37   *The honor of this house . . .*

In the violet twilight the noises of the day were gradually
fading, but the plantation bore the indelible mark of the day's
looting and pillaging, for the devastation was appalling. Vyry
stood and looked, and far as she could see lay the litter and
trash of the departed soldiers. Everywhere over the lawns and
yards and gardens they had built small campfires to cook
food or to burn valuable property on the plantation. The usual
sounds of domestic animals were missing and the night had
an unusual stillness. The air was damp and cool and it felt
refreshing to Vyry, who had spent the day in a hot kitchen.
She felt very uneasy, however, as though an ominous presence
were all around her and some terrible thing of frightening
dimensions, and yet indescribable, hung over her head.

She was bone tired, and, despite the fact that this was the
first day of freedom she had known in her whole life, she felt

dejected over the news that Jim had brought about Randall Ware. She could not believe he was dead. All her hopes for life and freedom were bound up with him. She reasoned, *Perhaps I'm foolish to expect him the first day the soldiers come. He may still be sick or weak from his sickness, but one of these days he'll come along. He's bound to show up here before long.*

She was about to call Minna and Jim, thinking they were nearby, when suddenly a strong arm grabbed her and clapped a big hand over her mouth and she found herself struggling and making muffled noises in her efforts to scream for help and free herself. Jim screamed, and Minna hollered, "Maw!" and then the man who was with the children came forward and beat off her attacker, who soon disappeared in the bushes. Vyry felt so shaken she could not speak. It had happened so suddenly that she still felt the bruising hand over her mouth although the man was gone. The children were still upset and Minna was crying, "Maw, Maw," while Jim kept saying, "Did he hurtcha, Maw, did he hurtcha?" They clung to her, and they had reached her cabin when she saw that her rescuer was still walking nearby. Now she turned to thank him.

"That's all right, ma'am. I'm glad I was still here. If you don't mind I'll sleep here in front of your door tonight and you and your little chaps'll be safe."

Vyry was mute with gratitude and she hurried inside, closed the door and quickly took the children to bed with her, where they slept on their pallets one on each side of her.

Day had not yet broken and Vyry had to fight herself out of the deep dreamless world of heavy sleep to answer the distressing call sounding so loud and clear, so near and yet so far away. There was a banging on her cabin door. The children, startled, grabbed hold of her in fear and said nothing.

"Who knock?" said Vyry.

"Vyry, Vyry, please come and help my mother! It's me, Bobby. Oh Vyry, please come quick!"

Vyry ran out in half her clothes and the man sleeping on the ground in front of her door sat up, too, with the noise. Jim and Minna were following their mother and Vyry ran up to the Big House with her heart in her mouth.

Miss Lillian! Miss Lillian! Vyry had forgotten about Miss Lillian all alone in the house with only Bobby and Susan, now that Caline and May Liza had gone off with Jim, the houseboy. In the house Vyry saw what damage the soldiers had done while she was frying all that chicken in the kitchen. She had not seen this part of the house since early morning when the man read the paper. Now she saw molasses all over the floor, walls dirtied, and chairs broken. She could hardly pick her way gingerly up the stairs to Miss Lillian's room, where she found her.

"Oh, my God," said Vyry, "I ain't never seen sitch a mess in all my borned days."

Aside from the fact that the room was in terrible disarray, with everything thrown in confusion, there were feathers everywhere. The feather bed had been split and all the feathers thrown out. They were all over the molasses-strewn floor. They were sticking to the walls. Little Susan sat hunched in a corner whimpering to herself with her face to the wall, and she was covered with feathers. Poor Miss Lillian lay on the floor in the sticky mess of feathers with her head in a little pool of blood. Her hand clutched feathers. One shoe was off but otherwise she was fully clothed, although the front of her dress was ripped as if someone had tried to tear off her dress. A gun lay close by, also bloodied, but it had not been fired.

Vyry was hysterically calling, "Miss Lillian, Miss Lillian!" but she was unconscious, so Vyry knelt down beside her to see if her heart or pulse were still beating and to her great relief discovered that the poor woman was not dead. Then she turned quickly to her Jim and said, "Jim, go get that man in front of our cabin and you and him go for help fast. See if yall can't get somebody to get a doctor here for Miss Lillian while I straighten up this mess and see can't I get her off this here messy floor."

Jim ran out in frightened obedience to his mother while Minna tried to comfort Susan, who was still crying and whimpering.

Afterwards Vyry wondered how she had managed. She found that all the feather beds in every room had been cut like this one, but she cleared a room of as many feathers as she could, first sweeping them carefully into a pile, and then she made a makeshift mattress of quilts, some of which had been split in rags but were still good, and using what she could find that was not smeared with either molasses or blood she managed to get Miss Lillian in a bed before the doctor came. Then she could see that she had been hit on the head with the gun. Her hair on one side was matted with blood, and her bosom heaved with heavy broken breathing, but she was alive. By the time the doctor came, the day was well along its way and Vyry had tried to clear away most of the debris, but evidences were everywhere of the tell-tale molasses and feathers. In the room where Vyry had found Miss Lillian there were also blood stains.

It was a grim doctor who picked his way through the soiled and wrecked home.

"Name of God, Vyry, whatever in the world did they do here?"

"I dunno, sir, no more'n you, and what you sees here. I was in the kitchen all day long cooking."

"Yankee buzzards! Nothing but scavengers out of hell, that's what they are! You should see what they did to the Crenshaw and Barrow places, burned them to the ground, that's what they did! And why? My God, why? The war is over, the niggers are free, now what more do they want, our last drop of blood?"

Vyry listened and said nothing. *He talk like he talking to Big Missy, and not me, the nigger, Vyry.*

Miss Lillian was still unconscious. She opened her eyes while Doc bent over her and she gave a little moan, but he could tell from the look in her eyes she could not tell him anything that had happened to her. After he had dressed the head wound, the doctor explained to Vyry that he thought the head injury was her worst problem.

"Try to keep her quiet and let her sleep, and we'll just have to let Nature take its course and see what happens."

As he went out again, he kept shaking his head.

"My God," he said, "the honor of this house is dead this morning."

He promised Vyry he would come back as soon as he could to see about Miss Lillian and admonished her to take good care, and Vyry said,

"I will, doctor. I'll do the best I can."

Howdy do, howdy do!
I want a jug of lasses.
Same price I paid before
When I worked on the railroad.

38 *My name is Innis Brown*

"My name is Innis Brown, ma'am, what might be your name?"

"My name is Vyry. Pleased to meetcha, Mister Brown."

And Vyry extended her hand in a friendly greeting to this "contraband" freedman who had slept and kept watch outside her doorway. Innis Brown was a maroon, what the slaves called a "meriney"-colored man. He was tall with crinkly brown hair and pleasant eyes that changed color, and his skin was that high brown that was heightened with yellow and reddish tones. He gripped Vyry's hand in a warm close grasp of friendliness while she looked him straight in the eye. It was hard to guess his age, whether he was twenty-five or thirty or somewhere in between, but he looked strong and husky and able to do a good day's work.

"I made friends with your little boy, here yestiddy," and he patted Jim's head. Jim was watching his mother's face to

see how she liked his new friend. "And your little girl, too,"
he said, lifting Minna's chin with his little finger. "You got
some real cute little chaps."

"Thankye sir. I sho wants to thank you for all you done for
us last night and this morning too, with poor Miss Lillian."

"How she making out now?"

"Well, it's kinda hard to say. The doctor say she may be
all right with rest, but I think it's gonna be a long while."

"Then you won't be moving on, soon?"

"Nossah, I don't hardly think so. I'm kinda waiting here
for my husband anyway."

"Oh, I see. Jimmy told me yestiddy you was waiting for
his daddy."

"Wa-al, yassah, I is. You see he went away before the war
started, but he sent me word to wait here until the war was
over and he'd come after me and the younguns."

"I reckon I oughta be moving on. I was hoping you folks
was moving too and I'd have company. I ain't got nobody
but myself."

Vyry said nothing, but the children spoke quickly.

"Don't go, Innis Brown," said Jim, "stay here a little while
longer with us. Maw, can't he stay a while with us?"

Vyry was embarrassed.

"Yall hush. Mister Brown say he gotta be moving on."

Minna asked, "You gotta be moving on, Mister Brown?"

Innis Brown laughed.

"Tell you the truth, ma'am, I ain't got no wheres to go and
I ain't got to do nothing I ain't got a mind to do. That's the
nicest thing bout being free. I ain't got to work for nobody
now but myself."

"Where'd you come from, Mister Brown, and what did you
do before Surrender? I reckon you was a slave, too, or was
you free?"

"Nome, I wasn't free. I been a slave all my life; ever since
I was big enough to hold a hoe I been working in old Marster's
field, tending taters, cotton, and corn. I ain't never had a
Maw nor Paw, sisters nor brothers to remember. I was a field
hand, ma'am."

Vyry looked disappointed. Yard niggers and field hands
didn't set so high with her, but she thought to herself, *I
mighta knowed it, from the looks of his clothes.* Innis Brown
was wearing the cheap sack clothes of a slave and his toes
were peeping through the cracks of makeshift shoes.

Vyry never did say to Innis Brown that he was welcome

to stay, but he made no move to leave the plantation. Vyry took her children up to the Big House and began to sleep there where she could be near Miss Lillian should she call out in the night. And Innis Brown began to sleep in Vyry's cabin. It seemed to be a natural arrangement that followed an unwritten agreement; while Miss Lillian is sick, and while Vyry is waiting for her husband, and since Innis Brown has no family and nowhere to go, he will stay.

Miss Lillian was like a ghost who crept back to life slowly, and yet seemed to leave half her mind and soul with the dead. The summer came like a sudden surprise. Vyry's corn was tasseling in the fields. She found sugar cane volunteering in the usual places and down near the creek beds she found rice paddies. Vyry was sure that if she took time to look she would find an old setting hen somewhere that had strayed off, but she looked at old bantam roosters in disgust.

"You ain't big enough to make a meal."

Blackberries and wild grapes would be theirs for the picking, both muskedines and scuppernongs. Down in the swamps there were pigs running wild. Innis Brown was a born farmer so he rustled up the scattered leavings of stock and mended a broken-down wagon. What was most amazing, he reckoned there would be enough cotton to make a bale. Meanwhile, Vyry took care of Miss Lillian, nursing her body back to a small measure of her former strength, but feeling her mind slipping away almost steadily. Sometimes it was clear and sometimes it was hazy. Vyry would take a rocking chair and put Miss Lillian on the veranda, but then if she turned her back she would suddenly find her patient walking off and wandering down to the Big Road.

"I thought I heard a band playing and I went to see who was playing the music, drums and bugles, and they were all waving flags."

"Honey, you musta dreamt it. Ain't no bands playing no music round here."

Miss Lillian's little son, Bobby, watched his mother with a growing fear. He set himself the task of watching her, and he tried to talk to her, to make conversation. Sometimes she would look lovingly at him and smile, sometimes vacantly and puzzled, but she almost never answered his questions. The boy grew irritable and Vyry found him frowning and trying to force back tears. When Jim would say, "Let's go play," Bobby would answer, "No, I don't wanta. I halfta watch my mother." Some mornings Miss Lillian did not know her little Susan but would talk like the child she had been when she and Vyry had played mud pies under the trees. This distressed Susan and she would cry as if her heart were broken and could never be mended again. As soon as Miss Lillian came to herself, however, and spoke normally to her little daughter, the child was whole and happy. Bobby, however, could not forget his mother's lapses. They worried him more and more.

Vyry found many supplies missing after the soldiers left. There was no coffee, no flour, no sugar, and no lard. One morning, to her joyful surprise, she heard a "moo-moo" and there at the back door stood a lowing cow, a cow come fresh with a new calf though Vyry did not see the calf and wondered where she was. Innis Brown took Jim and went looking for the calf, and before dusk he brought back the young calf in his arms.

A cow come fresh meant sweet cream and butter and buttermilk plus sweet milk and clabber too. But even though Vyry coddled Miss Lillian and tried to make her eat fresh eggs and drink fresh buttermilk, Miss Lillian was not interested in anything.

Innis Brown had always had a dream, a daydream, something like a castle in the air. He dreamed of a farm of his own, a place further west with a team of mules, with a house for a family, and a cotton crop of his own. Now as he struggled to tell Vyry his dream, she smiled.

"You likes to farm, doesn't you?"

"It's all I knows how to do."

"I can see you makes a good farmer, Mister Brown."

"I wisht you wouldn't call me 'Mister'; first place I ain't useta it, and second place I always calls you Vyry."

"Well, that's my name."

"And Innis is my name."

But Vyry did not want to get familiar with this man's name. She had another man's name written in her heart. The man she loved had always been free, and he had a trade, and a shop, and a grist mill, and a house. He was a town man, and not a farmer. He could read and write and cipher on his hand and he always carried a sack of gold. Someday, any day now, he might come home. And what would he think, if he thought, that is, if he saw she had "took up" with another man? Innis Brown, seeing how she kept her distance from him, knew she was dreaming of another man and wondered if sure enough that man was ever coming back.

Vyry lay on her bed at night and fancied she heard a night bird calling, a whippoorwill.

"He wouldn't have to slip now."

But the summer days wore on and she heard no word from Randall Ware. She was busy all the time. Occasionally she found herself singing. When she sang, the children would stop their playing and come closer to listen, for they loved all her songs—the old slave songs Aunt Sally used to sing, and the tender, lilting ballads of the war, too. In the twilight when the summer fires of the long hot days banked themselves until the smoldering ashes were cooled by the dusk and the starry night and the glistening dew, they sat out on Marse John's veranda and sang, the children and Vyry and Innis Brown with Miss Lillian rocking, apart from all around her. The summer then was like an idyll, a season of peace, when all the agitation of the violent world around them seemed suspended, and they felt secure.

39 *What you waiting here for?*

September days were clear and bright, but the waning summer heat continued to linger over a field of ripening corn and the open bolls of cotton ready to be picked. Innis Brown worked as hard in the fields as Vyry had ever worked in Marse John's kitchen. With the summer ending, Vyry wondered how they would have managed since Surrender if Innis Brown had not happened along.

Miss Lillian's head was completely healed, but she acted more like a child than ever. Vyry watched her in the mornings when they were just getting up, and unless she reminded Miss Lillian about dressing and combing her hair, the young Missy remained listlessly unconcerned. At first, Vyry would help her get dressed for the day and patiently encourage her to put up her hair, but gradually it became very plain to Vyry that Miss Lillian was not just uninterested, she was growing less and less capable of looking after herself. She was as docile and sweet as a child, but she would sit in one place for hours doing nothing, sometimes looking out of the window or rocking on the veranda with Bobby. He was always sitting on the steps or playing nearby.

Old Doc hadn't been out for several weeks, when out of a blue sky one September day he appeared. Miss Lillian was sitting on the veranda smiling to herself, and at first the doctor thought all was well. Bobby was sitting on the steps and he looked up apprehensively as the doctor stooped down to speak to him and then to his mother.

"Why, hello there, Lillian, you look like you're feeling fine this beautiful day!"

She smiled up at him and then said, "I'm waiting for Mama to take me to town. We're going to buy things for my trousseau." Shock wiped the smile off the doctor's face and he glanced back at the boy whose grim unsmiling look told him how aware the boy was of his mother's condition. The doctor kept on through the house and found Vyry, as usual, in the kitchen. She was taking a cake out of the brick oven and as she did she looked up into old Doc's face.

"That cake smells good, Vyry."

"Thanks, Doctor, I don't usually cut a hot cake but would you like a piece with a glass of milk?"

"No, I don't reckon so, I haven't got time to spare. I came to ask you how you think your young mistress is doing?"

"Well, Doctor, I just don't know what to say. She looks all right and I'm sure the place on her head is well. It healed a long time ago, but she don't talk right and she don't act pert."

"That's what I was afraid of."

"What must I do, Doctor?"

"I don't think there's anything you can do, Vyry."

"Doctor, you don't think she gonna stay this-a-way?"

"I don't know, Vyry. I just don't know."

"She been through a whole lot, Doctor, a awful lot, losing all her close kinfolks one right after another, right close together. She sho has had a bad time, and then getting that lick on her head didn't help none."

"Yes, I know. The war was awful, and it affected everybody some way or another. She's suffering from all the effects of the war, but I don't know whether it was the war or the accident that has affected her mind. It may be both."

"You think she's losing her mind?"

"Well, it's clear she's not always in her right mind."

"Oh, Lawd, have mercy! Poor Miss Lillian."

"I was wondering if you knew of any kinfolks left around here who ought to come and see about her."

For a moment Vyry was taken aback, and she caught her breath sharply before she answered.

"Some of Missy Salina's folks come here from Savannay for the wedding, but they was all so old I don't reckon none of them is still living . . . but, oh, yessir, they's some of Marster's kinfolks somewheres down in Alabamy. They useta come every Christmas to visit. Miss Lucy is Miss Lillian's auntie, and I knows she would come if she knowed about Miss Lillian's condition."

"You don't know her name nor whereabouts in Alabama she lives?"

"No sir, I sure don't, but I reckon either Banker Barrow or Marster Crenshaw might would know."

"Well, you know they've had a lot of trouble, too. Lost their home places by fire and then they've had sickness and death, too. But I'll inquire of some of them. Meanwhile, you do the best you can for Mrs. MacDougall."

"Yessir. I'll do my best."

Gradually the days turned golden in the sun; the autumn mornings and evenings distilled a thin mist from the baked earth leaving hazy fog over everything. The harvest time had come again. Innis Brown sensed that Vyry was disturbed, but whether she was worrying over no word from her free man who had not yet come for her and her children, or whether she was worrying about Miss Lillian, he could not feel sure. She did not speak to him at first about the doctor's visit, but he learned about it accidentally.

One day Vyry took Jim and Minna into the fields to help Innis Brown pick cotton. The children had never done any field work before and they were slow. Vyry admitted that she had never really worked in the fields either. "I reckon I never knowed before how hard this work could be."

"It ain't hard, if you useta it and you ain't got nobody driving you with a whip or threatening you with a shotgun," said Innis Brown. "I'd be happy to work in the fields the rest of my natural born life, if the harvest be mine."

"Brother Zeke useta say it ain't no more'n right for a sarvant to be worthy of his hire and make a living wage."

"That's what I'm talking about. I wants to work for myself. I ain't a slave no more, thank Gawd, and I wants to work for myself."

"Well, I reckon ain't nobody hindering you now."

"Does you mean by that I oughta go?"

Vyry was flustered.

"Naw, that's not what I said, but . . ."

"Well, I wants to go. I just been tryna make up my mind where."

"Has you decided?"

"No. But I knows the best way is to go west. That's where all the land is. I was just wondering how much longer you'n your chaps is gonna wait here for your husband. Sposing he ain't coming? And Miss Lillian, she well now, ain't she?"

"Lawd, no, Miss Lillian's troubles now is more worser than death."

"What you mean?"

"Doc talk like she done lost her mind."

"Well, you kinda knowed that, didn't you?"

"Well, I reckon I just didn't want to believe it."

"Well, you gotta mind to face it."

"I reckon so. Doc ask me about her kinfolks. Reckon now he done sent for Miss Lucy."

"Who's Miss Lucy?"

"She Miss Lillian's auntie. I reckon she'll come up here and see about her."

"Whereabouts is she?"

"I told him I think she in Alabamy."

"Then that mean she might take her back with her, and what's gwine become of you and your chilluns?"

"I reckon it ain't come to me what."

"Well, I'm asking you now to marry me and leave here. How long you reckon you can stay here when she go? Your free man may be dead. He sure coulda been here by now."

"Naw, he ain't dead. I knows he ain't dead. Some reason he ain't come, but I knows he ain't dead."

"Well, how long is you got a mind to wait?"

"I figgered he'd be here by lay-by time."

"Well that's right on us, ain't it? You ready to go now?"

"Naw. I ain't got my mind on leaving yet."

"What you waiting here for?"

"I can't leave Miss Lillian here by herself. You knows I can't go off and leave her helpless like and sick in her mind!"

"Well, when her auntie come, will you leave with me?"

"I dunno, I hasta think about it. Maybe. I dunno. If my husband ain't come by then, maybe so."

And Innis Brown, having pushed his point this far, said no more.

We will be de marster,
He will be de sarvant,
Try him how he like it for a spell;
So we crack de Butt'nuts,
So we take de Kernel,
So de cannon carry back de shell;
Look out dar now! We's gwine to shoot,
Look out dar, don't you understand?
Babylon is fallen! Babylon is fallen!
And we's gwine to occupy de land!

40   *One more Christmas on the old home place*

Vyry began to prepare for Christmas but her heart was heavy and though she worked against time trying to do many things, she felt leaden and empty by turns. She and Innis Brown took the children in the woods and found hickory nuts, chinkapins, and black walnuts. Pecans and peanuts were grown on the place, and as usual there would be plenty. There was a good crop of sweet potatoes, and Vyry's Irish potatoes and onions also made a good harvest. The cotton was picked, but the gin was permanently broken and the gin house burned to the ground. Vyry saved kitchen grease and made soap with wood ashes, and from a year's supply of tallow she made candles. The candle molds were not broken, neither was the spinning wheel, so Vyry tried hard to spin and weave and make warm things for the winter for the children.

Miss Lillian was no better. If anything, her mind seemed to go back farther and farther into the past, to happy days —times of her childhood and days when she was growing up in the Big House, before she married, and the happiness she had known with her husband, Kevin. All this saddened Vyry. She felt terribly unhappy over Miss Lillian and it seemed so strange that things had turned out this way for the little golden girl she had always adored since she was a slave child herself growing up in the Big House.

But it was not only Miss Lillian's condition that worried Vyry. She had a nagging worry about Randall Ware. She could not accept the word that he was dead, but if he was alive why didn't he come and get them?

Innis Brown wanted to take Jim hunting, but there wasn't a shotgun on the place. The doctor had taken the gun Miss Lillian had been holding when her assailant turned it to use against her. Not willing to be outdone, however, Innis Brown set traps, and to their surprise he caught a half dozen pieces of wild game, rabbits, squirrels, a possum, and a coon. Vyry decided they would kill hogs, too, and the young heifer born that spring. There would be lots of fresh meat and chicken, but no turkeys and geese for Christmas. She baked cakes and pies, egg custards, sweep potato custards, pecan pies and syrup pies.

"Miss Lucy won't find this cupboard bare even if Big Missy ain't here no more."

As the time drew near for the feasting, however, Vyry worried more and more about leaving the place and going off where Randall Ware could never find them. She was also upset over her promise to leave with Innis Brown. She had promised to marry him, but as she told him, "I'm already married and I don't know that he's dead!"

"Yes, but even so, the law don't hold a woman to a man when he been gone seven years."

"It ain't a question of no law."

"Well, I don't wanta press you against your will, but I don't think you can be too choosy. Of course you can go off some place by yourself and try to raise your younguns, but one thing's certain and two things sure, you ain't gwine stay here much longer."

The whole problem oppressed Vyry so much that one cold December day, just before Christmas, she got Innis Brown to hitch up the one old mule on the place to the make-shift wagon and all of them started into town. Innis Brown could not understand why she wanted to do this foolhardy thing.

"We may make it there and we may not, 'cording to how this here pesky mule has a mind to go."

The wagon was rickety and the mule was balky but they got to town, although they nearly froze before getting there. Vyry wanted to see Randall Ware's shop and grist mill and see if anybody was there or using them. The place was abandoned. The anvil stood cold. The grist mill was ramshackly, and there were big field rats running around looking for corn. At the livery stable nearby she saw only a couple of horses and few people idling there. Miss Lillian, in a very lucid moment, wanted to go by the bank, but there they found to their deep dismay that Mr. Barrow, the banker, was sick at home and the doctor said he was bad off with heart trouble. Minna and Jim had never been to town before, and they wanted to stay all day, but Vyry had accomplished her mission and she said to Innis Brown, "I reckon we might as well be getting on back before it gets late and dark catch us way from home."

After this, Vyry began to set her mind toward leaving. She told Innis Brown she would marry him at Christmas, and if Miss Lucy came, as soon as they could leave, she was willing.

Miss Lucy and her husband came three days before Christmas.

"I just couldn't come no sooner," she explained to Vyry that first night after they had taken off their coats and had eaten supper. Miss Lucy came out in the kitchen where Vyry was clearing away the supper things.

"When I first got the letter from Banker Barrow in the fall I sat right down and wrote if I could I'd come for Thanksgiving, but Mister Porter—that's my husband—keeps a store, a general delivery store, and we just can't walk off anytime. I always did come at Christmas, you know, till the war, and when the war came it stopped folks from going anywhere."

"Yes'm, I know. Wa-al, I'm sure glad you come. I knowed you'd come if you heard about Miss Lillian's condition."

"How long has she been this way, Vyry?" And Miss Lucy almost whispered, her face frowning with her concern.

"Ma'am, I just don't recollect how long. Now since I gotta studying about it, it seem to me she been going off ever since her Paw died, Marse John."

"Well you know I was here for the funeral and I remember how hard she took my cousin John's death. You know his mother and my mother was two sisters, but my mother married a poor man and we never did own slaves. We was always in trade or business and I guess you know how his wife, Salina, looked down on folks in trade. That's the way those high-toned dicty folks in Savannah always was. . . ."

"Well, ma'am, as I was saying, Miss Lillian got worser after the bad shock over her husband's death, but she still wasn't out of her good mind. She just didn't take no interest in nothing and she went down to that graveyard every single day to put flowers on the graves."

"Poor Lillian! She always was a soft, delicate little thing."

"But I reckon the real strain what broke her mind all to pieces, what with all of them dying one right after the other, her paw and brother and then her husband and her mother, was when she got that lick on her head the night the soldiers come."

"Oh, no! Whatever in the world happened to her?"

"Ma'am, we just don't rightly know. Caline and May Liza and Jim, the houseboy, left that evening with the soldiers and when I got through in the kitchen I went home to bed cause I was so tired, but they musta been a lot of them 'bummers' hanging round cause one liketa knocked me down and if it hadna been for my younguns screaming and Innis Brown, a contraband man, no telling what woulda happened to me. But anyhow, I was asleep when Bobby come down there screaming to come see bout his mama and when I got here, Lawd, Miss Lucy you never seen sitch a sight! Miss Lillian was laying on the floor and her head was bleeding and she didn't know nothing, and she ain't knowed much since."

"Oh, my goodness a-life, what did the doctor say?"

"He say the lick on her head was the worsetest. She wasn't hurt nowhere but that lick on her head."

"And she lost her memory?"

"She lost her good senses. She talk about things happened when she was a child and we was playing round the Big House like chilluns do. One day this fall I found her down to my old cabin talking bout she didn't have nobody to play with, everybody was gone, and could she stay and play with me."

Miss Lucy took her handkerchief and wiped her eyes.

Vyry cooked two Christmas dinners. She set the dining room table for Miss Lillian and her children and Miss Lucy and her husband, and placed before them a baked fresh ham with candied sweet potatoes and buttered whole okra and corn muffins and pecan pie and elderberry wine. She set the table in the kitchen for her children and Innis Brown, her new husband. She made ambrosia and cake for everybody, but for her family she cooked the possum with sweet potatoes and collard greens and okra and made a sweet potato pone because that was what Innis Brown said would be real Christmas for him.

She couldn't get excited about being married and she was not jubilant, but he was. Even though she knew this time the state of Georgia would recognize her marriage, she couldn't help remembering when she jumped the broom with Randall Ware and Brother Zeke had married them and everything was so different.

Jim ate so much his stomach hurt. While Vyry was washing dishes and Innis Brown was helping her in the kitchen, Minna came running and crying, "Maw, Maw, come quick! Jim got his head hung up in the pot!"

Vyry was nonplussed. "Hung up in the pot? What is you talking about, gal?"

"He got his head hung up in the pot!"

And Minna was crying and jumping up and down until Jim appeared in the doorway, screaming to the top of his voice but only making a muffled sound because he had his head completely caught inside a little black iron pot.

"My Gawd, boy," said Innis Brown, "what is you done to yourself?"

Every time Vyry tried to get the pot off the boy yelled louder. Finally Vyry got an idea. She took the skillet where she had cooked the possum and she filled her hands with grease, then she began to work around Jim's face and around his ears until she could get her hands inside the rim of the pot and gradually she worked him out. His face was full of possum grease and he was still bawling, but now that he was free everybody laughed.

Vyry figured it would take a week to get everything packed for Miss Lillian to take to Alabama, but Miss Lucy said, "We can't carry half this stuff, and we got nowhere to put it, if we did."

Vyry said, "This ain't all. We buried the best of Big Missy's things when we heard tell Gen'l Sherman was coming."

"I don't know as Lillian will ever be able to use all her nice things again, that is, her mother's things. I reckon all

her things she left in Oglethorpe are gone, just like every-
things else, on the wind."

"I dunno, ma'am, I dunno nothing bout that at all."

"But Susan should have some of her grandmother's things,
and Bobby, too. I think we ought to try to take the barrels
of dishes; Mister Porter said he would send a dray."

"What about all the furniture and linen and the silver and
stuff?"

"Well, Vyry, we just ain't able to carry all this stuff away.
And you oughta pick out something for yourself after Lillian's
stuff gets packed up. I just think it's no more than right for
you to have some of this stuff. Better than strangers coming
in and destroying everything."

"Well, they done that already."

So they unearthed all the hidden things. Innis Brown asked
Vyry why she told Miss Lucy.

"Well, it wasn't none of mine, even if she may be right
bout I got a right to some of it. And anyhow Bobby knows
we buried that stuff and way after while he would remember
and I don't want nobody saying I stole Big Missy's things
cause I ain't no thief. I couldn't carry all that stuff away
from here if I wanted to."

Miss Lucy's eyes popped when she saw the gold plate and
silver plate and the precious jewels and gold money. But she
contended to the end that Vyry should have a part. When
the week was nearly over and the house was dismantled, it
was Miss Lucy who asked Vyry again what her plans were.

Vyry didn't exactly know Innis Brown's plans, but she
knew he wanted to go west. She remembered that Caline
and May Liza and Jim, the houseboy, had gone into Alabama
following the army. Miss Lucy said, "There's plenty land in
Alabama. And you know, the United States Government
passed a law during the war, I think it was in 1862, giving
folks squatters' rights to the land for homesteading. I'm sure
you could find land there. And if you ever need anything
and we can help you, don't hesitate to come and see us.
Can you read?"

"Nome."

"I didn't think so. I was going to write down where our
place is, but maybe you can remember?"

"Yes'm."

"We live in the south end of Butler County at a little place
called Georgiana. If you can make it there anybody can
tell you where Porter's store is."

"I'll remember."

Miss Lucy and her husband were taking Miss Lillian and her children on the railroad cars to Alabama. The dray would carry the things. Vyry and Innis Brown had decided to go in the wagon and they put a cover over it so that it could provide a place for them to sleep.

On New Year's Day, 1866, Vyry was spending her last day on Marse John's plantation and watching the last of Marse John's family leave the old home place.

Just after midday dinner, old Doc came out to say goodbye. He visited awhile with Miss Lucy and her husband. For the first time that Vyry could remember the doctor complained of being tired and he was more down in spirit than she could remember. He said to Miss Lucy, "I never thought my own flesh and blood would harbor a Yankee. But Hilma had fed this Union soldier right in our own barn behind my back, and him a fugitive, too! Now to my great consternation she's married him and going up North to live. It's a real blow to me in my old age, but I've seen so much lately I never thought I would see, I try not to let anything surprise me. I came out to tell you that Banker Barrow died last week from heart failure. And that old hussy gal of his didn't let him get cold before she married the very varmint that used to oversee here on this plantation, Ed Grimes!"

"I thought he had a wife."

"Did, but she died in the war. I don't know whether she died from starvation or dysentery, but she was worn out with child bearing for one thing. She died up in the hills with her people, and looks like he felt it was good riddance of bad rubbish, he married again so soon."

"Wasn't the Barrow girl one of Lillian's friends?"

"Yes. That whole circle of girls has felt the bad luck of the war, all their eligible young men killed in the war. I hear the parson's daughter, Belle, is going to teach school. The Crenshaws have had a lot of bad luck too, but with their gun factories all over the South from here to Virginia, I don't think they've lost much even if their home place did burn down."

"Looks like all those girls have had one tribulation or another."

"Yes, all but that Millie Butler. Jeb Hendrix did come back last month from the war. He lost an arm, but he and Millie got married."

"Well, the war surely has changed things."

"Yes, and I don't know for the better or worst. It'll be twenty-five years before the South can get over all the setback of four years of war, especially after the Yankess have burned all our big cities and destroyed our whole way of life."

"Well, I always believe it's an ill wind that don't blow some good. I think the poor white people will have a better chance to prosper now that slavery is dead, at least down South, I don't know about up North."

"I don't know, I just don't know," said Doc, "I liked the Slave System all right, but then I guess it was because I didn't know any other, and I got along all right. Being a country doctor I look after everybody, black and white, poor and rich alike. Never made any difference to me."

Now he rose to leave. "Well, I'll say goodbye." He shook hands with Miss Lucy and her husband, but he kissed Lillian and her children, and to Bobby he said, "You're going to make a fine young man, Bobby, just like your father. You be good now, and look after your mother."

And Bobby said, "Yes sir."

Then the doctor went out in the kitchen where Vyry had almost finished dismantling everything and had pots and pans in a row trying to decide which ones to take.

"Goodbye, Vyry, you've been very good and faithful. I hope you and your children and your new husband have good luck down in Alabama."

"Thank you, doctor. I sho hopes so. If it's the Lawd's will, I reckon we will."

III *"Forty years in the wilderness"*
RECONSTRUCTION AND REACTION

I am bound for the promised land,
I am bound for the promised land,
Oh, who will come and go with me?
I am bound for the promised land.

41   Two weeks in the wagon

Nine months after Lee's surrender the South was still trying
to extricate itself from the wreckage of war. The roads and
railroads were in many cases in a poor state of repair, and
in some places were utterly beyond use. People were moving
from place to place, nevertheless, at great inconvenience.
The fact that Vyry and Innis Brown with two small children,
Minna and Jim, were on the road in January of 1866 looking for a place to settle where they could begin a new life
was typical of hundreds of thousands of emancipated Negroes.

It was bitterly cold. Vyry heated smoothing irons and
wrapped them in rags to keep the children's feet warm while
they sat in the wagon. Jim and Minna peeped out of the rear
over the tail board while Vyry and Innis rode up front with
more hot bricks and irons to keep them warm.

There was plenty of food for them, and provisions for the

mule. Vyry had an abundance of other things she considered necessary to give them a comfortable start in life. She had iron pots and kettles, a wash pot, skillets, smoothing irons, candle molds and tallow candles, tin plates and cups and dippers of gourd and tin, a china wash bowl and pitcher and a slop jar. She had quilts and croker sacks of cotton and feathers for beds and pillows, a precious spinning wheel, lots of potash soap, and most important of all she had sacks of cracked corn, water ground corn meal, and sacks of seed. She filled the chest with her most valuable keepsakes from the plantation and Big House and tied it on the wagon. She baked sugar cakes for the children and roasted peanuts and she filled sacks with hickory nuts, pecans, and black walnuts.

They traveled very slowly for three reasons. First, the mule was balky and would not move with a tight rein. Second, the hard roads had deep ruts and sometimes Vyry and Innis had to get out and help the wagon along by pushing through the ruts. The children would get out and help, too, and if the place was impassable, they had to relieve the wagon of some of the iron weight before they could travel onward again. Third, the wagon was old and rickety.

At night they stopped to make a camp fire and cook supper, then they went to bed in the wagon with the mule tied to a tree. Early in the morning Vyry would make a hot mush gruel for breakfast and fill their stomachs with hot food and hot sweetened water before they began another day. She kept cold pones of corn bread and cold roasted sweet potatoes with hog meat for their middle of the day meal. But sometimes they did not stop along the way to eat this, hoping to move a few miles farther during the daylight hours.

Everybody was feeling fine and in wonderful spirits. They laughed and joked along the way, planning what they would do with the years of freedom stretching a lifetime before them, and they sang. Vyry raised her melodious voice and filled up the valley with its rich and resonant tones:

> I'll be dar, I'll be dar
> When de muster roll am calling, I'll be dar
> sure's yer born.
> I'll be dar, I'll be dar
> When de muster roll am calling
> I'll be dar, sure's yer born!
>
> Oh, come you sinners, go wid me
> Oh, I'll be dar
> I'll take you down to Tennessee

Oh, I'll be dar.
Come and jine de silver band
Oh, I'll be dar
I'se gwine to fly to Canaan's land
Oh, I'll be dar.

The children and Inis Brown stared in awe at Vyry while she sang and when she finished Minna whispered, "Oh, Maw, you sing so pretty!" Jim said, "Maw, you sound so good, sing another one, Maw, please!" What the children and Vyry discovered to their delight was that Innis Brown could sing, too, and with his heart bubbling over with joy he taught them to sing:

Oh, boys, carry me long
Carry me till I die
Carry me down to the burying ground
Marster, don't you cry!

They listened in amazement as his voice, rich and dark, rose in his favorite song:

Oh, carry me long
There's no more trouble for me
I'm going to roam
In a happy home
Where all the niggahs am free.
I've worked in the fields
I've handled many a hoe
I'll turn my eye, before I die
And see the sugah cane grow!

Minna and Jim never tired of joining in the chorus. Vyry declared, "Time always seems to go faster when you sing."

And Innis said, "Don't it though?"

"Aunt Sally useta sing sometimes when I was running around no bigger than Minna here. She sho had a pretty singing voice. She sang at church, too, after Brother Zeke's preaching."

"Reckon we'll find us a church in Alabamy?"

"Don't, maybe we can get one started."

"Yeah, I reckon we can."

"I sho hopes so. I wants my chillun to go to school, too, and learn how to read and write and cipher."

"And I wants me a farm so bad I can taste it."

It took them a week to make the trip from the plantation to the Chatahoochee River, and there they found that the bridge on the old wire road was destroyed and they would have to travel to the Fort and cross the river on the bridge the Federal Army was still providing. This would take them into Henry County in the wiregrass country of Alabama, but beyond this point they did not know where they were going. At the Fort soldiers told them that if they went to Montgomery they could get aid from the Freedmen's Bureau which was helping Negroes get settled by homesteading or on abandoned lands, but Montgomery was more than a hundred miles away and they knew they could not make that trip in a rickety wagon with one old balky mule. General Swayne of the United States Army was in control of all civil affairs in Alabama. His office was in Montgomery, where he had a large detachment of men assisting him in his military and civil duties, which were all closely connected with the Freedmen's Bureau. Vyry and Innis decided against the risk of such a trip, so they stayed in Henry County and found a place in the low country below Abbeville and near the Chattahoochee River.

"Where is we gwineta stay?" asked Jim.

"We's gwineta build us a house, that's what we's gwineta do," said Innis Brown and Jim gaped in amazement.

When they had decided on a good spot in the midst of a virgin pine forest, and with a level piece of rich bottom land for farming not too far from the river, Vyry and Innis Brown began to set up stakes for their cabin. Then he began cutting down trees of different sizes, pine trees and oak trees with trunk sizes varying from six inches to a foot thick. He broke his ax handle twice and had to make a new one to wedge in the iron head. But he was quite patient, and when he was not singing, he was whistling at his work. As he cut down the trees for the logs to build the cabin, Vyry and the children would strip them bare of needles and leaves and small twigs and branches and bark, and then they would neatly lay them in piles. Innis Brown cut down trees for logs for three days, and when Vyry asked him if he might not get blisters from holding the ax so steadily and long, he said, "I got calluses in my hands long time ago holding a hoe. I ain't likely to get no blisters now. What you think I is, anyhow, a woman? I'm tough and strong, and right now I'm just glad to be living in this here new and brighter day!"

When the logs were cut and he thought he had a sufficient pile they made a big mud hole.

"We ain't got no stock now, but one of these days we'll have pigs rooting in that there mud!"

The mud was used to chink the logs. They measured off a space approximately twenty-five or thirty feet square, and then they began to roll the largest logs in place.

The great wonder to the children was the building of the chimney. First they mixed pine needles and sticks with mud and pebbles, and since there was no sun to bake bricks they made a cat'n'clay chimney, building it with the rocks and pebbles and the mud mixed with sticks and straw and baking it hard with fire. It burned into the hardness of bricks.

Innis Brown also built a loft at the top of the house where Vyry could store things and the children could have ample space for sleeping. In this loft Vyry put her precious chest and spinning wheel.

They thatched the roof with boughs of pine and oak complete with leaves and pine needles and they covered the open places left for windows with quilts until they could build shutters from saplings. The floor was only hard clay which they also covered with pine straw and rushes and more leaves, but soon this would be a raised platform of boards when Innis Brown could get some boards cut at the nearest sawmill. Inside, the mud walls would also take a longer time, and at first Vyry's chimney smoked a little but in time it drew the smoke upward. And in their joy to be building a home of their own, everything seemed possible.

Oh, Susanna,
Now don't you cry for me.
I'm bound for Alabama,
With my banjo on my knee.

42   *Bound for Alabama*

The man standing before the barbed wire fence looking at the deserted plantation in all its desolation read the "FOR SALE" sign a dozen times without believing what he read. It couldn't be true, everybody dead, everybody gone, the place boarded up and overgrown with weeds—all in a matter of months. There must be some mistake. He looked at the scraggly stray chickens pecking in the grass, the broken windows and doors with boards nailed across them. In the distance he could see the dusty brown and black shingles on the tops of old slave cabins where the rooftops were all falling or caving in. He was half inclined to disregard the "No Trespassing" sign nailed on a nearby post and climb under the fence to make a thorough investigation. But he knew it would be no use. There was nobody living here, he was sure.

Nothing he could do would prove that to his greater personal satisfaction. He must face the facts staring him in the face. Anybody in his right mind ought to be able to realize an unpleasant truth especially when he was looking at the evidence with his naked eye.

He had been gone more than seven years, it was true, but even so, there must have been people living here less than six months ago. He realized that two years had passed since he saw Jim in Atlanta, but he reasoned it was only last May that the slaves in this backwoods were set free. After all, Lee's surrender was still less than a year ago.

Randall Ware could not help remembering how the place once looked. In his mind's eye he still saw it as it had appeared in his imagination during all those long wandering years of his absence. He could still see Vyry in her cabin door or working in the kitchen, holding a baby in her arms with another child pulling on her long skirts and apron-tail. He looked again into her serious milk-white face, her solemn, sad eyes; saw her rope-wound sandy hair, and her thin lips turned down at one corner, and his heart longed again for a sight of that severe countenance.

He could easily see a bustling plantation with nearly a hundred people, with smoke coming out of chimneys, hear noises of domestic animals and children playing, see lights from a thousand candles and observe green gardens and lawns and carefully clipped paths and walks. There stood the shining white Big House with its square pillars and green shutters, the hitching posts for the horses, the stables and carriage house where he had shoed the horses, and far over the distance on a foggy gray morning with the sun just rising, or in the twilight of an early wintry evening, the patter-rollers disappearing from his alert and careful glance. Now here lay this place in utter desolation before his startled eyes. All of this seemed unreal. Every sign of life had gone except the pecking chickens and the thin black lines of birds wheeling around the trees and the cold chimney tops.

He turned with his shoulders sagging in disappointment and rode back to town. Perhaps, if he had come straight home, if he had not stopped to attend that First Convention of Colored People in Georgia, he might have made it in time and found them still here. He thought again about it and his bitter thought came out loudly spoken, "If I had not stopped . . ."

The furnace pit in his smithy was cold and empty of ashes, but the anvil was ready for the hot metal. He felt himself a strong man again with muscles and biceps that were hard as iron, and his hands itched to hold the hammer. He would bend the molten metal again, and he would shoe horses, too. He was ready for the forging irons. He could hear his hammer ringing and see the red and blue sparks flying. At least he was alive, and in Dawson, Georgia, again. Randall Ware was home.

Three or four weeks passed and he had no leads telling him in which direction Vyry and the children had gone, but his trade was picking up. Sooner or later everybody in a village comes to the blacksmith shop and somebody would happen along, sometime or other, whom he could ask. Gradually he re-oriented himself. He learned about the destruction of the major plantations in the area. He knew that the Barrow and Crenshaw places were burned; that Banker Barrow was dead and his daughter had married Grimes. Grimes might know what he wanted to learn, but he would not go near him to ask.

Those few Confederate veterans who had returned to Dawson were full of the talk of the war. He heard them arguing about the greatest of the commanders and generals. Every man respected most the man who had led him. Jeb Hendrix, who lost an arm in the war, was in the cavalry under Joe Wheeler with Johnny Dutton and the Winston brothers, who did not come home. Randall Ware listened to their talk but he was wary of every Georgia "cracker" who came to his shop. Most of these white people did not know he had also been in the war. He listened and said little, but he thought a great deal. He thought most about the vast social changes which Georgia, like all her other southern sister-states, was undergoing.

The Freedman's Convention he attended in Augusta, Georgia, raised his hopes sky high. He became a charter member of the Georgia Equal Rights Association and he returned to his smithy with the express intention of taking an active part in the political affairs of his county, town, and state. He was a property owner. He had served the Union Army honorably and was loyal to the United States Government, and he was literate. He intended to exercise his right to vote, to hold office, and to participate further in his local government. One day he expected to exercise this right of citizenship and to have his chance as a free man living in a free country. The war was over, a social revolution had taken place, and there was going to be true democracy in the land. The 13th Amendment was passed and ratified by the states. Sooner or later it was sure to be tested.

Georgia, however, had passed new laws restricting Negroes. To be sure, they were not as rigid as those in Alabama and some other southern states, due to the moderate leadership of ex-Governor Brown, but they were literally the same old laws that had restricted the movements of slaves and free Negroes before the war. Negroes were still forbidden to own fire-arms and to be seen on city streets at night after nine o'clock or they could be arrested for vagrancy and loitering. Every Negro who had no job and was not working for some respectable white man was a suspect.

Eventually there would be a showdown between the conflicting groups of citizens in Georgia who were holding these opposite views. Randall Ware had no doubt where he would stand. But at first he listened to the white man's talk. Those white men who brought their horses to be shod talked. Those who stood idle on the main street corners talked. Their talk seemed idle but it was salted with bitterness and peppered with resentment. None of the white people he heard talking liked the new government laws about Negroes. All of them felt that in one way or another the freed black people were a menace to the lives, property, and liberty of white people and their local government. They rarely addressed themselves to him personally, and when they spoke to him it was strictly about shoeing their horses, but he sensed their moods and caught the meanings of their undertones.

Less than two months after he reopened his shop and grist mill, old Doc happened by. Randall Ware was shoeing a horse and when he finished he looked up to find an old white man, whom he did not at first recognize as the doctor, staring intently at him.

"How long you been back here?" the doctor asked him abruptly.

"Do I know you, sir?"

"I'm the doctor and I asked you a question. How long you been back here?"

"Oh, two-three months, maybe, eight or nine weeks, I reckon, why?"

"Didn't you useta work on the Dutton plantation?"

"I shoed horses for him, yessir."

"I mean, as a slave."

"No sir, I never been a slave. I was born free."

"You mean Mr. Dutton didn't own you?"

"No sir. He sho didn't."

"That's funny. I don't remember free niggers around here since long before the war."

Randall Ware's eyes narrowed as the doctor talked about niggers, and he opened his mouth to speak, then closed it again.

"Well, were you gone before the war?"

"Do you remember the law said in 1858 a free colored man must either take a master and become a slave or leave the state of Georgia?"

The doctor turned red, but he said, "Can't say as I do, but what about it?"

"I left the state of Georgia."

"And you been gone all that time?"

"I been gone all that time."

"Why'd you come back?"

"I left a wife and children on the Dutton plantation, and besides I own this place."

"You must be the free-issue nigger Vyry had her children by."

"I'm their father if that's what you mean, and by the law of Georgia she is my wife."

"Oh no she's not, not any more, if she ever was."

"What you mean by that?"

"She got herself another husband, legal husband that is, and left here."

"What you mean 'left'? Do you know where she is?"

"Somewhere west of Georgia, I reckon. I heard she was bound for Alabama."

"Thank you for the information."

"You mean you didn't know?"

"I didn't know."

"Well, if I had known that, I sure wouldn't have told you. Vyry was a good and faithful nigger and I don't want you making trouble for her."

"I'm not interested in your opinions."

"Nigger, do you mean to be impudent to me?"

"Sir, I didn't look you up, and I'm not giving you any trouble. I'm on my own property, and I repeat I did not ask your opinion about me or my wife."

"Well!" huffed old Doc and left.

But the news had shaken Randall Ware. Not only gone,

but married again, was she? He would make certain first, and then if it was true he would forget her. The next time he had business in the courthouse he would search the records and see if she really was legally married to another man. He found the records of Elvira Dutton and Innis Brown, but forgetting Vyry·was not going to be that easy.

I'm gwineta lay down my sword and shield,
Down by the riverside,
Down by the riverside,
Down by the riverside,
I'm gwineta lay down my sword and shield,
Down by the riverside,
And study war no more!

43 Wiregrass country in the Alabama bottoms

Once they had completed the log cabin for shelter, Innis
Brown and Vyry made long rows for a field which they planted
with cotton seed and corn, sugar cane, rice, and potatoes.
They exulted in the rich bottom land, although it was largely
sandy loam, and they carried buckets of water up from the
river to water the rows, for the spring and summer were very
dry that year. Vyry detected a spring in the woods with
clear fresh water to drink, and for this they were most grateful. In the spring they explored the woods. There would be
wild fruits and berries and wild greens to add to their diet
of corn meal and hog meat. As they walked through the
forest where they lived, the children picked flowers and Vyry
found her precious herbs and roots for teas and medicine,
such as mullein, pinetop, penny royal, and sheep sorrel in
profusion.

They had their hardest time obtaining live stock, but soon there were chickens picking in the grass growing in wide stretches behind their cabin. Paw, as Minna and Jim now called Innis Brown, went to town in nearby Abbeville and brought back first a sow with a litter of pigs, and then a cow. He decided that for a while they could not manage another mule. And the wagon served many purposes.

Abbeville was a small country town and the county seat of Henry County. Innis Brown told Vyry he felt they would be better off the less they went into town.

"White man talked pretty rough to me where I fetched the pigs. Ask me who own me and where I live. When I told him nobody owns me, I'm free, he got mad. Told me niggers was made to work for white folks and all this free nonsense warn't agoing to work."

Vyry had made brush-brooms from young branches and saplings in the woods, and with these she swept her cabin and around her doorway. She was sweeping now as Innis talked.

"Did you tell him where we live?"

"Naw. I told him we was living in the country, and when he asked on whose land, I told him we was in the woods and the river bottom and wasn't nobody nearbouts to us with no land."

"What he say then?"

"He act kinda satisfied, leastwise he didn't say nothing else."

Innis Brown had taken his time building a barn and an outhouse, but across the summer when he was not working in the field, he was working on the barn. He located a sawmill and carried logs in the wagon to the mill near Abbeville. When he came back with the logs all sawed into boards he told Vyry, "White man offered me a job at the sawmill."

"Say he did?"

"Yeah, say he need help bad, and he would pay me."

"What you tell him?"

"I told him I was real busy now trying to git settled and fix me up a place to farm, but if he needed somebody across the winter, I would be glad to do what I can."

"Well, did he say he would hire you?"

"Naw, he got mad cause I say I can't come right now. Went to talkin bout no-good niggers don't want to work, and won't do nothin lessen you beats em."

"Well, I likes his nerve! That sho ain't no place to go work, neither."

"Naw, the way he talk he want to see cullud folks back in slavery."

"I reckon talking bout paying was just his way to bait you in."

"I dunno. I thought he was serious and meant well, and I was just telling him the God's truth."

"They don't wanta hear the truth."

"Well, we don't want no trouble."

"Naw, we ain't lookin for none from nobody and ain't givin nobody no trouble."

The summer days passed and although the weather was very dry they did not suffer from the heat with the forest all around them and the river so near. They rose early in the morning to feed the chickens and stock, and went to bed with the chickens. Innis Brown and Jim would carry buckets of water to the house for drinking and bathing and for Vyry's cooking, and they also kept the pigs and chickens and mule and cow supplied with plenty of water. In addition they had to water the fields. Little Jim complained, "All day long I gotta be toting water. I gits tired."

Vyry laughed and said, "Shut up boy. No sitcha thing as a youngun gitting tired."

And Innis said, "You gotta learn how to work."

"I thought we was free and didn't have to work."

"You keep on talking like that ever since Surrender. Boy, doesn't you know everybody gotta work to live and them what doesn't work doesn't eat?"

"Well, I'm just tired of so much work."

"What you wanta do?"

"I wants to play sometime."

"Play when you gits through working."

"That's just the trouble, I don't never git through."

"All right now, that's enough of your sass. Chilluns is suppose to be seen and not heard. I don't wanta hear no more that kinda shiftless talk. You keep on like that you ain't gwineta mount to nothing."

"Aw Maw!"

"Aw Maw, nothing, don't you answer me no moah."

At the end of the summer Vyry looked at her rows of canned vegetables, preserves, jam, and jelly and her provisions for the winter with great satisfaction. They dug potatoes and stored them in hills. She dried onions, and chopped cabbage and hot peppers for sauerkraut. She gathered okra and tomatoes and string beans and peas and corn and canned them. She dried meat and even dried some fish. She knew the value of rock salt and how to stretch her brown sugar and sugar cane syrup. Innis Brown laughed at her gathering her usual supply of nuts from the forest, measuring the peanuts she had grown, and saving sugar cane for the children to chew. "Ain't nobody gwine starve with you around!"

He still had no gun, and could not buy one, but he set traps and killed game, mostly rabbits and squirrels, some of which he salted and hung to dry. He made a squirrel cap for Minna and a raccoon cap for Jim and he promised them that one day he would make boots and shoes from hides for the whole shebang!

When the cotton was picked and the corn husked and shelled, Vyry decided to take the children and go into town with Innis to see about getting the cotton ginned and the corn ground. She made the children stay in the wagon while Innis carried in the croker sacks and she went in to do the bargaining and selling. To Innis's great surprise they had no trouble. All the merchants they encountered said, "Yes ma'am" to Vyry and treated her with the utmost consideration. On the way home Innis was silent for a long time. They had been completely successful in all their undertakings, bought matches and coffee and even white flour. They had sold eggs and vegetables and gotten their cotton ginned, and corn ground into meal. Vyry bought peppermint and horehound candy and some whiskey and there had not been a minute's trouble. Slowly the truth dawned on Innis Brown.

"They musta thought you was white."

"You reckon?"

"They treated you like you was, and you never told them no different."

"Does you think I gotta go round saying I'm a colored person to white folks?"

"Naw, I don't reckon so."

"I ain't said nothing, and they ain't asked me nothing escept one woman asked me if I was from Georgia, and she said she thought I was, and I told her yes, I was."

And then Innis Brown yelled and nearly burst his sides laughing.

"They not only thought you was a white woman, they figgered I'm your nigger."

This didn't tickle Vyry. She sat tall on the wagon seat with her back stiff and straight and her eyes on the road ahead.

"I don't care what them white folks thought, and you can

laugh all you wants to and make out like I was passing for white. We done our business and that's all I'm caring about, and we ain't had no trouble neither."

During the cold winter months when the ground was frozen too hard for field work and there were only the outside chores of feeding and watering their meager stock, Vyry and Innis Brown found much to do inside to pass the long winter nights and brief days. He made pieces of furniture for their cabin, some rather crude pieces, but others so expertly and polished with such loving care and with such interest and fine craftsmanship that Vyry marveled. He made chair bottoms with cane and corn husks; he made a fine trestle table of oak, and he promised the children a swing outside when the summertime came again. He was also good as his word about taking the hides of animals and making shoes. This was really his best work, working with skins.

"How'd you learn to do this work?" marveled Vyry.

"I learned on the plantation. Slaves where I was done everything. Just like you can make candles and soap and feather beds, rag rugs, and quilts, and spin and weave and sew, and cooking was your main job, I learned to do a lots of things 'sides working in the fields. I really knows how to make good shoes if I had leather and tools."

"Where I was they always bought shoes. Big Missy or Marster let Grimes buy shoes."

"But look how much you knows about herbs; you can doctor the sick like that."

"Well, I learned a lot from Aunt Sally. I was too little to learn all what Mammy Sukey and Granny Ticey knowed, but I sho learned a lot from Aunt Sally."

"Old folks didn't let you lay around lazy-like doin nothin. When you couldn't go to the fields on account of hard rain or freezing weather, you learned to work doing somethin elst."

"Aw naw!" said Jim, "work all the time?"

"Well I gits a pleasure outa this kinda thing. Some work you like to do."

Jim's idea was to tell stories and jokes and sing songs and eat nuts and candy to pass the time and Vyry and Innis grew impatient as they tried to pass on the skills they knew to the children.

"Idle brain is the devil's workshop. You ain't got nothin to do but set around and stand around you just thinks up deviltment."

"What's devilment?"

"Trouble, that's what, trouble and badness stead of decency and goodness."

Minna was more like her mother than Jim. She was industrious and wanted to learn how to do everything her mother did. She wanted to learn to sew and weave and card cotton. She wanted to spin, too, but her mother said she couldn't.

"You too little now, maybe another year or so, and you can spin. Lawd, I wish yall could go to school."

"Ain't no schools round here for them to go to and when they is they'll cost a heap of money."

"I don't care. I wants my chilluns to learn to read and write and cipher."

As the year turned toward warmer weather Vyry and Innis remarked they had never seen such a strange spring. The cold weather lingered and the frosts were black and biting, the days were gray and gloomy, and the earth seemed frozen and hard long past the time for plowing. Vyry watched the moon for the spring equinox for she wanted to plant on Good Friday. And then came what must have been the great spring thaw for the Chattahoochee River floated down from the north a caravan of ice and frozen patches of snow bearing them southward in a torrential rush. Innis Brown turned the hard soil with great difficulty. Vyry insisted on planting when the moon was right, although she muttered, "Look like it's too early, and it look like it's too late."

Somehow they got the seed in the ground. Frosty mornings were still numbing to fingers and toes and the sun brought little warmth when it dared to show its face. When the week after Easter set in with cold rain, Vyry felt that maybe they were right to get started with the planting. But it rained for a week. With difficulty, Innis managed to protect the stock in the cold wet weather, and then for ten days they saw no sun. Every time the rain slackened to a drizzle they thought the bad weather was breaking, but after two weeks of rain every day and sometimes all night, their faces puckered with worry. One morning after feeding all the wet, bedraggled chickens with cracked corn Innis Brown came inside and warmed himself at the fireplace, saying to Vyry, who was cooking breakfast, "I think the river is rising."

"Aw naw! What you reckon that mean?"

"I dunno, but I thinks I'm gwine raise up that pig pen today and get that chicken coop in the barn offa the ground.

I dunno what to do with that cow; she wants to get out and she don't like her feets staying wet like that."

"Sho ain't no place to take her up to higher ground, is they?"

"Naw, but I reckon I could try to get her up on some kind of platform in the barn."

"A cow ain't got no sense. You can't make her do nothing."

"Well, I sho would hate to lose her."

"You think this here mean high water?"

"It might. We right here in the river bottom. Maybe that's how come that white man looked so satisfied when I told him where we was."

"Ain't no usen us crying over spilt milk now. It's done. All we got is here and we got to make the most of it."

"Yeah, I reckon so."

All that day Innis Brown worked hard trying to prepare for high water, and Vyry did the same. She cooked extra food and they got extra buckets of spring water. On the river side of the cabin he dug a trench hoping to turn the water back from the foundation of the house. He had trouble trying to put the cow's feet up, but he moved the chicken coop and built up the pig pen and tied them to the barn with rope and wire. He put extra feed in the troughs for the pigs and the chickens and gave them water.

Inside the cabin Vyry put as many of her most precious things as she could in the chest and Innis put it in the loft or table-like half story that he had built high in the cabin. Then they moved everything that water could ruin off the floor.

Vyry said, "I prays it don't come."

But Innis said, "It's coming. It's already on the way."

When they went to bed that night all of them slept in the loft. Before day the water began to creep into their cabin and when daylight awoke them they saw six inches of water inside their log house. Innis told Vyry and the children to stay up in the loft while he went outside to check everything. It had rained all night, but now the rain was definitely slackening, only the water was getting higher. He found the chickens huddled together and the pigs all right. He untied the mule and the cow and after feeding and watering them, he turned the cow loose to wander free. Then he went back inside. They could not build a fire in the fireplace but the chimney was still warm and they were not too uncomfortable.

"Wonder how long it'll last?" said Vyry.

"No telling," said Innis Brown, "but I sho hope it goes down soon."

"Me, too," said Minna.

"Is we gwineta wash away?" asked Jim.

"Hush up, boy, you ask too many questions!"

But Innis was very worried and kept wondering out loud if the stakes of the house would hold or would the force of the water and mud move them away. The barn was holding, and the house should hold, too, but they were worried just the same. They ate and sat and slept in the loft, for there was nowhere else to go.

Vyry mused, "It's just like Noah and the flood in the Bible." Minna asked, "Who was they, Maw?"

"Well, it's a story Brother Zeke useta tell bout long time ago the Lawd got tired of the wickedness on the earth and he say he gwine destroy the world, all excepten Noah, what was his servant. So he told Noah to build a ark."

"What's a ark?" asked Jim.

"I reckon it was a house and a boat together. Anyhows God told Noah to build it big enough to put two of every living things in the world, animals, birds, insects, male and female, that mean boy and girl, and peoples too."

"And then what happened?"

"Well, the wicked folks laughed at Noah and says he was crazy and asked him what he was building, and when he told them what God had done told him they laughed some more, but he kept right on a-building anyhows and the floods come just like this here high water."

"And then what happened?"

"Well, I can sing it bettern I can tell it:

> Forty days, forty nights, when de rain kepta falling
> De wicked climb the trees and for help kepta calling
> Didn't it rain?

"Is that all?" asked Jim rather scornfully.

"Well, when the rain ended and the ark landed on dry ground up on a mountain top,

> God told Noah by the rainbow sign
> No more water, but the fire next time."

Late that afternoon it began to rain again in heavy torrents. All during the second night they heard the water churning in the grip of a storm. Through claps of thunder and flashing lightning they heard the snap of the trees and the lashing of the water. The house quivered, and although the children slept, Vyry and Innis Brown hardly closed their eyes in their anxiety. Early the next morning when Innis Brown went out to examine the stakes of the house he came back inside and told Vyry he thought the worst was over.

"I believe it's gwine blow over now."

"I pray to God that you is right."

"Well, if the Lawd spare us to see dry land agin we gwine move from this here place."

In the afternoon the skies were clear and when it was time for the usual sunset, Vyry called the children to see a beautiful rainbow arched across the sky. There was yet, however, another twenty-four-hour period of high water, and only on the third morning did they look down on the mud-covered floor of their cabin. The children wanted to scramble down at once and go outside, but Innis Brown said, "I better go first."

After climbing down from the loft on the crude ladder he had built, he began poking around among things as though looking for something, and then about to build a fire in the fireplace he found what he had been searching, a snake curled up asleep in the corner of the fireplace. After killing the cottonmouth moccasin he held it up for the family to see, calling Vyry.

"Oh, my Lawd have mercy, anything I'm feared to death of it's a snake."

Outside he was about to rejoice in their good fortune. They were all alive, and neither the house nor the barn were washed away. The mule, chickens, and pigs were safe, but he found the cow dead.

"I ain't surprised," said Vyry, "and ain't nothing you coulda done to keep it from happening. Silly old cow! I told you a cow ain't got no sense."

"If there'd been dry land or high ground we coulda saved her. We sho gonna miss her milk."

"Yeah, butter and cream, too, for awhile."

"I reckon we better not try no more cow here in this here place."

"Where is we gwine go?"

"God knows, but I gotta find us a place."

"Well, right now I gotta clean up this here mess and mud."

The children were so excited in the release from confinement in the loft after three days and nights they scarcely

wanted to come inside except to eat. Vyry cautioned them,
"Yall be careful, now, squishing your feets in all that muddy
water. I doesn't want you catching a cough or something."

There were extra large mosquitoes in the house and all
kinds of water bugs, grass and mud, and the usual silt covering
everything. Innis Brown was determined to skin the cow, and
he wanted the snake skin, too. But Vyry also cautioned him,
"Mind, you be careful with them dead things; varmints can
be pizenous and dangerous."

"Never mind, don't you fret none, I knows how to handle
em."

Vyry still had her doubts but she knew he was determined.

It was late that evening before they went to bed. Everybody was tired with the day's work, but Vyry insisted on
heating water so that everybody could have a hot tub bath
for the first time since the high water. The children were
caked with mud, anyway. Jim and Minna went to bed first
and Innis Brown was last. Before Vyry could fall asleep, however, Minna and Jim were both sneezing.

"See there, now what I told yall bout getting yourself in
them mud puddles this morning?"

In the night time Minna cried out for water and Vyry got
up to take a dipper of water to the bed. There she found the
child dry and hot with fever.

"Oh, my Jesus have mercy!"

"What's the matter?" cried Innis.

"She's sick. She got the fever bad. She justa burning up
with the fever."

"What kinda fever?"

"I dunno, but I got to work fast and see can't I break it."

"What you wants me to do?"

"Make a fire, and heat some water, I gotta make her some
hot teas and wrap her up and see can't I sweat it outen her."

And they slept no more that night.

In the morning Jim was sick, too. Minna would not eat,
and Vyry held her in her arms as she had when she was a
baby. Jim, too, lay listless, and Innis Brown was as worried
as Vyry.

"I dunno whichaway to go to find a doctor."

"I don't need no doctor. They'll be all right soon as I breaks
the fever."

"How long that gwine take?"

"I hopes I can get it outen them by morning."

"You means tomorrow?"

"I'll be lucky then, if I does."

"Well, does you think it's too serious?"

"It's serious enough, but I knows I'm gwine break this here fever with the help of the Lawd."

Innis was alarmed over the children's illness, but Vyry remained calm and refused to be alarmed. She fought through three nights without taking off her clothes and Innis only taking cat naps in a chair. But when the fever was broken, the children only normally warm and wet with perspiration, she sat down and cried. Only when she burst into tears did Innis know how frightened she had been.

The sick children were far from well enough to leave their beds and romp around when the fever was broken. Again Vyry tried to coax them to eat with very little success. She made chicken broth and egg custards, but they remained listless. She and Innis tried to think of various things to amuse them. Vyry made Minna a rag doll with shoe-button eyes. Minna smiled when she saw it and said, "Maw, what is it?"

"It's a play-toy for you, honey, a baby doll. I ain't never had no time to make you none before." And the little girl hugged her dolly. Jim wanted a toy, too, so Innis made him a puzzle with a jar top filled with dried peas and a painted face where the peas dropped into the indentations for eyes and nose and mouth. For the first time in three days Jim laughed aloud.

Innis moved the children's box beds in the loft down where they could be near the fire and Vyry could nurse them through the day. Strength crept back slowly, and they complained that their heads ached when they held them up.

"Malary. That's what it is."

"Don't that stuff stay in you all your life-time?"

"Not if you gets enough quinine. Later on I'll feed them some lasses and sulfur powder."

"We'll see can't we get some quinine."

"I'm gwine give em some chinaberries and whiskey and that'll help, too."

"All of that oughta git it."

When the children were convalescent and fully on the road to recovery they were harder to handle than when they were very sick or completely healthy. Vyry strove to keep her nerves in check, but she was very tired, and sometimes almost irritable. But she could never resist the slightest request from Minna and Jim. She and Innis sang songs until they were tired and then they resorted to story-telling. The children were propped up in chairs and wrapped in quilts before the fire-place. Vyry still insisted on their drinking the hot teas which both Minna and Jim protested were bitter and nasty.

"They'll do yall good and make you well," Vyry remonstrated, and while Minna drank a cupful slowly and Jim dawdled over it, Vyry said, "I'll tell you a tale if you drinks all of it."

"What kinda tale, Maw?"

"Oh, lemme see, one about a silly cat and a wise spider."

Jim's eyes were immediately alert and both he and Minna quickly swallowed the medicine as Vyry began.

"Aw, Maw, don't quit, tell another one please!" said Jim.

"I'm tired," said Vyry, "and I dunno no more."

"Paw, does you know one?" asked Jim.

"Yeah, I reckon I do. Don't know as I can tell em good."

"Well, thank God for that cause they ain't no more wore out than we is." And relieved to see them sleeping, both parents chuckled.

Every nigger's gwine to own a mule,
Jubili, Jubilo!
Every nigger's gwine to own a mule,
And live like Adam in the golden rule,
And send his chillun to the white-folk's school
In the year of Jubilo!

44   Forty acres and a mule

"Whichaway is we gwine now?"

"I dunno, but I gotta find us a place to stay."

"Where you figgering on looking?"

"I thought I'd just go see whereabouts I could find some high ground."

"Them soldiers at the bridge told us to go to Montgomery in the first place."

"Yeah, but how us gwine get to Montgomery with nothing but this here mule?"

"I just wants to get way from here quick as we can."

"Well, soon as I feeds the stock in the morning, I'm gwine start out looking. You reckon you and the chilluns gwine be all right?"

"What's gwine harm us here?"

"I'll do my best to get back early."

For several days he made hopeless and fruitless trips into town and the nearby countryside. He always had news of some other place to try.

"I seen colored soldiers in town."

"Naw."

"Yeah, they say this here state under military regulation."

"The army?"

"Yeah, the Union Army, ever since the first of the year."

"Sho enough?"

"Yeah, and I heard tell the gov'mint gwine give every colored farmer forty acres and a mule."

"Hush your mouth!"

"That's what I heard. That's all I needs to have me a real nice farm, forty acres and another mule."

"It sound too good to be true."

"Soldiers says colored folks been had them acres in Georgy on the ocean front for the longest."

"Well, they sho ain't none where we come from."

"Naw, I been studying bout it, and I wonders where they is got it, but they says the gov'mint gwine be good to colored folks cause they done already give us they word."

"What kinda word?"

"I dunno, but that's what they says."

"Well, when is we gwine get them forty acres and a mule?"

"I wasn't able to get that straight, but some says this summer and some says this fall and some says the end of the year, but they all says it's gwine be this year."

"Well, it sho would be nice if it's the truth."

"But I gotta find us a place to stay somewheres anyhow."

"I hopes you ain't figgering on setting down waiting until they gives us them forty acres and a mule fore you find another place."

"Now you know I ain't, but it's something to look forwards to just the same."

"I reckon."

They had little hope of any crop from the flood-soaked fields now covered with a thick layer of silt, but Vyry hoped to have something to eat for the winter, a late garden perhaps, and certainly her chickens and eggs and hog meat. She decided she would try another set of biddies in the spring.

"Just since they don't hatch in May. May chickens hard to raise, and they don't hardly ever live."

All the summer they were planning to move, only there seemed no place to move to. Innis Brown began to venture out of the county looking in any direction where he heard there might be land. He discovered that the poor white people were very much opposed to Negroes owning small farms. It was bad enough, they complained, in slavery time, when all the "nigger lords" or slave owners had the best land, and the poor whites farmed only the worst land. But now the "niggers getting all the good land" made the white people hostile to any colored people settling near their farms. This section of Alabama was almost entirely farmed by poor white dirt farmers. Innis heard that in some places the fight for land was increasing much hatred among the people and the more he went about the more he became acquainted with this white hostility. At first he was determined to find a place where they could homestead by squatting on the land and sitting out their claim. He wanted a farm of his own. He did not want to work for another farmer. He constantly heard about white owners of large plantations who were looking for Negroes to farm their land, but he did not want this for he understood the conditions were similar to those he had known as a slave. On several occasions when he was offered such work and refused he was met with such rebuffs that he narrowly avoided trouble. Once a white man cursed him so terribly he trembled in anger, but not wanting trouble he hastened away and arrived home so exhausted that Vyry could get no information out of him, although she suspected that he had had trouble. By the middle of the summer he was terribly discouraged.

"They says they's plenty land in Bullock County but black and white folks is fighting over there fierce."

"I sho don't wanta go where they's trouble, and I don't wanta git in that Black Belt."

"Humph, we ain't got much choice of nothing right in through here. These white folks is dead set agin colored folks farming for theyself."

About the middle of July he heard of a place which seemed to be vacant. Since it was more than a day's journey there and back, he told Vyry he would have to go and spend the night on the road.

"I hates to have you on the roads at night. Everything happening to peoples now and you ain't got no gun nor nothing. I reckon all us can do is pray the good Lawd'll take care of you."

Innis Brown found the place and discovered a white family was in the house. The man, a poor dirt farmer who was chewing tobacco seemed friendly enough to Innis.

"Yep. We is fixing to move. Got another place we's taking first of the fall."

"How long from now?"

"Wa-al, I reckon bout six weeks' time, bout the first of September. My wife just had a baby, and she ain't too strong yet. Soon as she gets over her puny feelings I reckon we'll move."

"I'd like to have a place for my family fore then, but if you is sho you is moving, bird in the hand bettern in the bush."

"Wa-al, we's leaving all right. I ain't had much luck here, myself, maybe wall'll do better."

"Who else do I hafta see?"

"Nobody. Just come on up here bout the first of September."

"We got flooded out where we is; bottom land and the river riz. I reckon ain't no danger of high water up here, is they?"

"Naw, that's one good thing you won't have to worry bout."

"And I sees you got a well. Water good?"

"Yeah, pretty good. Last year I reckon was the drought and dry weather done it, it liketa run dry, but it's all right now."

"Well, I'll bring my family up here in six weeks' time."

"You do that, now. I'll be looking for yall then."

Vyry could hardly believe the good news.

"And you sho you ain't got to see nobody else?"

"That's what he says."

"I wish we could move right now."

"Six weeks ain't long. We got a lot to do fore then."

"Yeah, I reckon so."

It was too hot to kill hogs, so Vyry suggested that they sell some and try to take what they already had salted down. Innis decided to put one hog in a pen and carry it with them, and sell the rest. Vyry also put her chickens in a coop to carry. They planned to buy a cow the first chance they could after they moved. Although they had lost a crop in the field they still had some cotton seed and some corn.

"Enough to start with, anyhows," said Vyry.

The children were slowly regaining their health, much dosed by Vyry with chinaberries and whiskey, molasses and sulfur, and with liberal doses of calomel and castor oil.

"If all that don't git it I doesn't know what will."

Despite the flood the woods yielded a great abundance of wild fruit and berries and Vyry had luck with her garden. The month of August seemed never to end and September brought relief from the heat and a long dry spell. That first week the Browns started out again with a heavily laden wagon. It was filled with furniture, iron pots and pans, sacks of seed and meal, a coop of chickens and a hog in a pen. The wagon was so full there was no room for the children and they sat up front with Vyry and Innis. This time they were hoping not to sleep in the wagon. The weather would be good for camping if it didn't rain.

When they were near the place, Vyry was surprised to learn that the house was up a steep hill and the ground was rocky all the way.

"It sho looks like rocky soil and nothing but nubbins of wiregrass growing here."

"Well, it's the best I could find. I hopes it ain't too bad."

It was late afternoon when they found themselves at the end of their long journey, and they had been on the road since daybreak. The sun was setting and Vyry wanted to fix supper and clean up before bedtime. To her great dismay the white family was still in the house. The man came out and welcomed them. He was very apologetic.

"I'm sorry yall had to find us still here, but we can't move before tomorrow. I got me a man with a team of horses coming to help me. We got most of our things packed up, but we ain't got no room in the house tonight for yall."

Vyry was still sitting in the wagon. Now gradually the white man's family appeared. His wife came out with a young baby in her arms, then following her one by one, in stair-step sizes, came their other five children. They were all thin and ragged. The little ones were sucking their fingers and Vyry could tell they were all hungry. There was a stove in the house, but no smoke was coming out of the chimney. Vyry got down from her wagon seat, but Minna and Jim were still gaping at the white children who, in turn, were staring at them. Innis looked confused as if he wondered what he should do. There was an awkward gap of silence before Vyry spoke.

"Mister, does you mind if I makes a fire out here and cooks my chilluns supper?"

"Why no, you just go right ahead," and he seemed happy with the thought. Meanwhile Vyry looked around and saw there was a barn.

"And if you ain't got too much in your barn, we might be able to stay there tonight."

"We ain't got nothing in it yall can hurt." And he laughed a bit sheepishly. Vyry directed Innis to get a fire going and take down her big wash pot from the wagon.

Innis asked her, "How come you gwine cook in your wash pot?"

"Sh-sh, can't you see these folks is hungry?"

First she heated water from the well and scalded two big fat chickens. Then after she had dressed them she had Innis half-fill the big iron wash pot with water. Into this she put the cut-up chickens, a rabbit cut up, fat salt pork in hunks, a pan full of potatoes and onions, a jar of okra, tomatoes and corn mixture, salt and pepper, and let the pot boil a long time until the aroma of the food began to rise on the wind.

The white woman and her children sat down on the front porch steps and at first watched. Then she came over to Vyry and whispered, "Is you got any snuff?"

Vyry was at first taken aback, then she answered, "Nome, I ain't. I ain't never used it."

"Well it keeps me from getting sick to my stomach when I'm in family way."

"I'm like that now myself," said Vyry, "but I ain't never used no snuff."

"We ain't had nothing to eat but fried meat grease and hominy since day before yestiddy. Your pot sho smells good."

"Yas'm, it sho do, if you thinks your chilluns would like some you is welcome to share what we got, sich as it is."

"Is you got enough?"

"Ma'am, I got plenty."

"Well it would be mighty kind of you. Paw, she says she would be glad if we'd help her and her younguns eat cause they got too much."

The man's pride was involved, but he said, "Honey, yall eat some, I ain't hungry."

But when Vyry dished up the steaming hot stew she fed every one of the white family as well as her own and made the poor white woman and her husband feel they were doing her a favor. Then to Innis's great surprise, Vyry quickly cleared everything away, saw that the fire was out, and after heating another wash pot full of water and washing up her children, comfortably bedded down her family in the barn among the hay and animals.

Next morning she was up early fixing breakfast. Before the white family was on its way, loaded into their wagon and a borrowed one with a team of fresh horses, Vyry again filled their stomachs full of hot food.

The white woman asked her, "Did you make a crop this year?"

"Nome, but we made a good one last year. This year we had high water."

"Well, we been here three years and we ain't made one yet. I hopes yall does better, but this here soil ain't nothing but rocks and wiregrass."

"Oh nawl" said Vyry and she felt so weak she had to sit down.

When Vyry walked into the house to take possession she found much to her displeasure and a few things that pleased her. The house was dirty and she resolved at once to scrub the floor with potash soap and sand.

"I reckon that poor woman ain't had strength enough if she had a mind to clean up, but I just can't stay here till we gits everything scoured down."

In the kitchen she found a small wood stove, such as she had never used before, and she was also pleased to find the well so convenient to the back door. The house had three rooms and they seemed snug and sound. The boarded walls were rough and devoid of paint as were the outside walls but this she did not notice and she liked having a porch in front and back. Later she would explore the grounds.

There was much to keep them busy and two days passed without incident. On the third morning they were awakened by a loud knock at the door. When Innis opened the front door there stood a strange white man. He seemed as shocked to see Innis as the knock had shocked them.

"Where's the Coopers?"

"The Coopers, sir?"

"The white family who was here?"

"They've gone sir, they left day before yestiddy."

"Oh, they did? Do you know where they went?"

"No sir, he didn't never tell me. Never said a word bout where they was gwine, did they Vyry?"

"Naw, but we never asked them neither."

"Well, Goddam his soul in hell, he went off owing me!"

"You means you owns the place?"

"Why of course, you didn't think he did, did you?"

"I dunno sir," and Innis, weak with worry, sat down. The children were still asleep in bed and he and Vyry were in their night clothes.

"Oh, my Lawd have mercy," said Vyry, "Mister we didn't know."

"I know you didn't."

"Well sir, can we stay?"

"Why, I guess so, soon's you sign the contract."

"Contract?"

"Yes. You agree to work the farm on shares. You get the house rent-free and we advance you any seed and food you need and at the end of the year when you make the crop, you pay us and get your share. Fair enough, don't you think?"

Innis looked at Vyry and back again at the man. The man also looked at them as though trying to read their minds.

"Of course, if you don't sign you have twenty-four hours to get off the place."

"We'll sign," said Innis, and Vyry nodded. "Only I can't write my name," said Innis.

"Well, that's all right, just make a mark. Here, I'll show you where. What is your name?"

"Innis Brown, sir. And this is my wife, Vyry."

"Well, my name is Pippins."

"Yes sir, Mr. Pippins."

"You sure you wanta stay a year?"

"We would like to try it at least a year, maybe longer if we does well."

"Oh, I have no doubt you'll do well. All it takes is hard work. You can't make a crop if you're shiftless and lazy, but a good hard-working couple like you two seem to be should do all right."

"Yes sir."

"Now here is where you sign. Just make a mark right here."

"Yes sir." And Innis made his mark.

Oh, brother, I'm working in the high ground,
Gwine to git to heaven by and by.

45 New land and higher ground

The land was very bad. It was hard with rock and full of the
nubbins of grass Vyry had noticed when they were arriving.
But the house was a good shelter. When Vyry had scoured it
to her satisfaction, she began to brighten it with curtains hung
over the shuttered windows, large wooden flaps crudely con-
structed, and with rag rugs on the floor. The furniture Innis
Brown made for the log cabin was quite suitable here, table
and chairs and beds. The wood-burning stove in the kitchen
had two cooking eyes on top that Vyry's pots and pans fit
perfectly, and a real oven. The fire-box was not very good, but
Vyry was as happy as a child with a new toy.

"I'll have to get useta it first, but before long I'll be baking
biscuits and egg bread and pies and cakes same as usual."

The two other rooms shared a chimney. With two fireplaces
and a stove they would be warm in winter. Innis Brown told

Jim, "We gotta cut a heapa firewood so's your Maw'll have enough for cooking and we'll keep warm through the winter."

Jim was not happy with the prospect of carrying wood; and even less happy about going to the woods and chopping down trees. He preferred to pick up chips from the woodpile and gather pine-knots for kindling.

The first time Innis made a fire in the kitchen stove the smoke nearly ran them out of the house. It took some time to understand the damper in the stove pipe and then they discovered the whole pipe had to come down and be cleaned. The black soot clogging it was like thick black rags. Once it was clear and clean there was danger of letting the fire get too hot or the pipe would turn a burning red and frighten them with the imminent danger of fire.

When he explored the grounds Innis Brown reckoned that there were twenty-five acres of land on the place. After the first week he discovered on the back another farm adjoining his land. On one side the land sloped down to a creek and on the other side there was a thick grove of pine trees separating them from another tract of land.

"It don't look like this land's been worked in I dunno when. Was a field of corn cause I seen a heap of corn stalks laying there rotting, and musta been a few pickins of cotton cause they's some left in the fields, but they's places look like they ain't nothing but solid rock. Even much can't hardly raise hay to feed the mule."

"We's got to raise something," said Vyry, "else we'll come near starving like them white folks done."

"I was just thinking if I had me a good load of barnyard manure I might be able to fertilize a few acres."

"Don't look like to me that barn been cleaned out in I dunno when. It don't smell bad, but I bet you could scrape up a whole wagon load."

"Well, we ain't gwine have no fall crop no how this year, and by the time I gits ready to plant in the spring I'll have that land in shape."

"I don't reckon you can make good land outen bad land but you can make the best of what we got."

Vyry tried to have a small kitchen garden with collards and winter turnip greens, but Innis had to do most of the work. She was getting too heavy on her feet to do much outside work.

Much to his surprise Innis found a number of fruit trees on

the place, most of them in very poor condition, but with some attention they might bear.

"We's got several peach trees and some wild plums voluntary, and a real scraggly fig tree. They's blackberry bushes and a crab apple tree, and I believe I sees a wild persimmon. Don't know yet if they's bearing, but over the winter I can kinda nurse em along and we'll see what we'll see in the spring."

Vyry was overjoyed to hear this. Although she would miss the fine pecan trees she had known in Georgia, there were bound to be some hickory trees somewhere near them.

"We's gwine make out somehow. I'm glad we got seed and we got some food to carry us 'long, I hopes, through the winter. I don't wanta have Mr. Pippins advancing us nary bit of seed and food."

"How come? He says we can pay when us makes a crop."

"Yeah, but that there white woman told me they ain't made no crop in three years, and no telling how much he charge for his feed and seed and stuff like that. We can make out without it, Paw."

"Well, if we can."

"We can."

One night in November sitting before a fireplace fire when the children had gone to bed, Vyry said to Innis Brown, "Paw, is you ever seen a baby born?"

"Naw, I ain't."

"Well, you fixing to see one, and you gotta help me cause I ain't got nobody else."

Innis's eyes widened. He had seen Vyry preparing baby things for weeks and days. He watched her slowing down when she prepared food, sitting to roll out her biscuit and pie dough, and for the last week or so cleaning and cooking and sewing long past bedtime. Now he was really frightened, but he dared not let Vyry see his fear in the face of her own courage.

"First, make a fire in the kitchen stove and git the house real hot. Put a pot of water in each eye so it'll git hot fast, and build up this here fire too. You ain't got to do much else, just mind you do like I say and we'll be all right."

"Does you want me to try to find somebody?"

"Who is you gwine find, and where you gwine this time of night? Ain't no granny round here and we don't know no doctor nohow, ain't got nothing to pay one if we did, as if I needed one in the first place, but I done told you before I never needs no doctor."

For the next few hours Innis Brown lived through the most harrowing fit of nerves he had ever had in his whole life, but under the calm, controlled, and steady direction of Vyry he helped her bring their first child into the world. When he heard the baby cry he broke into a broad grin, but he was not sure whether the water on his face was from tears of joy or relief or streams of perspiration. Anxiously he followed every step Vyry outlined to him and when he heard the roosters crow for day and saw the broad daylight creeping into the house he realized he had not taken off his clothes to lie down during the long night. Vyry and his new boy-baby were clean and warm and asleep, the baby washed in a warm bath of melted tallow. He was exhausted, but as he realized his paternity and his baptism of fire into the ritual of life he was so excited he forgot about sleep and he went out to feed the chickens and the one big fat hog.

When Minna and Jim awoke to find a new and tiny baby asleep beside their mother, who was still in bed, they were shaken by the wonder. Minna said, "Maw, whose is he?"

Vyry laughed and said, "He's ourn."

Jim was skeptical and said, "Where'd you git him, Maw?"

Vyry laughed again. "A big brown bird brung him down the chimney last night while yall was asleep."

"Can we keep him?"

"I reckon. Ask your Paw."

Innis came in just then with another arm load of wood for the fires and he asked, "How you like your new baby brother?"

"Paw," said Minna, "can we keep him?"

"I reckon so," smiled Innis, "I don't reckon nobody else want him as bad as we do, and he too little right now to run away."

With an additional mouth to feed Vyry and Innis Brown worked hard and they were determined to make a success of the bad land. Vyry made Christmas a happy time. Innis killed the fat hog and they had two hundred pounds of fresh meat. Vyry made sausage and liver pudding and crackling bread, cooked chitterlings, and made souse from the hog's head and feet. They salted and sugar-cured with molasses the hams and shoulders and middlings. Vyry cooked so much tenderloin, backbones, ribs, and neckbones that Innis declared, "We sho is had enough fresh meat."

"Now we ain't got no more hogs, but we'll get us a couple of shoats in the spring."

"Yeah, be all we can do to feed two."

"They never eats nothing but slops from the table no how."

"Yeah, but ain't no big oak trees round here for them to root in the woods."

"Naw, and no pecans neither."

In the spring of the new year Minna was big enough to be left alone with little Harry while Vyry took Jim to help Innis in the field. They realized they could not raise rice here. They hoped to make a crop of cotton and corn, but Vyry felt sure they would succeed most with vegetables. She had a bright idea about planting a field full of greens and okra, tomatoes, squash, pumpkins, gourds, peanuts, sweet and Irish potatoes, onions, beans, peas, and cabbage.

"How come you think we oughta plant more of them than cotton and corn?"

"'Cause this here soil ain't gwine make but so much and we can peddle the vegetables good as we can sell cotton and feed, if we make much."

Despite their diligence they were unable to plant all the acreage. Having one mule and no extra help, they could only hope to cultivate a portion of the land, anyway. In the summer, Vyry harvested a good crop of fruit and berries.

"They ain't as juicy and plump as usual, and I got quarts stid of pecks but they'll make good eating as jams and jellies and 'zerves."

As Vyry had predicted, the vegetables were doing better than the cotton, and in a summer that was more than usually dry the corn was stubby, too. Just before harvest, Mr. Pippins came to see them and looked out over their fields.

"I understand," he said, "you haven't been buying much feed and you didn't buy any seed nor any fertilizer from our store."

"No sir, we didn't buy no feed neither," Innis hastened to say.

"Say you didn't? That's funny. I understand you bought about six sacks of feed, twenty-five pounds each."

"Who say so?" asked Innis bristling.

"My storekeeper, that's who. Says he's got your mark to prove it. He's a fine honest man, been doing a business for us for many years and never had his word disputed, that is before."

Innis opened his mouth to argue this point, but he saw Vyry's tight face and she was shaking her head to give him a high sign, so he said nothing. Mr. Pippins changed the subject.

"You look like you gonna make a good crop."

"Well, sir, we doesn't know yet. We ain't started laying-by."

"When you think you'll finish?"

Here again Vyry gave Innis a look and he subsided into a mumble.

"I just can't say right now, sir, but I hope to start any day now."

"I'll come back in a month or six weeks' time. By that time you oughta be through."

"Yessir, I hopes so, sir."

Innis was terribly upset when Mr. Pippins left, but Vyry tried to steady him with consoling words. Maybe there was really nothing to fear and Mr. Pippins could not make trouble for them without reason.

"And since we ain't giving nobody trouble, ain't no need in us looking for trouble."

Innis Brown had some notion that the best way to prepare for sharing crops was to fill a croker sack for Mr. Pippins every time he filled a sack for himself.

Vyry said, "He didn't say shares half and half, so we just don't know."

"I don't reckon he'd want more'n half of what we got."

"Well, we just don't know, but don't look like he would." For every sack of cotton and every sack of shelled corn that he counted for himself Innis counted one for Mr. Pippins. Vyry did the same with their vegetables. But to their surprise when Mr. Pippins returned he did not figure the bargain in what they had produced, but in money.

"I figure you owe us a hundred and twenty-five dollars for rent alone."

"Rent, sir? Is you talking about house-rent?"

"Why, of course. That doesn't count the land yet, nor the crops, and what you owe the store."

"How much us owe the store?"

"Don't you know how much you bought?"

"No sir. I disremembers buying airy nickel's worth of stuff from your store."

"Your memory's mighty short then. I've got it all set down right here and your contract, too."

"But I told you sir, I can't read and write."

"That's your hard luck, and none of my business at all. Ignorance of the law is no excuse. It has nothing to do with the hard cash you owe me."

"Well, sir, how much us owes you altogether?"

"Well, how much crop have you made?"

"What you means?"

"Have you sold the crop? How much will the crop bring?"

"No sir, we ain't tried to sell nothing yet. I dunno how much it'll bring."

"Do you want me to try to sell it for you?"

"Well, sir, we wasn't figgering on selling our part. We was counting on having something to feed us through the winter."

"Well, I don't know how you expect to pay me my money if you don't sell the crop."

"How much money you figure we owe you?"

"I can't say that till I know how much money you got."

"Well, sir, we'll hasta go to town and sell first fore we can tell."

"That's perfectly all right with me, just since you get my money."

"How much, sir?"

"How many times do I have to keep telling you the amount is conditional. I can't figure my share until I know the whole amount."

Vyry could see the white man, Mr. Pippins, was getting redder in the face and his voice was more irritable. He kept putting his hand in his pocket as though he were fingering something. She spoke quietly.

"That's fine sir. We'll get you all the money we can get for the crop just as soon as we can go to town."

Slightly satisfied by her quiet tone which was also suggesting an end to the conversation, Mr. Pippins cast a baleful glance from Innis to Vyry. Then turning to leave he said, "See that you do."

Cotton was selling for fifty cents a pound and when his crop was ginned Innis Brown had five hundred pounds, which was a small crop, as he and Vyry had known when they were slaves on a big plantation, but they had two hundred and fifty dollars for Mr. Pippins, and they thought this should be satisfactory. Corn was not nearly as highly priced as cotton, but Innis Brown had seventy-five bushels of corn varying in size from nubbins to half-filled ears. Vyry estimated they needed

ten bushels for food, to be ground into meal and made into
lye hominy. Innis felt he also needed fifteen bushels for feed,
some cracked corn for chickens, and some for the mule, which
was a real necessity since there was very little hay. This would
leave fifty bushels of corn and twice as much as they had for
themselves. Corn would not bring more than a dollar a
bushel, if that much, and this meant at the most fifty more
dollars for Mr. Pippins. Vyry's vegetables, not already canned
or stored for the winter, would barely fetch another fifty dollars on the market, but Innis Brown felt quite happy when
he counted three hundred and fifty dollars in money to Mr.
Pippins for his share.

"It's all the money we is got in the world, but we knows
you wants to be fair with us, and so we . . ."

"Hell, nigger, I ain't running no Sunday school society. You
owe me one hundred and fifty more dollars on this year's
crop."

"But sir . . ."

"I know you say this is all you got, and as you say, I want
to be fair with you so we'll just mark that up to next year's
bill. You can pay me back the hundred and fifty dollars you
owe for this year when you make another crop next year.
That's fair enough, isn't it?"

And when Innis looked from Vyry back to Mr. Pippins
again as though wondering what to say to this turn of affairs,
Vyry hastened to say, "Yessir, I reckon that's fair enough."

"Well now, just sign the contract, here with your mark
again."

And Innis much bewildered and disturbed signed again.

But as soon as Mr. Pippins was gone, Vyry said, "We's
gotta get away from here right now!"

"But you seen me just sign for another year."

"I knows that, but I don't care, we ain't staying. That white
man means trouble, and we ain't never gwine git outen his
debt. Another year he'll tack on some more, and knowing us
is ignorant will just make it worser and worser. Talking bout
us owing him for feed when we ain't bought no feed! Naw,
Gawd knows we gotta get away!"

"When?"

"Right now. Soon as we can get our rags and junk together.
Naw, Lawd, we ain't staying on this here bad land and letting
that white man get us more and more in debt until we can't
even much eat."

"Well, where is we gwineta go? You knows how hard it was getting here."

"Yeah, I knows that too, but ain't no use'n your thinking we can make it here because we can't."

"Maybe we could get them forty acres and a mule."

"Whereabouts?"

"Maybe if we goes to Montgomery?"

"Well, I dunno if we can make it to Montgomery or not, but we can start out trying. Anything better'n staying here."

"Well, we is just getting out in the road now with no place to go."

"It ain't wintertime yet. We can find us something. I ain't in family way neither like I was before and us can take our time."

"I dunno. Maybe, but I just don't rightly know."

"Well, I knows one thing, if we doesn't leave here now we gwine be sorry."

And so after hastily getting their things together once more they got in the wagon and started northwest toward Montgomery. They had to stop and ask directions, but they did not breathe easily until they left the county line behind them and started again across the wiregrass country.

I'm a-rolling, I'm a-rolling,
I'm a-rolling through an unfriendly world.
I'm a-rolling, I'm a-rolling,
Through an unfriendly world.

46   Brand-new house with windows
from the mill

The wagon broke down on the outskirts of Troy, a little
town that was the seat of Pike County. The axle gave way
and the wagon dropped to the ground. Fortunately, no one
was hurt, but this was just one more problem added to their
homelessness.

"I gotta find a blacksmith to fix this wagon, and I dunno
if he'll come out here or no."

"Somebody gotta come here. We can't take the wagon to
town and the axle broke."

The mule refused to budge, so Innis walked to town and
Vyry sat in the wagon with the children until he came riding
back on a horse with the blacksmith jogging along beside
him, tools and all. When the wagon was fixed and the stubborn mule off again, it was dark and they entered the bustling
village with no place to go. They were putting up the mule

in the livery stable where the blacksmith had offered them a stall until they could get located when a well-dressed white man inquired from the blacksmith if he knew anybody who wanted work. He looked at Innis Brown and Vyry, and Innis stepped forward.

"Sir, we'd be much obliged to you if you'd hire me. I'm able to do most anything."

"Can you cook?"

"No sir, but my wife can."

"Where do you live?"

"Sir, we's hunting a place right now."

"What all have you got?"

"Well, sir, we's got our three chilluns and a wagon load of stuff."

"That's no trouble. I own plenty nigra houses, but there's no place for your mule and wagon."

Innis arranged with the blacksmith to return the wagon and mule to the livery stable once they had moved their belongings, and if he could not find a place later, perhaps the blacksmith could sell them for him.

"My name is Jacobson and my wife'll be mighty happy if your wife can cook. We haven't had a decent cook since the war ended."

Mr. Jacobson did indeed own a number of houses for Negroes in a settlement near the railroad tracks and not very far from his house where Vyry and Innis were hired to work.

"What I'm to do with my chilluns when I'm working?" asked Vyry.

"We'll figger out something," said Innis, who was so relieved to find shelter and work on their first evening in the town. When the Jacobsons learned how well Vyry could cook they said they would pay a combined twenty-five dollars a month for the services of both Vyry and Innis.

"You won't have to buy food, and you can have the house rent-free."

"It sounds all right to me," said Vyry, and Innis nodded his head in assent. What was even better, the Jacobsons did not ask them to sign a contract. Mr. Jacobson owned a lot of land and several businesses in the town, so that he was quite wealthy. His wife seemed much relieved to have help and she was quite nice to Vyry. Gradually the Browns learned that the Jacobsons owned half the town and controlled most of the people in it. After the first week in the town, however,

Vyry knew she did not like the community where she was living.

"First thing, these colored folks is too low-class and just nothing but riff-raff."

"What you mean?"

"All night you can hear folks hollering and screaming. They's razor cutting and shooting and drinking. I ain't useta sitch and I don't like it, and I never will."

"They works in the sawmills and the turpentine camps round here and I reckon they wants some pleasure when they's off from work."

The first Saturday night Vyry and Innis Brown and their children were in Troy they had gone to bed when they heard such yelling and cursing and horses and dogs that Vyry and Innis sat up in bed. He was about to make a light in one of the new kerosene lamps they had recently acquired when Vyry said, "Don't you make no light!" They got out of bed and went to the front window to peep out and they saw a big commotion in the streets. There were six horses and riders. The riders were all dressed in white sheets and had masks on their faces that covered their heads with only holes for their eyes and nose and mouth.

"My God in glory, what is them things, ghostes?"

"Lawd knows, I ain't never seen nothing like it."

One of the white-sheeted riders was pounding on the door of a colored woman who lived alone in a house not far from where the Browns were living. While he knocked another man was screaming, "Come on out of there you goddamned whore, we gonna teach you black bitches a lesson tonight."

Suddenly three of the men rushed the door and in a few minutes they came out with the woman in her nightgown. They were dragging her out of the house while she screamed, "Help, Lawd have mercy, help!" Evidently nobody dared go to her assistance and Vyry and Innis Brown could hear the woman screaming as the riders galloped away with her and until they were out of earshot.

Next morning bright and early the Negroes in the community were congregated in the streets talking about the night before. To Vyry's horror Innis Brown told her the men had visited the woman and Ku Kluxed her and she was back in her house right now. They took her off and tarred and feathered her in the woods and she had dragged herself home before day in the morning. Innis Brown finished by saying, "They say she was entertaining white mens."

"Well, how come they ain't took the white mens?"

"Is you crazy?"

Vyry went to the woman's house later in the day to carry her some food and see how she was and she came home more agitated than ever.

"I thought I would just go up there and see if I could do something for her, but ain't nothing to be done. That woman gwine die. They poured hot tar all over her and she is just blistered from head to foot. Then they covered her with chicken feathers, and just ain't no ways to help her at all. Even if you gits the cold tar off without tearing off her skin and her flesh she still burned black underneath it. Jesus! I knows we can't stay here."

"Aw now, Vyry, we ain't a-fixing to move again on account of that there woman, is we?"

"What you reckon?"

"Naw!"

"Well-er-rer I doesn't know what you figgering on but the quicker we gits away the better I'm gwine to like it."

The Jacobsons paid so well, however, that Vyry and Innis agreed that if they saved their money they would soon be able to get another place, maybe one of their own. With this in mind, Vyry tried to make herself satisfied for awhile.

"Mister Jacobson done offer me a job in his sawmill."

"Well, I doesn't want you to take it."

"How come? I'll make more money and we'll be ables to get us a farm."

"You ain't got no business working with them low-class folks in them sawmills and turpentine camps. Them is the worstest folks, just nothing but roustabouts."

"Well, I done told him I'll do it."

"Well, you gwine be sorry."

"I don't know about that."

"Wait and see."

Innis lasted two weeks before Mr. Jacobson decided to shut down work at the local sawmill near Troy and go down deeper in the piney woods.

"Now I reckon you wants to hear me say I ain't got no complaint?"

"Well, is you?"

"Yes, I is. That means you gwine down there to live with them peoples what doesn't do nothing but drink and give they money to them bad womens."

"Well, I ain't no drunkard and I ain't got no money for

bad womens. I wants to make a home for you and the chilluns and I wants to do it fast. I doesn't like no town living and I wants to get away from here, too."

"Well, all I got to say is I doesn't like it, your gwine off and leaving us here by ourselves."

In the end, Vyry persuaded him not to go, but when Innis was talking to Mr. Jacobson about it, he was surprised at the white man's reaction.

"Vyry's right, of course. A lot of prostitutes hang around the sawmills and turpentine camps, and it is a bad environment."

"I knows she's right, sir, she always is, but I was just trying to raise us some money fast so's we can have our own farm. We ain't use to city living and city folks and ways, and we likes it better in the country. Farming is all I rightly knows."

"Well, that's no problem. There's over a million acres of public land right here in Alabama, and the government says all you have to do is stake your claim and prove up by staying there five years."

"Yessir, but we ain't never been ables to find none of that good land. I heard tell, too, they was gwine give every freedman forty acres of land and a mule, but I ain't never seen none."

"Oh, that's just hearsay. I don't think that's ever going to happen, at least not here in Alabama, but you could homestead on public land."

"Whereabouts, sir?"

"Let me see if I can't find a tract nearby. We don't wanta miss Vyry's cooking."

The place Mr. Jacobson found had exactly the forty acres Innis Brown wanted. There were fifteen acres of heavily wooded land, and the rest would be open to cultivation. They picked a lovely site for a house, high on a hill, and even found water on the place.

Little Harry was a toddler, Minna was ten years old, and Jim was nearly thirteen, but all were willing to help Paw build the new house. With Mr. Jacobson's sawmills nearby, they could have a house with real lumber and glass windows made at the mill. Vyry decided that she wanted a house with four rooms and a wide hall through the center of the house. This wide center hall was really another big room with two rooms opening into it on each side. The front and back doors also opened into this hall, and there were front and back porches.

While Vyry and Minna were planning the house and deciding where each chair, table, and bed would go, as well as the chest, the spinning wheel, and Vyry's brand-new churn, Innis Brown concerned himself with a barn, a hen house, an outhouse, and other outbuildings. Now at last they would have a real home and a farm of their own. The work took a long time because Vyry was still cooking for the Jacobsons and Innis did many odd jobs, so that any time Mr. Jacobson needed him he put down his saw and hammer and went to town to finish off another job before working again on his house.

During the entire time Vyry was working for the Jacobsons she kept the children, Minna and Harry, with her. Sometimes Innis kept Jim with him, but there were times when Jim, too, stayed with his mother. They played in the Jacobsons' back yard, and Minna was helpful in sundry ways, as a nurse for Harry, as an errand girl, and doing odd jobs that Vyry had taught her. From the first, Vyry put her foot down against leaving them at home. She did not trust the neighborhood, and she said, "I feels better when I knows where they is."

"That's all right, Vyry, you know they're always welcomed and free to play outside and if they get cold they can come inside and warm themselves."

"You been real nice and kind, Missus Jacobson, and I appreciates it. I really does. Truth is, I wants my chilluns to go to school, but we ain't never been near no school for them to go to."

"Well, that's one of the big issues up now all over the state about free schools for white and colored. There's a lot of feeling against mixed schools and I can see why, but the big question is how to pay for schools. I believe most of the people want common school education, but there are some against the school tax and unless the schools are supported by a tax on all the people we couldn't have free schools."

"How much would this here tax be?"

"Oh, not much. I don't think more than fifty cents or a dollar a year for every male of voting age."

"What is voting age?"

"Twenty-one. Didn't you know?"

"Nome. I ain't never heard much talk about voting. Fifty cents or a greenback dollar don't seem like too much a year to me, especially if my chilluns could go to school."

"Of course, you know the churches have got schools too,

private schools where you have to pay. And I believe I heard once the Freedman's Bureau is setting up schools for the children of former slaves all over the South, but then you hear so many things, good and bad, you don't know what to believe."

"Yes, ma'am, that's the sho-nuff God's truth. Course I wouldn't care what kind of school it was as long as my chilluns could learn to read and write and cipher."

"Well, I tell you what, the first thing they would need would be two or three books, maybe one, and a slate, I don't know. I don't have as much education as my husband, but I have had the rudiments of schooling. I can read and write and figure. I'll see if I can find a book for Minna."

Vyry struggled to control her emotions before she tried to answer her employer.

"Ma'am, that would be real good of you, and I wants you to know I wouldn't never forget your kindness."

Throughout the fall of the year they were building the house. It would be Christmas when they moved. Vyry decided that she would work throughout the winter for Mrs. Jacobson, but she and Innis Brown seemed to take it for granted that they would take the time off from any other work to get spring plowing done, and after that Vyry would stay at home. Sometime after the middle of the summer she was going to have another baby. They put the finishing touches on their brand-new house with loving care.

"Now we's got to have another cow," said Innis.

"Yes," said Vyry, "and a new team of mules."

"I thinks we got the money."

"Yes, bad as it has hurt my pride living among them low-class folks, this year been real prosperous."

"We can thank God we's doing more'n just living."

As he had promised, Innis bought Vyry a new churn when they moved into the house. Her precious chest and spinning wheel and the new churn had places of honor in the back hall. She had a big blue jardiniere from the Dutton plantation to grace her front hall. Minna was learning to sew and she helped her mother make curtains for every window in the house.

"I heard tell they's got a new preacher come to town talking bout opening up a church and a school house."

"Whereabouts?"

"Well, right now they's a little ramshackle shanty ain't nobody using belongs to Mister Jacobson, and he say if we wants to fix it up on our own time and expense colored folks can have it."

"What kinda preacher is he?"

"Baptist."

"That sounds real nice. I hopes it ain't just talk."

"You means like the forty acres and a mule?" and Innis grinned. Vyry smiled back at him and nodded her head.

"Well, ain't no law agin finding out. They's gwine be a meeting called come Sunday night."

Vyry could hardly believe that all she and Innis wanted seemed so near the point of coming true, their new house and farm, a chance for Minna and Jim to go to school and learn to read and write, and the organization of a new church. Her heart felt full to the breaking point. It was their happiest Christmas since Surrender, although Innis reminded her that their first Christmas was his marrying time and would always be special.

"Look like everything come right at Christmas time."

"I reckon."

Spring of 1869 was a turbulent spring in Alabama. There were Negro soldiers in the streets of Troy as well as many northern white strangers. The local white people and the northern whites clashed and there were scuffles among the Negroes and between the Negroes and whites. Vyry and Innis kept thinking how glad they were that they lived on the outskirts of town on top of one of its many hills. They went back and forth to the Jacobsons throughout the month of March and meanwhile they were going on Sunday nights to church meeting.

The question of a new Negro school had created some controversy. The whites wanted to know where the money was coming for "nigger" children to read books when there were fields that needed to be worked, sawmills, and turpentine camps that were going idle. Mr. Jacobson told Innis he didn't know how it was all going to work out, that they should be careful. Innis told Vyry that it was all right for Minna, but he thought it might be a mistake to send Jim to school.

"Why?" asked Vyry.

"He's old enough to work, that's why."

"But he got a right to learn, too, ain't he?"

"That ain't the point."

"What is the point?"

"The point is we needs him to help work."

"I wants him to go to school."

"Well, the white folks is saying . . ."

"I don't care what the white folks is saying. I wants my chilluns to learn to read and write."

"Well, they is *agin* it."

The subject became a sore topic even between Vyry and Innis. When the fifty cents tax was levied, the white folks claimed the Negroes would not pay, and Innis said, "We ain't got the money."

"We is got the money, Innis Brown, and you knows it."

"But we can't afford it."

"What else can we afford more'n book learning for your younguns?" And, stricken by the conflict, she looked at him and he dropped his eyes.

April came and time to leave the Jacobsons and Vyry was surprised to see that Mrs. Jacobson had not expected it, did not like it, and was not only bitter but almost nasty about it.

"You mean you're going to stop cooking for us now that you've got yourself a house and a farm?"

"Well, ma'am, I figgers my husband needs me to help work the place."

"What about Jim? Can't he help him?"

Vyry felt a pang of fear, but she continued to look steadily at Mrs. Jacobson while she spoke, "Yes'm, Jim can help, but I figered whilst all the spring plowing and planting's going on they can't hardly manage by themselves."

"Can't Minna keep the baby and look after the house?"

"Yes'm, she can," and now Vyry was twisting her apron in her hands, and her agitation must have been visible to her employer at this point.

"Oh, I know, you want them to go to school, is that it?" And Vyry could tell from the accusing tone of Mrs. Jacobson's voice that she really didn't like the idea even though it was she who had given Minna her first book.

"Well, ma'am, I was thinking you more'n anybody else would understand."

"Yes, I do understand. I understand how you colored people don't want to work the way you useta. What's more you won't work the way you useta. You expect everything to come dropping in your laps, houses and land and schools and churches and money, and you want to leave the white people holding the bag. We've done everything we can for you, my husband and I . . ."

"Yes'm, you sho is," said Vyry miserably trying to avoid a big misunderstanding by interrupting, "and we appreciates it, ma'am, we does."

"It doesn't look like it now."

"I wasn't planning on quitting working for you for good, Missus Jacobson. I just wants to help him get the cotton and corn and taters in the ground."

"Oh, yes, you want everything at your convenience and none at mine. You take off any time at all and you need not come back." And Vyry, with her head bowed, sorrowfully turned away.

One April morning Vyry and Innis and Jim were hard at work in the field. It was nearly noon and they would soon stop working and go to the house for dinner. Minna was in the house with Harry. She could clean the house and wash the dishes and tend Vyry's cooking pots while the others were in the field. When Harry was asleep she tried to figure out the words in her picture book which Mrs. Jacobson had gvien her. She had worn it hard and thin and she fussed with Jim if his hands were dirty and messed up her book while he tried to read it in the evenings. They would have fought over that book if it had not been for Vyry. This was a bright, sunshiny morning, a Friday, and although Minna did not exactly understand the difference in all the days yet, she was learning. She knew it was Friday because Vyry kept track of church meeting night and there were two more nights before Sunday. Minna put down her book and went to look at the pots on the stove. Standing in the back door were three half-grown white boys or young men, and they were walking into the house. Minna was startled and stepped back toward the room where Harry was sleeping.

"Hey, nigger-gal, what you cooking?" And one of the boys moved toward Minna, while the other two giggled. Minna backed quickly into the bedroom and grabbed Harry. Awakened suddenly from a nap, he hollered.

"Make him shut up, nigger-gal, or I'll cut his black throat with my razor."

They were still coming in the room and Minna, now frightened out of her wits, had Harry in her arms and was backing into a corner. When he screamed again and she saw the boy flick the razor she put her hand over Harry's mouth and muffled his sound. The boys were still grinning, and one said, "We wants a drink of water, nigger-gal, come on outside and give it to us." But they stood blocking her path and when she made an effort to move they laughed and moved in closer. Now the third boy looked at his friends and then back at Minna and Harry, and pointing his finger from one to the other he began to mimic,

> Eeny, meeny, minie, moe,
> Catch a nigger by his toe,
> If he holler let him go,
> Eeny, meeny, minie, moe.

And they were laughing loudly when suddenly coming through the house were Innis, Vyry, and Jim. The boys were startled when they looked up and saw three their size. One of them wanted to stand his ground and get ugly, but after a moment's hard silence another said, "Come on yall, let's git outa this nigger house. It stinks." And laughing loudly again, they ran out. Minna was near the point of hysteria and she collapsed in Vyry's arms screaming, "Maw, oh Maw!"

Innis and Jim were unable to utter a word but they fully understood Minna's terror and the whole family was stunned into silence. Saturday morning Vyry did not go into the field with Innis and Jim. She knew she could not leave Minna alone in the house again, even though they were so near.

"I'm just thankful it wasn't no worse than it was."

"It was bad enough, Maw. They nearabouts scared me to death."

"I knows they did. Your Paw and me keeps wondering what they come up here for in the first place."

"I guess they was just out in the woods and wanted water, so they come over here and then they seen me here by myself and started meddling."

"I dunno. I just don't know."

Vyry and Minna were cooking and baking for Sunday as well as Saturday.

"We's gwine have the new preacher for dinner tomorrow and then we's all gwine to town for evening meeting."

"All us?"

"Yeah, your Paw says so."

Although Vyry worked hard all day scrubbing and cleaning and cooking and baking, and sometimes singing from long force of habit, she was deeply troubled over the boys' intrusion on Friday. She wanted to tell somebody like the

Jacobsons, but she knew Mrs. Jacobson was still angry. "She'll just hafta git over it, I reckons."

"What did you say, Maw?"

"Nothing, Minna, I was just thinking."

Sunday was a merry day. The new house shone with Vyry's best. Everybody was happy to have company. Once, when Jim was gulping down chicken and dumplings faster than seemed company manners, Innis roughly reproved him, "Sirrah, there boy! Ain't nobody running you no race. This food ain't gwine no place." But to the preacher he said, "Eat hearty, Reverend, if they ain't enough my wife'll cook some more."

And they laughed, for Vyry always had more than enough.

They were climbing the hill that night between nine and ten o'clock. Innis was riding Harry on his back. Vyry was still deep in the mood of the meeting, hearing the singing and the preaching and the stirring testimonies. She could still feel the intense joy of the song she was humming,

> Tell me how did you feel when you come out the wilderness?
> Come out the wilderness,
> Come out the wilderness,
> Tell me how did you feel when you come out the wilderness
> Leaning on the Lawd?

She had Minna's hand in hers, and the little girl was looking up at the sky full of stars and the house at the top of the hill that was home, when suddenly she cried out, "Look, Maw! Paw, looka-there!"

It was happening so suddenly they hardly realized the stunning impact. They saw a half-dozen white-sheeted and hooded figures, some on horseback, some holding horses, and others busy on the ground. Then they saw them hoist a huge rough cross-like structure tall as a tree and flaming with fire, and it rose up on the hill against their house. Suddenly they felt the earth rock under their feet, and they smelled the strong fumes of kerosene oil, and they heard an explosive noise break forth on the spring night, while expertly directed flames licked their beautiful new house and it burst into a roaring fire. As the blaze leaped up the white-sheeted riders galloped away and vanished into the spring night.

Innis began running and Vyry, with her heart in her throat, tried to run, but she felt herself stumbling forward heavily and weighted as though in a dream. Jim and Minna were running and screaming and thinking this must be a nightmare and not their brand-new house with windows from the mill. Innis was fighting the flames to pull out Vyry's new churn, her chest, and her spinning wheel. They were blackened with smoke and the smoke was choking him, so they were all that he managed to save.

Tis the song, the sigh of the weary.
Hard Times, Hard Times, come again no more.
Many days you have lingered
Around my cabin door.
Oh Hard Times, come again no more.

47   *Bad luck and hard times*

As the first mist of morning rose over the hills, Vyry poked among the rubble and the warm ashes of her gutted home trying to salvage any possible possession. At first, she was just another part of the gray mist that enfolded her, the gray shawl she was wearing, and the gray sky against whose grayness she was stooped alone in gray relief. Occasionally she found an iron pot or a fork and a spoon in the charred remains piled near the blackened chimney that had been the chimney of her kitchen. A little wind blew among the ashes, and sometimes the dust blew into her face. Then she would slowly straighten up and, carefully blinking her eyes, let the tears wash her eyes clean before bending down to continue her dismal search.

"I oughta be glad we is living. I oughta be glad ain't none of my chilluns got burned up in that fire. I oughta be glad me and Innis is still strong and can build us another house. I oughta be glad we is got food saved, and if we ain't got nothing but the clothes on our backs I can make more. I oughta be glad for the chickens and the cow and the pigs, for the new team of mules, and for the crop we got planted in the fields. But I ain't. Lawd, I ain't glad about nothing this morning. You knows I ain't. This here ain't nothing but a gray morning for me when I can't see no sunshine shining nowhere, Lawd. I done tried and tried. We is done been from pillar to post, and just when I thought we was bout to git us a home at last, they done burned all we got to the ground. Why, Lawd? Just tell me, why? And maybe I'll try to understand. What is I done to them white folks? Lawd, what is I done? Is you punishing us, and is I just ungrateful? Jesus, I sho can't understand nothing this morning. I'm trying, Lawd, I'm sho trying to understand. But here we is outa doors and no place to go, got three younguns and me fixing to have another. What is the reason, Lawd? What is we done? If you tells me now, I'll try to understand."

She stood up again because the tears were blinding her eyes. Standing there in the gray morning she looked around her as the fog lifted. She looked far beyond the other hills of Troy shrouded, too, in mist. She watched the sun rising, only a thin streak of blood penciling the sky, and in the midst of the sounds and sights of a new day dawning she gave a deep sigh. She was breathing out her heaviness upon the morning, but it would not leave her. She heard birds singing, brown meadow or field larks taking flight, blue jays and mockingbirds twittering noisily, roosters crowing lustily, and above them she saw the first flames of light running wildly through the sky. Her day's work was calling. She thought first of her chickens, and then guiltily she remembered her children and her husband sleeping in the barn. *Not even quilts left to kiver them! I better git some breakfast cooking.* But when she remembered she was standing in the ashes of her kitchen, she sank down to the ground and began sobbing again. Covering her head with her shawl she rocked herself back and forth.

Innis Brown thought he was waking from a bad nightmare. He often had these bad dreams at night, thought somebody was running him, or lashing him with a whip, or he heard bloodhounds on his heels. "Musta been something bad bout to happen" he thought, and waking, he remembered.

"Great God-a-mighty, they burned down the house!"

He looked around him, wondering why he felt so stiff and sore. Jim was curled up alone in a big bundle of hay with all his clothes on. Minna was sleeping with the baby, Harry, asleep in her arms, and in her sleep she was crying. Her little body sobbed with a heaving motion, and a tear ran down her cheek as though she had cried all night in her sleep. And they were all in the barn. Now he realized that Vyry was not there. He jumped up and ran looking for her.

At night when Innis prayed he was most grateful to God for Vyry. His whole life had changed with Surrender and Vyry. She and her children and little Harry had brought him more happiness in four years than he had ever known in his whole life before they met. She was his reason for living, to please her, and make a life for her, and go through life working by her side. She made every day a bright adventure. It was she who lifted his spirits when he was down because she could always see things getting better. He was very proud of the house because it made her so happy. Now in the morning's confusion his first clear thought was of Vyry. The second thumping in his heart was for that little stranger they were expecting in the late summer or early fall, he couldn't remember which.

And now, we got no house. Maybe we oughta build another one right here. We's got us a field planted. We's got a good barn and a hen house and we's got some land. I still got my tools and I still got a little money. I reckon we can still make out if Vyry thinks we can. In the daylight he took a few minutes to accustom his eyes to the sunrise. *I musta overslept. Time to feed.* But he was looking for Vyry. He didn't want to startle her or wake the children by yelling for her. When he didn't see her feeding the chickens nor drawing water for breakfast, he looked out at the smoking ruins of their house. At first she was so buried in the gray ashes he did not recognize her, but as she rocked he saw her moving gently and he ran to her.

When he touched her, she looked up, her face contorted with crying and the ashes dirtying her face and all her clothes. He knelt down beside her and tried to dry her tears. It distressed him to see her sobbing and he didn't know what to say.

"Aw, honey, please don't cry. I just can't stand it if you cries. I don't know what I'll do if you is to just give up and keep on crying like this."

"What *is* we gwine do?" she wailed, and then he saw she had been crying a long time. Her eyes were puffed, her bosom heaved terribly with heavy broken sobbing and the tears ran down her smudgy face. The note of abject hopelessness in her voice jolted him. Automatically he put out his arm and drew her to him. She fell against him sobbing in a fresh spurt. For an empty moment words failed him and then he blurted out, half asserting himself, half questioning her,

"Do? What is we gwine do? Ain't we gwine do what we's always been doing, try again? Maybe we can build us another house right here."

She stopped her sobbing at once and stood up.

"Anh-anh, Innis Brown, we ain't building no more house here."

"Well, all right then, let's us just wait until we can git ourselves together, again. We sho ain't fixing to build nary notha one right now, but I was just thinking we's got us a field planted here, and we's got a barn and a well, and chickens, and I got my tools, and . . ."

"Naw." She spoke dully with deep dejection. "Doesn't you knows yet what them Ku Kluxers means?"

"Naw, what they means?"

"They means git! 'Nigger don't you let the sun go down with you still in this town.' They means *GIT!*"

The children in the barn awoke fully clothed, got up, and stretched, and came out blinking in the daylight, looking for Maw and Paw. Their solemn faces expressed their memory of the terrible night that had passed. It was morning and time for breakfast, but now they saw again that their brand-new house, with windows from the mill, was all burned down. Harry whimpered and clung to Minna, but he called for his mother, "Maw!" Vyry heard him and started out of the ashes, slowly moving to her children standing in the sunlight and shadowed by the barn. They were all smudged with smoke and ashes and dirt and they looked bedraggled and woebegone. Vyry looked at her downcast family and tried to set their day in motion.

"Paw, I reckon you better make a fire out here and put my wash pot on with water to boil. We's all could stand some washing up. I'll try'n fix something to eat by the time you gits through feeding and milking." Vyry's voice was so dull and toneless, Minna said, "Maw is you feeling po-ly?"

"Naw, honey, your Maw is all right."

But Innis heard her in disbelief. His shoulders sagged as he looked out over his planted field and all his half-finished work. Every pail hanging in the barn was smoked and dirty, bue he took one and turned to get water for the chickens and the stock.

It would have been impossible for the people in the town of Troy not to see the Sunday night fire that blazed on one of its surrounding hills, and Monday, as the day grew, people not only inquired about the fire they had seen, but many of them came out to the hill to see what had happened. Usually a fire attracts a crowd immediately, but the big fiery Ku Klux cross that heralded the flames was a frightening thing and Negroes were not likely to venture out in the night. Those whites watching it were either sure it was none of their business and not their place to interfere, or they were amused to see flames destroying another "nigger" house. But in the morning people started gathering to see the damage.

There were some people who came to ask Vyry and Innis if they could help them. Among these was the preacher they had fed the day before. He was also the teacher of the one Negro school newly organized in Troy and the sign of the Ku Klux house burning was not of little importance to him. He said to Innis Brown, "You know you have to report this."

"What you mean? Who I'm supposed to report it to?"

"To the government."

"Whereabouts is the gov'mint?"

"I mean to their headquarters here in the town."

Vyry heard them talking and she walked over to where they were standing.

"Reverend Whittaker says I gotta report the fire."

"Report it? Report it for what?"

"Well, Mrs. Brown, it's the law. They're trying to find out about all this lawlessness and trouble colored people are having everywhere."

"Well, what is it us gotta report? We seen them white-hooded mens upon they horses and we seen them hist that there big burning cross up in front of our house and the next thing we knowed, pouf, the house went up in a blaze and they was gone." And she threw out her hands in a hopeless gesture.

But there was further support for Reverend Whittaker's

ideas when two Negro soldiers on horseback rode out about mid-morning.

"Sir, can I help you?" Innis asked.

"We come out here to help *you*. When did all this here fire happen?"

"Last night."

"Did you see anybody?"

"Yes sir. We sho did. We seen bout six mens on horseback hist up a burning cross in front of our house and I reckon the fire musta caught from that. But I ain't sho cause I just don't rightly know."

"Did you find any empty cans or buckets around?"

"Yes sir. I found a bucket and a big empty can look like it'd hold a drum of coal oil."

"Where is it?"

"I got it in the barn, sir, you can come over this a way."

"What did you say the cross looked like?"

"It was a great big thing looked like it was tall as the house and they musta had it wrapped in something and soaked with coal oil and then set afire cause it was justa blazing when we seen it from the bottom of the hill."

"Was there an explosion?"

"You means a big noise?"

"Yes."

"Yes sir. They was. They was something heavy-like what rocked the ground under us."

"Like dynamite?"

"No sir. I figger it wasn't nothing like dynamite."

"Well, we'll take this evidence back into town with us. Meanwhile, what are you going to do?"

"Well, sir, if it was left to me, I'd stay right here and try to raise my crop I got planted in the fields and maybe I could build me another house, but my wife is scared to death. She fixing to have another youngun, and she don't want to stay here even much tonight."

"I don't blame her, myself. The best thing is to go somewere else where you will feel safe. These Kluxers means business when they does something like this."

"Trouble is, we ain't got nowhere to go. All we's got is tied up in this crop and was tied up in this house. We ain't got a stick of furniture, no more'n the clothes we got on our backs, and we ain't got no money."

"Well, the Government will help you."

Now Innis Brown's irritation surprised them.

"Gov'mint? Gov'mint? Gov'mint you say? I done heard that word Gov'mint until I'm sick to my stomach. The Gov'mint gwine give you this, the Gov'mint gwine give you that. The Gov'mint gwine give every nigger forty acres and a mule. The Gov'mint got good land. The Gov'mint will help you get settled. The Gov'mint gwine have free schools for colored. Sir, does you want to know what the Gov'mint done give me? Nothing. Not nary nickel's worth of nothing. Do you hear me?"

They listened silently and somewhat amused at his exasperation.

"Mister, did you ask em?"

"No sir. I ain't never been ables to catch up with the Gov'mint. All I knows about since Surrender is I'm supposed to git to Montgomery and I'll find the Gov'mint representation there."

"Mister, the Government is everywhere. It's right here in Troy just like in Montgomery. You got your freedom on account of the Government. And that's just what we doing out here, now, we suppose to help you on account of that's what the Government is for. They *is* helping colored folks get land and go to school and vote in the elections, too. That's how come the Ku Kluxers is getting so bad. They's mad with the Government on account of you and me. Mister, don't carry down the Government. That's all the friend us colored folks is got. Did you know that Gen'l Ulysses S. Grant is now the President of the Newnited States?"

"Naw!" said Innis, "you don't say!" And he shook his head in amazement.

"Then I reckon you didn't know colored folks' votes helped to put him there."

When the soldiers went back to town, they promised Innis Brown and Vyry they would be back and told them to get their things together to leave. Vyry and Innis began to take stock of what they had to carry. Vyry had salvaged most of her pots and pans and her iron skillets, some tin plates and a few knives and forks and spoons that didn't have wooden handles. Some of her things were only half burned, some were blackened with the smoke and a little cleaning and scouring would restore them to their original brightness. They had stock, a cow, pigs, chickens, and the new team of mules. This time they would not sell anything but carry all they could manage. There was still some seed they had not put into the ground, but only a very little. There was always meat hanging in the smokehouse, and this would last until they could smoke more.

Curiosity seekers after midday watched Vyry in her sad preparations. The children, always excited about a journey, were not happy about leaving this time. They took their cue from Vyry, who was frightened, tense, bewildered, and deeply depressed. She remembered with distress all her rows of preserves and canned and pickled goods, jellies, and jams, all lost in the fire. She looked at her blackened chest, her spinning wheel, and her churn, but none of these things brought her joy. She moved through the day in a daze and she found, when the afternoon sun advanced before them forming long shadows, that the day had rushed away in a gray fog of confusion.

In the afternoon Mr. Jacobson came out to see them.

"I heard about the fire in town and I came out to tell you how awfully sorry we are. My wife says if you want to come back, Vyry, she'd be glad to have you."

"No sir, Mr. Jacobson, but I thanks you just the same. I reckon we gotta be moving on."

"Yes, I don't guess you have much choice."

It was with Innis, however, that he had real business and it was to him that he addressed his next question.

"Where do you think you will go?"

"I dunno, sir. We don't know where we's gwine."

"Well, now you can forget about anything between us that's owing."

"Oh, but sir, I knows an honest debt and I means to pay."

"No. You got nothing now to pay with, and the fire has burned up the debt. Do you need any money?"

"Well, sir, we ain't got any but I reckon we'll do the best we can, cause we always been ables to make out."

"Well, my wife sent out some bedding. She says she's sorry she's got no clothes to fit the children, but she put some things in there you and Vyry might be able to use. I hear that the preacher is getting some clothes together, too."

"Sir, we sho do appreciate it. I reckon we's worse off for clothes and bedstuff than anything else."

"And here, this is just a little money to help you till you can get settled. Take it, Innis, because you're going to need it."

"Sir, I don't know how to thank you."

"Don't try. Things get out of control every once and a-while, especially after a war. But I hope things will quiet down soon and you and your family can get settled on a farm."

"You think, sir, it's just the times . . . our getting burned out and all?"

"Why, of course, you're just caught in something that's a bigger thing than we are and the changes are not good. But you are good people and eventually you'll be all right. But I must be going. Good luck to you all, now."

"Thank you, sir."

"Goodbye, Mister Jacobson."

It was early dusk when Reverend Whittaker returned with a small bundle of clothing for the children, some bedding, and a purse of money he had collected from the Negro community.

"I heard you talking this morning as though you might be leaving at once. If I had a few more days, I could do better."

"Thanks, Reverend, we appreciates what you done. We sho hates to leave just when they's a church and a school and everything, but I reckon it's the Lawd's will."

"Not that you got burned out. I don't believe that. But I do believe God will provide for you wherever you go."

"Yes sir, I reckon He will."

"I was counting on having you two in church and Minna in school, but I know you got to go. I'm glad I got to eat one good meal in your house. Do you know where you're going?"

"No sir. We dunno nothing but we got to go."

"Well, I pray you find a good safe place and get settled on a farm of your own before long."

"Thankye sir, thankye very much."

"Goodbye, now, and God bless you."

"Goodbye, Reverend."

In the evening the two Negro soldiers returned. They asked Innis, "Are you ready?"

"Yes sir, we is ready."

In the darkness they put the coop of chickens in the wagon, croker sacks of cotton and corn and potatoes, the iron kitchen utensils, the chest, the churn, and the spinning wheel, and tied the cow on the back of the wagon. There were three squealing baby pigs and a sow put in a pen and set down in the wagon with the children. Vyry and Innis drove the wagon.

They set out in darkness, but Vyry was anxious to go. Innis said to the soldiers, "But where is we gwine?"

"Don't worry; we're taking you clean outen this county, into Crenshaw County, and we have orders not to leave you till you're settled."

"Well thank God for that," said Innis. Then turning to smile at his tall thin wife who had not smiled all day, he said, "Does you feel better, honey?"

And looking up in his face she smiled tightly and nodded her head.

I sit upon a hornet's nest
I dance upon my head;
I tie a viper round my neck
And den I go to bed.
I kneel to the buzzard
And I bow to de crow
And eb'ry time I wheel erbout
I jump jis so;
Wheel about and turn about and do jis so,
Eb'ry time I wheel about I jump Jim Crow.

48   *Ku Klux Klan don't like no Koons*

The first morning Randall Ware worked in his shop after
the expulsion of Negroes from the Georgia Legislature, he
had a caller. Ed Grimes appeared in the open space where
Randall Ware was shoeing a horse and said, "Nigger, do you
own this land?"

Startled, Randall Ware looked up and caught his breath
before answering.

"Mister, you are standing on my property, and if you
doubt it you can find the deed recorded in the courthouse."

"I didn't ask you for any of your impertinence. I've seen
the records. Looks like you own nearly all the good land
around here."

"I own a fair share of the land around Dawson. I happened
to come by it honestly."

"Well, you've got a piece I want to buy."

"Where is it?"

Grimes went to the grist mill adjacent to the blacksmithy and he pointed diagonally across the railroad tracks to the land he had in mind.

"I'm sorry," said Randall Ware, "but it's not for sale."

"Nigger, are you telling me no?"

"I'm saying I don't want to sell."

"Well, we'll just see if we can't find some way to make you change your mind."

And with that, he turned on his heels and left the place. Randall Ware thought no more about the incident as the days passed and he was busy working in his shop. He learned from Henry Turner that the Negroes were going to appeal to Congress and beg to have Georgia removed again from the Union, but Randall Ware said he would have to stay near home for awhile. His journeyman was afraid to stay on the property alone.

It was late October and great masses of the Georgia people were more distracted than ever, for with the approaching presidential elections there was high feeling between the local whites and the black Republicans. Negroes everywhere were being urged to vote the Grant-Colfax ticket for the Republicans while the Conservative Democrats were stumping every section of the states for the Seymour-Blair ticket.

Randall Ware kept busy at his trade but on the eve of the election, at Turner's insistence, he began attending more Loyal League meetings and working to encourage local Negroes to hold fast to the Republican ticket. Sporadic spurts of violence were erupting around him, but since there had been no incidents in his immediate vicinity Randall Ware was caught unaware one night on returning from a political meeting. He heard a crowd of horsemen riding up to his shop. He turned to face them, the white-sheeted callers with their faces covered and saw them throw at his feet the body of a man. It was Jasper, his journeyman. Pinned across his bloody chest was a piece of foolscap also stained with his blood and with the crudely printed words:

DEAD, DAMNED, AND DELIVERED

Jasper had been shot in his right temple, but evidently before they killed him he had been brutally beaten with sticks for his flesh was cut and bleeding and his shirt was bloody and in shreds.

Randall Ware was alone. He needed someone to help him with the body of poor Jasper. He first made a cry in the streets for help, but nobody came. Then he made a light in his house, and went out again to find help. He had to walk about three-quarters of a mile to a Negro community, but when he returned with two men to help him, he found Jasper's body was gone, and his shop and the back-room serving as his living quarters were in shambles. He thanked the two colored men, who were wide-eyed with terror, and he told them he guessed he could manage alone. He would try to put his place to rights.

At four o'clock in the morning the riders came back again. He was again unprepared for violence and he made no attempt to run or try to escape. They grabbed him. Ware was a powerful man and he struggled until he felt himself hit on the head with a blow that felt like iron. He lost consciousness and when he came to himself they had him in the woods. When he opened his eyes he saw three men standing over him as he was lying on the ground. They came at him with blows about the head and face and although they were disguised he thought he recognized the voice of one who kept pounding and yelling,

"Nigger, who do you think you are? You think you good as a white man, don't you? You think you just as good, going to the State House and dressing up like a white man and owning all our good land. Don't you know you ain't nothing but a nigger? We know just what to do with a big black ugly baboon like you when you get so uppity you too big for your nigger britches."

Randall Ware wondered why they did not shoot him and kill him and get it over with. Why were they merely beating him? Did they mean to cut him to death and shoot him afterwards? Then he heard one whisper, "Why don't we kill him now?"

"Naw. I say naw. He got all them papers in the courthouse, ain't he? How we gonna git that land if we kill him? Beat him an inch of his goddamned life, but don't kill him."

It was broad daylight when they rode away on their horses. For a long while Randall Ware lay on the ground, half conscious, bleeding, and so sore he could scarcely move. His lip was cut, and he knew there was a bad cut over both eyes, and his face was swollen twice its size. He also had a large, painful lump on his head, and about his back and shoulders they had beaten him with what felt like wooden clubs but were actually stripped branches from the trees. He got to his knees but when he tried to open his eyes the blood ran down his face. He tried to stand and found he could not, so he began to crawl on his hands and knees out of the woods.

It was late afternoon when he finally made it into his shop, and then he was so exhausted he fell on his bed to sleep. In the darkness he awakened and lighted a lamp. He began to care for the cuts and bruises on his face and head, when he heard such a loud commotion in the streets he looked out and saw riders coming again. This time he would not wait. He quickly put out the lamp and ran into his grist mill. There he made his way to the great wheel that pulled the mill by water power and lowering himself quickly he dropped down into the water while holding to the rim of the half-submerged mill wheel.

He was not a minute too soon. He heard their voices and knew they were in his shop and house again. They ransacked the place again and began yelling and cursing and calling his name.

"I told you we oughta killed that black bastard."

"We got to teach him a permanent lesson."

"How long can we waste time here looking for him?"

"He ain't going nowhere. We can come back and git him later on."

And they left. But Randall Ware, now deathly afraid, waited another full hour before he came out of his grist mill after hiding under the water and holding on to the great wheel that ran the mill.

Early the next moring he had another caller. This time he would not answer, and he peeped out stealthily to see who it was. It was old Doc and he was banging on the door.

"Let me in. It's only me, Doc. Let me in, Ware. I know you are in there."

Randall Ware let the doctor in. At first, the black man glared at the white doctor, his swollen face and lip and half-closed eyes making him look like some half-mutilated animal. The blood was still on his head and face, and his body ached from the terrible beating.

"Look like you had an accident."

"Yeah, I reckon so. Accident strictly on purpose."

"Well, you better let me take a look at you. You need a doctor."

"Is that why you came here? To offer me your doctoring services?"

"Why not? I'm a doctor, am I not? And I don't think there's another one for miles around."

"Are you sure you weren't sent?"

"Well, what difference would that make? You still need the doctor, don't you?"

Randall Ware grudgingly admitted that he did. The doctor went to work on his face and head and he flinched under the probing of the sore and cut places. At first old Doc was strictly professional.

"Hmmm, that's a bad one. You took a mighty bad beating."

"Didn't I though? Wonder why they didn't kill me?"

"Oh, you know that answer as well as I do."

"On account of the land?"

"Yes. Are you willing to sell, now?"

"Do you think I've got any choice?"

"Not if you want to live and continue working here."

"And if I don't sell?"

"I'd advise you to leave, but you would be a fool to leave everything you've got just because of a little piece of land. Sell the land. You'll get a fair price."

Randall Ware snorted with a bitter sounding grunt. The doctor worked awhile longer in silence.

"And when I sell this piece, they'll want another and a bigger piece and that will keep on till I don't have any left."

"Oh, I don't know about that. There's a limit to most people's greed."

"For money or for land, for votes or for power?"

"Well, now, you might as well give up the idea of power and voting. You are going to get yourself absolutely killed if you don't quit all political activity."

"I thought you came to bring me a message."

"I can carry back your answer if you desire."

"And if my answer is not what they like?"

"Well, I couldn't say what might happen. You might have night visitors again, and this time you might end up like your journeyman, Jasper. It's not necessary to go that far unless you don't value your life and property."

"More than my liberty?"

"More than your liberty."

"Well, I guess I had forgotten your role on the Dutton plantation. You are a real humanitarian doctor!"

"At your service anytime. Shall I tell them you will sell?"

"I need some time to think about it."

"They won't be giving you much time."

"Yes. Damn them, yes! Tell them I'll sell. Tell them I'll leave. Tell them I'll leave off politicking. Tell them to save my miserable neck I'll cease resisting and desisting. Tell the hellish rebels I say *Yes!*" And he burst into a fit of oaths. He put his head down in his hands and when his shoulders had ceased shaking he looked up and found the doctor was gone.

49 *Keep the niggers from the polls and we'll return to White Home Rule!*

Violence in the state of Georgia reached a pinnacle during the national elections of 1868 when the Ku Klux Klan rode for three days and nights. A trail of blood and death was spread across the state evoking such horror and fear that the nation was aroused. Congress demanded a full investigation into the activities of this vigilante group when the nation realized that the Klan was well organized all over the South and was terrorizing loyal Unionists as well as all Negro voters trying to exercise their rights of citizenship. But Randall Ware was as good as his word to old Doc. Trembling in his boots he ventured to the polls and cast his vote, but nothing Turner could say could persuade him to run for office on the local, county, or state level.

"But the Government promises to protect us."

"The Government can't protect us."

"Why do you say that?"

"Because of the way the Klan operates and because the Ku Kluxers are represented on every level of southern politics. They are sitting in Washington. They are in the State House, and they are gradually pushing back into control in every county, town, and hamlet. The Government can't protect every Negro in the South against all his white neighbors and their friends. They mean to enslave us again or kill us. That is their real intention."

"But have you heard about the investigation? The Government is taking statements from as many victims as they can get to give testimony, and then Congress is going to act on it."

"Well, that all sounds fine, if you can live to see the results. But I tell you nothing will come of it. This is a war of white against black and it's a night war with disguise and closed doors. The first white man you see in the morning could be the very man who beat you within an inch of your life the night before. No, they have begun a reign of terror to put the Negro back in slavery. They will never accept the fact that the South rose up in rebellion against the Union North and the North won the war. They mean to take out all their grudges on us."

"I suppose you know that Congress has thrown Georgia out of the Union again for expelling us?"

"Yes, I know that, and they'll get back by the same ruse they used before. They'll let all the niggers come back and then insult us again, only *I* won't be there."

"Ware, I never thought you would prove a coward. I trusted you, and counted on you as my friend."

"And I am your friend, but it looks like Mr. Bush is my lawyer. Right now I'd rather make a good run than a bad stand. I feel like it's better to have folks looking at my back saying 'yonder runs that stinking yellow-bellied coward' than looking at my corpse saying, 'don't he look natchal?' "

Children grumbled on the way:
Ah wisht ah hadda died in Egypt's land.
Children they forgot to pray:
Ah wisht ah hadda died in Egypt's land.

50 Burned out and running for our lives twice in a row

Daylight was struggling to break through murky clouds hanging over the railroad station, and wisps of gray fog rose and floated over their heads as Vyry and Innis Brown entered the sleepy little town of Luverne, Alabama. They had been riding in the wagon all night, and the children were still asleep. Against the eastern horizon there was the faintest blush of color pinking the sky. The sleepy town was waking up. The horses' hooves clattered on the cobbled streets. Here and there they saw gray figures moving like ghosts through the town. Passing rows of ramshackly houses, Vyry noticed the grim faces of thin-shouldered white people, their eyes wide and staring. She had a ghostly feeling and she tensed in the hostile atmosphere. As the light broadened a path before them she looked into the faces of more people sitting on steps, lounging before stores, just opening doors, and driving teams of horses that were beginning to clutter the roads.

"What's the matter with these peoples?" And at first she breathed her question in such a low husky voice that Innis could hardly understand what she was saying.

"Hunh? Hanh? What you say?"

And now she spoke loudly enough for the two soldiers to hear. They were leading the way as they had done all night and were riding on either side of the mule team.

"I say, what's the matter with these peoples?"

"What you mean?" asked one of the soldiers.

"They looks so hard and skinny, so raw-bony and so mean."

"Well, I don't know about they meanness, don't know whether they's mean as they looks or not, but I knows why they looks so skinny and so raw-bony; they is hungry, that's why."

"Hungry?"

"Yes'm. This here part of Alabama has been in a famine ever since the war ended. I guess you know near bouts a hundred thousand white folks starved to death while the war was going on."

"No sir, I ain't never heard tell of that before."

"Well, they did, and this here is one of the places where a lot of them starved in Alabamy."

"I thought most of them peoples what was so hungry was hill peoples," said Innis.

"Well, they was. Them mountaineers done they share of starving but famine run through here, too, and all through the red-clay hills, specially after the Union soldiers come. What little the peoples ate give them dysentery cause I reckon they ate meal with bugs and worms, cause they didn't have no flour, and they had sick pigs and chickens so they lived offa greens and wild berries and sitch."

"Lawd have mercy! Jesus, is we gwine starve too?"

"Ma'am, I wouldn't think so. They raises a lot of green vegetables round here now and peanuts and pecans and some cotton."

"Well," sighed Innis, "I ain't got me no farm no more to raise nothing."

"Well, you probably will just be here temporary, and if you looking for a farm I'm sho the Bureau will try to help you find one."

"We ain't got no money to buy with, even if we was to be lucky enough to find us a piece of land. And then I'd be feared to build. These white folks looks worser than them we seen in Troy."

"You probably won't find a farm here, maybe not even in Crenshaw County. You might have to go over in Butler County."

Vyry perked up her ears when he mentioned Butler County. "Butler County? Whereabouts is South Butler?"

"Butler County is the very next county to this one. Does you mean the south end of Butler County by South Butler?"

"I reckon. Whereabouts is it?"

"Well, ma'am, if you knows some particular place maybe I could tell you better."

"Yes, sir, I knows a place. It's a place called Georgiana."

"Oh, I knows right where that is."

"Well, soon as we can get settled here in a house I wants to go there. Is it a far piece from here?"

"Nome, it ain't so far. Not much farther than yall come last night."

"Well, I sho wants to go there, I sho do."

Vyry and Innis were not too happy about the three-room shack at the end of a long row of houses where colored people were living in Luverne, but it was a roof over their heads and better than nothing. They were not happy moving. Vyry declared the place was dirty and caked with stale and rancid grease. It was shut tight and had little light.

"It smells like somebody died in here. Open up them shutters and let some fresh air come in and blow out this stink."

They deposited the cow and chickens and pig pen in the skimpy backyard wondering how long they could leave them there. Innis followed the soldiers back to town to the office of the Freedman's Bureau where they suggested that he hire himself out driving a dray by the day since he had a team of mules and a wagon, so that first day he went to work and he took Jim with him. Innis Brown was deeply distressed, however, because there was not a bed nor chair nor table for his family to use.

Vyry used her chest for a table, and they sat on croker sacks and boxes. Before they could sleep that night beds must be improvised. Vyry said to Minna, "If we ain't got no quilts and feather beds nor mattresses, we is got them things Missus Jacobson give us and what Reverend Whittaker brung us. We can make pallets now, and soon as we can we'll make some more mattresses with pine needles or corn husks or cotton or feathers or something or another, I reckon."

Vyry tried hard to be her cheerful and optimistic self, to buoy up the children's hopes, and bolster the sagging spirits of Innis, but often in those first days in Luverne, Minna would come upon her mother crying.

In less than three weeks after they moved to Luverne, Vyry lost the child she was carrying. She had hardly made any acquaintance with the Negroes in the community, but Innis ran out and found a granny who came to help Vyry. This time Vyry did something she had never done before when her children were born. She screamed and cried and lay in labor for hours before the baby was born dead. The granny explained, "He was born foot-foremost, and with the cord wrapped around his neck." Vyry lay weak and listless while a solemn household moved around in gloom. When she got out of bed ten days later she dragged around in tight-lipped silence.

They crossed the Conecuh River when they were moving from Troy to Luverne, and now they discovered that the land around Luverne, especially to the south, was swampy. Much of the high country was piney woods land and the chief occupation of many of the people was lumbering and sawmill work. Brantley, a little settlement, only a few miles away, was a turpentine camp and had a sawmill. It was often Innis's luck to find nothing to haul but logs or lumber, and he almost depended on the sawmills for daily work.

Vyry seemed to have neither energy nor interest in a garden, but Innis persevered after his long working day and tried to bring some order into the chaotic circumstances in which they found themselves. He found pasture for the cow. Early every morning Jim led the cow by a rope to pasture, fastened her to a stake, and then late in the afternoon brought her back again. Innis built a pig pen nearer the swamps and carried slops to the pigs morning and night. This left their meager backyard free for chickens and a small garden. Out of his first money, Innis bought an iron bed for Vyry, and then he worked late in the evenings making box beds for the children. Eventually he made chairs, but at first he brought home boxes, and for a long time they continued to use the chest to sit on after it was replaced by a real table for meals.

Innis Brown sensed among his striving, however, that there was no joy in his household. Joy had disappeared and he missed it so much he kept fumbling after something to restore it. He worked hard for long hours and came home bringing first one trinket after another for Vyry hoping thereby to

brighten her eyes with a smile, but she remained dull and
dour. She would reprove him for buying her anything, and
say, "We ain't got no money to waste on trifling things. You
better be saving your money to get us a farm."

The hot summertime passed miserably. The scorching and
oppressive heat filled the house in the day and smothered
them at night. Vyry complained, "I ain't never seen so many
flies and skeeters in all my born days. It looks like they'll just
take the place." Innis bought long pieces of sticky fly-paper
and hung them up in the house to catch flies, but when the
papers were black with the annoying insects they were still
pestered. Mosquitoes made singing noises all night long and
were a nuisance from first dusk till daylight. Vyry set smudge
pots in the backyard and on the front porch burning pungent
green wood to drive away the insects but the low swampy
ground and the open house with pigs and cows and horses all
close to the houses only complicated their problems and made
the summer misery one of heat and stench and insect bites.

Late in the summer, after they had been in Luverne at least
three months, Innis came home on Saturday soon after twelve
o'clock and said he was taking the afternoon off.

"The Gov'mint mens at the Bureau is done found us a
farm."

"Whereabouts is it?" asked Vyry.

"Well, the land is over in Butler County near a place called
Greensville."

Vyry perked up considerably when she heard the place was
in Butler County, but her first instinctive reaction was to be
wary about any strange place until she knew what the people
were like. Innis noticed her silence and did not understand the
conflict in her mind. Alone, he was uncertain, half-fearful of
her reaction, but he blurted out decisively,

"I just thought we'd all go over there and take a look at it
and see how we like it."

"When, today?"

"Yeah, this evening."

"Can we go and come before night?"

"Naw, I don't reckon so, cause it's all of twenty-five miles."

"Well then, how come we don't go tomorrow? You ain't
working cause it's Sunday, and we could get away real early
in the morning, bout first daybreak and then we might make it
home by tomorrow night."

"Well, if we did, it would be way over in the night when
we gets back."

"Is the soldiers gwine with us?"

"I ain't asked them, but I reckon they would."

"Wa-al you ask em to go, cause we might get lost or something."

"Ain't no danger, Vyry, if that's what you is scairt of."

"Who says I'm scairt?"

"Well, ain't you?"

"I might be, a little bit. Anyhows it won't hurt none to ask em to go with us. I would feel more safer."

"I'll ask em if it'll make you feel any better."

"Well, how you like it?"

"I likes it all right. Is they any more farms around here?"

"Why? Does you wanta look at another one?"

"Naw. I just wants to know whereabouts is the nearest one, and do it jine us?"

"I dunno. I ain't asked."

"Well, is they white folks or colored?"

"Do that make a difference?"

"It do, if they doesn't want us."

Innis was puzzled, but Vyry had decided after the fire that they would be certain about their neighbors before they built again. She had never voiced her fears to Innis. She didn't want him to think she was foolish, but she didn't want to see another house go down in fire and smoke to ashes. This was something Innis wouldn't understand and wouldn't know how to prevent. He would just think they had to take that chance, and she knew that as bad as he wanted a place he would grab at the first thing. She wasn't that eager.

The land near Greenville was high, well drained, and fertile. There were stands of pine trees, a brook with clear water trickling over smooth stones and running down hill out of a thick grove, and wide acres of land for cultivation. Once again they could build on a sloping site where the air blowing from the pines was pungent, fresh, and invigorating. Vyry listened as the Government men explained to them that there was already a community of Negroes in this old Alabama town, that there would be a school for the children, and that this particular land was choice, and the site was one they could never regret.

Innis could not understand Vyry's reluctance.

"I like it all right. It ain't got nothing wrong with it, and I reckon we could be real happy here. But we ain't gwine build right-a-way, nohow. We can't, can we, Innis?"

Once again Innis was confused and he looked at her help-lessly. Sometimes he believed that the fire had affected Vyry's mind. She always seemed to be studying something and she was slow to make the decisions she had been so quick about before the fire. Now he looked uncertainly at the Government men.

"Well, I don't know what to say."

Vyry spoke up quickly, "You ain't gwine turn it down, is you?"

"Well, I was waiting on you to say if you wants it."

"Sho, we wants the land. We just gwine wait a while until we get ables to build."

Innis breathed a sigh of relief and told the man, "Well, sir, I reckon that settles it."

Riding back to Luverne Innis tried to get a conversation started with Vyry about the land, but she seemed abstracted and not following what he was saying, so he gave up in his usual bewilderment and despair. Suddenly Vyry asked him, "Innis, you member that soldier said Georgiana ain't a far ways from here? We's in Butler County, now, ain't we?"

"Yeah, but we can't go traipsing down to Georgiana now, Vyry, and you knows that."

"Yeah, I knows it. I was just wondering . . ."

"Wondering what?"

"Aw nothing. I'll just wait until another time." But Vyry had Georgiana on her mind. She intended to find Miss Lucy. She had a hunger to see Miss Lillian anyway, and before they built another house she was determined to see Miss Lucy.

The enervating heat of summer gradually lessened, but they faced the fall with little hope for any immediate respite from the atmosphere in which they lived. Innis lived now with the hope that in another year he could move his family once more to a farm of his own, so he worked harder and harder, driving himself with such fury that he was all nervous energy. His husky body was reduced to the raw-bony look of all the people around Luverne. There was one good thing he and Vyry agreed to. They decided to have the cow bred so that she would surely come fresh in the spring. "Then," said Vyry, "with any luck we might have plenty of milk and butter, and we oughta have eggs to sell."

The winter set in early with slow dismal rain. For days there was the steady drip of depressing showers. The cold, wet weather dampened their spirits and around the house they were surrounded with sour mud. As the winter progressed the main thing Vyry associated with those dreary months in Luverne was the way everything got bogged down in miry clay. Innis struggled morning after morning to get his team going while the wagon wheels sank deeper in the gooey red mud. She could hear him in her sleep talking to the mules, "Yah, yah, git up there, git up, git up, yah, yah . . ." What was even more aggravating they were always tracking in mud on their feet despite the folded croker sacks on the rickety front and back porches. They never seemed to hear Vyry's constant admonition, "Wipe your feets good fore you come in the house." All winter long she was sweeping and scrubbing daily to keep out messy sour mud and dirty tracks all over her clean scrubbed floor.

At Christmas time they killed hogs and had more fresh meat than the house would hold and there was no smokehouse to keep it. They hung up the meat on the back porch, hams and shoulders and middlings in feed and flour and meal and sugar sacks. Vyry said, "You almost needs a gun to keep watch for fear somebody steals it."

This gave Innis Brown an idea. Christmas day he brought home a small rat terrier for the children. Vyry quickly said, "He ain't gonna stay in this here house. We ain't got room for us much less a nasty stinking dog."

The children were hurt and Innis was crestfallen.

"I thought he might make a good watch dog. He suppose to have some wolf in him and when we gits a farm again we gwine need a dog."

Vyry had not thought of this, and she was slightly mollified, so in spite of her fussing, it was she who fed and watered "Tricks" and taught the children how to give their new puppy a bath.

There was always food and this year lots of peanuts and pecans.

Vyry made molasses candy and taught the children how to pull the taffy. Minna and Harry always seemed in good spirits and enjoyed family fun, but Jim was not a happy boy. He worked hard all day with Innis and he was growing tall and thin as a rail. Vyry declared she could never fill him up.

"Boy, you eats so much you is just poor to carry it."

At Christmas he wanted more than anything else a real gun, a rifle that would shoot. Innis surprised him and said, "You and me'll hafta share it together," when the boy happily turned over the twenty-two calibre rifle on Christmas morning.

Vyry was against the gun—"too much like killing"—but she was glad to see something put a smile on Jim's face. He had been so miserable and unhappy since the fire, and his face was always glum. But he had never told his mother what his real problem was. He had a secret yearning to go to school and now that was a complete impossibility. He had to work and help support the family. Even if there was going to be a school in Greenville, he knew already that Innis Brown did not intend for him to go. It would cost too much money and they needed him to work. Work was all he ever heard, and he hated work.

When spring came again to Alabama early in 1870 Vyry was like a new person. She took Minna and Harry to the woods for brush brooms and dogwood blossoms, and she stood in the pine forest and sniffed the air hungrily. The sap rose in the trees and strength rose again in Vyry.

"If it's the Lawd's will, we's gwine make a change this year. I feels like it gwineta be a good year. I just feels it in my blood and all through my bones!"

Innis was happy to see her new enthusiasm. He listened to her optimistic plans with joy. Maybe she was finally getting over the fire.

They were delighted when the cow came fresh. Vyry got out her churn and scalded it and told Minna she was going to let her churn and make butter. Suddenly Vyry's interest turned toward making a new little garden. She began to fuss with her chickens and count her setting hens. Then to Innis's great amazement she began peddling her wares through the country side. At first she worried about leaving Minna and Harry alone in the house, but this time the doors had locks, and there were friendly neighbors nearby.

Innis told her that the Government man said they must take possession of the land and begin to exercise squatters' rights at once or it would have to go to someone else. They were not ready to build, but they had to move.

"What'll we do?" asked Innis, "when we ain't got no house?"

"Let's-us camp out awhile."

"Woman, is you crazy?"

"Naw. The weather is mild and we ain't got no barn. We could just take the cover we useta have on the wagon and make us a tent."

"It ain't gwine work, I can tell you right now. Soon as it rains we'll be in a mess."

"Well, you ain't got your materials together nohow, now is you? And you needs a barn, first off."

Innis could not understand her great reluctance to build, but he began to make preparations to leave Crenshaw County.

Vyry kept her butter and egg and milk money in a fruit jar. When she had filled one jar with silver money and copper pennies, she told Innis she wanted him to hire her a gig.

"What for?"

"I'm gwine down to Georgiana."

"By yourself?"

"Well, I can take Minna and Harry if you and Jim will be all right."

"How long is you gwine stay?"

"No longern than I can come and go, maybe one night I might stay, if they's any place for us."

"Well, I hopes you won't be sorry."

"Sorry bout what?"

"Sorry bout bothering them white folks again, that's what."

"I ain't gwine bother nobody. I just gotta hankering to go and I ain't gwine be satisfied until I does."

Innis Brown saw her leave with reluctance but he said, "I reckon me and Jim'll be all right. Don't you fret none about us."

"I ain't gwine fret. Jim, you behave. Obey your Paw and help him all you can."

"Yes'm."

Vyry found her way to Georgiana and Porter's Store without any trouble. She saw the house next door joined to the store, and she saw a woman rocking on the porch. She got out of the rig and told Minna and Harry to wait for her. Vyry saw Miss Lillian before she got to the porch, but the shock almost made her turn around and go back. It wasn't just the fact that she was still wearing the old, out-of-date clothes she had before the war. It was mostly her frowsy hair and her empty eyes that disturbed Vyry, who was seeing her after four and a half years of deterioration. Miss Lillian did not recognize her when Vyry spoke, but she stood up and walked away from the rocking chair talking rapidly in a high childish treble and monotone.

"I'm not crazy. I know who I am. I know my name. My

name is Lillian. . . . I'm not crazy. I know who I am. I know my name. My name is Lillian."

Vyry began to cry. A young girl about Minna's age came out of the house when she heard her mother's excited voice. She stared at Vyry and said, "Who are you, and what do you want?"

Vyry answered, "Susan, don't you know me?"

"Oh, you must be Vyry!"

"Where's your Aunt Lucy?"

"She's in the store, and Bob is too. Wait, and I'll call her." When Miss Lucy came running out from the store, Lillian was quiet again and rocking dully on the porch saying nothing.

"Oh, Vyry, I'm so glad to see you! How you getting along? Come on in. Is that your children out in the buggy? Why don't you bring them in? I can leave the store awhile anyway. Have you had dinner?"

"I fixed a lunch, Miss Lucy, and we ain't hungry. I just wanted to see Miss Lillian again. She ain't no better, ma'am, is she?"

"No, Vyry, I can't say that she is. Sometimes I think she's worse. We were just talking about you the other night and wondering where you were."

"Well, we fixing to move to this here county. We is just been from pillar to post since we seen you. First we settled in the river bottom over the Georgia line here in Alabamy and the high water run us outa there the very next spring. Then we worked on shares on a place where the land wasn't no good, then we went to another place called Troy . . ."

"I know where that is."

"Well, we built us a brand-new house there but we was burned out and had to run for our lives. That makes twicet in a row. And now to tell you the truth, we is found us some more land but I'm scared to build for fear we can't stay there neither."

"Oh, I'm so sorry to hear that. Wait'll I tell Mister Porter. He'll be in any minute now for his dinner. Whereabouts did you say this new land is?"

"It's here in this here county, up around Greenville."

"I'm sure Mister Porter knows somebody in Greenville. Here he is right now."

"Howdy Vyry, how you getting along?"

"I was just telling your wife, Mister Porter, we is been from pillar to post since we seen you last. We is been in a flood and been burned out and had to run for our lives twicet in a row."

"You have been having trouble. Where you living now?"

"We's still in Crenshaw County in Luverne . . ."

"I know where that is."

"But we's fixing to move here to Butler County, up around Greenville."

"Oh, that's fine. You'll be much closer, and if you need any help, maybe we can help you."

Miss Lucy said, "I was just thinking maybe you could go up there and straighten out their business and see about recording their claims and everything."

"Why, yes, I guess I could. I sure could. Would that help any, Vyry?"

"Yes sir, I believe it would. Me and Innis doesn't understand no writing and papers and sitch, and if you was to come and see about it, I reckon it would be a big favor."

"When are you going to move?"

"Well sir, we moving any day now, but we ain't building yet. We's planning to build though, sometimes this spring."

"Well, you all go on and move and try to build if you can. I may not get up there before six or eight weeks, but you can depend on me. I'm coming just as soon as I can."

"Thank you, sir. Thank you so much. I'll feel much more safer if you was to come."

"Well, now, Vyry don't you worry none," said Miss Lucy, "if Mister Porter gives you his word you can rest easy on it. It's just as good as his bond."

Miss Lucy insisted that they spend the night there, and although Vyry could hardly bear to look at the frowsy Miss Lillian with the vacant eyes she knew the return trip would be easier on Minna and Harry if they rested awhile, so she stayed. Early the next morning she got up and prepared to leave. She noticed that Bobby was a tall boy but he seemed sullen, almost hostile, and withdrawn, and he had little to say to them. Susan was a sweet girl but highly nervous. Miss Lucy said she and her husband were thinking about sending both the children off to school, but hadn't fully decided where. Minna and Susan had little in common to talk about, but they spoke shyly to each other. When Vyry left she hugged and kissed Miss Lucy goodbye and then Miss Lillian, who began repeating her chorus. "I'm not crazy. I know who I am. I know my name. My name is Lillian." Vyry soothed her saying, "I know you ain't crazy, and I know you knows who you are. Honey, don't you fret none. I knows you knows your name." Miss Lucy explained that some awful woman had frightened Lillian one day by screaming, "There's a crazy woman" and then running in fright.

Vyry rode away with Minna and Harry knowing she had accomplished her mission but feeling very sad about Miss Lillian. All the way home she could hear ringing in her ears the agitated sing-song words, "I'm not crazy. I know who I am. I know my name. My name is Lillian . . ."

Great Day!
Great Day, the Righteous marching.
Great Day!
God's gonna build up Zion's walls.

51   *Don't look like free schools and land reform is ever coming*

In the spring of 1870, five years after freedom from chattel slavery, Vyry and Innis Brown were still unsettled. Vyry's longing for her children to learn to read and write and cipher on their hands was still unfulfilled. Innis Brown was preparing to settle on another farm, but Vyry had learned from bitter experience that the white world around them deeply resented Negroes settling the lands and building new farms.

When warm weather came to Luverne, Alabama, and the mud puddles before their door were disappearing, the wagon moving on dry land once more, Vyry and Innis Brown packed up their belongings and set their faces toward Greenville. It was the first month of spring and Alabama was in bloom. The dogwoods were lovely, the grass under their feet was green, and the earth felt spongy. In the woods there were clumps of wild azaleas and bird foot violets. The mockingbirds kept a chattering school in the trees, and the blue sky was like a new canopy of silk shining behind cotton clouds.

In the wagon the children and grown-ups were silent. It was as though they were holding their breath, half in anticipation and hope, half in memory of the past and fear that it would repeat itself. Innis Brown kept his dreams to himself, for no longer did he feel that Vyry was optimistic and in that blissful rapport they had felt when they left Georgia. Vyry was studying ways to solve the problems she suspected were ahead of them and which she could not articulate. Jim seemed more silent as he grew older. His thoughts were his own private secrets. He felt he had no one who shared his life with understanding, and he could not have expressed his confused emotions if he had tried. He deeply loved his mother and his sister, Minna, but he had an undefined feeling of jealousy and resentment toward Harry, who had taken his place in his mother's affections and was the obvious joy of a doting father. Although he had been so fond of Innis Brown from that first day when the soldiers came, now he felt that his stepfather considered him a workhorse, and that his mother gave her silent consent. Minna was still an innocent, sweet little girl who loved her mother in every possible way, but she wanted to go to school, too, and she wanted to learn so much that sometimes at night when she went to bed she prayed to go to school, to have books and a slate and to be able to write. Sometimes she dreamed it happened, but she always woke to find the cold reality of morning when her dream disappeared with the darkness. Only little Harry, unconscious of fear or worry, rode along in happy creature comfort, close to all who loved him, pointing in childish excitement to the bright birds that crossed their path.

"Look-a-yonder, over there's a red bird!"

"Naw, Harry, that's a blue bird. That's a blue jay. You always mixing red with blue."

But the birds were a pleasure to watch and the spring morning was brightened with their colorful plumage, their gay chatter, and their flying back and forth.

Twenty-five miles in the wagon was a long trip, but Innis was now equipped with a strong wagon and a dependable team, so they rode along without fear of breaking down or being delayed by that old balky mule who had moved along so slowly.

Vyry and Innis seemed destined to stay in South Alabama where the farming land was not good and where the largest numbers of Negroes in the state did not live. South Alabama was more timber or lumber country with turpentine camps and sawmill towns scattered throughout the region. The wiregrass country bordered both the piney woods country and the farming sections of the Black Belt, and between these two sections they seemed to have cast their lot. It was really a section of poor white people. They always worked in the sawmills and turpentine camps.

Wiregrass country was also a place of mass illiteracy. Neither white nor black people in Alabama had ever been to school in large numbers. The law prohibited black slaves from learning and lack of money had prevented the poor whites from having an education. Only the rich planters' sons had been educated before the war. Now both blacks and whites were hoping for common schools. The only state with fewer people who could read and write than Alabama in 1870 was Georgia, where less than 10 per cent of the total population was literate.

The post-war problems of black and white were now enormous. Their first need was to survive. Throughout the whole wiregrass section it required very hard work to make the soil produce. In some places it was rocky and hilly, in others it resembled the sandy loam of the nearby coastal plains. And most people insisted on one crop—cotton. The price of cotton was high after the war, but there was also the cotton tax and the super-human difficulty of raising a good crop.

Tax was also the problem with the common school situation. Every Peoples' Assembly and Convention that met in the South during Reconstruction years had instructed each State Legislature elected to provide for free common schools. Some Legislatures went so far as to appropriate money for higher education among the Negroes as well as among the whites, but there were always three hindrances to the successful execution of such legislation.

To begin with, there was a widespread reaction against any education for the Negro people newly freed from slavery. Poor whites who had never been to school themselves had mixed reactions. The question of sending white and black to school together was always answered by a storm of protest, and violence erupted every time there was an attempt to put such schools into operation. The Negroes themselves were crying for education, and by 1870 the Freedmen's Bureau had established a few schools in every southern state. These schools, of course, were not free.

Thus there was the question of financial support. Every adult male between the ages of 18 and 45 was to pay one dollar a year for the school tax and in most instances the children in the schools were expected to pay tuition, about fifty cents per child or in some cases, per family. But the poor people claimed they could not pay and the whites cried loudly that the blacks would not pay.

And then there was the problem of teachers. Where would you find teachers in a region where the people as a mass were largely uneducated? Obviously they had to come from outside the South if they were to be found in large numbers. And this antagonized the southern people who boasted of their long ante-bellum tradition of colleges despite the obvious lack of trained teachers when the war was over. The teachers who came from New England, that region of highest literacy in the United States, brought with them their Puritan ideals, their Union sentiment, and their liberal ideas of education. All of these were repugnant to the white South which declared this infamy the result of Negro rule and Carpetbaggers. They vilified the New England schoolmarm, declaring all grossly immoral, and visiting all manner of persecution and violence on these ladies who dared come South to teach black and white children alike. Some of them were visited by the Ku Klux Klan and given the usual treatment of beatings and intimidation. There was even some loss of life. The white South declared it wanted only teachers from the South, white or black, but no northerners, especially no missionary Yankees, with their anti-southern sentiments. In their evident need for education the southern white people, nevertheless, reacted much as a mad dog suffering from every illness imaginable, full of fleas and ticks, drooling at the mouth, even howling in agony, yet daring and threatening every agent of mercy who came near on pain of death. The war had left their land devastated and the people in economic depression, social dislocation, and political turmoil. If education was to be the cure of their diseases they had not yet discovered a palatable way to swallow the medicine. Such was the state of affairs in the spring of 1870.

The long day was ending as Vyry and Innis Brown with their children and their wagon load of possessions were climbing the slope on their new land. The tall pines were casting shadows and the sun was disappearing behind red clay hills. Birds were seeking their nests and the peace of night was descending. Deep in their hearts Innis and Vyry and their children were praying that at last they had found a permanent home.

Now ain't them hard trials
And great tribulations?
Ain't them hard trials?
I'm bound to leave this land.

52   *Where's the money coming from?*

Innis felt he had enough money saved to start building their
house, but Vyry said no.

"I don't like our sleeping outdoors like this," said Innis.
"It's downright dangerous. Wild animals all round here, and
snakes too."

"Innis Brown, you ain't afraid of no snakes, nor wild animals neither. I ain't seen nary one since we been here, and
I doesn't see why you fussing so. We needs the barn first off
anyhows."

Innis was busy plowing and Jim worked with him in the
field. He also cut timber from his own place and they loaded
the logs in the wagon. When he went to town he brought back
lumber from the sawmill. He told Vyry the lumber would rot
if it got wet and lay on the ground too long, but none of this
moved her.

"We ain't ready yet."

"Ain't ready to build?"

"Naw."

"Well, what is us waiting for? I wants to get us settled whilst the weather is good, and I got me a lot of work to do in the fields, and anyhow I doesn't like your running all over this here country trying to make a dime selling eggs."

"Well, where's all the money coming from that we needs if I doesn't help you make every copper cent I can?"

"What is you got in mind doing with so much money?"

"I wants my chilluns to go to school."

"I done told you right now we ain't ables. We can't afford no school tax money and no high learning prices."

"I knows what you says. I heard you the first time you driv up."

"And what's more, I done told you I needs Jim in the fields to help me."

"I heard that, too."

"And you ain't in favor what I says?"

"I ain't in favor."

He stared at her in anger, but he controlled himself and turned away. In the meantime Innis had been taking Vyry to town twice and sometimes three times a week to sell eggs, butter, and occasionally some buttermilk. She walked out from the main street of the town into the white settlement. At first it didn't dawn on her that her customers thought she was white, but gradually as the poor whites engaged her in conversation—rich whites didn't buy since the Negro cooks met her at the back doors—she often noticed that they talked about the niggers. At first Vyry was tempted to bristle and get angry, but she controlled herself enough to listen. She could never learn through a better way how her prospective neighbors felt about her race.

One day she stopped at a place where an old woman was sitting on a rickety porch. When Vyry turned in at the gate another woman, evidently the old woman's daughter, came out.

"We can't buy nothing today. I ain't got a nickel."

"I was just wondering would you give me a dipper of cold water?"

"Why sho, wait a minute and I'll bring you a drink from the well."

Vyry was drinking the water when the woman suddenly

said, "Ain't it awful how the niggers is moving in here on all our good farmland?"

Vyry's eyes bucked and she nearly strangled on the water, but she finished drinking and then she said, "I've heard a lots of folks say they don't like it, ma'am."

"Like it? Like it, you say? How can anybody in they right mind like it? Them peoples ain't got no business in here, at all. They was much better off in slavery, and I says that's where they needs to be right now. Why, it's tore up our country just something awful! Instead of us prospering like we thought we was gonna after the war and everything, them grand rascals what the Yankees has brung down here ain't done nothing but set us back a hundred years. No telling when we'll git a living wage, and they even got the nerve of trying to open up mixed schools. Is you got any chilluns?"

"Yes'm. I has three."

"Well, I knows you don't want them going to school with niggers. 'Twas bad enough when the nigger lords had all the land and decent white folks couldn't make a living. Now we got to divide everything we got with the niggers. I don't know what it's coming to, myself, I just don't know. I'd like to have some of your fresh eggs, but I ain't got a dime to my name, but when you come back I'll buy some. Is you coming back next week?"

"Yes'm, I'll be back then. And thank you so much for the water."

The older woman had not spoken one word. Now she spat out a big mouthful of brown tobacco juice and as Vyry looked at it on the ground, and then at the old woman, she remembered the poor dirt farmers where they had been before they went to Troy. Now she looked again at the younger woman standing, arms akimbo, on the porch and Vyry smiled and said,

"Goodbye, ma'am."

There were many places where people did have a dime to buy eggs and not every place did she find people making conversation, but when she did, she never heard anything good about "niggers." One day she had a basket of fresh young turnip salad and a woman stopped her to admire the greens and buy some.

"It's getting so lately you can't hardly afford nothing fitten to eat; they has got us so taxed and ain't nowhere to git the money less you is got a money tree. They wants cotton tax, and land tax, and school tax. Tax is bout to eat us out of house and home and we ain't gitting nothing for the tax right on. They is already took all our rights from us and give em to the niggers. Hmmmmmm, these is sho good turnip salad. When you git some big with the roots be sho and bring me some cause I sho do love turnips!"

Vyry smiled understandingly and pocketed another dime. Then she wondered as she walked away, *What kinda rights is us niggers got what we taken from the white folks?*

But her worst experiences were overhearing two conversations that were so harrowing they left her feeling faint and ill. She dared not repeat what she heard to Innis for it would only discourage him at the outset, and his hopes were steadily building around the new farm and farmhouse and getting his family finally settled.

She had finished selling her goods one afternoon and was walking toward the place where she always waited for Innis or he met her with the wagon. A group of white men and boys were standing on a corner laughing and talking among themselves. One was recounting a night adventure with the Ku Klux Klan. They had lynched a Negro man after torturing him nearly to death, and Vyry heard one of the men say, "If you'd seen that nigger's face and seen him down on his knees praying for mercy you would have died laughing. I ain't never seen nothing so funny since before the war and they had that two-headed man in the Side Show what come here with the circus one time. We whipped and cut the blood out of that nigger and then we cut off his fingers and toes, and I got me a black ear for a souvenir."

Vyry's path led in different directions each week, only occasionally retracing her steps for steady customers. One Saturday Innis was angry and would not drive her to town.

"You ain't got no business traipsing around amongst all those poor white trash selling eggs. I done made up my mind not to carry you no more, and that's all I got to say about it."

"Well, let me tell you one thing, Innis Brown, don't no one monkey stop my show, and I knows more'n one way to kill a cat sides skinning him."

"Well, you just go on and skin your cat by yourself. This here is a bad Saddy and you hang around down town amongst these here evil white folks until dark and you gwine be sorry. That's all I got to say."

Vyry hitched up the team herself and went away. She left the wagon and team of horses at a livery stable and walked out as usual with her wares. It was later in the afternoon when she started than was her custom and she remembered Innis's warning. She did not intend to let darkness catch her away from home. But it was a slow day. She had not sold many eggs when she met an old couple living nearly a mile from town. There were a few small children playing in the dust before the ramshackly house. It had evidently seen better days for it was a large two-story dwelling with cupolas and turrets and gingerbread trimming, but the paint was peeling, the porch was sagging, and the steps were rotten.

"How you sell your eggs?"

"A dime a dozen."

"That's cheap enough. Mammy, does you want any?"

"Yeah, Pappy, course I do, if you is got money to buy."

"Reckon I got a rusty dime. Lemme see now, I wantsta make sho it ain't no worthless Confederate specie, heh, heh, heh!"

Vyry looked startled and wondered if he was crazy. While she transferred the eggs to a pan "Mammy" provided, the old man chatted away steadily. At first she wasn't paying close attention, but something he said made her know he was talking about the war.

"And when I heard tell how our folks was starving and Mammy wasn't gitting no greens and corn pone, I just quit the nigger-war and come home."

"Nigger-war?" asked Vyry.

"Yeah, that's all we fit for, the niggers and the nigger lords. I figgered I ain't had no niggers and wasn't likely to have none, so I just quit and come on home so Mammy could have her greens and corn pone. They come after me, mind you . . ." Here, he stopped and spewed a stream of tobacco juice across the yard. "So I just went on up in the hills." Now he started cackling and laughing and slapping his thighs. "Lord, I wisht I had me the greenbacks for them army mens what's buried up in them hills. Every time they come up there hunting desertions, we kilt them. No telling how many of them is buried up in them hills. And ain't none of us went back to the nigger-war."

As Vyry walked away she could still hear the old man cackling and she felt cold shivers go up and down her spine. The next Saturday passed and she made no move to go to town. At supper Innis ventured to ask her, "You ain't had no cat to skin today?"

"Naw."

"You ain't selling no more eggs?"

"Naw."

"Is the hens quit laying?"

"Naw."

But when he opened his mouth to question her again she saw the twinkle in his eyes and said, "You leave me lone, Innis Brown, I ain't pestering you none now, so don't you pester me!"

De Camptown ladies sing this song,
Doo-dah, doo-dah!
De Camptown race-track five miles long,
Oh! Doo-dah-day!
I come down daih wid my hat caved in,
Doo-dah, doo-dah!
I go back home wid a pocket full of tin,
Oh! Doo-dah-day!

53   *I reckon I can be a granny in a pinch*

June came to Alabama with a burst of warm weather. The days were dazzling and the sky shimmered like a precious sapphire. The roadsides and the pasture and all the uncultivated fields were pink with primroses, their cups holding a pot of gold, and their blossoms waving like a rosy sea when the gentle summer breezes blew. But Innis Brown was still fuming with his stubborn wife who insisted they were not ready to build a house.

"How come we ain't ready?"

"I don't know, but we just ain't."

"Well, when is we gwine be ready?"

"I dunno, but I knows we needs to wait."

"Why? Cause you is scairt, fraid somebody's gwine to burn us out again?"

"Maybe. I dunno. These here white folks ain't friendly to colored folks. I knows that much."

"Well, is we got to wait until they is friendly? What they got to do with us building us a house? Supposing they doesn't never be friendly? Ain't you asking too much?"

"Maybe so, but I'm still troubled in my mind; I doesn't feel easy bout nothing."

"Wellum, you been that way ever since the fire."

"Yeah, I is, I reckon so, and even much gitting this here land ain't raised my spirits none."

"Wellum, I figgers it's partly on accounta you lost the baby, too, and that didn't make none of us happy. But now, if we was to have a nice brand-new house . . ."

"Naw!"

"Vyry, we's got to have a house. We's just got to trust God and go ahead. We can't figger we's gwine to be burned out everytime."

"Naw. Not yet, we ain't ready to build. I knows you right, we gotta trust God and go ahead. I knows we's got to have a house, and I knows we got to git over that fire, but Innis, just wait a little while longer, please, I'm begging you!"

"Well, all right," he said, knowing he could not refuse her anything she asked in reason, and also realizing that the deep shock of the fire had left her profoundly disturbed.

It was her brooding solemn face as she went about her work that disturbed him. Whether she was cooking outdoors, washing clothes, helping in the field, churning inside their makeshift tent, or trying to keep things in order, she reflected this worry about settling among hostile people. She seldom sang unless her song was also a brooding melody, haunting in its plaintiveness, and pitched in a minor key. Although she had a large garden thriving now, she talked no more about peddling her wares. In desperation Innis relented about taking her to town and the first Saturday in June after midday dinner he asked her if she didn't want to go. She looked at him in surprise.

"Take the chillun, too?"

"Not unless you wanta. You can if you wants, or you can leave them here."

"You reckon they'll be all right?"

"We coming back before dark. Jim can look after Minna and Harry, can't you, Jim?"

"Yes sir."

"Well, I did wanta buy something, but I ain't got much

money. My butter and egg money don't go far and I been saving to buy things for the new house."

"Ain't you got nothing you wants to trade?"

"You means vegetables and eggs?"

"That's what you been selling, ain't it?"

"Yeah. I ain't got no extra butter, but I is got eggs and plenty greens."

Vyry still hesitated about leaving the children, but Minna and Jim reassured her, and although Harry cried to go, too, they left him at home.

Vyry sold most of her goods in town at the stores, so that she had only a small portion to carry into the white settlement. She was walking briskly when she thought she heard a woman scream. She looked around but didn't see anybody and the nearest house was still more than a hundred feet away. She quickened her steps and heard the woman scream again. Now she was sure it was coming from the nearest house. There was a picket fence with a gate and she had trouble unfastening it, when suddenly a young white man, little more than a boy, rushed out, his face red and perspiring and his eyes looking wild, and he cried, "Oh lady, help me please, my wife's having a baby, please come in quick!"

Vyry ran into the house and found the young child-wife screaming and crying and tossing to and fro on her bed. Vyry went to her and touched her and spoke quietly but firmly, "Here now, you gotta quit thrashing around like that. Does you wanta kill your baby before it's born?"

The girl hushed at once and stared at Vyry.

"That's better. Now lie still on your back and I'll hold your knees for you and when you feels the pain again, close your mouth and grit your teeth and bear down hard like you is on the pot."

The distraught woman ceased to tremble and cry and when the birth pangs caught her again and she started to open her mouth and yell she looked at the forbidding face of Vyry and obeyed. In less than thirty minutes after Vyry entered the house the baby was born. The baby was a squalling, healthy, large boy, red-faced, his eyes shut tight, and thin wisps of white hair on his head.

"I ain't got no scissors with me, but any pair you got in the house'll be all right. Find em while I ties this knot."

The dazed young man fumbled for scissors and luckily found them. Then Vyry wrapped the baby in a soft cloth, and turned to finish helping the young mother. In an hour's time she had cleaned the baby and dressed him, and left the mother, clean and comfortable, ready for sleep. Vyry promised she would come back the next morning.

"My Paw's s'pose to bring Maw tomorrow to stay with me, and my husband hasta go to the Depot and meet em. If you was to come, we'd be most obliged.

"I knows I can't pay you what you is worth but I'm willing to pay you whatever you charge. You saved all our lives. I was going outa my mind and Betty-Alice was going to break that baby's neck if you hadna come along."

"I don't charge you nothing. And I'll be glad to help till your Maw gets here."

When Vyry got back to the appointed place with Innis she told him her experience.

"Now you done got yourself into something!"

"Well, I reckon I can be a granny in a pinch."

"I ain't talking bout that. How come you promise you'd come back and help her out?"

"Well, tomorrow's Sunday . . ."

"Yeah, I knows, and I was gwine bring you and the childrens to church in town anyhow."

"That's so. Well, I'll hasta miss church. I'm sorry, but I feels like it's my duty to help anybody I can wheresomever I can. That gal ain't nothing more'n a child."

"She old enough to have a baby, she grown."

"Well, it's her first one, and I members when I had my first baby Caline and May Liza was both there to help me. A woman sho enough helpless when she having a baby."

"I reckon I done found out how helpless you is when Harry was borned."

And Vyry laughed.

The next morning Vyry and Innis Brown and the children went to town early and while her family went to church, Vyry returned to the house where only the day before she had become a granny. Betty-Alice and her baby were fine but the poor husband and new father was struggling with a household of chores completely unfamiliar to him. Vyry relieved him of all the work and told him she would take care of everything.

"We didn't get your name yestiddy nor where you lives nor nothing. Our names is Fletcher and we going to name little Baby Buster here Henry Fletcher, Jr. Ain't that a purty name?"

"It sho is. My name is Brown, Vyry Brown, and we live on

the other side of town on the Big Road going over into Crenshaw County. We's farming out there."

Mr. Fletcher had fed his wife, so Vyry fixed sweetened water for the baby. She bathed the little boy and dressed him. Then she brought water to bathe Betty-Alice, helped her put on her prettiest night-gown, combed her hair and tied ribbons in it. Then she cleaned the house. There were dirty dishes in the kitchen, disarranged furniture, and the clutter naturally expected when the housewife is not in charge.

Shortly after Vyry arrived the proud Mr. Fletcher set out to meet his wife's parents and bring them to their new grandson. In his absence Betty-Alice kept a running chatter. At first she played with her sleepy son while Vyry worked in the kitchen. The house was new. It was very small but furnished nicely, and Vyry said, "You got a real purty place, Mrs. Fletcher."

"Oh, call me Betty-Alice, everybody else does. Henry fixed the place. Henry's real nice and he's always teaching me something cause Henry is real smart and he knows lots of things I don't know nothing at all about."

"Well, he was pretty scairt yestiddy long about the time I come along."

"He sho was, and I was scairt too. He ain't easy scairt and I ain't neither. I don't know much I'm scairt of excepten big old black bears and other wild animals and niggers."

"Niggers?"

"Yes ma'am. I'm scairt to death of niggers."

"You is? How come?"

"Why, ma'am, if a big black nigger was to put his hands on me, I believe I would die!"

"Well, I don't reckon they's no danger of that cause I can't think of no reason why one would put his hand on you."

"Well, that ain't what Henry Fletcher says. He says all black nigger mens wants white women."

"Say they does?"

"Yes ma'am. Ain't you never heard that?"

"Nome. I sho ain't."

"An you knows they has tails?"

"Tails? Who got tails?"

"Nigger mens."

"Aw naw, now, you must be joking?"

"Nome I ain't. Henry says nigger mens is got tails."

"And you believe that?"

"Yes'm. I sho do. Henry is smart and Henry knows . . ."

"Well, now wait a minute here, I can't listen to no more stuff like this. What if I was to tell you I'm a colored woman and I has got three children, two boys and a girl, and I ain't never yet seen no colored folks with tails?"

"You ain't no nigger!" And she laughted scornfully. "Who you funning?"

"I'm a colored woman."

"You trying to joke with me. You whiter skinned than I is."

"I can't help it if I am. My Maw was sho a black woman."

"Your mother was black?"

"She sho was. And I don't reckon I hasta tell you what my daddy was?"

"A real light skinned colored man?"

"No ma'am, he wasn't. He was my white marster, that's who he was. He was my mother's marster and my marster, too, and I was a slave on his plantation till Surrender and the soldiers come and declared us free. Of course now, he never did own me for his child and I wasn't nothing but his piece of property to work and slave for him, but I sho didn't cost him nothing, that is as a price on the slave market, cause he never had to buy me—I was always his."

Betty-Alice was struggling to get her composure, to rearrange her conversation, to change her manner—without any luck—when her husband and her parents came in, and then she blurted out, "Henry Fletcher, Vyry Brown says she's a colored woman and she ain't never seen no nigger mens with tails!"

Henry Fletcher was so taken aback and so acutely embarrassed the red blood quickly suffused his face and he said, "Aw, Betty-Alice, I told you not to tell nobody that, cause that was just our private secret talk."

"I wantsta know how come you said it if it wasn't so?"

Now her parents interfered, "What kinda talk is this? Betty-Alice, what you getting so upset over? You ain't gonna have no milk if you gits all excited."

"Mama and Papa, I'm real glad you come. Look at the baby, ain't he purty?"

"Don't he look like me?" said Henry Fletcher.

"Naw, he don't," said Betty-Alice, "he look like the Shackelfords, now don't he?"

Vyry was getting her things together to leave. Betty-Alice's mother spoke to her, "My son-in-law told me how you saved our baby's life yestiddy by coming here in the nick of time and all you done for him and Betty-Alice and I'm much obliged to you."

"Ma'am, it wasn't nothing. I was glad to help. It ain't no more'n my Christian duty to help anybody I can."

"What's this I hear about colored peoples? Is you a colored granny?"

"I'm a colored woman, yes ma'am."

"Why Lawd! Betty-Alice, the best grannies in the world is colored grannies. They doesn't never lose they babies and they hardly loses they mothers. They is worth more'n money and you is real lucky to had a colored granny. I must say, I took you for a white person myself. You sho don't look colored."

"Well, ma'am, I is. I wasn't trying to hide my race from nobody, cause I ain't ashamed to be colored, but I does feel real bad and hurt deep down inside when I goes around and hears all the things the white folks is saying bout the colored peoples. What's so bad and what hurts so much is half the time they don't know what they talking about, they doesn't even much know us and what they saying is all lies they has heard and stuff they has made up. Me and my husband and my chilluns is been from pillar to post since the war. We ain't been ables to stay nowheres in peace. We's been in a flood and we's been burned out when six white mens purposely set fire to our brand-new house right in front of our very eyes. And it ain't nothing we done to them made them do it. We ain't even much knowed who they was. We's got us a place now out on the Big Road and we's been planning to build in this here community, but after all the terrible stuff I has heard just going round selling vegetables and eggs and stuff I'm scared for us to build, and I'm gwine tell my husband we's gotta be moving on."

"Well, I'm sho sorry to hear that. I can tell you is a good woman and a Christian woman, too. I thank God for what you done for my child and I wants you to know I wishes you well."

"Well, thankye ma'am."

And Vyry left.

She repeated very little of what had happened or what she had heard to Innis when they went home that Sunday afternoon. He could tell, however, that she was more down in spirit than ever because she was singing Aunt Sally's song,

> I been buked and I been scorned,
> Lord, I been buked and I been scorned,

Lord, I been buked and I been scorned,
I been talked about sho's you borned.

She moaned and groaned that song while setting the dinner table and feeding them and when she cleared away the dishes. They sat in front of the tent looking over the land late that afternoon until the sun went down. Night was falling when they saw two men coming up the hills. The children had been playing games but now Vyry stopped them, and as the visitors approached, she sent them inside and told them to go to bed.

"I wonder what they wants with us?" speculated Innis.

"I dunno, but I don't reckon it's good if they's white," said Vyry and Innis looked at her, surprised to detect a hint of bitterness in her tone.

"Well, we ain't got no house for them to burn down," he said.

As they came closer Vyry could see that one of the men was Betty-Alice's father and the other man was a stranger. They came close enough to face them, then Mr. Shackelford said, "We looking for some colored people name Brown. Oh, there you are. Ain't you the one who was granny for Betty-Alice yestiddy?"

"Yes sir," said Vyry, "I'm the one."

"Well, my wife told us what you said, and we went right out and talked to some of the folks in this settlement. They's a lot of young folks around here, some just married, and a lot of them is raising families, some of them expecting babies right now, and all of them agrees they needs a granny round here, cause they has been losing babies something awful, and we heard how you was fixing to build but you was afraid to, on account of so much ill-will, and we come up here to say if you'll stay here in this here community we'll come up here next week and help you build your house. I'm a contractor myself and I does nothing but build. I built all them new houses round Betty-Alice, and we has the word of the people that if you will stay we guarantee yall won't have nothing to fear, ain't nobody will bother you, do, we'll protect you instead. We'll put you up a house in a day. The women folks'll come too and have a quilting bee, and in a day's time we'll have you under your roof just like you want it. Now, how do that sound to you?"

"Mister," said Innis, "it sho sounds good to me." Then they turned to Vyry.

"It sound like God ain't dead and the devil ain't ruling the world. We sho can't thank you enough."

"All right then, we'll be here Thursday morning bright and early."

"Yes sir. We'll be looking for yall."

As the two men went down hill, Vyry and Innis went into their tent, so joyful and stunned by the good news that they could scarcely speak. Innis turned to her in the dark and said, "Well, honey, it looks like you done skinned that cat all by yourself."

"Naw, I ain't. I'm a praying woman, and I figgers with a little time the good Lawd'll show us which a way the wind gwine blow. I done prayed hard, and them folks is done had a change of heart."

I got a home in that rock,
Don't you see?
I got a home in that rock,
Don't you see?
I got a home in that rock,
Debbil in hell can't bother me,
Don't you see?

54   *We got new neighbors now*

Monday morning Vyry and Innis Brown began preparing for
guests on Thursday. Innis was so excited he ran in and out
of the fields and the barn and the tent checking with Vyry
on all his materials and what she thought he ought to have
so there would be nothing lacking.

"I got me a keg of nails. I got three wagon loads of lumber: some yellow pine and some white pine and some hard
pine. I got some bricks for chimneys and fireplaces fires, and
I got bricks for foundation pillars. I got me some tar paper
and some of them new-fangled wood shingles. I is got the
windows and the window facing and the glass panes and the
putty and I got my solid doors already cut out. I got my two-
by-fours and two-by-sixes, and I got me my ladder. I got
sand and I got cement. What you reckon I ain't got yet?"

"I don't know, Innis Brown. You is just making me so

nervous. I has had to stop three times and recount my quilt pieces and study bout my pies. I'm torn between blackberry pies and fresh peach pies, and I dunno how many chickens I got put up to fry! I dunno no more bout building a house than you does, and look like to me by now wouldn't nobody hafta tell you nothing. This gwine be the third house you done built since we come outa Georgy. I can't make up my mind whether or no to mix my turnip sallet with mustard or cook me some purple hull peas and okra or whether to fry some ham or boil it with the vegetables. I keeps hoping buttermilk and coffee and pitchers of lemonade will satisfy thirst. Course I is got some 'simmon beer and some elderberry wine, but I ain't got a plenty and I doesn't know if I oughten offer them white folks wine or no."

"Woman, you is gwine have plenty something to eat, you ain't got nothing to worry bout. I'll be in a awful fix if we runs outa stuff to finish up the house and hasta keep all them mens waiting. I ain't gwine have that, no sirree. I rather have too much than not enough."

"I feels the same way bout vittles. Six families plus my own is a heapa mouths to feed. And you ain't never built me them quilting frames, neither. Is I gotta build them myself?"

"Does you need them Thursday?"

"Of course I does. I done told you time and again we's gwine have a quilting bee whilst yall is building the house. I got to have the midday dinner and I doesn't want nobody leaving here hungry."

"I doesn't see how you makes out cooking all them fine things when you ain't got no cook stove. Lawd, that's what I keeps on forgetting I got to buy!"

"I can't see how you can forget it, I mentions it every single living day the Lawd sends. Is you sho you ain't got no roasting ears big enough?"

"I done told you yes a dozen times bout that, too. I is got plenty roasting ears and I'll have two-three dozens for you to boil or roast come Thursday. I even much got watermelons ripening on the vines."

"Well, I musta forgotten bout them roasting ears, but I'm saving plenty butter."

"Lawd have mercy, woman, you makes my mouth water just talking bout it."

"I means to have plenty something to eat. I done spun some

thread and got it wound on sticks. But I wants you to build me them quilting frames, today!"

"Today?"

"Yeah, and I don't want you putting it off no longer. And, oh yes, Innis Brown, is you done forgot we is got to set up at least three long tables to hold the peoples if we doesn't need more'n that?"

"Vyry, I ain't forgot. Now for the Lawd's sake, calm down!"

"Whose excited, me or you?"

"Well, to tell the truth, I reckon I is."

"Well, old man, you ain't by yourself!" And they both laughed.

Thursday was a delightful summer day with the same weather that had favored the Brown's camping out since spring. Early that morning their place began to take on the festive look of a summer carnival.

Vyry and Innis had long ago decided on the exact spot for their house. It would crest the hill, and there from the front porch they would look off along the Big Road and beyond it into the thick woods and pine forest that rose on high red-clay hills bordering the road to Crenshaw County. The back porch would be built up a story high from the ground with a long flight of back steps and space to walk under the back of the house. In the northern direction were more red-clay hills, and the morning sun would filter through the kitchen windows. On either side of the house were stands of pine trees. Down the back hill a path led to the brook with clear water running over round pebbles and stones with a clear view of the veins of golden sandstone rising in a wall of graduated steps to its source, an underground spring bubbling in another thicket of jack oaks, sweet gums, pines, and dogwood.

"I'm gwine love every inch of this here ground. I loves a hill and always did. Look like you can see far places of the world and you is high enough to reach up and touch the sky and God's face comes down close enough to look in your eyes."

Innis listened to Vyry's praise song and hoped that at last the dark night of her depression was ending.

"We's gwine do well here. I feels it in my bones. God's gwine bless the plowing and the sowing, the reaping and the thrashing. He's done give us a home, and me a farm at last."

Between six and eight o'clock that morning their neighbors

were arriving. They came in buggies and with their mule teams. Every man brought his own tools, his hammer and saw, his plane and lever, his mitering box and his trowel. Some of the women brought small children with them, and every family brought a quilt ready for the frames.

Vyry had big pots of hot coffee waiting and bowls of fresh peaches and the first ripe dew berries with pitchers of sweet cream and milk, and she was frying ham and eggs and offering breakfast to all those who had not already eaten or were hungry again. She had pans of hot biscuits cooked under covers on an open campfire and in hot coals. Vyry's pies were baked and cooling when the neighbors arrived. Her dinner pots were full; her chickens cut up and salted and ready to fry.

Mr. Shackelford, true to his word, arrived early and was directing the carpenters himself. By nine o'clock that morning the men were working on the foundation. At noon the framed house stood as a skeleton with the rafters going up and the upper supporting the long two-by-fours forming the main support of the roof.

The easygoing, friendly spirit these people extended to the Browns was amazing to Innis, but he watched his serious wife move quietly among them with her generous spirit of hospitality and wondered how she could keep so many things going at one time. He had her tables ready, her quilt frames made, ears of corn gathered early, and melons cooling in the spring, but his excitement over the new house was still uncontrollable.

The house was enough excitement, but Vyry fairly burst with pride and interest in the quilts. There were six quilts and each housewife had a different pattern. Mrs. Shackelford was making the Rose of Sharon for her daughter, Betty-Alice, and every woman "oohed" and "aahed" over her workmanship. She was going to quilt it with the big rosy flowers known to some as the single hibiscus outlined in her most exquisite stitching. Mrs. Lapsley was quilting the Star of California and she had used a combination of red and blue calico for the huge six-cornered star, while a third lady, Mrs. Flake, was making the Star of Texas in brilliant red and white. Perhaps the most original pattern was a monkey wrench used by Mrs. McElroy with each monkey wrench in a different color on a field of white and brown. The double wedding ring was Mrs. Medford's pattern with pastels for the interlocking circles. Vyry was making pomegranates with deep orange fruit, green stems and leaves, on a white background. Each woman sewed industriously through the morning and at dinner time they compared notes with admiring glances and comments to see how much they had accomplished.

At noon work stopped for Vyry's fried chicken and biscuits and buttered ears of white field corn, turnip greens, okra, blackberry pie, and coffee. Later the taut quilt frames with their colorful sides were turned up to the bright sun as the energetic women bent over them, while Jim and Innis Brown ran to the beck and call of the busy carpenters, sawing and hammering and fitting the pine boards together.

It was hard to say who had had a more satisfying day, the neighbors who had built a house of good will with their good deeds, or Vyry and Innis in their humble gratitude for this fine gesture of friendship and understanding from their new neighbors. Moving into the house could be a gradual thing, but the Browns would all sleep under a new roof that night.

Come by heah, Lawd!
Come by heah!

55 *Freedom don't mean nothing, him allus driving and whupping me to work!*

Summer 1870 seemed to bring the supreme fulfillment of all Innis Brown's hopes and desires. He had a farm and his family settled in a home of their own. Here in this brand-new house they could feel secure at last, thanks to Vyry's errand of mercy and the new vein of good will she had struck in their neighbors. They certainly did need a granny, and often in those early summer weeks Vyry was called to practice her new role of midwife. She kept a little package ready with her scissors handy and a small bag packed, for sometimes she was gone overnight or several days. She worked very hard at home to keep her family from suffering during these sudden absences.

The summer months were full of the halcyon days one dreams and scarcely believes are real. All of the month of June the days were clear as glass and when the month of July set in with intense heat and sultriness they felt the relief of afternoon showers.

"It's dog-days now," said Innis, "it gwine rain some every day."

That was, in truth, the pattern of July. They awoke every morning to a blazing hot day that by noon would seem unbearable, and then in the afternoon the rain would settle the dust with sudden showers that poured down in big drops but did not last long. Sometimes the sun shone fiercely through the rain and that explained the saying, "Raining in the sunshine, rain again tomorrow." Innis had a fine crop of watermelons and Vyry would put the children on the back porch where they washed their faces in the sweet red juicy fruit and ate down to the rind.

But Jim felt that the summer they got the new house began a period of torture and unbearable labor for him. His stepfather got him up at the crack of dawn, before sunrise, and together they did the chores of feeding and watering stock before they ate breakfast. As soon as breakfast was over they went to the fields. Innis Brown had half his cultivated acreage planted in cotton and he believed this was his most important crop, but it was also the most back-breaking work. His second crop was corn and a quarter of the cultivated land was planted in it. The remaining land was planted with vegetables—peas and beans and potatoes and peanuts. Vyry had a large garden in addition to Innis's fields and she and Minna and little Harry tended the garden after the plowing was done. Jim hated to plow. He hated to hoe and cultivate. He hated to weed and to tassel corn. He hated to drive the mules and he hated to bend over in the hot sun handling the hoe. He told his sister, Minna, "I believe Paw's losing his mind. He must be going crazy. I can't stand the way he's driving me to work. I just can't stand it. I'm always so tired and I don't no more'n git to sleep at night before he's waking me up to git up and go to work. I'm tired, I tells you, I'm tired of Innis Brown driving me like I'm a mule to work his fields."

"Aw, Jim, Maw says you always complaining and you always did ever since you was little; they says you just don't like to work."

"Well, who do? I ain't nothing but a work-horse. I ain't even much good as a horse. I'm a mule. It's just like slavery time round here with Innis Brown."

But nobody seemed to understand him or pay attention

to his complaining how he could not stand the hard work Innis Brown was putting on him.

At night Innis complained to Vyry, "That boy sho is good for nothing and trifling bout work."

"I hears you grumbling bout him all the time, but it looks like to me he working all the time."

"What you mean? That boy don't work half the time. He claim he tired and got to stop and sit down and rest awhile. Make out like he bout to drop he so tired. Soon as he start to work again he gotta have a drink of water or he got business in the out-house. After dinner he sleepy and long before time for dinner or supper he hungry. Something or nother's wrong with him all the time. And Lawd have mercy if he ain't glad when the showers come. Lil drop of rain and he fairly jump up and shout, 'Whoopee, Paw, it's raining. Let's us stop.' I tells him, lil rain ain't gwine hurt nobody, ain't no needs stopping for lil dog-days shower."

"Well, you knows he ain't a man like you is and I expects he do git tired sometime and I don't think you oughta keep working in no shower neither. That's something Grimes didn't even much make the field hands do on Marse John's plantation in slavery time."

"Yeah, well I ain't got me no hands like he had and anyways we's working for ourselves and we gotta work harder than if we was working under a whip for a marster or a overseer-boss driving. Ain't nobody driving us with no whip and no gun. I ain't got nobody but me and Jim and we's got to work just twice as hard."

"You right sho you ain't driving him?"

"Driving him! Driving him, you say? That boy's stubborn as a mule. Can't nobody drive him if they tries. How you figure I'm driving him?"

And Vyry hushed because she was sure there was no way for Innis Brown to see Jim's side, but she also understood how anxious Innis was to make a crop, and she didn't want to encourage laziness in Jim. She knew he did not like to work, but he was growing up and he needed to know how to work. All summer their feuding continued, Jim and Innis Brown both stubbornly contending the work was too hard and too much on one hand and the work was not enough on the other. Vyry had a plan in her mind for the winter time after harvest. She wanted Jim and Minna to go into town to school. She heard there was a school in Greenville for Negro children, but it wasn't free. She didn't intend to start

Innis Brown again on that subject of how they couldn't afford it. She was saving every nickel and dime she made with the full intention of sending Jim and Minna to school.

Innis Brown was especially proud of his stock, as proud of his hogs and team of horses and cow as Vyry was proud of her chickens. When they moved to the land in the spring he realized at once that everything here was ideal for healthy growing stock. There was fine pasture land for a cow, ample wooded sections with coverts for game, and natural springs of water. As usual he built a pen for his pigs far from the house in the woods. He was trying now to build up his stock of pigs and his hopes lay in breeding them. He had two large hogs, one fattening for winter that he would kill at Christmas, and one large sow which he hoped would have a fine litter of pigs late in the summer. This big sow was free to roam in a corner of the woods where there were acorns and even pecans, and where the shade of the trees sheltered her from the hot summer sun. There was a big mud hole for her comfort fed with water from the hillside spring which Innis had cleverly turned into a small irrigating trench or ditch. The summer was hot and humid, but despite the daily showers, not an especially moist or wet summer, hence they needed the ditch. Mornings and evenings either Innis or Jim carried slops to the hogs and saw that they had enough water.

August was a hot, stifling month. There were few showers, an occasional downpour relieving the oppressive dryness, and doing little more than settling the dust. Every morning and night Innis tended his stock with care, sometimes dividing the labor with Jim. Always he questioned Jim at breakfast or supper or dinner about his watering or feeding the hogs. Jim always answered him "Yes sir" but his hostility to Innis Brown had grown to boiling point over the summer. Stealthily he rolled his eyes at Innis or kept his eyes on the plate of food he was eating, sometimes jumping up from the table and running outside in anger when Innis remarked about his table manners or called him a glutton. Jim told his mother that Innis Brown was "picking" on him.

"Aw, son, I don't reckon so. You is just touchy."

"No, ma'am, I ain't. He grudges me my something to eat, won't let me finish my food in peace, and then he shaking me before day and hollering to me to git up and go to work. If he ask me about that sow one time he musta asked me bout her six times yestiddy."

Vyry could hardly repress a smile, knowing that Innis was really anxious about that sow, who was due to have her litter of pigs any day now. It was the end of August, and as the summer ended the morning mists and evening dews that cooled the baked earth were more frequent. Innis was looking forward to an early harvest. He had grown thin under the pressure of the summer, and now Vyry noticed that he was so wrought up he slept poorly and tossed in his sleep at night. He was always awake by four o'clock in the morning, sometimes up and dressed and waking Jim, and at night, when it was dark and time to go to bed, he was restless and trying to figure ways he could make the work go faster.

Toward the end of the mouth of August, the twenty-ninth, late in the morning, Vyry was preparing midday dinner when she heard Jim sobbing and running up the back steps of the house. He burst into the house and ran into the kitchen where his mother was. He was sobbing hysterically and screaming incoherent words between sobs.

"I ain't gwine stay here no longer! I ain't gwine stay where nobody beat me like I'm a animal and driving me like I'm a dog and then beating on me too. I'll kill him, Maw, I'll kill him. I got to git away from here, elst I'll kill him!"

To her horror his shirt was in shreds and sticking to his skin and she saw his back was bleeding. He had his rifle in his hand and her heart jumped in her throat.

"Calm down, boy, and tell me what in the world is the matter with you?"

"Can't you see? Can't you tell? Can't you see how he done beat me unmerciful like I'm a dog? Can't you see he trying to kill me? I hates to leave you, Maw, but I gotta go. I ain't staying here no more, you hear me? I ain't gwine stay here with him no more. I'll kill him, I tells you, I'll kill him!" And he ran into his room.

"Jesus have mercy! Boy you stop talking bout killing before I goes crazy clean out of my mind. Does you want to kill me? I'll die, I tells you, I'll lay right down and die, if you ever kills anybody."

Jim was first fumbling among his things for his clothes. Now he stopped at his mother's words and sat on his bed. He was still sobbing, his thin shoulders hunched, and great gulps of sobs tearing him apart. Minna and Harry stood looking at Jim. Vyry saw the tears rolling down Minna's face to see Jim hurt. Even Harry was whimpering.

Vyry heard the back door slam and heard Innis come in. She met him in the kitchen.

"Where is that good for nothing trifling low-down boy? I ain't begun to beat him. I feels like skinning his hide!"

Vyry's eyes went wild at the sight of him with a big green stick in his hands, trembling in his nervousness and rage. She stood in his path between the kitchen and the door to Jim's room and she grabbed one of her iron skillets from the stove.

"Do it, Innis Brown, and I'll brain you with this here skillet!"

Deeply shocked, Innis stepped back, completely inarticulate before her rage.

"If you hits him one more time, I ain't gwine be 'sponsible. Don't you hit him nary nother lick or I'll send your soul to Kingdom Come."

"Woman, is you outa your mind or is you just now losing your senses? Does you know what that boy done done?"

"Naw, and I don't care. You done beat him unmerciful now, don't you hit him no more."

"You don't care? You don't care nothing bout him killing my sow what fixing to have pigs and all my money done gone down in that there mud?"

"Killed the sow? Lawd, have mercy, is the sow dead?" And the news weakened Vyry so she sat down.

"And that ain't the worst of it, he let her mire herself down in mud, all on account of his carelessness. Does you know what he was doing? Shooting birds, that's what he was doing."

"It wasn't none of my fault, Maw, it wasn't none of my fault! I tried to git that sow outen that mud. I done all I could to keep that sow from getting in that mud and the more I tries to git her out the deeper she goes down in that mud. It wasn't none of my fault, Maw, I told him I didn't go to do it and I was sorry, and he just cussed me out and went to beating on me with a long green switch like he losing his mind."

"Yeah, and I'm gwine beat you some more. Cause I faults you for it, and I oughta skin your hide."

"Naw, Innis Brown, I done told you naw, and I means what I says. That sow is dead now and that's a pity and a shame, but beating on my boy ain't gwine bring that sow back, now, you done beat him enough."

Minna was so upset she ran up and said, "Please, Pa, don't kill my brother, you done cut the blood out of him!"

Innis, still bristling with rage and bridling under Vyry's threats, turned to Minna and raised his hand to strike her, "Git away from me with your sass fore I slaps you in the mouth and knocks the fire out of you, too."

"Aw, naw, Innis Brown, I knows you crazy now! Don't you lay a hand to hurt her, do, I don't know what I won't be crazy enough to do."

"Woman is you trying to tell me your childrens is too good to be whipped? I ain't gwine stay under no roof with no young uns I can't chastise."

"Oh, pshaw, that ain't shot from taw, Innis Brown. I ain't said no sitcha thing and you knows it, but I wants you to know you ain't gwine browbeat and mistreat nobody here, not long as I'm living and I can help it. You ain't gwine hit Minna lessen it's over my dead body, now does you hear me? I'm a little piece of leather, but I'm well put together, cut the holy man!"

"What you means by that?"

"I kivers every inch o'ground I'm standing on. That's what I means."

"You ain't all that much trouble you is kicking up now."

"I ain't no trouble at all long as you behaves yourself, but when you comes in here talking bout skinning Jim's hide and slapping the fire outa Minna, you is gwine find out you is done run into *me*, and that's just the same as meeting your granddaddy drunk. I ain't gwine stand for it. That's what I means."

"What you gwine do about it?"

"Try me and see."

"I ain't never thought I'd live to see the day you would carry on like this, Vyry Brown. I's done everything I can to please you and I ain't never been trying to do nothing to harm you nor your younguns. All I been doing was for them and you much as for myself, if not more. I ain't trying to mistreat and 'buse nobody. God knows I's been willing to work my fingers to the bone for you and these childrens. Is I got to let them destroy everything I'm trying to raise to make a living for us? Is I got to let them run over me and sass me to my face and then you takes up for them? Naw, God, I ain't going that far. I loves you and I loves them and I been willing to die for alla yall, but I'm a man too, and I ain't gwine take down low under your younguns. I'm just as much a man as you is a woman, and I wants to tell you now if you thinks they's gwine run me and do like they please whilst you is planning and holding them up in they devilment, you think like Parker dreamt, he dreamt he farted and he shit. Naw. God knows this here brand-new big farmhouse ain't gwine be big enough to hold alla us. Now you can put that in your pipe and smoke it whilst you is kivering your ground so big."

"Is you through?"

"Naw. I just wants to let you know I knows what you been thinking. You ain't never wanted Jim to work in no fields. You ain't never been much for field hands no-how. I knows your kind of dicty Big House Miss Ann's nigger servants. You wants your childrens to be like they fine daddy was, a free man what had learning in his head, books and a trade. You wants Jim to go to school, that's what you wants. You figgering on sending him over my head even much though I tells you we can't afford it and I needs him to work. You got your own money and you figgering on doing like you please. You gwine run me and your childrens gwine run me, too, and I ain't nothing but a ignorant field hand what you despises. You ain't been the same nohow since that there fire, but if you is swallowing me for a fool you is gwine belch up some sense, and if you burns me for one you is gwine lose your ashes. That's all I got to say."

"Well I reckon that's big enough mouthful for one day. Ain't nothing never hurts a duck but his bill. I done heard you, Innis Brown. I hopes you right sure you ain't said too much so's you won't have to eat up nothing you is done said."

It was a very bad morning and it turned into a very bad day. Nobody had any appetite. Vyry warmed tallow and put it on Jim's lacerated back and when Innis went back to the fields, he went alone. Jim slept all afternoon. At supper time the house was still wrapped in gloom. Innis ate his supper in silence. Jim would not come to the supper table, and this distressed both Minna and Harry. Afterwards, Vyry tried to coax Jim to eat but he insisted he wasn't hungry and didn't want to eat food when he wasn't welcome. He even refused watermelon and the other children left their half-eaten slices on the back porch so that Innis had to carry the rinds in the slops to the one remaining hog. Vyry watched darkness descending with a deepening despair. Although she moved about her usual tasks she felt mechanical. She acted from force of habit, but inside she was a sea of seething emotions.

One of the concessions they had made to Jim's growing up

was a room of his own. The iron bed that Innis had bought
for Vyry was now his. They thought when they built the
house that if he had his own room with privacy it would make
him happier, but of course it did not. Minna and Harry were
sharing a room. Vyry and Innis had a big air-swept bedroom
where she could keep both a spinning wheel and a loom, and
where eventually she hoped to have a sewing machine. The
big center hall in this house, like that in the gutted house in
Troy, was their living room for company. Cross ventilation
made this room very pleasant in summer.

Vyry had said nothing to Innis since their midday outburst.
Now feeling the awkwardness of the awful day, Innis asked
her, "Wife, is you mad?"

Vyry swallowed hard before answering. "I'm more hurt
than I is mad."

"Well, did you ever hear the story bout the man and his
wife with the plank in the bed?"

"Naw, and I doesn't wants to hear none of your dirty
under-my-dress-tail stories neither."

He was taking off his shoes, but she had already gone to
bed. Now aggrieved, he turned to her to say, "I wasn't gwine
tell you no dirty under-your-dress-tail story, I was just . . ."

"I says I doesn't want to hear it, Innis Brown!"

So he did not come to bed. Next morning she awoke earlier
than usual, still too troubled in mind to feel that the night
had been restful or had lessened her distress, and discovered
that Innis Brown had made himself a pallet in the big center hall.

The house was so gloomy that morning that Vyry felt as
though it were overcast with the pall of death. Everybody
ate in silence and nobody paid any attention to Harry's chatter
or the dog, Tricks, who was barking for scraps from the table.
Inins did his chores and went again to the fields without
Jim. Vyry finished her morning's dishes, again moving me-
chanically and then she and Minna straightened the house.
Vyry was so abstracted that the children stopped trying to
talk to her. By nine o'clock in the morning she felt so leaden
she told Minna to mind Harry, and, saying nothing to Jim,
who was still sulking in his room, she went out of the back
door and down the high back steps and began to walk aim-
lessly toward the woods.

It was a still morning, but luminous and clear. A thousand
thoughts were crowding her troubled mind, and an equal
number of emotions were surging through her. She felt as

though her world had broken like a china bowl and lay scattered around her in pieces. It was no small matter that the sow was dead. She knew what a blow this meant to her husband and his hopes for the fall. It was also not a simple matter that Jim felt as he did. He was fifteen years old and feeling himself a man. Innis Brown said more than once during the summer, "I think he smell his pee." But she also had deeply sympathized with Jim in his aversion to working in the fields, and though she had never spoken one way or the other, Innis Brown had read her mind like a book when he chided and accused her of her secret thoughts and ambitions for Jim. It was, moreover, very disturbing to see her warm, happy, and loving family split and bursting with strife. She did not know at first why she felt so stricken, so cut in two parts. Innis Brown had tried to be a good father to her children, and he had been as fine as he could be. He deserved the right to chastise them as much as she did. It wasn't just a matter of prejudice that Jim was her first-born child and she loved him dearly. But all that confusion in her house yesterday went back to something in her life that she thought she had forever escaped. It brought back all the violence and killing on the plantation when Grimes was driving and beating the field hands to death. It brought back the horror of the deaths of Mammy Sukey, and Grandpa Tom, the branding of Lucy, and burning the old men to death, the plague, and the hanging, murder, and fire, when the slaves all knew their lives were not worth a copper cent with a hole in it. It went back to the war and all the bloody fighting and killing and dying, the death of all her master's family one by one, and the final assault on Lillian that had left her mind wounded for life. It was part of all the turbulence of the Ku Klux Klan and the fire and all the evil hatred she had felt before the house was built here. Now this awful hatred and violence was threatening to destroy her happy home and her loving family. It was in her own brand-new house. What could she do about it? What must she do? Must she stand by and watch this same terrible hatred and violence destroy everything and everybody she loved and held most dear? Deeply shocked, she knew she herself had been capable of killing Innis Brown yesterday. She knew that Jim repeatedly threatened to kill Innis Brown, and that he owned a gun. She knew that Innis Brown cut the blood out of Jim in a hot passion of anger and frustration and talked about skinning his hide. She was sick of killing and violence. She was sick of the hate that went with it. Was this kind of evil going to follow her all the days of her life?

Before she realized where she was going she found herself deep in the woods. Around here there was a chapel-hush. She heard birds softly and sweetly singing, but most of all she felt the silence of the thickly soft carpet of pine needles under her feet, and looking up she could faintly see the blue sky in thin scraps of light through the interlacing of tender young leaves and green pine needles. She found herself a rock, and instead of sitting down she dropped to her knees. Instinctively she began to pray, the words forming on her lips at first in a halting, faltering, and half-hesitant fashion, and then rushing out:

"Lawd, God-a-mighty, I come down here this morning to tell you I done reached the end of my rope, and I wants you to take a-hold. I done come to the bottom of the well, Lord, and my well full of water done run clean dry.

"I come down here, Lord, cause I ain't got no where else to go. I come down here knowing I ain't got no right, but I got a heavy need. I'm suffering so, Lord, my body is heavy like I'm carrying a stone. I come to ask you to move the stone, Jesus. Please move the stone! I come down here, Lord, to ask you to come by here, Lord. Please come by here!

"We can't go on like this no longer, Lord. We can't keep on a-fighting, and a-fussing, and a-cussing, and a-hating like this, Lord. You done been too good to us. We done wrong, Lord, I knows we done wrong. I ain't gwine say we ain't done wrong, and I ain't gwine promise we might not do wrong again cause, Lord, we ain't nothing but sinful human flesh, we ain't nothing but dust. We is evil peoples in a wicked world, but I'm asking you to let your forgiving love cover our sin, Lord.

"Let your peace come in our hearts again, Lord, and we's gwine try to stay on our knees and follow the road You is laid before us, if You only will.

"Come by here, Lord, come by here, if you please. And Lord, I wants to thank You, Jesus, for moving the stone!"

Now with the morning rocking around her like a storm shaking through the earth beneath her, she waited till the thundering sound of crashing trees and trembling worlds had ceased, and she got up from her knees. She looked around, startled and almost amazed that the day was still so hushed and still. The sunlight dappled through the trees and she put her hands out to touch the absolutely motionless leaves. In wonder she looked again at the blue sky, and then in a sudden lightness of movement, feeling that once again she was a feather, she began to pick her way out of the woods. She touched her wet cheeks with one exploring finger and, drying them on her apron, she spoke out aloud, "My eyes must be red and I must look a sight. I reckon I better wash my face in the brook before I goes back to the house."

Jim was still in his room when she got back to the house so she went inside where he was sitting on his unmade bed.

"Good morning, Jim, how you feeling?"

"I'm all right, Maw," he mumbled.

"Well you don't ack like it, you ain't put on no clothes, and you ain't ate nothing. I don't reckon you is planning on staying in here all day, is you?"

"Nome. But I ain't gwine back to no fields and work with Innis Brown."

"Well, I reckon if you doesn't, I'll have to."

"Why?"

"Cause he got to have somebody help him, that's how come. He overworked now trying to make a good crop. That's how come he been so overbearing with you. He trying hard to make us a living."

"I don't want him to make me none. I'm gwine to work for myself."

"Whereabouts, son?"

"I dunno, Maw. But I can't stay here no more, Maw. Don't ask me to stay here. I'm big enough to work for myself if I'm big enough to work for him. And I knows one thing, I'm too big to take a beating. I ain't gwine take no beating offa nobody, Maw, no more in this here life, does you hear me?"

"Well son, I don't blame you for not taking nothing you don't hasta. That's where you is different from me. I has been taking all my life, and I ain't never been ables to say what I wasn't gwine take, cause I was always beholden to somebody elst."

"I knows that, Maw. That's cause you was a slave all your life, but I ain't no slave no more. That man read that paper say I am forever free. And I thought that meant didn't nobody have no right driving me to work and beating me like I'm a dog. I don't see no difference in slavery time and working for Innis Brown. Freedom don't mean nothing with him always driving me to work and beating me like I'm a dog."

"He ain't always beating on you like you is a dog."

"One time is enough. I felt like killing him, Maw, yestiddy. Let me go way from here before he makes me kill him."

"Son, is you got murder in your heart for your Paw?"

"He ain't none of my Paw!"

"He's almost all the Paw you is ever known. And he been mighty good to all us."

"I knows he's your husband, Maw, and maybe you feels like you got to stick by him and turn against me, but I ain't got to stick by him and I doesn't wanta be round him no more."

"Son, you can't carry hatred round in your heart like that."

"How come, Maw?"

"You gotta forgive, like you expects God to forgive you."

"I'll forgive him, but I ain't never gwine forgit him."

"Then you is still hating, and you ain't forgiving."

"Well, I ain't Jesus Christ and I ain't no hypocrite."

"Who is you calling one?"

"Nobody, Maw, it's just I ain't gwine make like I feels forgiving and loving towards Innis Brown when he done put whelps on my back and cut the blood out of me."

"Well, you ain't gwine be hurting nobody but yourself when you goes round with a heart full of hate."

"How does you figger that out, Maw? I sho didn't beat myself."

"Keeping hatred inside makes you git mean and evil inside. We supposen to love everybody like God loves us. And when you forgives you feels sorry for the one what hurt you, you returns love for hate, and good for evil. And that stretches your heart and makes you bigger inside with a bigger heart so's you can love everybody when your heart is big enough. Your chest gets broad like this, and you can lick the world with a loving heart! Now when you hates you shrinks up inside and gets littler and you squeezes your heart tight and you stays so mad with peoples you feels sick all the time like you needs the doctor. Folks with a loving heart don't never need no doctor."

Jim listened and then he laughed. He laughed until the tears rolled down his cheeks. Then he hugged his mother, and said, "Maw, you is the most wonderful Maw in the world! I loves you, Maw. Don't worry none. I ain't gwine kill nobody. I might even get so I can stand Innis Brown and think about loving him. But I'm warnnig you, Maw, that's gwine be a long, long time before I gets a heart that big!"

Vyry listened to Jim. His laugh sounded so strange, so grown-up, and yet so familiar. His voice was changing, and suddenly with a pang at her heart she realized he reminded her of his father, Randall Ware.

The tension in the house began to ease that second afternoon. When Innis came home for his dinner he found his favorite food on the table, and that night a fresh-grated sweet potato pone. His eyes lighted and he looked at Vyry, who only smiled steadily back at him. The next morning, without any word from anyone, Jim appeared at the breakfast table. The charged feelings in the house were dissipated as once again the family life revolved around the quietly confident Vyry, whose presence exuded her own inner peace.

Twice that morning, however, whether from nervousness or abstraction, she dropped her cooking spoon, and Innis Brown remarked, "Sho must be somebody coming here ain't never been here before. That's twice you dropped your cooking spoon."

"Well, it ain't gwine be no stranger cause it wasn't none of my fork nor my knife. But I been thinking the same thing, two-three days now. It is somebody coming here cause the end of my nose been itching all this week."

Company appeared that day at noon in the shape of Mr. Porter from Georgiana.

"Howdy, Vyry, I told you I'd be here. Didn't think I'd be so long. Yall got a nice place here, a real nice place."

"Yessir, Mr. Porter, thankye. We likes it fine. How's Miss Lucy?"

"She's fine."

"And Bob and Susan?"

"They're fine, too, fine as split peas. Bob's going off to school next month, matter of fact he's going next week. We're thinking about Susan going too, just haven't found the right place yet. Bob's going to military school."

"Yessir. You don't say! I don't reckon it do no good to ask about Miss Lillian. She stays the same?"

"She stays the same."

Vyry set company dinner table to feed Mr. Porter. After dinner he took an hour's time to ask detailed questions about their claim. He said he was going to town to the courthouse and check the registration. He came back unexpectedly and walked around the back. He walked up the steps and startled Jim, washing up after having been in the fields. Jim's shirt was off so that his back was bare. Mr. Porter's eyes bulged when he saw the angry welts on Jim's back and when he went inside he spoke to Vyry in front of Innis Brown.

"Humph, that boy's back looks bad, Vyry. He musta caught a awful whipping."

"Yes sir, he did," said Vyry and said no more.

Mr. Porter must have felt the tension his remarks aroused and noticing their awkward and guilty faces he said no more on the subject.

"I'm going up to Dawson, Georgia, this week, Vyry. You got anybody up there you want me to give a message or say howdy?"

"No sir, I don't reckon I knows anybody there excepten old Doc and I don't reckon it matters none to him."

"I'm bound to see him. Got to see that hound dog Grimes, too. He's the banker now and there's a big confusion over the Dutton property and affairs. The way I understand it, looks like he's trying to take everything over."

"Is that so? Well, I hopes you can straighten out everything."

"That's just what I'm going up there to do, see if I can't protect the interests of Bob and Susan."

"Well, sir, I hopes you have good luck."

"Thanks. Well, you are all right. I can assure you on my honor these papers are in order. Take good care of them now. In five years this land will be yours free and clear. And don't fail to keep up your taxes."

"Yes sir. We sho thanks you."

And Mr. Porter left.

Well, I've done all I can do,
And I can't get along with you,
So meet me at my office pay-day!

56   *The blackest man I ever did see*

The first Monday morning in September, Vyry was sitting on
her front porch teaching Minna how to piece quilts and showing her how to make tiny neat stitches. The little girl's eyes
would frequently tire and wander away, and now looking up
she saw a man coming up the lane leading from the Big Road
to their new farmhouse. Minna strained her eyes and looked
again.

"Maw, who is that? That's the blackest man I ever did see
in my life!"

Vyry looked up. She had just threaded her needle and had
a snip of thread on her tongue. Now she made a knot and
spit out the thread.

"That look like your daddy," she breathed quietly. As the
man came closer she looked again and said in the same quiet
tone, "It is your daddy."

One reason the man looked so strange to Minna was that he was not only black but he was dressed in black clothes and his clothes were unlike any she had ever seen a black man wear before. He didn't have on work clothes or the cheap homespun that she knew. He was dressed in store-bought clothes and he had on a tall black hat. Now as the man approached them Vyry knew she was not seeing a ghost but that all her hopes and fears were true. He walked up the lane to the steps, took off his hat, put his foot up on one step, smiled broadly, and said, "Howdy!"

Vyry answered, "Howdy yourself."

Minna saw that his teeth were as white as the milky kernels of corn that had ripened in the fields. His eyes were twinkling, either in fun or mischief, but if Vyry's knees had turned to water no one could tell from looking in her face.

"Where is Jim?"

"He's in the field."

"Well, get him, cause I come after him."

Vyry got up and took the quilt pieces in the house, rolling up her needle and thread and thimble in the little bundle. Then she put on her sunbonnet and started to the fields for Jim. Randall Ware sat down in her chair and took Minna in his arms. He kissed her and he saw her squirm when his beard and mustache tickled her.

"Gosh, but you are surely a pretty little girl! How'd you like to come with me and go to school?"

Minna's heart leaped for joy. Going to school was what she had dreamed and what she wanted more than anything else in the world. Then she looked out and saw her mother in the field, going after Jim, her sunbonnet flapping as she moved.

"Will Maw come, too?"

"I don't know. Maybe."

"Well, if Maw ain't going, I ain't going neither."

"Well, one of these days you're going to get married and Maw won't come then."

"Annh, annh, I ain't never leaving my mama."

He laughed and kissed her again, and again she squirmed.

"We'll wait and see if a man won't change your mind."

Minna frowned. She wanted to go to school more than anything else in the world, but she knew she couldn't leave Vyry because her mama needed her. And about marrying a man, she didn't like anybody teasing her about a man making her leave her mama. She told him so, and he only laughed again showing those beautiful white teeth. And when he laughed he sounded just like Jim. Or was it Jim sounded like him?

Vyry crossed the field with Jim, his hoe held over his shoulder, his bare feet dusty, but his heart leaping with the joyful news that his own father had come for him. They left Innis Brown in the field, too stunned by the news to come to the house for awhile.

When they got to the house Randall Ware said, "Let him take a bath and put on some clean clothes. I'm taking him with me."

Vyry said, "When? Today? This evening?" In her mind afternoon was evening and that meant only a matter of two or three hours. Randall Ware took out his gold watch hanging on a long chain and looked at the time.

"I'm planning on taking that afternoon train to Montgomery where we change trains for Selma."

"What's in Selma?" asked Vyry.

"A Baptist School for the training of Negro teachers and preachers."

Jim's eyes widened and his face broke into a grin.

They moved into the house while Jim took down the big wooden tub hanging on the back porch. He built a fire in Vyry's cooking stove and put on a tea kettle to heat water. One kettle of boiling water would only take the chill off the buckets of cold water he needed to fill the tub, but that one kettle would help. When the boy's bath was ready and he was undressing, his father opened the door Jim had closed and went into the kitchen as Jim was getting in the tub. Randall Ware then called Vyry. She saw rage moving through every muscle of his face as he looked at Jim's back still showing the marks of the beating.

"I got a mind to put Innis Brown in jail for beating my boy like this!"

Frightened, Vyry answered quickly without thinking but also without any heated temper.

"White folks around here won't stand to see Paw go to jail."

"White folks? So the doctor was right! You are a good and faithful nigger! White folks can't help themselves if I swear out a warrant for his arrest. After all, Jim is *my* boy."

Vyry trembled visibly now, and her knees felt so weak she had to sit down. Then she looked Randall Ware in the eye and said, "And he's mine too. Now listen here, Randall Ware, as you say, Jim's your boy and you got a right to take him if you wants. Maybe it's the best thing in the world you can do is to take him, but you ain't got no business coming here making trouble for the man what's been taking care of us when you wasn't here and couldn't. You ain't got no business coming here and stirring up trouble for Paw after all he's done for me and your childrens. If push come to shove, I'll stand with Paw and I'll say Jim is careless and stubborn and don't like to work, and if he'd been paying attention to what he was doing that sow wouldn't be dead and he wouldn't have that beating. Course I know Innis beat him too hard, and I told him so, but Paw ain't no cruel man and that's the first time I knows he's ever beat that boy and he done it then through a passion of temper and anger, a sinful passion I grants you, but I knows he didn't know what he was doing or-ruh he wouldn't never beat him that bad."

Randall Ware listened to her words and watched her face while she talked. He also watched Jim, and Jim was assenting to his mother's words.

"Maw sho give him what-for about it, didn't you, Maw?"

Vyry looked at Jim and caught the happy ring in his voice and she smiled, but now Randall Ware changed to another tactic, "How come you didn't wait for me where I left you like I told you? Didn't you get my message saying I would come for you and the children when the war was over?"

"Yeah, I got your message and I waited. We waited and we waited till we couldn't wait no more. Everybody was dead and gone excepten Miss Lillian and she had done lost her mind, and the poor kin come to git her and her childrens and they was putting up the place for sale, boarding up the doors and windows and we had to leave. We couldn't wait there no longer."

Now Randall Ware looked at his watch a second time. Vyry threw a clean ironed feed-sack to Jim to use as a towel and wrapping it around him he ran in his room to put his clothes on. Vyry bent to empty the tub, but Randall Ware stopped her.

"You don't lift that tub. Either I'll do it or you call that boy back here. You wait on everybody hand and foot just like it's still slavery time." And he emptied the tub.

"I don't mind. Yall ain't gwine before dinner, is you? I got to get his few rags together."

"I can buy him some things in Montgomery, I guess, but I don't see why we still can't make the three o'clock train. Seems like it's about five miles walking out here from town."

"Paw'll take you in the wagon, but you got plenty time to eat before the train time."

When Innis came in at twelve o'clock dinner time he thought he was ready to face Randall Ware, but he was unprepared for the man. He thought, like Minna, that he had never seen a blacker man in his life. But he was uneasy in the face of this black man's clothes and gold watch, most of all in the face of his casual arrogance and his smoth, cultivated speech. For all his blackness, Innis Brown was forced to concede that Randall Ware was a very handsome man. His broad shoulders, quick alert eyes, sparkling white teeth, and his carefully clipped mustache and beard made him look more distinguished than Innis had expected to see in a common blacksmith. He also noticed how Minna was clinging to her father, how Jim's eyes were on fire with a light from another world, and worst of all, how Vyry was so excited she had brought out the finest things from her chest and from the plantation; things he could not remember ever seeing her use before, such as a real linen tablecloth and silver and china dishes. She had a bowl of flowers on the table. She had put the big pot in the little pot and she had fried chicken and made two kinds of pie, candied sweet potatoes, and okra, and lima beans and ham, and biscuits and corn bread and, no! the elderberry wine!

Vyry looked at Paw's face out of the corner of one eye and saw how miserable he was. He looked like he wished the ground would open up and swallow him. *He thinks I'm honoring Randall Ware when I'm just plain showing off.* If she were not so nervous and uneasy and excited she could enjoy the fun, but here sat two men facing each other who were strangers to each other but intimately familiar to her. She had carried babies for both and though one had come back from the dead, she was still wife to both. Every time she thought about Jim she wanted to say, "Glory be!" and every time she thought about herself all her confused mind came back with was, "What a mess!"

Harry had evidently been sleeping half the morning and when he suddenly appeared Randall Ware's eyes widened and he said, "Who is that?"

Vyry said, "That's my baby, Harry. Harry come here and say 'howdy' to this gentleman."

Harry said, "Howdy," and shook the hand Randall Ware held out to him, then Randall looked at Vyry and said, "How old is he?"

Even as Vyry got the words out, "He's four," Innis Brown was asking Randall Ware in an almost sullen and stunned tone, "How'd you find us? How'd you know where we was at?"

Randall Ware was now playing with Harry, who was fascinated by the watch and gold chain. He took the little boy on his knee and was showing the watch and chain to him when he heard Innis Brown's question. He looked up into the hostile face of the other man and answered easily, glancing back and forth from him to Vyry, "Old Doc brought a man in my shop Friday said his name was Porter and he had just been down here. Told me he saw all of you and told me somebody had beat my boy unmerciful and if I thought anything of my family I'd at least come and get that boy. I would have been here long before now but as God is my judge I did not know which way to go before Friday. I didn't even take time to arrange my business. Today is Monday and you see I am here."

Vyry was shocked to hear what Mr. Porter had said, but she dared not look at Innis's face now that Randall Ware had answered his question. She hoped he would drop the subject then, but he did not.

"I don't mind telling you that I was mad about the boy's back, but after hearing my wife explain everything, I feel better, but of course I'm taking my boy just the same."

"Your wife? How you figure she's your wife?"

"How you figure she's not?"

"Your *legal* wife?"

"My legal wife. According to the law of Georgia, which regulated all slave marriages, she's still my wife, that is if she wants to be."

"Even if she hadn't heard from you in seven years when she married me five years ago and you been gone all that time, sight unseen?"

"She heard from me."

"If she had known where you was and you was coming anytime soon, she never would have come away with me. She married me when all hope of seeing you again was gone. I ain't never heard tell of the law holding a woman to a man after seven years."

"I tell you by all the laws of God and man she is my wife, whether you like it or not, and unless she can produce a bill of divorcement from me she is a bigamist."

"What's that?" asked Vyry.

"A woman married to two men and both of them living. Now how does that suit your religion?"

Poor Vyry stared at him and said nothing. But Innis was bristling and ready to fight.

"You ain't trying to tell me you was looking for Vyry to be setting right here waiting for you after all them there years, and her a right young, pretty woman, too; a clean, decent woman and helpless with two childrens. You must think you is a Black Jesus!"

"Well, you just now told me she thought I was dead or she never would have married you."

Hearing this, Innis subsided into silence and Vyry said, "Yall eat now, and hush!"

While they ate Vyry's good food, Innis said little, but Randall Ware kept a running conversation about Dawson. He looked around their new and pretty house, visibly impressed by Vyry's neat housekeeping, and said, "You have a very nice place here. How long you been in this house?"

"We just now got it this summer. We just had been from pillar to post . . ." Vyry looked up and saw Innis scowling and she dropped her eyes but she continued talking in a more subdued tone. "First we was in the river bottom and we got flooded out when high water come the next spring, then we was sharecropping on a dirt farm for a year, and then we had us a brand-new house with windows from the mill and the Ku Kluxers burned us out. We lost everything excepten the clothes on our backs."

"Humph! So they bothered you, too?"

"What you mean by that?" asked Innis.

"Ku Klux Klan just as bad in Georgia. They killed my journeyman, Jasper, beat me nearly to death, tore up my house and shop looking for me . . ."

"O, Jesus have mercy!" said Vyry.

"And where was you when they was looking?" asked Innis.

"You know the big wheel of the grist mill that stays partly under water so the water furnishes the power to turn the wheel and run the mill?"

"Yeah, I knows what you talking bout," and Innis Brown was now listening, deeply interested for the first time in Randall Ware's conversation.

"Well, I got down in that water and hung on to the wheel with both my hands till they got outa my shop. Then I climbed out of the water, but I stayed in the dark in the grist mill a long time after they had gone. The next day old Doc came along and patched me up. He was their go-between and he told me I would be forced to sell my land that Grimes wanted to buy and if I didn't want to sell they would kill me. They've practically taken my land for a song. Half of what I had is already gone."

Now Innis stood up. "Well, Mister Ware, I don't see how come you is got to rush off now when Vyry and the childrens ain't seen you in sich a long time. You welcome to stay long as you likes, but I sho thinks you oughta spend at least one night with us. I likes your conversation but I gotta be getting back to my field work."

"Well, that's real kind of you, Mister Brown, I guess we do have a lot of things to talk out even if you don't recognize we are both married to the same woman."

"Well, as you say, that's her decision. She can make up her mind whichever one of us she wants, and I ain't gwine think hard of her if she don't choose me. I knows it's hard to split a family. We's all got childrens and I specs we loves em. I'm gwine bide by her choice and trust it'll be the will of the Lawd."

Randall Ware stared at the man. Then he looked at Vyry but her face was impassive and he could not read what she was thinking. On impulse he decided to spend the night. He told Jim, "We'll go on the morning train, son. I think it leaves about eleven o'clock." Then turning to Innis he said, "And since we'll spend the night, I'd like to look at your land."

> Lawd, ah doan feel no-ways tired,
> Oh, glory hallelujah!
> For I hope to shout glory when this world is on fire,
> Oh, glory hallelujah!

57   What will happen to poor colored folks now?

The children followed Innis Brown and Randall Ware around the farm until supper time and then they came in chatting and hungry for supper. Everybody was suddenly in a holiday mood, laughing and smiling and talking so enthusiastically that Vyry could sense the contagion of their excitement. The two men were talking animatedly as though they had always known each other. Innis shared Harry with his guest and the little boy rode piggyback most of the time from one to the other, while Minna kept her hand tightly in Randall Ware's. Jim was bursting with the thrill of a first ride on the railroad cars, going to school, and having his own father come and take him away. He was suddenly a very happy boy. Vyry looked on and smiled, understanding each separate individual's emotions and thinking how different things had been only a few days ago. She felt like a mother hen clucking over a brood, but her feelings were more mixed and confused than any of the others. She was very glad and thankful that things had worked out so Jim could go to school. It seemed a major solution to her problems. But what she would say to Randall Ware when the time came to speak she really did not know. How could she tell him there would be another baby in the spring when even Innis didn't know?

Everyone was eating heartily. Innis said to Randall Ware, "Whereabouts did you say you is taking Jim to school?"

"Selma. It's a place out from Montgomery where the Baptist Church has a school."

"Well, I sho hopes he do good with his books, cause he sho ain't no good behind a plow."

"Maybe he takes after me. I never did like farm work. Mind you, I've done it, when I couldn't find something else to do, but I never liked it. I've been working at the trade of blacksmith ever since I was his age, but he hasn't got the body-build for a blacksmith. He's built like his mother and he never could swing that big hammer. I'm going to make a teacher out of him."

"A teacher?" blurted out Vyry. "You means he can make a teacher?"

Jim beamed, and the other children smiled at him with awe and admiration.

"Of course he can. He's always been quick and he'll learn fast. Sure he can be a teacher. That's what our race needs now more than anything else. It might take from five to seven or eight years, but by that time he'll come home a teacher, able to help his people."

"You thinks education gwine raise up the colored folks?" asked Innis. "I always been told education don't do nothing but make a nigger a fool."

"Well, that's the white man's attitude. He says an educated Negro gets ideas in his head about being free and equal, and that's the truth. When you can read and write and the white man can't make a fool out of you, he never likes it. You know it was against the law in slavery time to teach a black person to read or write. The white man must have had some fear about educating colored people or he wouldn't have had the law. He knows as long as we are ignorant people we are helpless."

"I knows that's the truth you speaking now. They sho will take vantages of you. That's just what happen to us at that share-crop place when I made my mark on them papers I couldn't read."

"Well, I thought once, right after the war, that colored people were going to reach the Promised Land with land, education, and the vote just because the Government said so. But I've learned different. Nobody is going to give us anything. We're going to have to fight and struggle for it just like it took years of fighting and struggling to end slavery. The white man is fighting education, land, and the ballot for Negroes. The Ku Klux Klan rode night and day in the last elections."

"Say they did?"

"Didn't they ride here? I heard they rode all over the South."

"Well, they's bad, I knows that. We ain't been in no bad trouble since they burned us out, but Vyry here been selling stuff round the neighborhood and one while she heard a lot of stuff about the Ku Klux Klan killing colored peoples."

"Well, there's going to be a big Government investigation and for awhile they may be quiet, but the whole truth about it is the southern white man is not going to rest until he puts the black man back in slavery."

"Oh, naw!" said Vyry, "colored folks won't stand for that. I reckon all us would die fore we'd go back to that there misery!"

"Well, they're not going to have it the same way. Freedom won't mean much more than they can't buy and sell us on the auction block. Even the Confederates abolished the slave trade. But they mean to keep us down under some kind of different system, controlling our labor and restricting our movements, and not allowing us to vote, and trying to keep us ignorant. The Ku Klux Klan will be just like the drivers and the patter-rollers were in slavery time."

"Air, Lawd! Air, my Jesus, what you reckon poor colored folks can do about it?"

"Well, not much, that's why I say one of the first things we have to do is to educate our children. We do have schools, that's one good thing we got under Black and Tan conventions and Radical Republicans, and I don't think even the white folks will let the common school go down, although I hear they are going to close down the 'nigger' school as soon as they get back White Home Rule."

"What in the name of God is that?"

"Government the same as usual before the war."

"Well, is they winning?"

"I'm afraid so, though I don't know how much longer it will be before they get back complete control, but they're going to get it. And the northern white man is going to let them keep it. I tell you I heard the white man up North talking about the Negro and let me tell you one thing, don't fool yourself, the colored people haven't got any friend in the white man, North or South. Average white man hates a Negro, always did, and always will."

Vyry was clearing away the supper things, but the men continued to sit at the table when the children were excused. Now Vyry interrupted.

"You sho sounds mighty bitter, Randall Ware. Does you figger every white man hates every nigger?"

"Well, Vyry, you might as well face it, the white man is your natural enemy and he regards you as his natural enemy. It's just that simple. Fundamentally, yes, every white man, deep down in his heart, believes that a black man's color makes him less than a white man and he's supposed to treat you like a brute animal because he believes you are."

"I don't believe it."

"Well, you don't have to, but I'm telling you the truth."

"I don't believe the world is full of peoples what hates everybody. I just doesn't believe it. I knows lots of times folks doesn't know other folks and then they gits to thinking crazy things, but when you gits up to peoples and gits to know them, you finds out they's got kind hearts and tender feelings just like everybody else. Only ways you can keep folks hating is to keep them apart and separated from each other. Of course I knows they's plenty evil peoples in the world, look like they's just born evil and the devil's they companion, but I just doesn't believe its cause they's white or black. I doesn't believe every white person's evil and every black person's good. It ain't that way, Randall Ware, it just ain't that way."

"Well, Vyry, I keep forgetting that you're half-white and you love white folks bettern you love colored folks."

"That's a lie, and don't you say no sitcha thing to me."

"I didn't mean to make you mad."

"That's the second time today you done told me I'm a white folks' nigger. What is you, some kind of devil out of hell come here to torment me?"

Innis Brown looked startled to hear the angry tone in Vyry's voice, but Randall Ware only laughed. He knew that he and Vyry had always disagreed and sparred with each other, and now he answered jokingly, "Looks like you're red hot and still a-heating!"

"Yes, I got me a lay-low to catch a meddler, and I'm gwine set with the sick till the poorly gits better!"

And the kitchen fairly lighted up with the sparks that flew between them. Innis Brown said, "Let's set out on the porch where the air's cooler. Look like to me it done got *hot* inside." And the three of them laughed.

Outside they watched the September sky fill with stars. They hung so low in the indigo heavens they sent out jagged points of glittering light which made the red clay and wet green grass glisten in the moonlight.

"You know one thing, Randall Ware," mused Vyry, "Jim, the houseboy, told me you was dead."

"When'd he tell you that? I wasn't dead the last time he saw me, or I wouldn't be here now!"

"Well, he said you was so sick until you was on a litter, and you was so poor and wasted away until he didn't see how you could last another week. He said you had the fever. He come by Marse John's plantation the day the soldiers come and set us free, and he asked me to gwine way with him and May Liza and Caline cause him and May Liza was gitting mar-riaged."

"Say they were? Think of that! Well, I was sick, and I guess they had given me up for dead, cause one morning I woke up and they had drawn the sheet up over my face and I was too weak to take my hands and push it back, but you oughta seen me puffing and blowing hard as I could so when the dead detail come in they saw that sheet rising and falling so they knew from my breathing that I wasn't dead. That sickness is really what kept me away from Georgia so long. I was still in Chattanooga after Surrender, I lost so much weight I could see the bones in my rib cage. I had malaria fever and dysentery, and it's a wonder I didn't die, but come to think of it now, I never did think I was dying. I kept fight-ing to live. During the summer I picked up right smart, but it was fall of the year before I began to feel strong enough to make my way south again and I was in Georgia at Christmas time, but I stayed in Augusta for a meeting in January and I guess that's the way I missed you. When I saw the Dutton plantation abandoned and didn't know where you had gone, I figured if I hadn't stopped in Augusta for that meeting I might have made it to you in time."

"Time for what?" asked Innis.

l, what was in it for them? What were they going to
being nice to you?"

u sounds so bad. That's what you does, you sounds bad.
uspicions everybody. What you means what was in it
um? Six families come here, mens and womens and
ole day gitting us in this house. I doesn't think

"In time to keep you from going off with my family where
I didn't know where to find them, that's what, in time for
that."

Innis's eyes widened but he didn't say anything further just
then.

"Well," said Vyry, "I guess it was just one of them things
meant to be."

"Yeah," said Innis, "the good Lawd's will."

Both Vyry and Randall Ware caught the hint of bitterness
and sarcasm in his voice and they looked at each other, then
Vyry said, "But I just wants you to realize I had cause to
believe you was dead."

"But did you really believe it? Did you honestly think I
was dead?"

"Naw. To tell you the truth, I never did. I never did have
the feeling that you was dead. I figgered it was strange you
hadn't never come, and I thought a lot of things, but I never
did believe you was dead."

Now Innis Brown and Randall Ware exchanged significant
glances. For awhile they sat in silence, feeling the refreshing
night winds blow in their faces while the air cooled the
sweating earth. Vyry went in the house and came back with
pans of roasted peanuts and a few of last year's pecans.
Randall Ware commented that they were uncommonly good.

"Getting on back to your conversation this evening when
we was eating dinner bout the white folks trying to put us back
in slavery, and bout us got to git education for our younguns,
and the political vote and all that . . ." Innis Brown and
Randall Ware were both eating peanuts and while Innis was
shelling nuts and talking to Randall, the latter was eating and
looking at him and nodding his head waiting for Innis to
finish:

"I feels like this, if we gits a piece of land like we's got
this here farm and we tends it good and makes a living and
don't bother nobody and uses the mother-wit what God give
us, we'll git along all right. They was a man not so long ago
made a speech round here and he says the colored peoples
got to forgit about the political vote and tend our farms and
raise our families and show the white folks we ain't lazy and
ain't stirring up no trouble for nobody, but we is for peace
and we's good citizens and all that, and that'll do us more
good than anything else. I kinda believes like that man . . ."

"Well, I don't," said Randall Ware. "There's nothing wrong
with that as far as it goes. Yes, we need land and farms and

we need to work them and be good citizens, but when you've got all the land you can get and you got no education and no vote with it, the white man is still going to make a fool out of you. He'll come pretty near trying to make a fool out of you when you got all of that, but he's sho going to take advantage of you when you can't help yourself. You're not a citizen as long as you can't vote. I learned that much from Henry Turner."

"Who was he?"

"Well, you know when I got back to Dawson, and Vyry and the children were gone and I didn't know where, I started working again in my shop, and the reason the Ku Klux Klan took me out and beat me an inch of my life was I ran for the state Legislature with this friend Henry Turner and we won."

"What you talking bout? Ain't no niggers been in the Georgia State House! You ain't talking bout that is you?"

"That's just what I'm talking about. I sure went there. Henry Turner was elected from Bibb County and I was from Terrell County. We went, all right, even if they didn't let us stay long. We were in the Georgia State House, and twenty-six more colored people besides."

Vyry's eyes were shining now and when she spoke Innis could detect the great respect in her voice.

"Randall Ware, you is been a real big nigger since I seen you last. Standing up in the Georgia State House and all that. I never thought I'd see the day that a nigger would go where Marse John done been."

"Well, I reckon that was the whole trouble. White folks couldn't and wouldn't stand for it. They put us all out. Oh, they were wrong and they threw us out on the basis of our being black and all that was wrong, but they just couldn't stomach the very idea." Randall Ware had seen the light of admiration in Vyry's eyes and he wished he could keep it there, but something told him he must be as honest this night as he ever had been in his life, so he continued.

"But it was Turner who was the big man. He made the speech defending our right to be there because we were duly elected and all that, and he made the speech defending the black man to the white people, too. It was Turner who kept on fighting, and still is, but I must confess the Ku Klux Klan made a coward out of me."

"What you means by that?" asked Innis.

"Well, as I was saying, Turner got me into politics. Oh, he didn't get me interested, I was already interested, but I didn't

"Forty years in the wild[...]
know anything about it, and Turner did. I fig[...] 402
war was over that a free people could express t[...]
vote, and I knew I was born free, I had property i[...]
I could read and write, and I thought I had a right li[...]
body else in America to take part in my government.[...]
found out I was wrong."

"You mea[...]

"...you means we ain't got no right?"

"I mean the white man is determined to keep us down or kill us when we try to do anything but lick his boots and say 'yassah, Mister Boss-man' to him."

"You is talking bitter again, now ain't you?" asked Vyry.

"I guess I am, but I'm not like Turner. You can't tell Turner from a white man. He's just as white as Vyry is, and the white people didn't know he was a Negro until he stood up and defended the colored people's right to sit in the legislature. He went on to tell them that black men were kings and emperors when white men were still swinging from trees like monkeys!"

"Annh, annh, now Randall Ware, does you know what you is talking bout or is you just making all that stuff up?"

"I'm telling you what Turner said, but if you don't believe me what difference does it make to you whether it's true or not? I'm not like Turner. I'm a black man, and I'm a proud black man. I don't believe in licking any man's boots. I've always had gold in my pockets and I always felt like I was just as much as any man, a lot better than some. But I'm telling you now the white man is using his Ku Klux Klan to make us all eat dirt and stay down where he can keep his foot on our necks."

"Randall Ware," said Vyry, "I thought you told me once everything you got in the world two white mens give it to you?"

"Who you talking bout? Mister Wheelwright and Robert Qualls? Well, it is true Mister Wheelwright did leave me his land all legal and clear, but you got to understand a northern Quaker like Mister Wheelwright and an abolitionist like Mister Qualls were always friends to Negroes."

"Well, yeah, I heard you say that same thing back in slavery time. You says that they was plenty white folks up North sympathize with colored folks and wants to help us. Now you come here talking bout every white man ain't no good. Does you know how we got this here house? Our white neighbors come here and helped to put us in it, that's how we's in this here house."

spent the whole day _____ _____
that sounds like every white person ain't no good."

"Yeah, but I asked you, what did they want from you? They must have wanted something. What did they want from you?"

"They want us to stay here, that's what, and they told us they want us to stay here."

"Why? Why they want niggers so bad unless nigger got something they want?" Randall Ware's voice now was taunting, and at first Vyry was so angry she was flustered.

"Aw, you is a bowdaciously outrageous colored man! Just cause I can be a granny in a pinch, you think that's a whole big thing for me to do when they is making it possible for me to sleep in my house at night and not be scairt? They ain't needing me no worser than I is needing them, that's what. We both needs each other. White folks needs what black folks got just as much as black folks needs what white folks is got, and we's all got to stay here mongst each other and git along, that's what. You ain't got no God in you, Randall Ware, that's your trouble. You is ate up with hatred, that's what you is. You ain't got no God in you at-all."

"Maybe not. You can keep your white Christian God along with all your good white friends because I never could stand hypocrites. I still say you've got white man's blood in you. That's the way he made the black slave docile and a good nigger in the first place. Black African slaves right out of the jungles use to die before they'd take a whipping and let the white man stomp them down in slavery, but he mixed his blood with them and then he made good niggers. You got his color and his blood and you got his religion, too, so your mind is divided between black and white. I know you can't help it. He made you that way."

"My God," said Innis, "ain't you scairt when you dies you'll go down to old Nick stead of up in the sky to heaven?"

"Up in the sky? Up in the sky? Don't tell me you believe that nonsense?"

"Randall Ware, is you a infidel?"

"Ah naw now, I believe in God all right. I'm not an infidel

but I know damn well there ain't no hell in the ground and no heaven in the sky when I die, either."

Innis Brown looked shocked and Vyry stared oddly ahead of her. Randall Ware continued, "You don't mean to tell me I shock and surprise you? Sure I believe in heaven and hell too, but I don't have to wait till I die to go to either place. If you want to know what I think, I've seen saints act like devils right out of hell, and the devil himself turn into a saint when it suits his purpose. Most people got as much evil in them as they got good, maybe more."

Vyry and Innis still sat listening to him.

"Why, my God, I'd be a bigger fool than if I didn't know my ass from a hole in the ground if I went around with all that sanctimonious self-righteous stuff in my head, and anybody who tries to tell me, that has got more nerve than a brass-ass monkey!"

"All right now," said Vyry, "I'm sitting here."

"Well, I see you, don't I?"

"I can't stand that vile language you is putting out."

"Oh, I forgot about that prissy old white woman who was mistress on the plantation where you come up. You oughta seen her. Did you ever see her?" And Randall Ware turned his question to Innis who was struck dumb by all that was transpiring, and he shook his head "no" because he was too dumbfounded to speak.

"Well, that old white woman looked and talked and acted like she was Queen Victoria. Big Missy, they called her. She reared all the niggers and white folks around her just as prim and prissy as you please. She had a son who thought he was Prince Charming. I heard he was killed in the war, and she died too. I wonder what ever happened to her stupid daughter that she bossed around when she was full grown?"

"Who you talking about?" asked Vyry, "Miss Lillian?"

"Listen to her, *Miss Lillian!*" And he mimicked poor Vyry, who was shocked out of her wits to hear Randall Ware discuss her white folks in such sacrilegious terms. "Yeah, that's the one, *Miss Lillian,* whatever become of her?"

"I told you she lost her mind, and I don't think it was one bit funny neither."

"Well, what would you expect from somebody never taught one day in her life to look the truth in the face. How was she gonna cope with real life when you pull the rug out from under her and she no longer can sit on a cushion and feed upon strawberries and cream? Well, what I started to say was you couldn't have told that old white woman she wasn't fit to be an angel. She was a pious Christian lady if ever I saw one, and just as pr'm and prissy as you please. She left her prissy mark on everybody around her, including Vyry. That's why she can't stand bad language. And so far as education is concerned, I tell you it may not be the only way for our people but it is the main way. We have got to be educated before we know our rights and how to fight for them. All the violence and killing that colored people have suffered since Freedom may just be a drop in the bucket to what they put on us in slavery time, but God only knows what it will be in the future."

"Well, all I got to say, Randall Ware, is I can't understand you no more'n I can understand evil white peoples what ain't got no shame and ain't got no God. But I ain't gwine try to beat the white man at his own game with his killing and his hating neither. I knows deep down in my heart that they is a God and He ain't gwine never forget his childrens no more'n I'm gwine forget mine whilst I'm living in this world. He's above the devil too, that's what He is. I knows I'm a child of God and I can pray. Things ain't never gwine get too bad for me to pray. And I knows too, that the Good Lawd's will is gwine be done. I has learned that much. I'm gwine leave all the evil shameless peoples in the world in the hands of the Good Lawd and I'm gwine teach my childrens to hate nobody, don't care what they does. I ain't gwine teach my childrens hate cause hate ain't nothing but rank poison. I knows they is evil peoples in the world and I knows everything don't always turn out like we think is right, but I also knows like the song say what we sings in church,

> A charge to keep I have
> A God to glorify
> A never dying soul to save
> And fit it for the sky.

You been talking all day long now and I been listening. I knows how much hell the white man can raise and I knows how much the black man can raise and I 'spects hell ain't gwine have only white folks in it and neither is they gwine be just colored folks up in heaven cause, as the song says, everybody talking bout heaven ain't gwine there, and mighty few is bound to make it in, but down here in this here rain-washed world we's all got trials and tribulations. We's all got to fight the devil and his wicked imps of the devil. Poor colored folks ain't gwine have no more put on us than we is able to bear. We's done come through slavery and we is free at last. I knows we's got to wander awhile in the wilderness just like the children of Israel done under Moses, but when the battle's over we shall wear a crown. I ain't gwine git tired of well-doing cause I'm gwine to shout 'Glory' one of these morning's when the wicked world is on fire. God don't prom-ise . . . easy Jesus, I reckon, wore his crown of . . . . f evil more'n I does. You done called me a white folks' nigger and throwed up my color in my face cause my daddy was a white man. He wasn't no father to me, he was just my Marster. I got my color cause this here is the way God made me. I ain't had nothing to do with my looking white no more'n you had nothing to do with your looking black. Big Missy was mighty mean to me from the first day I went in the Big House as a slave to work. She emptied Miss Lillian's pee-pot in my face. She hung me up by my thumbs. She slapped me and she kicked me; she cussed me and she worked me like I was a dog. They stripped me naked and put me on the auction block for sale. And worsetest of all they kept me ignorant so's I can't read and write my name, but I closed her eyes in death, and God is my witness, I bears her no ill will. Old Marster was my own daddy and he never did own me for his child. I begged him to let me marriage with you and go free and he say no. He ain't punish nobody when he stand to see them beat me . . ."

She stopped and looked at them frightened, almost panic stricken, for in working herself up to this pitch she suddenly realized that she had never told either one of them that she had been beaten. But they caught her words and suddenly they were both standing over her.

"What did you say?" asked Innis.

"Who stood to beat you?" asked Randall Ware.

Then both of them together said, "When?"

Now Vyry was crying and she realized she had gone too far not to go on. She was fumbling at her waist and her apron, at the buttons fastening her clothes. Suddenly, snatching at her clothes, she tore them loose and bared her back.

"That's what they done to me that morning when I was trying to meet you at the creek. That's how come I got them there scars."

Hysterical now, she had thrown off piece after piece of her

clothing, and now in the moonlight the two men stood horrified before the sight of her terribly scarred back. The scars were webbed and her back had ridges like a washboard. Innis Brown's face was working and he covered his face to keep them from seeing him cry. He knew and understood now why Vyry went wild when she saw him with a whip in his hand after Jim. Randall Ware was swearing terrible oaths and chorusing them with "Oh, no, my God, no! Oh, no, my God, no! Look at what those bastards have done."

Vyry was still weeping, but inosen and threw her apron off her clothes she recovered herself and threw her apron around her shoulders to cover her back again and began to draw her skirts closer. Now she was drying her eyes and trying to compose herself.

"I may not understand much. I'm just a poor colored woman traveling through this sinful world, like Brother Zeke useta sing,

> I am a poor way-faring stranger,
> I'm tossed in this wide world alone.
> No hope have I for tomorrow,
> I'm trying to make heaven my home.

I wants you to bear me witness and God knows I tells the truth, I couldn't tell you the name of the man what whipped me, and if I could it wouldn't make no difference. I honestly believes that if airy one of them peoples what treated me like dirt when I was a slave would come to my door in the morning hungry, I would feed em. God knows I ain't got no hate in my heart for nobody. If I is and doesn't know it, I prays to God to take it out. I ain't got no time to be hating. I believes in God and I believes in trying to love and help everybody, and I knows that humble is the way. I doesn't care what you calls me, that's my doctrine and I'm gwine preach it to my childrens, every living one I got or ever hopes to have."

It was after midnight but they were too wakeful now to think about sleeping. Randall Ware knew from the moment he looked on Vyry's lacerated back that they could never go back to what had been before he left. It was too late. Innis Brown knew that this woman, who had stood so much outrage, had a wisdom and a touching humility that he could never cease to admire. It was more than her practical intelligence, or her moral fortitude; more than the fundamental decency and innate dignity that marked her character as an unusual one in the face of both these men that night. Randall Ware had hinted that she was a prudish woman as though he had forgotten any moments of passion between them when he had controlled her and her face was neither impassive nor cold. But Innis Brown knew that she was touched with a spiritual fire and permeated with a spiritual wholeness that had been forged in a crucible of suffering. She was, in that night, a spark of light that was neither of the earth nor September air, but eternal fire. Yet it was not that she stood there in pride for them to worship her or be in awe of her deep integrity. She was only a living sign and mark of all the best that any human being could hope to become. In her obvious capacity for love, redemptive and forgiving love, she was alive and standing on the highest peaks of her time and human personality. Peasant and slave, unlettered and untutored, she was nevertheless the best true example of the motherhood of her race, an ever present assurance that nothing could destroy a people whose sons had come from her loins.

And now, like an ancient chorus lost in the air, Innis added a strange and pathetic voice in his sequel to all that had been said, "I has listened to, and I has learned from listening to what yall has to say. I ain't never figgered I would have a chance in the world to be anything. I never knowed my mother, nor father, sister, nor brother, and I was sold three times before I was grown. But I always wanted a piece of land of my own, a farm to raise me a crop with my own house and my own loving family. When Surrender come I just got out in the road and follows the peoples what was following the Union Army and the soldiers, and I come down to the Dutton Plantation in Georgia where Vyry and her younguns was. And you know who I took up with first?"

Randall Ware said, "No."

"I took up with your lil boy, Jim. He was the cutest lil boy, and he had so much sense, I just fell in love with him and his sister, Minna. He look like he was just crazy bout that gal he told me was his lil sister and she was just as crazy bout him. That was before I ever seed Vyry."

"Yeah, and if it hadna been for Innis that night no telling what wouldn't have happened to me, maybe the same thing what happened to poor Lillian, one of them bummers tried to attack me and Innis run him off."

Randall Ware looked again at Innis, but Innis was embar-

rassed and said, "I wasn't gwine tell that part. But she was
just as honest as she could be. She told me she was waiting
for her children's daddy. She say you went off before the war
and you sent word for her to wait there until you come after
the war for her and the younguns, and she say she was duty
bound to wait and she wasn't gwine with the army and she
didn't plan to be moving on soon. But here was the first time
I had ever seed a colored family what looked like they was a
loving wholeness together, a family what slavery hadn't never
broke nor killed. I just couldn't leave there until I knowed
what was gwine become of them."

"He worked that place like a dog all by hisself, Innis done
it, to help me with Miss Lillian and the childrens."

Randall Ware was now walking up and down agitatedly,
pacing back and forth before the house, his head down, but
suddenly he turned as though pivoting on his heels and faced
Vyry.

"Well, I reckon you all don't have to say any more. I'm
trying hard to understand. Vyry, have you made up your
mind?"

"You know I is. I doesn't want to hurt nobody, but it's too
late for us now, any more. They's too much water done run
over the dam. I reckon you knowed that when you come."

"In a way I did, but I don't mind telling you both I got up
fresh hope when Porter told me about you beating the boy.
I figured a man like that wasn't likely to be making Vyry
happy, crazy as I know she is about her children, but I see
now it was just one separate incident."

"Yeah, in a way, it was a accident. Jim ain't no easy boy
to handle, and if you is round him long you gwine see what I
means. I guess it's good you come to git him cause he was
gitting clean out of our control and I couldn't scarcely speak
to him 'thout he wouldn't puff up and git mad."

"Well, it's just his age. I was the same way. If you knew
me, you'd understand him. He's just like me. But as I started
to say, I knew you two were married ever since I got back
to Dawson five years ago."

"You knowed it?"

"Yes, I didn't know where you were, but I knew you were
married and I wouldn't have come but for the news about
the boy."

"Innis and me has got a marriage, Randall Ware. We has
been through everything together, birth and death, flood and

fire, sickness and trouble. And he ain't never thought once about hisself first; he always thought about us. You and me didn't have no chance to make a marriage. Slavery killed our chance. I use to dream I would see you coming down the Big Road, I wanted you to come so bad—but you didn't come."

Randall Ware sensed the sad note of regret in her voice for something that might have been, but never was, and his own words echoed with regret.

"I figured, too, when I came, that I could offer you everything, and I can—anything your heart desires, Vyry, fine home, money, education for our children, everything!"

She shook her head.

"Big House don't matter to me. I was a slave in a Big House and I knows that don't mean warm loving home and peaceful night's sleep. Your money was always gwine buy everything, even much me and my freedom, but it was a dream, Randall Ware. I tells you it wasn't nothing but a dream."

"And I guess I had a dream, too, of you that didn't come true, and it's not your fault or anybody's else, I guess. I guess we just got caught in the times."

"That's what Mister Jacobson say when we was burned out," echoed Innis. "He say it's just the times and the changes ain't good but yall is good peoples and I hopes you gits settled somewhere soon."

"The times have changed so fast since Vyry and me first met, we're living in another world."

"But I prays God's blessings on you and wishes you well and good luck, Randall Ware, I sho does."

"Thank you, Vyry, I know you do."

"And you welcome to come again whenever you wants," said Innis.

"Naw. I won't come back any more. It was hard for me to come this time, but I had to see about Jim. I won't come back. I'll keep in touch with you and if you need anything I've got you know it's yours, but I'm going to find myself another woman now and make her my wife."

The day was breaking. The eastern sky was streaked with rainbow-hued ribbons like the flames from torches or runners who were racing across the world. The three had talked all night. It was time for Innis to feed his stock, for Vyry to start her day, and time for Randall Ware to think about starting another journey.

"Why don't you come in here and stretch out and take a nap until the younguns wakes you and it's time to wash for breakfast?"

And Randall Ware, spent in body and spirit, said, "I believe I will."

eeing her brother go. When they were ready to leave
standing in the house, Minna sidled up to Jim and
ere, Jim, here's something I made for you." To
e's amazement she produced a square white cotton
e size of the white linen handkerchief she had seen
Ware use the day before. She had neatly hemmed the
with tiny stitches for her brother. Jim was so surprised,
ulsively hugged Minna saying, "Thank you, Minna,
you so much. It's just what I been wanting." Smiling
other they fought back their tears. Harry could not
stand at first what was going on, then he said, "I got
hing to give you too, Brudder, dear," and he produced
rize possession, a round rock from the brook. At first
aid, "Naw, Harry, I ain't gwine take your rock what
ikes so much."
rry protested, "But it's all I got and I wants to give you
thing too." So Jim took the rock.
nis Brown capped the gift ceremony by giving Jim his
pocket-pen knife with which he whittled and carved. Ran-
Ware started to say, "I'll buy you . . ." but he saw the
Jim's eyes shone and the happy look on Innis Brown's face
he knew better than to say anything. Vyry knew, too, that
reconciliation was now complete.
ding in the wagon to town, Innis apologized for the jolting.
Ve ain't got no buggy, but one of these days I'm gwine
'yry a buggy so's she and the younguns can ride in style."
This is better than walking, the way I did yesterday," said
dall Ware.
ry sat between them and said little. She was staring down
road. Minna and Jim and Harry rode in the back of the
on and tried to think of everything they should remem-
to cover the vast time of their parting.
And don't forget to feed Tricks, Minna."
won't. And Jim, when you learns how to write, write me
ter, please!"
Vill you know how to read it?"
I bet I learns just as fast as you does."
yry listened to them talking.
wisht you was going with me, Minna."
knows, Jim, but you knows I can't leave Maw. Maw
ds me." And Vyry smiled.
t the railroad station there was a crowd of people, but
t of them were not going anywhere—just came to look at
train and the people who were going somewhere. They

Oh, come and go with me
To my father's house,
To my father's house,
To my father's house,
Oh, come and go with me
To my father's house,
There is joy, joy, joy!

58   *Howdy and goodbye, honey-boy!*

Vyry was moving around quietly in Jim's room hoping not to
disturb him, but then she felt his eyes on her and saw he was
awake.

"Maw?"

"Yes, Jim."

"I sho hates to leave you, but I sho is glad to go to school."

"I knows, and I'm glad for you. I been praying for a way
to send you to school. It wasn't gonna be easy to send you to
town to school this winter and your Paw needing you here on
the farm."

"I knows. And he was saying he wasn't gwine spend the
money."

"Yeah, but he's gonna miss you just the same. Much as he
grumble, it's gwine be worser when he ain't got nobody to
help him."

"Yes'm."

"I wants you to promise me you is gwine study hard and make us proud. Your daddy say he gwine make a teacher out of you. That's gwine make me proud."

"I know, Maw, and I'm gwine study real hard. I'll miss Minna and Harry too, and I dunno when I'm gwine see all yall again."

"If it's the Lawd's will it won't seem long before you is home again."

"Yes'm."

"And Jim, I wants you to be good and try to git along. Mind your manners and make friends with peoples. Friends and good manners will carry you where money won't go. You is born lucky, and it's better to be born lucky than born rich, cause if you is lucky you can git rich, but if you is born rich and you ain't lucky you is liables to lose all you got. But you gotta use mother-wit long with education elst you won't be nothing but a fool. Get up in the morning early and say your prayers. Early bird catches the worm. And don't you be mean and ugly in your heart toward nobody. Remember, sweet ways is just like sugar candy, and they catches more flies than vinegar. I'm praying for you to be somebody. I wants you to be good and make a real man out of yourself. You is got a great big chance, now, don't mess it up. I'm sorry you ain't got no more fitten clothes, but your daddy say he gwine buy you some more in Montgomery on the way to, what you call that place?"

"Selma."

"I ain't never heard tell of it before, but we is been trying to git to Montgomery ever since we left Georgia. I reckon this morning you is gwine be there."

"Yes'm."

"I gotta be gitting in my kitchen now and cooking. You git up now and clean yourself up and put on them there clothes and straighten up this here room. I reckon this gwine be Harry's room now when you gone."

"Yes'm."

And Vyry went out and closed the door.

At breakfast the three adults were sleepy-eyed, rest-broken, and jaded. But the children were so excited they talked incessantly. Vyry, Randall Ware, and Innis Brown were smiling at the children and thinking their own very different thoughts about the day. Innis Brown lingered over his blessing saying a prayer for Jim and the stranger at the table who

was one of them. Harry renewed his fasc[...] Ware's watch where he had left off yeste[...]ing and [...] fast was over, Innis Brown went out to hi[...] and still [...] his wagon to take everybody to town. Ra[...] said, "[...] and reached down in his pocket and brou[...] everyon[...] greenbacks, so big the children's eyes popped[...] cloth th[...] agreed to each other, "Big enough to choke a[...] Randall[...]

He took half of the money and handed it [...] square [...] first protested, "I don't want to take your n[...] he imp[...] Ware!"   thank [...]

"Don't be foolish, Vyry. This is yours, I owe[...] at eac[...] more besides. I'm sorry to leave you knowing I [...] under[...] forever as my wife, but you're still the mother[...] somet[...] children, and who knows whether I'll ever have[...] his p[...] Buy yourself something pretty. I know you wor[...] Jim s[...] me for a dime, but you're forever welcome and I'[...] you [...] make sure you have this much. There's going to b[...] H[...] in Greenville open in the fall, maybe this month, a[...] some[...] Minna to go. You see to it that she goes. Promise [...] In[...]

"I promises," and Vyry's eyes welled with her te[...] dall[...]

"Here, Minna, this is for you. Your mother will [...] way[...] something pretty to wear to school. I'm going to [...] and[...] some school dresses and some more money, and you[...] the[...] and let me know when that man comes along to m[...] leave your mama, cause I'm going to send you your [...] dress!" And he handed Minna as much money as sh[...] git[...] hold in one fist.

"Harry, come here." Randall Ware stooped down [...] Ra[...] spread out several bills like a fan in his hand. "Tak[...] the[...] you want." Harry looked solemnly at the money, tou[...] wa[...] greenback tentatively with one finger, made one sw[...] be[...] though to gather all the money in his fist, and then pus[...] bills aside to touch the gold watch and chain. All o[...] laughed.

"Oh, so that's what you want? You're a bright boy.[...] a l[...] give you this watch, but one of these days soon I'll se[...] one. Now try again with the greenbacks."

Vyry had packed a wicker basket with a lunch for J[...] Randall Ware. She had lined it with a clean ironed fee[...] Minna whispered to Jim, whose eyes got wider and [...] "It's got fried chicken and fried ham and home-mad[...]   ne[...] wheat bread and boiled eggs and ripe tomatoes and ca[...] cold sweet potato pone and pie and peanuts and pecar[...]   m[...] But Minna was trying hard to cover the great pain o[...]   the[...]

were early and Randall Ware had bought Jim's ticket so they stood in a little knot talking until the train came. Vyry and Innis told Jim a dozen times, "You be good now, Jim."

Vyry hugged him so tightly he winced in pain from the still sore back. "Goodbye, honey-boy, you be good now and study hard and don't forget to pray!"

Jim kissed his mother and felt her tremble. "I will be good, Maw, don't you worry none, and nome, I won't forget."

Innis kept chorusing, "You behave yourself now, Jim, and study hard so you can make your maw proud."

"Yes sir. Yes sir, Paw, I sho will."

Randall Ware had first thought how ironic and smiled to hear the boy call Innis Brown, "Paw," but he nearly burst with pride and pleasure when he overheard Jim saying proudly to Minna and Harry, "Our daddy said so. My father says . . . and that's what my daddy says."

The loud, black, iron horse came blowing in, chugging and rattling, scattering soot and cinders over the bystanders. The white trainman started yelling, "All aboard! All aboard! Colored up front! White ladies to the rear! All aboard!"

Randall Ware's lip curled, the hate leaping out in his eyes as he frowned, but Vyry pulled him out of the path of the irate white man just in time. Instead of knocking into him, the hostile trainman glared at the black man and moved on. Now as Randall Ware bent forward and kissed her on her cheek Vyry tried to stand rigid and look ahead, but even Innis could feel her tremble.

"Goodbye Vyry, take care of yourself."

"Goodbye, Randall Ware. God bless you always. We sho glad you come. Good luck and God bless . . ." and she could say no more.

Randall Ware shook Innis's hand and said, "Well, goodbye, I'm glad we met, Innis Brown."

"Goodbye sir, we glad you come."

Randall Ware picked up Minna in his arms and kissed her. His mouth was unsteady as he said, "Let me know when that man comes along!" Minna frowned and shyly hung her head and everybody laughed to see her teased. Harry held out his hand and Randall Ware stooped to take it and kissed him, too. Then he and Jim, who had hugged everybody around twice, got on the train. Their chorus rang out, "Yall be good, now. Yall be good."

The colored people shared half their car with the baggage and the freight including squawking chickens, pigs, and a goat. Randall Ware found a seat for Jim and himself as far back as he could. They sat beside the open window, smiling out at Vyry and her family waving and smiling, too. Jim's and Vyry's eyes clung as the train moved away. They were still waving and smiling broadly, but neither one could see the other's face for their tears.

It was a very quiet little group returning to the farm house. Even Harry had little to say. Innis spoke once to Vyry, "Look like we'll have a good harvest, do this weather keep up."

And Vyry nodded her head. Then, on impulse, she told him about the baby. "I hopes this next child will be a gal. Gal babies don't never want to leave they maw easy."

Innis looked at her stupidly, then he nearly jumped out of his seat and said, "Whoopee! Hey, giddyap there! Naw, what I'm talking bout, steady . . . steady!"

But the day was a long day for Minna. After noon dinner, when Harry was asleep, her mother went down in the fields with Innis. Minna went in her mother's bedroom and looked at the big beautiful oak bed that Innis had made for Vyry. She looked at the high mounds of feather mattresses with the snowy counterpane, crocheted, tasseled, and fringed with white matching shams that Vyry had made for herself, and Minna dived under the bed, under all that magnificence where nobody could see her and cried her heart out until she went to sleep. When she awoke the long fingers of shade from the afternoon sun were lying across the bed, and she heard her mother outdoors feeding the chickens.

Vyry stood and looked over the red-clay hills of her new home where the shadows of the tall pine trees were following the sun to darkness and to sleep. She thought of herself another day, one morning long ago, standing on top of Baptist Hill watching the sunrise, seeing the Central of Georgia Railroad chugging along the track far below, chasing that dominicker hen, and hearing Aunt Sally call her back to the Big House and to work. Now, with a peace in her heart she could not express, she watched her huge flock of white leghorn laying-hens come running when she called. This time she was feeding her own chickens and calling them home to roost. It was this call Minna heard her mother crooning:

Come biddy, biddy, biddy, biddy,
Come chick, chick, chick, chick!